# TEAMWORK

## BOB ROBUSTELLI

ISBN: 146622195X
ISBN 13: 9781466221956
Library of Congress Control Number: 2011914500
CreateSpace, North Charleston, SC

# DEDICATION

To Nana and AR…We miss you.

# PROLOGUE

East Berlin, Germany
September 21, 1986

His head ached from the cheap vodka he drank most of the night. As always, he stayed out too late and drank excessively. *But what else is there to do in East Berlin?* Since the Communists had taken over, they were never really sure what was going on. Work was scarce, and, as far as social activities went, he only attended the soccer games on Sunday afternoons. Dances or social gatherings weren't an option, but the neighborhood commies who ran the streets had several meetings. The apartments had little heat, and the store shelves were just about bare. Even if they had products, no one could afford to buy them anyway. Things weren't going very well in East Berlin.

As the day progressed, Gerhard Muller was alone in the three-room apartment where he lived with his wife and three children. He could barely make ends meet, but enough money was always around to buy a bottle to share with his friends or see a good soccer match. He was glad the wife and kids had gone to his sister-in-law's for a birthday party. Nothing was worse than waking up to three screaming kids and a nagging wife after drinking all night. No food was in the cupboards, so he changed quickly and left the apartment. Maybe he could find something to eat at the corner kiosk.

He didn't have steady work, but one of the lieutenants in the neighborhood council would occasionally let him do odd jobs in the munitions factory around the corner from his apartment. It was more of a laboratory than a factory, located in a building not far from the Wall on Behrenstrasse.

The Wall was probably the ugliest thing Gerhard had ever seen. Construction began on August 13, 1961, and took years to finish. The night before the East German leaders started the Wall, they met in a farmhouse on the outskirts of East Germany to celebrate and sign the declaration to begin building it. They closed down the border at midnight, tore up the roads, and placed barbwire entanglements along the ninety-seven-mile stretch.

Gerhard worked on it from the start, as a day construction worker hauling stones and cement to the mason in charge. It was brutal work, and he knew what was being built wasn't a good thing.

While he walked along the street, he was deep in thought, not looking where he was going. He halted by the Wall and turned around to start back to the munitions factory. *The kids are growing up too fast. We need to get them away from East Berlin if they are to get anywhere in life. This isn't an easy way to live. More is out there, but I have to go get it.*

When he neared the factory, he looked back to the Wall that he helped build. *If only I had known at that time what it really represented.*

He turned away from the Wall and continued on his walk. At four thirty in the afternoon, a massive explosion knocked him off his feet. The fire was everywhere, and the damage was devastating. People were running out of the factory, engulfed in flames, burning to death, but no one could do anything for them. The whole block was on fire, and the flames spread to other buildings in the area. The wind had shifted, and the paint factory and fertilizer plant down the road exploded in flames. The explosions shook the hell out of this section of East Germany. No one in the neighborhood was sure what had happened.

After the firefighters had extinguished the flames, the neighborhood looked like a war zone. Nobody knew the exact amount of causalities, and it would take a while to figure it out. *What the hell had happened?*

Miles away, in an office in the center of Moscow, a man was slumped over his desk with half his head blown off. On his desk, in among the brain fragments, was a bottle of vodka, a gun, and a remote control device.

On the other side of the Wall in West Berlin, Pete Martin called Mickey Rossetti in Moscow. *What a day! I'm glad it's over.* "Mickey, is that you? How are things in your neck of the woods? " It was a loaded question, but he wanted to be sure Mickey was all right.

"We're fine over here, but it was friggin' unreal," Mickey answered. "How the fuck did you ever let me get involved with this shit? Oh, yeah, I fucked up big time in Mexico. That's how!"

# CHAPTER 1

Benny Rossetti and Pete Martin started off their morning with a cup of coffee, and a short meeting in Benny's office. Rossetti Enterprises specialized in travel programs and incentives, sports marketing, player representation, and anything else that came its way through Benny's contacts from his days in the NFL. The offices were in Stamford, Connecticut, about thirty-five miles from New York City.

Only Benny was sure what Pete's real background was. Rumors suggested he was somehow connected to the CIA or some other government organization.

A few days earlier, Pablo Ruiz had called Benny to talk about starting a professional football league in Mexico City. Benny and Pablo had met when Benny had played for the Los Angeles Rams at the beginning of his career.

"Do you think there's anything to the call we got from Pablo the other day? The concept of starting a professional football league in Mexico City is intriguing. I know they've been playing the game for years, but are they ready?" Benny asked.

"I've checked out the people involved. Based on our conversation, it looks like it's real. I think we should go down and meet with them to find out more."

"I'm not sure. You know how the Mexicans can be with the graft and corruption. Worst-case scenario, we could get ourselves involved in something and have it backfire on us. We've had a good reputation with everything else we've done, so we need to be sure."

"I talked to Pablo early yesterday, and then had a conference call later in the day with some of the partners, including Colonel Morales. They've made a deal to play the games at the military stadium in Mexico City, and it has the government's backing. I think it's worth a shot."

"And how did Pablo seem?"

"As far as I could tell, he's fine. I think this is his chance to shine in the eyes of some of his friends. He was really excited."

The last time Pete had seen Pablo, they were at the 1971 Hall of Fame dinner in Akron, Ohio, when Benny was inducted into the NFL Hall of Fame. Pete smiled when he recalled the start of Benny's speech that day.

"Rossetti's on the forty, the thirty. He cuts to the right and avoids a tackler. The twenty, the ten. Touchdown!" Benny put both arms in the air, mimicking the referee. "The loaf of bread under my arm was the closest thing I ever had to a football. Schuyler Avenue on the west end of Stamford, Connecticut, was predominately Italian and poor. The Church of the Blessed Mary was in the middle of the street, and the barbershop where my dad worked was at the far corner near the Amigone funeral home. When I ran through the streets, some of my neighbors cheered me on as I made my moves. Others yelled, 'You crazy paisan! But I didn't care. I always thought I'd make it big someday!"

*And make it big he did.*

"Okay, Pete, let's set up a meeting in Mexico City with Pablo and his partners. Let's take Mickey with us. It's time to get him involved in the international side of the business, and this will be a good place to start. Do you think he's up to it?"

"You know how I feel about Mickey. If he ever sets his mind to something, he'll see it through. Maybe this is just what he needs."

*Mickey is having some problems, but maybe he could handle what we put in front of him. He's a good guy. He just needs something to hold on to.* Just coming off a divorce, Mickey's drinking and drug use were already a problem.

Later that morning Pete called Mickey to meet him for lunch at Tino's Café across the street from the offices. "We just got a call from Mexico City. They want us to consult on an American football league. We've checked it out, and your dad thinks it has possibility. He also wants you to be part of it. Are you up to it?"

"You bet I am. I want to start some international business, and it seems like a good opportunity. Do you have more on the program?" Mickey was eager.

"Pablo Ruiz is sending a brief later today, so we can start with that. In the meantime see what you can find out about the ball being played in the colleges and what standard they're at. Pablo told me they were close to Division II here in the States, but we need to be sure."

"Okay, will do. Anything else?" Mickey couldn't wait to get started. He had wanted to do this type of thing for some time. He loved to travel internationally, and with things going the way they were he needed a change of pace.

"Yeah, call Pablo and firm up the dates for the trip. Then get to the airlines and let me know the travel schedules so we can confirm it with your dad." Pete left the office.

Two weeks later Mickey, Pete, and Benny were on their way to Mexico City, and Mickey's life would change forever.

# CHAPTER 2

As soon as Mickey got off the plane in Mexico City, he coughed. "This smog is enough to choke you," he said to no one in particular. It was early afternoon, and it was hot as hell.

Pablo and a contingent of Mexican businessmen who were there to meet Benny met the trio at the airport.

"Buenos días, Señor Rossetti." Pedro Guzman, a lawyer, was the first to greet Benny.

Next was Alejandro Perez, who ran one of the largest newspaper and magazine companies in the city. The last two were Armando Roblas, the youngest at thirty-eight, and Don Emilio, definitely the money behind the group. Don Emilio's wealth came from old Mexican money mixed in with a little drug money lately, and he carried his status very well. Pablo Ruiz just stayed in the background and watched the proceedings.

"Please call me Benny. Any friend of Pablo's is a friend of mine. This is my son Mickey and my good friend Pete."

Pablo directed the three guests to the limousines waiting for them at the curb. The men were taken to the Sheraton Isabella hotel in the heart of the city. Traffic in Mexico City was horrendous, and the ten mile drive took them over two hours.

"Is the traffic always like this?" Mickey asked Pablo.

"The government is finally trying to get a hold on it," Pablo explained. "Starting next week, they will institute a plan to try to cut down on the congestion and exhaust fumes. The cars with license plates ending in an even number will be allowed in the city on Monday, Wednesday, and Friday the first week and then Tuesday and Thursday the following week. Odd number plates will be the opposite, so we'll hopefully be cutting the number of cars that would be in the city in half."

They checked into their rooms and met the group down in the Restaurante Isabella. The Mexicans, a fun-loving people, treated their guests like family. Pete had advised Mickey and his dad to initially discuss anything except business.

After an hour of pleasantries, Pablo looked at Benny. "As you know, we wanted to discuss an idea with you regarding a professional football league in Mexico called the *Liga Nacional de Futbol Americano*. We've been playing football here since the 1920s. In the past several years, the game has expanded. Currently, we have seventy-six colleges playing the game, with the biggest percentage of them being in Mexico City and Monterrey. We think it's time, and we need your help."

"Do you think you're ready for that type of commitment, Pablo?" Benny looked around the room.

Pablo glanced at his partners. "We've done the research needed to see if it's a viable project, and all reports were positive."

Alejandro explained, "Through our various media outlets, we conducted research and surveys on the public response to the game in the Mexico City area. We also did some sponsorship work and discussed the possibility of TV rights with our contacts there."

"I'd like to see the reports," Benny said, "but I think it might be too early to look at TV rights until the product is good enough to attract the right advertisers. Start-up sponsorship is a little different, but we can discuss that later."

"We're willing to pay Rossetti Enterprises a good sum of money to get involved," said Don Emilio.

"With all due respect, Don Emilio, it's not only about the money. The partners need to trust each other and anyone else involved in the league. If the product isn't entertaining, it will fail. There also needs to be a structure to the league with checks and balances on all funding and money. We should look at it very carefully."

"Benny, we understand that and feel we have taken the appropriate steps," Pablo said.

"Where do you plan to play the games?" Pete's concern was about security.

"We've worked out a deal with the Mexican military and an officer named Colonel Morales to utilize the military stadiums. He reports directly to General Punta, who is very excited about the league. There are enough players and coaches for four teams to start," Pablo replied.

"What type of assistance would you need from us?" Benny asked.

"As you suggested earlier, we need organizational and sponsorship guidance to make it work. I'm sure you know what it takes to get it done, and we'd like to persuade you to help us. My corporations will be funding the league," Don Emilio said. "Please allow us to show what we've done, and we can go on from there. I think what you see will please you, Mr. Rossetti."

"Will you be willing to do as we say without hesitation? Rossetti Enterprises won't be a dictatorship, and there will be discussion on all points, but, in the end, the committee we appoint together will make the final decisions. This must be clear from the start." As far as Benny was concerned, this one stipulation wasn't negotiable.

Don Emilio stood up and walked directly to Benny Rossetti. "It will be as you say."

Benny thought for a second. "Let's see what you have done so far, and we'll take it from there. If it makes sense, we'll let you know before we leave."

Pablo was all smiles. "Let's go watch practice. Later we can introduce you to some of the players and coaches.

That night Mickey found himself in a little café in the Zona Rosa with Armando and Armando's friend Pepe. Pepe was from the area and knew everyone in the place. Mickey was in his element, and it wasn't long before he was looking to buy some cocaine.

Pepe was the man. He controlled all of the distribution in Zona Rosa, his home turf. He had held out some of the better stuff that was left uncut for Armando and Mickey, as he had been told to do by Colonel Morales. He passed the package to Armando and saw Mickey look over. The first part was going as planned, as the colonel knew it would.

"Want to take a little walk, Mickey?" Armando asked.

"Fine with me. Just lead the way, and I'll follow." Mickey could feel his palms getting clammy. After he closed the bathroom stall door, Armando showed him the rock, and Mickey's nose started twitching.

"Holy shit, Armando! He just gave that to you? At home that would cost us over four hundred dollars."

"Let's just say I help Pepe out with the upper-class clientele, so whenever I need something, he takes care of me. He's been handling this part of town for many years, and I've been with him for about eighteen months. Business has been great, and it's only going to get better."

After the first blast, Mickey felt a lot better. When they left the bathroom, Armando gave Mickey the rock.

Mickey noticed her as soon as he came back: a beautiful Mexican girl with a great body and an adorable face. She was with a bunch of other girls, and by the way they dressed and acted, he knew they all had money. Before he knew it, the group was on their way toward him and Armando's table.

"Good evening, Señorita Emilio," Armando said. "Please allow me to present Mickey Rossetti from the United States."

After the introductions the group got up from the table and walked to a private room at the back of the club. Mickey had never seen anything like it.

The room was set up with a big table in the middle, with little alcoves that led to bedrooms and living room areas. A total of thirty people were in the room, all friends of Ana and Armando. They kept leaving and coming back into the room. They drank, snorted cocaine, and danced, as if there was no tomorrow.

"Armando, I can't believe you guys parade this right out in the open. I know the door is closed, but a lot of people are coming in and out." Mickey looked toward the dance floor. Ana was doing the sexiest dance he had ever seen.

"Don't worry, Mickey. Me and Ana have important fathers, and they'd never bust us here."

Mickey was just about to say something when Ana walked over. She took the seat next to him, leaned over, kissed him on the cheek, and put her hands on his thigh.

*What's happening? I can't believe it. I'm here with a pretty young Mexican girl with money and smarts. Only one thing could make the night better, and that might happen before dawn.*

Ana abruptly got up and led him to the alcove furthest away from the table. Ana made Mickey sit on the couch in the back of the room. She was dancing again, and Mickey felt his body start to relax as she pushed her hips against his crotch. It was like a great lap dance except there was a good possibility he was actually going to get it. She started to moan, and that was it. *I can't believe it. I'm actually going to get laid.*

Mickey all of a sudden thought he heard something through the door.

"Ana, is there a problem outside?"

She didn't respond as she was into the lap dance, but at the same time, the door bust open.

"Both of you stay where you are!"

Under different circumstances, Mickey would have loved to oblige, but, as they had guns in their hands and wore police uniforms, he thought it best to sit up and try to look alert. *What the fuck is going on?*

"Señorita Emilio, please put your clothes on and come with us. Señor Rossetti, get dressed and wait at the table in the middle of the room outside. Someone will be right with you."

After Mickey dressed, he slowly walked outside into the private room and took a seat next to Armando. At the table was Pepe.

"What the fuck is going on, Armando?" Mickey asked. "I'm in a bunch of shit right now. I can tell you that. Who the fuck are these people?" *I've done it again. When am I going to stop fucking up? One of these days, my luck is going to run out.*

The door opened, and in walked Colonel Morales, who went directly to Pepe. "Pepe, I told you to watch what you've been doing, but you never listen, do you?"

The punch cracked Pepe in the head, and he fell to the floor. The colonel looked at him on the floor and kicked him in the side. The pain on Pepe's face said it all.

"Sergeant, please get this piece of shit out of here," the colonel said.

They helped Pepe off the floor and dragged him out of the room.

"Armando, I'll deal with you in the morning at my residence. Be there by eight and bring your father. Tell him anything you want, but I assure you that he'll learn the truth when he gets there. Get out of here."

Armando got up and left the room. The silence was deafening to Mickey. *What's coming next?* Left alone in the room with the colonel, he was scared shitless.

"If Don Emilio ever gets wind of this night, Mickey, he'll cut off your balls. You and Armando are lucky I know what's going on, or you'd both be in real trouble, and I could probably do nothing for you. Don Emilio would kill you as soon as look at you. A car outside is waiting to take you back to the hotel. Not a word of this to anyone."

After Mickey left, he could finally breathe, as he knew he had escaped again. *I can't let anyone know what happened.* Just the thought of getting out of this situation made him sweat. He got in the car and went back to the hotel.

The smiling colonel sat at the desk. The door opened, and in walked Pepe and Armando.

"I guess he bought it. A well-executed setup if there ever were one." The colonel was quite proud of himself.

# CHAPTER 3

Mickey wasn't sure what the hell had happened the night before. He knew it wasn't good, but there was nothing he could do about it now. *Why the hell do I always get in trouble lately? I have this great chance to do business in Mexico City, and I screw it up. Will I ever learn?*

Mickey had the day off, but dinner was planned for the evening and he was apprehensive.

"Pete, who do you think will be at the dinner?"

"It will be the full committee and probably the restaurant owner. Why? You have someplace else to go?" Pete suspected Mickey probably had a señorita waiting in the wings.

"No, just asking. I wanted to know if I had to be on my best behavior."

They were driven to La Mansion, about fifteen minutes from the hotel. They sat around a table for ten. On his left was Armando; on the right was Javier Pena, the establishment's owner. Don Emilio, who, at the moment, was in deep discussion with Pete and Benny, also employed Javier.

"Our specialty here is Argentine beef, slowly roasted over coals, and served with empanadas and a Chilean red wine. If we can order for you, I think you will enjoy what we serve," Javier said to them all.

It was fine as far as Mickey was concerned, and he was glad to get the evening going. Dinner was served, and it was delicious, as Javier said it would be. Over cordials, the group broke off into little groups, and Mickey found himself outside with Armando, the colonel, and Javier.

Colonel Morales took the lead. "Don Emilio is finalizing the football matter with Benny and Pete in the other room. The league will undoubtedly be successful, and we want all of you to be a part of the success. It will be a three-year contract, and your father will put the organization in order and then find someone to run it for us. We have asked that he let you, Mickey, be in charge of sponsorship for the league, and he agreed so you will be working with us on that aspect."

*Things are moving too fast. But what do I know?* It would be great to go back and forth to Mexico City, see Ana, work on the league, and snort cocaine. But he was unprepared for what came next.

"After your little episode last night," said the colonel, "we'll be going to Cocoyoc in the morning for a few days to discuss the rest of our deal. It stays between us unless you want your dad to know about your little cocaine problem. Pablo is in way over his head with Don Emilio, and you are going to help him out of it. Enjoy tonight, and we'll see you tomorrow."

Pete waved to Mickey that it was time to go. They said their good-byes and were on the way back to the hotel. *What will tomorrow bring?*

Mickey, Armando, Colonel Morales, and Javier were meeting at the hotel for a little talk about the situation in Mexico. Mickey and Armando left midmorning and hoped to be there by noon.

"The countryside is beautiful, Armando," Mickey said. "What's the name of the hotel?"

"Hotel Cocoyoc. The hotel's a three hour drive from here.The name Cocoyoc loosely translates into 'place of the coyotes' and is steeped in Aztec history."

"How long do you think we'll be staying here?"

Armando actually liked Mickey, so he gave it to him straight. "I'm really not sure but I have to tell you. The colonel isn't someone you should mess with. I don't know him that well, but I've heard terrible stories about him and what he has done. Be careful, and do what he asks."

"Thanks, Armando." *Shit, I've done it this time.*

After the three-hour drive, they pulled up to the hotel and checked in. Their sleeping rooms were in a lovely courtyard and done in simple but classic Mexican style. The room had terracotta flooring, a large bed, and high ceilings painted an azure blue with antique Mexican artifacts hanging on the wall. Mickey sat in his room. *What's going to happen next?*

He walked into Javier's suite and noticed the lines of cocaine on top of the glass table, three different types of tequila, and sangrita. Mickey looked at it, and Javier nodded. After a few lines and a couple sips of tequila, he took a seat.

Colonel Morales explained, "Pablo owes Don Emilio over a million dollars from gambling and bad business debts. It has been going on for over twenty years now, and Don Emilio figured it was time to get it back, plus anything else he could get. The idea is very simple. Get Pablo's friends from America—Señor Martin and your father—to assist us in starting a professional league in Mexico City. Then we can get his friend's son—you—to start a cocaine distribution center for us up in New York."

*There it was.* Growing up in Stamford, near New York, and being part of the cocaine set, Mickey had relationships that could assist in the business. It was a diverse city, and when someone is doing and selling drugs, it's not uncommon to find him on the other side of the tracks with the Mexicans or at the seedy night-clubs. *Maybe these contacts could help me.*

"How do you plan to distribute the product once it is packaged?" Mickey asked.

"We have a network in place from a little marijuana operation we have been running on the south side of Manhattan with the Mexican mob, and we'll expand that to all parts of the city," the colonel explained. "We'll get the cocaine to the border, and you'll fly it into the States to get it ready for sale. How you do that is up to you."

Mickey looked over at Javier and then back to the colonel. "And if I say no?"

"We kill Pablo and his family, and we send your nose to your dad!"

"Then let's do it." He took a few more lines and sips of tequila. "What do we do next?"

The *Liga Nacional de Futbol* was an immediate success with the Mexicans, and two teams were added the following year in Monterrey. The cocaine business started at the same time, and Mickey's group slowly got a hold on the market in the New York area with the Mexican population. This naturally started to spread out into all ethnic areas, and before they knew it, they had a pretty good thing going.

Pablo stayed alive, and Mickey kept his nose!

# CHAPTER 4

The annual meeting for the EFL was taking place in the Italian seacoast town of Rimini. Along the beach stood the rental shacks for the chairs and umbrellas and the seaside bars with outside seating. The Italian men were all dressed in similar fashion with white linen pants, white mesh shirts opened at the chest, and gold chains glittering in the sunlight.

*No wonder they never took off their shades,* Mickey mused.

If they weren't dressed for casual dining, they wore those small, tight-fitting swimsuits where everything bulged out, whether they were a Roman god or Vinny Boombotts.

Pete, who wasn't present, set up the luncheon with the Russian representative through his contacts in Mowcow. Tommy Amendola, a former coach who worked with Rossetti Enterprises in Europe, and Mickey were seated under the Chinzano umbrella, waiting for their guest.

"How the fuck did Pete arrange this meeting so fast?" asked Tommy.

"I'm not really sure, but I never question Pete on how he gets things done. You should have seen him in Mexico when we were setting up the *Liga Nacional.* I never saw things move so fast."

The waitress brought over the wine and fried sardines that Mickey ordered. Right behind her, walking to the table, was their Russian contact, Ivan Sakolov. A skinny Russian man with light skin and hair, indicating his Armenian background, Ivan wore grey pants and a blue shirt with stains under his armpits. His demeanor came from his father, a bigwig with the Dynamo sports club. As a youngster he didn't excel in sports, but he was intelligent and spoke English. He looked to be about twenty, but he was actually thirty-three, a few years younger than Mickey.

"I'm Tommy Amendola, and this is Mickey Rossetti. We're glad to meet you and excited about Russia looking to start its own football federation." Tommy, who had a way of making someone feel accepted, shook Ivan's hand.

"Likewise," Ivan said. "It's a pleasure to meet you both."

"Where did you learn to speak English so well?" Tommy asked.

"Our Russian schools teach us what we need to know in order to succeed in the outside world. We're not all shoe-banging communists. There's a lot that the Western world doesn't know about us." Ivan answered confidently. "Didn't you coach at Yale, Tommy?"

"I was there for twenty years before I retired. After a few years I got involved with the European Football League and opened EFL Clinics Inc. with Rossetti Enterprises."

Mickey wasn't sure about the Russian right off the bat, as he had an air of superiority about him that he didn't like, but he realized that, if he and Tommy could get involved with him, it would open up many avenues for business. "Glad to make your acquaintance, Ivan. How far along are you in establishing the league in Moscow?"

"The federation is being formed now, and we've been meeting for a few months. We know the game is new to us, but we have set a goal to be the best in Europe within two years."

*Could this Russian really think they would be the best in Europe that fast?* Mickey paused before speaking so he wouldn't offend his guest. "That's a little quick, don't you think?"

"Anything is possible in Russia, and if we're going to do business, you better understand that. In Russia, if we wait that long, we'll be removed from the federation. We have the money, facilities, and contacts to get things done. It's just our way."

Ivan called over the waitress and ordered a Peroni beer. "Tommy, how long have you been working with the EFL?"

"I've been with them for a few years now and running clinics mostly in England, Italy, and the Scandinavian countries. The other federations are beginning to catch on, but it all takes time."

"What about the EFL as a whole?" Ivan asked. "Do you think the concept would work?"

"If run properly it should, but right now it's a loose organization of fourteen federation countries trying to learn the game. It's not an easy sport, but they realize what needs to be done. An expat in London named Billy Whitemore started it, and the league has been running for three years. If they keep on the path they're on, it just might work."

Ivan sat back and stared at a bikini-clad honey passing by.

"Mickey, what's your background, and how did this all come about?"

*Could he really be this arrogant? This Russian honestly believes they could be the best in two years and Russia could run the league.* Until now Mickey was just listening and trying to get a read on Ivan. "To make a long story short, Rossetti Enterprises has been involved in a Mexican football league for three years and EFL Clinics Inc. for two years with Tommy in Europe. We've been very successful." *I'm damn sure not going to give Ivan too much information at this point.*

"I may need some background on both companies and some letters of reference."

*I don't like this guy at all.* Mickey pretended he didn't hear the last comment. "What about equipment, footballs, and yard markers, not to mention offensive and defensive plays?"

Ivan gave him an impish grin. "I thought that is what you were here for? We'll need help, but once we get the hang of it, we'll give the NFL a run for its money."

*I can't believe what I'm hearing.* Now Mickey let loose and dropped the business speak. "Ivan, you're fuckin' kidding me, right? In ten years you won't be able to beat the best high school team in the States. Shit, you haven't even kicked an extra point yet!" *This isn't the way to get business, but I'm not gonna let this Russian push me around.*

Before Ivan could answer, Tommy got between both of them to try to calm the situation. Ivan had a smug look on his face, and at that moment what Pete said to Mickey came back to him. *The Russian contact will be arrogant and think he's superior, so let him think it. Hold your ground but don't get pissed off.*

*Oh well. A little late, but at least I remembered,* Mickey recalled to himself.

"Ivan, it's a little late, and I think we might have had a few too many drinks," Mickey said. "We'll continue this tomorrow."

Tommy and Mickey said good-bye to Ivan and headed back to their hotel. On the way they stopped along the sea and sat on a bench to catch some fresh air.

"Is that Russian arrogant, or is it me?" Tommy lit a cigarette.

"He can kiss my ass. In two years they should be the best in Europe? Who the fuck does he think he is? They haven't even scored a touchdown yet, and the Russians are the European champs. Better than the NFL? What do you think?"

"I guess they have the people, size, and numbers, but they have no idea of the talent needed at certain positions on the offensive side. Defensively it will be easier, but they'll still need to learn the game like everyone else. It will take years. Shoot, they need to run clinics, watch film, and learn the strategy of the game. Ivan has no idea what it'll take."

"I'm not sure we can trust this guy. Does he have the power and money to make the deals? He's an arrogant bastard. That's for sure. But I need to call Pete to be sure this guy is on the level. I know he set it up, but we need to be sure before we offer him anything." *Do we want to deal with this guy on this type of venture? Getting Rossetti Enterprises into Moscow would be great, but I need to be sure it would work.* "I want you to be the good guy and let me play the bad cop. Shit, I did a pretty good job already. We need to keep this guy off balance a bit and close the deal if Pete okays it."

"Not a problem. Just let me know what you want me to do."

"I think we should invite him to join us on the remainder of our trip. He can see what we've done so far with these other countries and then maybe, with the help of the Scandinavians, we can close the deal before we go back to the States. What do you think?"

Tommy lit another cigarette. "That's a pretty good plan, and with our meetings and clinics the rest of the week, Ivan will get a good hands-on feel for the program. It's worth a shot."

"If he comes with us, we'll try to close the deal in Finland before we all leave for home. I'm guessing he's under a little pressure to get this done. If we move forward, I think we need to up the ante to fifty thousand for the initial plans. If he pays it, he should mean business."

"The numbers are up to you. I handle coaching the game."

"Then that's it. We finish the trip with Ivan and then head home to settle some business in New York. Get to Ivan and see if he can join us for the next few days."

"I'll talk to him tomorrow and see what he wants to do." Tommy stamped out another cigarette.

"You better stop smoking. The shit's going to kill you."

They got up from the bench and walked back to the hotel. Mickey needed to call Pete to clear things, and Tommy couldn't wait to sit on the balcony for another smoke.

The meetings the next day lasted well into the night, but when it was over, Ivan, Tommy, and Mickey went for a late-night snack at the corner gelato shop. They were all tired, but time was of the essence, and they needed to discuss things.

Ivan didn't hold back. "Are these people full of shit, or is it me?"

"Why?" Tommy retorted.

"They sit here and think the NFL gives a shit about what they're doing. Then they argue over the dumbest things and never agree on anything."

Tommy and Mickey looked at each other and laughed. How the Russian had figured that out so quickly was beyond them, but it was exactly how they felt.

"Ivan, excuse us for laughing, but you catch on pretty quick. Italy, England, and the Scandinavians, especially Sweden and Finland, seem to know what is going on. All the other federations are getting smoke blown up their asses and can't smell it," Mickey said.

Mickey looked at Tommy and then at Ivan. "If you want to work with us, Ivan, we gotta cut the bullshit and work together. There's no way you're gonna run over Europe in two years. You might do it in five to ten, but that depends on how much time, effort, and money Russia is willing to put into it. I won't even discuss the NFL."

"You must understand that we don't have a lot of time. Others in the USSR are trying to get a league together, and we might have competition. I need to do it fast and show results."

"How do we know that the other people aren't already ahead of you?"

"They aren't, and honestly you'll probably never know or be able to find out. You'll have to trust me if we move forward."

"Trust comes from being up front with each other and watching each other's back. These countries don't trust each other, and they probably don't trust you either. That's the one problem with the EFL." Mickey looked directly into Ivan's eyes. "You want to work with us? That's fine, but it goes two ways...not one."

They let the conversation drop for a few seconds so Tommy could light another cigarette. "Ivan, we thought it might be good if you joined us on the last four days of our trip in Europe? I know it's kind of quick, but the opportunity is there. You'd get a firsthand look at what we do and what we're all about."

"I could work that out, but I need to show some type of progress from this trip. I've been assigned to assess the situation and decide which direction we go in."

"You seem to be under a little pressure?"

"You must understand. In Russia the pressure is constant. The federation has been approved by the Soviet Sports Commission, but the business behind the federation is also a major part of the program. It is run by the Vladikoff's who will also be involved. I must show progress."

"Why don't you just join us and see where it goes?" Mickey asked. "We'll be with the four best federations, and at least you'll be able to provide a good report when you get back to Moscow on the state of American football in Europe. We can also discuss how we can best assist you in the process."

Ivan hoisted his glass. "I'll contact my people back home and advise them on my new plans. As you said it'll give me a chance to assess the whole situation in a week's time."

*I'm surprised he agreed to the trip so quickly. He must be under more pressure than I thought. I'll need to get more insight from Pete on the Russian manner of doing business.* But Mickey's gut feeling said that Ivan needed to make a deal.

They left Rimini and headed to Milan, where they met Giuseppe Pronto who was in charge of the Italian federation. Most of the football was played in the north in the industrial cities rather than the resort towns of the south. The best two teams were in Milan and Parma.

After the meeting Mickey, Ivan, and Tommy caught a quick dinner at the airport in Milano.

"The Italians seem to have a pretty good feel for the game," Ivan said.

"They've spent most of their time on clinics, at first with coaches and players, rather than just rushing into the whole program. That's why I told you it would take time." Tommy paused. "The key is to take a systematic approach to the game and to slowly grow it. A lot of countries usually think they can jump right in and play. Football is a complicated game."

"We need to be sure we approach it cautiously but have the momentum going in the right direction at the same time. The worst thing we could do in Russia is take too much time. We must be the first to be up and running."

"I understand that, but there's more to this than just learning the game. Mickey works on the other aspects as well so our plan isn't only the Xs and Os, as we say, but about making money to keep the sport going."

This was Mickey's hint to start his sales pitch. Mickey and Tommy had sold the concept a few times and worked well as a team. "We've also laid the groundwork for sponsorship and product marketing. Italy, England, Finland, and Sweden are the best because they have followed our plans for the last two years and they're beginning to see results. Italy won the European Cup last year, and the only countries to show profits are the ones we deal with directly," Mickey added. "Not a bad track record."

"Your sponsorship and marketing will be new concepts to us as I learned in the EFL meetings. We'll need to see how this fits into our business method and adapt it where we can. Monies for Russian sports come through the federations and the government."

Mickey realized a lot of the concepts—not only business but operationally—would be new to the Russians and the learning curve could be high. As in the sport, he might need to take a systematic approach to it. "Ivan, the marketing of the league is as important as the game itself. Initially there will probably not be any TV, but we still need to get butts into the stadiums. It's important to be able to get sponsorships lined up before the opening game to promote the season and the teams. The sponsorship dollars help offset the cost of running the league."

"I have studied a little on these sponsorship methods and marketing, but we need to have a better understanding on how we work these through our Soviet system. Getting the sponsors should be easy when we work with the Vladikoff brothers. If the deal goes through, we can meet them when you come to Moscow."

They boarded the Alitalia flight to London and arrived late in the evening.

Lance, the English federation's rep, met them the next morning at the hotel and brought them out to their offices in Wembley. "We just finished the facility, and we're looking to get a few sponsors to help with the cost of maintaining the area. Without sponsors this game doesn't succeed. At least that's how it is in England."

"As I said earlier, you need to have a well-balanced approach to keep the league alive, Ivan," said Mickey. "The games can be good, but if there aren't enough people in the stands and companies providing monetary support, the league won't last long."

"I just don't understand. In Russia the government, through the federations, pays for what is needed. Why would I need anything else? Doesn't the government assist with sport programs here and in the U.S.?"

Mickey stepped back for a minute and realized he was making a mistake that Pete had advised him against many years ago. *Don't think the only way is the American way. Remember other countries do things differently.*

"Ivan, we can discuss our way of supporting the league, and we'll need to see how you do things in Moscow. There's probably a way to incorporate both ways of doing business to make the Russian Football League a success." He paused to think. *The upside of the situation is that, if the Russians subsidize the league through the sports organizations, then the extra revenue generated by sponsorships and in-kind programs would have a bigger impact on the program.*

"Let's look at both systems, and then we can decide what to do later. We'll be working the program in Moscow, not New York," Ivan replied.

*Ivan is right. I might need to adapt my way of thinking to the Russian business model,* Mickey pondered.

The rest of the day, Ivan, Tommy, and Mickey were with the other members of the federation watching the Wembley Bulldogs practice.

"Ivan, see the quarterback over there running the passing drill?" Tommy pointed to the player. "He starts for the team, but part of his responsibility is to teach the English players the finer points of the game. This can be in physical drills or the mental aspect of the sport. Both are important."

Ivan watched and absorbed everything. When practice was over, he sat with Tommy in the stands. "How long before we could get two or three coaches, a couple quarterbacks, and a few wide receivers over to Moscow?"

"If we can draw up the papers in Finland to start the ball rolling, we should be able to get the players and coaches over in a few weeks. You need to be sure you pay these players and coaches the standard EFL rates that have been established for these programs."

Ivan looked at Tommy. "Let's talk to Mickey and see if we can incorporate the whole program into the initial agreement. I want to start working on the marketing concepts, along with the operations of the game. My father's wrestling federation will fund this once the papers are signed and until we can get a football federation in place. That's how EFL Clinics Inc. and Rossetti Enterprises will be paid."

At a local pub near the pitch, a bunch of the players wanting to meet them were already there. Ivan was working the room pretty well. *Maybe this is going to work? I need to be sure this works properly. It's a huge opportunity with a chance for a lot of profit.*

Mickey found Tommy at the bar and ordered a pint of bitters. "Tommy, has Ivan mellowed a bit, or am I imagining things?"

"No, he looks comfortable, and we talked this afternoon about starting the paperwork for EFL Clinics Inc. and making Rossetti Enterprises the sole supplier to his federation. I would have told you sooner, but this is the first time we've been alone." Tommy said with that crooked-toothed smile of his.

"What makes you think he's relaxed?"

"I think we gave him a good look at what this is all about. He's met a lot of people from different countries so maybe he realizes the Russians have a long way to go. Who knows? Maybe he just likes us." He slapped Mickey on the back, and they both knew they were in for some journey.

At the end of the evening, they went back to the Cumberland and had a nightcap at the hotel bar.

"So Ivan, did you get enough information for one day?" Mickey asked.

"Sure did. I'm glad I came with you on this trip."

"Speaking for both me and Tommy, we're glad you did, and I think we've accomplished a few things."

Ivan downed his beer. "I spoke to Tommy earlier today about initiating the paperwork for EFL Clinics and Rossetti. I'd like to try to get the initial contracts in order before I go back to Russia." Ivan knew that, if he could get this done, he'd get a head start on the competition.

Mickey looked at Tommy. "Ivan, I think we can. We can work on the initial letter of agreements and start the contract process in Helsinki. Once you get them signed and send the first payment to us, we'll release the initial plans to you. You can also get another look at how Finland and Sweden have adapted our plans to their needs. That's a work in progress and can't be detailed in the agreements, but it's normal. Would you be able to get the agreements to Moscow?"

"As soon as I get them, I'll pass them on and let my people know that we'll need to review them, make any necessary changes, and get them back signed to you. It shouldn't take long."

They shook hands, and all three went to bed. In the morning they flew to Helsinki to meet Ari Bruun and Peter Erikson from Sweden to finalize the deal.

Tommy, Ivan, and Mickey were walking down a path on the outskirts of Helsinki, and ahead of them was a cabin with a small chimney. It was twilight, and the sun was going down.

"Mickey, it looks like Uncle Tom's cabin," Tommy remarked.

Tommy looked at his watch. "Hey, Mickey, it's almost midnight, and the sun is still out. We could hold four practices a day if we lived here."

Mickey just shook his head in astonishment. The cabin, split in half, was no more than the size of a small bedroom. The first part was a simple sitting room with wood benches and a few pails filled with beer, soda, and ice. A small entry was in the next room, and in the corner were a fire pit and a chimney. Sitting on the ledge of the pit were sticks with sausages cooking slowly from the heat of the fire. The saunas that Mickey had been in were small and had units with electric coils and stones to create the heat, but nothing like this one. They undressed in the outer room and sat by the fire pit, as was the custom.

"It's called a *savasauna,* and they're very popular in Finland," Ari advised. "In the old days, this was how it was done, and we made sure we've kept up the tradition. After we sweat for a while, we'll go out the side door and jump in the lake."

Mickey looked over at Tommy, who was sweating profusely. Ari put a few more twigs on the fire, and the smoke and steam filled the outer room. When it was time to jump in the water, their bodies were wet with perspiration. Like a fire drill, they followed one another and hit the lake. Mickey and Ivan laughed aloud when Tommy came up for air.

"Holy shit!" Tommy yelled. "It's freezing but feels good."

After a few minutes in the water, they dried off and went back into the sitting room.

"Pass me a beer, Ivan," Tommy asked.

Ivan was still laughing, thinking about Tommy hitting the water and the look on his face. He handed him a beer, and they went into the sauna to start the cycle over again. After the third time in the lake, they dressed and discussed business.

Mickey took the lead. "We want to have Sweden and Finland as part of the process, Ivan. Travel between Moscow and Scandinavia, although not easy, is doable, and the teams and coaches in Scandinavia are pretty good. They might not have the talent of the English or Italians, but they're good guys, and proximity to Russia is important."

"We have been working with Peter and Ari for three years already, and the program has made great strides. They have embraced our concept, and we're looking at plans for the next two years to take the game to the next level," Tommy said. "We can do the same in Russia."

"We need it faster in Moscow," Ivan retorted. "I can't waste time, and I need to get it done. Can you guarantee that we'll be further ahead than Sweden and Finland in the next two years?"

"No, I can't, but I know no one can do a job better than the people in this room," Tommy said. "A lot will depend on the talent level, and I'm guessing that Russia has it."

Peter took over for the Scandinavians. "Ivan, we know your culture better than Tommy and Mickey do, and we know you have more talent and numbers to pull from than we could ever hope for. The NFL isn't going to do anything to teach you the game. EFL Clinics and Rossetti Enterprises' concept works and adapts to what you'll need."

"Thanks for backing us up, Peter." Mickey knew Ivan didn't have too many options. "Ivan, if you think someone better is out there, please go and find him. There's no guarantee, but we promise to do our best. We have the plan in place and the people to do it."

Ivan looked around the room at all present, but his eyes landed on Mickey. "You can draw up the papers but know that my ass is on the line."

"If your ass is on the line, then so is ours," Mickey concluded.

Ivan had accomplished what he had set out to do, although not with the Italian federation, and was quite pleased with his progress. Tommy needed to get home to start preparing for the Russian league, and Mickey had other business he needed to attend to.

# CHAPTER 5

"The next shipment from Monterrey should be in any minute," Pedro Medina said to Mickey over the phone.

Pedro was the operational manager down in Texas, and nothing came in without his knowledge. He had been in charge for a few years now, and the amount of shit being brought in was getting pretty big, and the operation was growing.

"Pedro, that's fine, but when do you think it will be ready to transport up to New York?" asked Mickey. "A few guys are interested in buying the whole operation, and I need to give them a heads-up. I want to be there when it gets here. I want to show them the cutting and packaging operations in the Bronx and introduce them to all the players. It's time to sell what we have and get out of this business. Starting to get a little too big for us, and I think it's time."

In three years Mickey hadn't saved a penny. Any profits went up his nose.

"That's up to you, boss. The shipment should be in by next Tuesday. I'll get back to you as soon as I have more." Colonel Morales had given them the okay to sell the operations to the Italian Mob. Pablo's bill was paid off, and the league was in its fourth year.

Mickey couldn't wait to get out. He couldn't believe it had been three years since they first brought in the cocaine from south of the border. It had actually been pretty easy with the contacts from the Mexican football league. Colonel Morales was doing as he promised by keeping the Mexican federales off their backs, and the quality of the product was unbelievable. The stream of drugs was steady, and the process had become quite easy. The Mexicans, headed by the good colonel, brought the bricks to an old military base outside of Monterrey, and then the shipment was flown over the border to Zapata, Texas. On the American side, Pedro picked it up and drove to Laredo, where he repackaged the product for shipment up to New York. The packaging house was on the outskirts of the town, right off the highway, so it was quite isolated. When they had a full load, Pedro loaded it in a semitrailer and drove it up to the Big Apple. He didn't trust anyone else.

Roberto Luis Gonzales headed the cutting and packaging operation in New York, and nobody was any better. The formula he used was his alone, but his cutting powders were a mixture of baking soda and benzocaine. At full production a total of ten workers cut and packaged the cocaine for distribution in the area. When the product was received, the key was to turn it around as soon as possible and get it out. Once it was packaged, it was a simple process of getting it to the main suppliers in the markets, who would then move it on to their people for sale to the public. Risky but well worth it, and for three years now, all had gone as planned.

"Not Benny Rossetti's kid!" Captain Jack Morgan said. Jack was head of the State Police in southeastern Connecticut, a big fan of Benny's, and had known the man for many years. "Why the hell do these kids need to get involved with this crap anyway?"

The FBI agent just shook his head. "Jack, I don't know why, but the bust is going down tomorrow, and we can't do anything to stop it. We've been watching the operation for eighteen months now, and our inside man tells us something big is going to happen tomorrow. I wish it were different, but seeing that it's in your district, we had to let you know, and we do need back-up."

The FBI had been watching Mickey and Pedro for a while now. The operation was getting too large, and the person interested in buying it had been on the FBI watch list for four years. When the agents moved tomorrow, they would be solving two problems at one time. Whatever was happening south of the border didn't interest them. They had all the evidence they needed, and they only needed to catch all the parties at the Bronx warehouse. The game would be over.

"What time do we make the bust tomorrow?" Jack finally asked. *I need to get to Pete to protect Benny, but timing is critical.*

"We move in at four if everything goes according to plan."

Jack and Pete had known each other for a long time, and went through school together. After WWII they stayed in contact periodically when either one needed a favor. In this case Jack was giving Pete a heads-up on the son of Pete's best friend.

"You're shittin' me, Jack," was all Pete could say. *I'm gonna kick his ass when I see him.*

"I wish I was, Pete, but this thing is going down tomorrow afternoon, so if we do anything, we need to start making some serious moves. How do you want to handle it?"

"We'll just have to be sure that Mickey never shows up to the meeting." Pete knew he had to help Benny. "I can't believe this. How the hell am I going to tell Benny? He'll kill Mickey, and who knows what kind of deal I'll need to make to resolve this? Mickey is going to owe someone a big favor. Hopefully he'll be able to walk after his father gets finished with him."

"Mickey, you fucked up big time," Pete said. "How the hell did you get yourself involved with these people?"

"It's been a long time now. The Mexicans were going to kill Pablo...I've had this coke problem for a while...they set me up. I let everyone down, but I gotta take what's coming and move on. It won't be easy, but it has to happen. I'm at rock bottom, and there's only one way to go. I just got caught up in it all with the way things went, and it's time to look at doing something positive for a change. Help me, Pete. Please! I'll owe you big time!"

"I'll see what I can do, but I can't promise anything. I'll let you know what needs to be done, but I'm sure you'll be on your way out of the country later tonight. Go home, pack your bags, and wait for my call. I need to go see your father, who I'm sure is not going to be too happy."

The meeting with the FBI took place the following morning in New York City. Pete had advised Benny of the situation the night before, and although Mickey was over thirty years old, he got the shit kicked out of him, as Pete suspected. Mickey was on a plane that night for Paris, where Pete's friends would pick him up and take him to a little farmhouse in Rouen. He had no idea what was in store for him.

"Benny, there wasn't anything else I could do," Pete said. "If I didn't make the deal, he'd be facing twenty years in prison, and your name would be dragged through all the papers. It was the best I could do."

"I realize that. I guess I'm just still pissed at Mickey. He has so much to offer, but he always gets himself caught up with the bad things. This is a little drastic, but maybe this will snap him out of it."

"He doesn't really have a choice. If he messes up again, he's on his way to prison, but I'll be around to help him out. Russia will be good for him. You and I both have faith in him, and I know he can do it. He's like a son to me. You know that. He just needs the right direction, and this has to be it. I'll watch over him. I promise."

That afternoon the police, along with the FBI, raided a warehouse in the Bronx and confiscated a ton of cocaine, along with a bunch of cutting and packaging paraphernalia. Pedro Medina of Laredo, Texas, was arrested, along with Donald Pervasi of the Braccia crime family from Long Island. The papers hailed it as one of the largest drug busts on the East Coast.

As he himself traveled to France, Pete put everything in order. When he landed at Charles de Gaulle Airport, he was actually happy to know that he had helped an old friend. *Who knows? Maybe Mickey would make a good CIA agent after all.*

# CHAPTER 6

"First time to Moscow?" the stewardess asked. Mickey had noticed her during the flight, but she was serving the first class section. She was pretty with soft blue eyes and light brown hair. Her Russian accent had thrown him off a bit.

Mickey looked up and smiled. "Yes, it is, and it all looks rather grey and gloomy."

*Flying into Moscow is like flying into another world.* He could only see things that looked grey and massive. Everything was dirty. Nothing looked new. The fields were rotting, and the buildings all had a blackish hue. *Something is wrong with the whole picture.* All the times he practiced hiding under his desk in grammar school, just in case of a nuclear attack, came back to haunt him. *Shit! it looked like they dropped the bomb on themselves!*

"It's not as bad as it looks, but be careful, Moscow can be a tough city at times," the stewardess said. "Once you have a chance to see the country and meet some of the people, it's rather nice. Is anyone meeting you outside of customs?"

"Yes, I believe so." Mickey wasn't sure he was ready to take on Moscow.

Ivan was sure to be there. They had spoken before the flight, and Ivan was to meet him once Mickey got outside immigrations and customs. The line at customs was long as hell. *This is going to take forever.* But he figured this was how it was going to be for most of the trip. *Didn't everyone wait in line in Russia?* He looked up and saw Ivan, right outside the customs area, pointing him to the left. When he glanced over, he saw two uniformed agents.

One motioned him over. "Mr. Rossetti, this way."

Mickey was both a little surprised and a little nervous. *Is Ivan this connected?* In the time he had known him, he thought he might know a few people, but this was a little more than Mickey expected.

"Thanks," Mickey replied.

They took him to a very small room with just a desk, a few chairs, and the plumpest *babushka* he had ever seen. Once they went through the formalities and she made sure all the papers were in order, he went to the baggage claim, got the bags, walked through customs without a hitch and met Ivan.

"Nice flight?" Ivan smirked.

"It was okay. But who do you know? I mean, it took me less than forty-five minutes to get through customs and immigration."

Ivan just looked at him. "The car is waiting for us outside."

They walked through the terminal and out to the curbside. Mickey noticed that everything was grey. The ceiling, the floor, and the wall decorations all had a dusty film on them, like they had never been cleaned. He put his bags in the trunk and squeezed into the backseat.

"What type of car is this?" Mickey knew he was in for some type of ride.

"It's a Lada, the people's car made in the Soviet Union. If it misses a bump, it goes back and gets it." Ivan laughed as he rolled down the window. "Just smell that fresh air."

Mickey wasn't sure what was going on. First he landed and got whisked through customs and immigration. Then he was put in a car without shocks. The driver, Dmitri, made Mickey feel uncomfortable by just looking at him, and the scars on his face, along with the bulge in his jacket, added to the discomfort level. Plus, the smog was unbelievable.

"Do you have the football plans we discussed with Tommy the last time we were together?" Ivan asked.

"The deal was that we would sign the papers and the money would be transferred to the Rossetti account. After that, we would hand over the outlined plans and start with the clinics. So far we haven't seen the money. We have received the contracts, but without the cash, we can't let the plans go." Mickey wasn't sure if the cash was on its way or if Ivan were playing a game.

"The fifty thousand should have hit the bank this morning. We sent it five days ago. Check with your office later and see if it's there. We need to get going on the program as fast as we can."

"I'll check back home, and then we can discuss the outline. We'll look at getting Tommy over here quickly. Has the federation bought into the overall plan?"

"So far they have, but they want to see something tangible. They aren't used to being put off. I know they checked out Tommy and you, and all reports have been favorable. But here in Moscow, the government federations and sports clubs run the show. They are used to getting what they want."

"Tommy is the best at what he does, and his process has worked in other countries. They will get what they paid for…if they ever pay."

"They will, but they'll watch the process every step of the way. That's the Russian way."

"Well, if the money is in the account, we'll release the plans. Until then I can't get approval to release anything."

Ivan wasn't too thrilled with the last statement. *Who the hell did this American think he was playing with?* But Mickey had his orders from Benny and Pete. "We do this our way, or we don't do it," they said.

"The Vladikoff brothers aren't going to be too happy with that, but hopefully the money will be there before we see them tomorrow. For your sake I hope so." Ivan was sure that Boris would kick Mickey's ass if he didn't show up with the plans.

"They can kiss my ass, Ivan. We all know the game, and it's not going to change just because the brothers don't like the way it's played."

Mickey wished he could back up what he just said. *If the Vladikoffs pressure me tomorrow, I'm not sure what I would do.* He reached over and opened the window so he could get a little fresh air.

Although the airport was only eighteen miles northwest of the city, the ride in on the Leningradskae highway took over an hour. The road was full of potholes, and the traffic was unbelievable. *This is worse than Mexico City. I hope the hotel is okay?* They pulled up to a building that had seen better days and was one of the ugliest buildings Mickey had ever seen.

"Welcome to the Sovietsky Hotel. This will be your home away from home," Ivan said.

Located in the city center, the hotel was in terrible shape. After check-in they sat at the hotel bar for a few drinks to catch up on what was going on. Mickey hadn't seen Ivan for a few weeks, but with all that was happening, they needed a little time together.

This being Mickey's first time in Moscow, Ivan made it a point that they did the vodka and caviar thing. After two bottles of vodka, a few tins of caviar, and some brown bread and butter, Ivan looked Mickey straight in the eyes. Both men were drunk.

"You better hope that money hits the bank and you can release the plans tomorrow. Boris will break you in half if he can't get his hands on the outline. I like you, Mickey, but I can't do much. I hope Boris is in a good mood."

"Fuckin' Russians! You think you can make up the rules as you go along. I don't give a shit what you think, and we won't be pressured into releasing the plans." Mickey took another shot of vodka.

"You Americans have no idea what life is all about. In Russia we have everything, but we have nothing. All you see around you is yours, but you can't possess it because it belongs to everyone. We have the arts, the ballet, and the best hockey team in the world, and it's mine. You people in the West can't say that. What you think about that Amerikanski?" Ivan banged the table with his fist.

Mickey sat as straight as he could in his chair. He was having trouble seeing, and he was bobbing and weaving a bit. "You're full of shit, Ivan. Did the U.S. tell you to embrace communism and all the great stuff it had to offer? Is it our fault you have no food and little in the way of products to send to the world? Except maybe that fuckin' Lada car or whatever you call it? Oh yeah, you're great in sports, but that's because Russia doesn't have any professional leagues and the Olympics, where you always win, is against amateurs. Didn't we just beat you in hockey at Lake Placid?

"The American hockey team was lucky, and if we played you ten times, we'd beat you nine."

"Maybe, but when the chips were down and it counted, we kicked your butt."

Ivan stood up and wobbled. "Fuck you, Mickey. Have another drink and go to bed. One thing I know for sure is that our women are superior to yours. Until you've been with a Russian girl, you've never made love. We're the best at everything we do, and in time you will figure that out." He turned and stumbled out of the lobby bar.

Mickey sat there shitfaced and finished the caviar, along with the last drop of vodka. *Ivan thinks I owe him something because I'm from the West, like the United States and all the wealth in the country should be at his disposal. It's not the West's fault that Russia is so fucked up.*

Mickey wasn't sure how he found his room. The space was old and musty, the toilet paper was like sandpaper, and the bar of soap was so small that Mickey thought he was supposed to take it with a glass of water in the morning and call the doctor. Without any hot water, the shower sucked. Plus, the towel was as big as a dishrag. When he went to turn on the TV, the knob fell off in his hand. *Well, that's a lost cause.* "No wonder they drink so much vodka," he said aloud.

So far Moscow didn't impress him. *The best thing they could do in the U.S. is to send kids over here at the age of sixteen and let them see how the other half lived. No one would ever badmouth the U.S. again. God, this is awful!*

The knock at the door startled him. *What now!* Outside the door stood two lovely, scantily-dressed ladies with an interesting proposition. It had been a long day, and he was looking to possibly a longer night. One was prettier than the other was.

"Hi, we're here to make you welcome to Moscow. I am Sasha, and this is my sister Mika. You can have one of us, or you can have us both! Ivan says whatever you want!"

*I might have to rethink this Russia thing after all!*

The phone rang. Mickey looked at the clock. It was six thirty in the morning. He picked up the phone.

"I hope they didn't get you drunk and then send you a few girls?" Pete asked.

"When the heck were you going to tell me their game?" Mickey knew it was part of their plan, but it was too good to let slip by. He might have given in even without the vodka.

"Some things you need to learn by yourself, Mickey. You got through the first night. Remember to listen and learn, but promise nothing to them at this time. We'll talk when you get home. No more phone calls after this one. Watch yourself, and be really careful."

So far what Pete had told him was right, and he didn't forget his final piece of advice. *When you think you have a deal, you probably don't. Stay with them, and be sure they follow through with the plan. They'll use you and forget you if you're not careful.*

"All right, Pete. See you soon, and say hello to everyone for me. Has the money hit the account?"

"I will, especially to your mom, and yes, the money hit the Rossetti account this morning, so things are okay. Let the plans go." Pete hung up the phone.

Mickey was glad for the last piece of news.

The morning was greyer than yesterday. Mickey didn't shower because it would have made no difference, and he used the Metro section of the *Izvestia* daily newspaper to wipe his butt. Anything was better than what hung by the toilet. Breakfast consisted of hard-boiled eggs, brown bread, butter, green hot dogs, and something they called coffee. Naturally no milk, but they did have sugar. *Things are looking up!*

Ivan picked him up shortly after nine with the same driver and same scars, but the car was a black 1981 Cadillac with red leather interior. *A little bit better than the Lada from the airport run yesterday. Now if I could only get an upgrade on the hotel, things would be a lot better.*

"Ivan, are all the roads eight-lane highways around here? Why is everything so grey and big?" Mickey thought he knew him enough to be direct. They passed the McDonald's and the Pizza Hut where the lines were huge.

"Our country has been struggling, but as you can see, we're trying to get current. We've had a shortage of food for years. Our buildings are old and need work, but they're majestic in their own right."

"The people seem dull, and their clothes seem to match their mood. The lines outside the bakery and the food stores are longer than the ones at McDonald's."

"Yes, that's all true, but we're proud of our country and our heritage. The city was built on the Moskva River, and it's the largest city in Europe. Our architecture is magnificent, and Moscow is home to the Kremlin, the Red Square, as well as the Bolshoi Theater," Ivan said with pride.

It was a lot to take in. During the first few hours of daylight, Mickey saw all the well-known sites, and the grandeur of some of the buildings impressed him.

They sat in silence for a while until Ivan broke the mood. "Sleep well?"

Mickey laughed his ass off and couldn't stop. He still wasn't sure what he was up to, but after last night, he figured to just play along and see where it went. "Mika was better than Sasha, but I guess you already knew that. Where are we going?"

Ivan just looked at him with that Russian smirk as if he were supposed to trust him.

"The money hit the account yesterday, so I have the approval to let Boris see the plans." Mickey thought he saw a bit of relief on Ivan's face.

"Thank goodness for that. I'd hate to think what might have happened. Boris is a nice guy, but when he gets mad, he gets fuckin' nuts. I wouldn't have been able to help you."

Later that afternoon the car stopped outside the Intourist Hotel, located near Red Square. It was no different than any other Russian monstrosity of a building, ugly, grey, and big as shit. *Hell, everything is big in this country!*

"And where are you taking me now?" Mickey asked.

"We're going to meet the Vladikoff brothers. Their offices and living suites are on the top floors of the hotel."

Mickey was a little nervous as they got into the elevator, and Ivan could sense it. "Relax, will you? These are the guys you need to know if you want to do any kind of business in Moscow or, for that matter, in all Russia. Shit, if they can help Ted Turner, I'm sure they can help you."

Mickey was impressed, but he didn't like Ted Turner because he hated the Atlanta Braves and he thought CNN was the most liberal station on TV.

The door opened, and the receptionist escorted them to a seated area. "Take a seat over there, and Boris will be right with you."

A lot of action was in the offices with phones ringing and people in and out, all in a language that was unintelligible to Mickey.

When the two guys came in and dropped off the brown paper bags, with what could only be cash in them, he only knew that this idea was pretty crazy. The cash had to be from drugs, prostitution or the black market. Mickey had seen this all before. The Vladikoffs had to be part of the Russian mob. *How the heck did I ever get myself into this mess? Oh yeah! Mexico and selling cocaine!*

Ivan added at the last moment, "We need to get the blessing of Boris and Mikhail, or no one will even see us. Trust me on this, okay?"

Boris and Mikhail were like brothers to Ivan, as his father Viktor took them both under his wing. They had grown up in the Zomoskvorechye district of Moscow. Mikhail was the oldest by three years, and he had the brains of the family. He was a man's man. He grew up on the streets of Moscow, and at sixteen, he ran the roughest gang of them all. He laid the groundwork for his younger brothers to take over for him, which they did when he was arrested and sent to prison at eighteen. After his release three years later, Ivan's father rescued him and got him enlisted in the Soviet army, which probably saved his life in the end.

Boris approached them, and took a seat opposite Mickey. "Ivan tells me you big man in American football," Boris said. "You think you big enough to knock me over?"

*Not bad English for a Russian who stands six-foot-seven and weighs around three hundred twenty-five pounds.*

Boris was the biggest Russian Mickey had ever met, and from what Ivan had told him, he wasn't as dumb as he looked. He was a mountain of a man but as gentle as they came. Although physically stronger than Mikhail, he always knew they needed each other. He was the brawn while Mikhail was the brains.

"I'm not sure if I could knock you over, but I sure as hell could outrun you," Mickey replied.

The big Russki laughed and hit him so hard on the back that even Ivan felt it. "You fun guy. Why come to Moscow and want see us? You want business, you want American football? Ivan say good guy and can help Russia do football good game. You have paper Ivan promise?"

"The money hit our account yesterday, so here are the outlines of the plan for the clinics as we discussed. I'm glad the money came in." Mickey looked him over. *This guy is pretty scary.*

"Money…no money I get plans today. If not maybe you not leave hotel." Boris glared at Mickey. He was quite serious, and Mickey knew it.

Up until this point, Ivan hadn't uttered a word, and as it was his meeting, Mickey was waiting for some kind of response. He knew Russia was a tough place to do business, and he wasn't sure how to proceed.

Ivan finally spoke. "Boris, you have the plans as promised, but we want to be able to come to you with any ideas we have to start doing business together. We'll need to start small and grow, but before we started the process, we wanted to be sure you and Mikhail were okay with it and hopefully get your blessing and your backing." Ivan thought for a moment. "My father would really appreciate it."

*What does that mean? Maybe Ivan can explain later.*

Boris looked up at Ivan, and Mickey thought he saw something in his eyes. It wasn't a tear, but it was an emotion he didn't expect from him. Boris drifted back to his wrestling days at the gymnasium with his favorite coach.

Viktor Sakolov, head coach of the Russian weightlifting team, was leaving the gymnasium when something caught his eye. Off in the far corner was a man sitting on the floor mats, near total exhaustion, gasping for air. He knew all his team members, and this boy was one of his favorites. He had seen this many times before, and the man's stamina and work ethic amazed him. He found him when he was fifteen years old in a small gym near his home, and he had been working with him ever since. The boy had grown into a man right under his eyes and become his second son.

The boy was Boris Vladikoff, and he was ready to be a major part of the team at the upcoming 1980 Olympics to be held in Moscow. He worked hard over the years, and the time had come to prove himself.

"Boris, if you don't slow down a little, you will never live to see the torch," Viktor said. "You've proved yourself and made the team. Take it easy."

"I know, little father, but I must keep strong and fit to do my best. I'll be all right, so don't worry. Go home to your wife and son. I'll see you later." Boris was always thankful for what Viktor had done for him and would do anything for the man.

"I love your dad like father. I talk to Mikhail."

Boris got up. The meeting was over.

Mikhail could always be found at the lobby bar in the Metropole Hotel, a few minutes from Red Square and close to the KGB head-quarters. A secret passageway was allegedly near the back of the kitchen entrance and led to the basement of the KGB building. No one ever confirmed this, but many people checked in to the hotel and never checked out. Because both were regulars at the bar, finding his older brother was no problem for Boris.

"Mikhail, I think it's time we found a new place to hang out. I just heard they will be closing down the hotel for renovations. It needs a lot of work. Shit, it was built in 1899." Boris took the seat next to his brother.

"Where will we go, Boris? Everyone knows us here, and they treat us like royalty. They can build around us for all I care. Is there something else on your mind?"

"Ivan Sokolov came to see me with the American he has been working with. Looked a little spooked, but I guess he should be. They want to know if it's okay to start doing a few things between them outside of the football deal we already are working on and asked for our blessing. At least they're going about it the right way."

"Do you think the American has the contacts we need? If we're going to get involved, I need to be sure he can come through with what he says and can expand into other products. What type of stuff were they talking about?"

"Ivan mentioned cars and maybe food as a start, and then based on where it goes, we can see what else he can get. If the football works out, who knows what else we could get involved in? We need a lot of shit in this country."

"I hate working with the fuckin' Americans," Mikhail said. "They look down on us like we're second-class citizens and think we should bow to everything they say. You think this guy is any different?"

Boris saw the concern on Mikhail's face and knew the tension he was under. "I think he may be, and I think it's worth a try."

Mikhail made all the final decisions, as he was the one who answered to the powers above. Their little empire couldn't be possible without the approval of the KGB and the government. The Russian mob had its hand in everything in Russia, and anyone who said they weren't involved in politics wasn't connected in the first place. All hands knew what the others were doing, and the KGB knew the most. They were the nastiest people in the world. Not only did they have control of the money, they controlled anything that had anything to do with Russia.

Mikhail's direct report was to the second chief directorate, a third-generation KGB officer named Yakov Passov. In his early years, Yakov was on the wrong side, if there were one. He grew up in Leningrad during WWII and did the best he could based on the circumstances. After the war Yakov spent a few years in Leningrad, but his uncle asked him to come to Moscow to help an old friend, Alexei Popov, a rising star in the KGB, with a problem he was having. His position was to watch over the Vladikoff empire and monitor it for the State. Not many organizations were as well organized as the Committee for State Security.

The brothers' operations within Russia were basically the same as any mob in any country. Drugs, prostitution, money laundering, and bribery were the staple, but the black market was by far the most lucrative, especially in a country like theirs. Getting a hold on products that were better than the ones made in Russia or products someone couldn't even get was the way to make money. The network went all the way back to the U.S. and the Russian mob in Brighton Beach. Bribes were paid on both sides of the Atlantic, and the customs agents on the take on the Russian side not only made money, but also robbed a little from the shipments.

"I'm not sure on this one, Boris. I might need to get Yakov involved and check him out. You remember what happened the last time we just went off and did what we wanted with that guy from Sweden?"

"How the hell were we to know it was a scam? A golf community at Odessa on the Black Sea was really quite interesting. It sure looked real, and the guy isn't shooting too many birdies on the bottom of the Gulf of Finland now, is he?"

"Don't be a wise guy, Boris, and don't talk so loud. I got in a lot of trouble and don't want to go through that again. Let me have a talk with Yakov, and we can get back to them. Do you think we should start the automobile operation in Leningrad if Yakov gives us the okay? We can ship them directly to our people up there. Once we establish the procedures, we can look at getting them to Moscow. It also might be a good idea to try to get a supplier from the U.S. rather than dealing with the Germans?"

"We need to reestablish ourselves in Leningrad," Boris said. "If we can show Yakov that we can bring products into that area, it would help."

"It sure would, but we need to work with Yakov on the final percentages and the way we do business. If he gives us another chance, we better not blow it. I think he'll put us in touch with Stephan Petrov, and we'll need to work with him."

"Do you think we can trust Stephan?" Boris asked. "Remember when Yakov pulled some of our business from Leningrad? It went to Stephan."

"Stephan isn't my main concern. Yakov will make that choice for us. But can this American get us what he says? We need to be sure on the products, and I think we should let Ivan stay with him. Let me talk to Yakov."

"Maybe this American can help us out. If we could use him to bring American football into Russia and start from the bottom up with clinics and equipment, it would establish him as a legitimate businessperson," said Boris. "Shit, we might even be able to get an NFL game here if he has the contacts. We can then also bring in cars for the operation up north and build from there. It might be worth discussing with him." Boris looked at Mikhail and waited for an answer.

"Not a bad idea. I knew you had it in you. Talk to Ivan as soon as you can, and get back with a plan. This might just work. Imagine an NFL game in Moscow. Who would have ever thought?"

# CHAPTER 7

Olga Nikolsky and Yakov Passov had been partners for nine years, and each knew exactly how the other one worked. Twenty-three years his junior, she was more like a daughter to Yakov, and for the last few years of their partnership, he had begun to worry about her. At thirty-five it was about time she got out of this racket and settled down. Not many women were allowed at this level of the KGB, and it was very rare that they were as good as Olga. She stood five-foot-ten with blue eyes and light brown hair, and she was simply gorgeous.

Olga was just finishing her lunch when Yakov entered her office. "Can you believe what these two brothers want to do now? Mikhail wants to bring cars in through Leningrad, and I gave him the okay to look at it. He met an American who is involved in football and wants to start the sport in Moscow. He's actually talking about trying to get an NFL game here in a few years. You can't make this stuff up."

"Any idea who the American is?"

"Some guy from Connecticut, Mickey Rossetti. They met through Ivan Sakalov. I want Petra to get close to Mikhail so we have another set of eyes and ears on this. Check with immigrations to see how and when Rossetti came into Moscow. Also check his background with our embassy in Washington, and get back to me on this guy."

"I'll get right on it."

"Check out another guy, Tommy Amendola. He was a coach at some university in the States, and he may be coming over for the football program."

"Will do." Olga paused. "Have you heard anything from Petra? We should have heard from her by now."

"No, I haven't. Let me see if I can track her down."

"I think she needs a little more time off, but that's up to you, Yakov." Olga always watched out for Petra, and she was concerned this time. Petra had been on sabbatical for over a month, and Olga had only heard from here a few times.

"At this point I'm not sure if I can give her any more time off. We're up against a lot, and I have this gut feeling that something is about to break. I'll discuss it with her when she checks back in. I want you to work with Ivan Sakalov on this project with the American and keep me informed on what's happening. Olga, are you listening to me?"

"Yeah, how close is close?" Olga already knew the answer.

Petra Volkova and Olga had been lovers for over six years now. Moscow-born Petra was raised in the wealthy part of the city but got disillusioned with the bureaucracy and the state of affairs in Russia. She wasn't beautiful but rather a handsome girl with looks much like Katherine Hepburn. While she traveled around the world, she realized that what she had wasn't as good as she thought it was, and she determined that Russia, in its current socialist state, was in trouble.

Her last assignment had taken most of her skills, and when she got back, she advised Yakov that she needed a little time off. She decided to travel to Greece, relax in the sun, and decide on what she wanted to do with the rest of her life. She wasn't sure what effect she was having on the state of affairs in Moscow and was wondering if it all made any sense.

Olga was closing out the day when her direct line rang. She thought about not answering the phone, but in the end was glad she'd decided to pick it up.

"Hello, love," Petra said after Olga answered the phone. Olga's heart skipped a beat as she recognized the voice. "I miss you and will be back soon."

Olga just sighed and sobbed. She had been with many men in her life, but no one made her feel the way Petra did. There was a softness to her that only Olga knew and Petra kept hidden from everyone else. No one fulfilled her sexually or mentally, for that matter, as much as Petra did, and she feared for the day when it would all end. They were friends and knew that, in this business, nothing was for sure and nothing was forever. "Are you okay, Petra?" Olga wanted to ask more, but she was sure the office phone was bugged.

Petra heard the tears in Olga's voice. "I will be in a few more days. We can talk when I get back, all right? Please tell Yakov I called and will be back in Moscow tomorrow."

Olga hung up the phone, smiled, and thought about their next assignment. At least they would be working it together and crossing paths occasionally. No one could know, but that was the fun in this relationship. She couldn't wait to see Petra again, and now she knew it would probably be tomorrow.

"Yakov had the American checked out, and he seems to be above board. There aren't any connections with any government agencies, and his dad Benny is in the NFL Hall of Fame," Mikhail reported to Ivan.

Boris was also at the meeting and smiled at Ivan. The office was quiet since the day had ended a few hours earlier, and all the employees had gone home. Mikhail wanted to discuss the situation with them in private without any interruptions. The movement in the office during the day was nonstop, and trying to do anything in secret was almost impossible.

"Good call, Ivan. Maybe this will work out." But Boris was more interested in the football plans he was reviewing than the other business at hand.

"So it's all right to research the other businesses we discussed?" Ivan couldn't wait to get started.

"We need to start with the football project first, Ivan. Because there isn't a Soviet football federation, the project is wide open, and we can establish the rules not only for the league, but for the other aspects of the game. This will open up a wide range of possibilities, and the prospects are endless. Boris will work with you on it," Mikhail answered.

"Can we start on anything else at the same time?" Ivan pondered hopefully, *They should at least look at one other project.*

"I think we can start doing some work on the cars and move on from there, but our main objective is football for the time being. Let's see if we can get the cars established, and that will open up the entry and distribution points for the other products. Do you trust this fuckin' Rossetti guy, Ivan?"

"Mikhail, I've only known him for a few months, but he seems all right. I met with him and Tommy Amendola a few times, and the football deal is going as planned. They are sticklers for correct procedures, but we'll need to work on that. Money needs to be in their accounts before they do anything, so we'll need to be sure that happens."

"Let him know that the contractual and money agreements will be met. We'll have to see what we can get over to the bank accounts without them knowing it."

"That may be tough," Ivan answered. "But let's get the business started, and we can deal with it later."

Boris hadn't looked up from the paperwork on the outline of the plan for the equipment and the clinics. He waited for them to finish. "If we work the equipment through the federation, we might be able to charge more and skim a little off the top. As long as we pay Mickey what he wants for it, they'll never know what we charge our own federation."

An impressed Mikhail patted Boris on the back. The big Russian smiled as wide as a big *babushka's* butt, and Ivan couldn't help but laugh. "Boris, you never cease to amaze me."

The knock on the door startled all three of them, and Mikhail darted furtively to see who it was. He knew everyone should have been gone.

When he opened the door, Dmitri stood there with a basket of food for the brothers and Ivan. "I thought you might be hungry, boss." He put the basket on the table and walked back out of the room.

"He's some guy," Mikhail said. "I'd trust him with my life."

"Ivan, we'll be bringing the cars into Leningrad and working with Stephan Petrov. You can rest assured that he'll test you the first couple times you meet with him. Don't let him push your buttons. He's a competitor, but not an enemy," Mikhail said. "I want you to watch the American and not get too close to him."

"Why's that?"

"We might need to use him and then get rid of him. I'm not sure how long we'll want to be partners. One last thing, we need to know everything that's going on. Yakov has agreed to it, but he told us a controller would be in place to work with you and Mickey. She'll need to know most everything, but she doesn't need to know it all, if you know what I mean? You report to us only, and we'll discuss how to best handle her. Whatever she advises Yakov is up to her. You will tell Mickey she works for me and Boris."

"Whatever you say, Mikhail, but I'll need to travel to the U.S. a few times to set things up and need the proper paperwork to do so. Do I just come to you?"

"You will come to us for everything, and we'll provide whatever you need. We're counting on you. Don't let us down."

The two Georgians guarding the elevator were very impressive, as was the list of people invited to Mikhail's birthday party. No one was sure how old he was, but everyone knew his importance in Moscow. All the significant people from the government were there, and the sport celebrities were out in droves. The women were beautiful.

Olga and Petra had come with some of the dignitaries from the government and stood off in the corner talking. They hadn't seen each other for a few weeks, so they needed to catch up but also needed to be sure to get their business done. Yakov was conversing with Nicolai Stropov, the starting goalie for the Russian Olympic team, and the discussion was getting pretty heated. There was some question on the status of the starting line. Mikhail was getting drunk, and as usual Boris was monitoring him.

Ivan and Mickey were running a little late, but they were on their way to the festivities. "What time do you want to get picked up for your transfer back to the airport tomorrow?" Ivan asked.

"I was thinking around one if that's okay with you? I want to be sure to have enough time in case the lines are long."

Ivan just looked at him and laughed. "Were the lines long on the way in? I'll pick you up at two, and we'll have no problems with the lines. I plan to have a long night anyway, and you might need another few hours of sleep."

The party was going strong by the time Ivan and Mickey arrived. The music was blaring, and the food was pretty good by Russian standards. Olga and Petra had slipped away for a while and taken care of their own business. Petra was ready to infiltrate Mikhail's little empire; Olga was just about to introduce herself to Ivan. Yakov was nowhere in sight, but that was the plan, as Boris and Mikhail actually had no idea who the girls were and what they looked like.

Boris and Mikhail were in the office suite with Vladimir, who was in charge of the prostitution part of the business. There had been a few problems lately with the girls, and Vladimir was supposed to keep all this under control. The take the last few weeks had also been short, and the word was out on the street, so Mikhail wasn't in the greatest mood. The worst thing a boss could have happen was to have one of his officers taking money off the top. In the brotherhood this wasn't a good thing.

They were seated at the desk, and Boris was keeping Vladimir's right hand pinned on the desk.

"Vladimir, I'm going to cut your balls or your fingers off. Which one do you want it to be?" Mikhail stated. "I won't put up with this bullshit, and if you aren't doing it, you better find out who is. Do you understand me?"

When Vladimir went to speak, Mikhail pulled out his knife and cut off his pinky. The blood shot out to the left all over Boris' pants, and the scream was horrid. Boris put his hand over Vladimir's mouth to shut him up. The pinky just rolled off the desk to the floor. When Vladimir bent down to pick it up, Mikhail finished the job and put the knife into Vladimir's side. At the same time, Boris released his hand and snapped his neck. Vladimir never did get to his pinky.

"Boris, have someone clean this mess up and then meet me outside." He left the room and ran right into Petra, nearly knocking her over. He excused himself and returned to the party and his guests. He looked back and noticed the slit in her dress and the look on her face. He knew he would have to find out who she was and what she did for a living.

Ivan was totally taken by Olga. Even before she introduced herself, he was mesmerized. Mickey had never seen anything like it. It was like Ivan had never seen a girl. She was dressed in a short beige miniskirt with a loose, low-cut white linen shirt and brown leather boots up to her ying-yang. She had pulled her light brown hair into a tight ponytail, but it was a soft look, not a hard one. Her eyes were a bright light blue. When she finally spoke, Ivan almost melted.

"Hello, gentlemen. My name is Olga, and it's my pleasure to meet you."

Ivan's knees buckled, but he held himself up. His mouth wouldn't work. Mickey was amazed. *This self-assured Russian is unable to speak.* "Hi, my name is Mickey, and this awestruck gentleman standing here is the infamous Ivan Sakolov. He really can talk."

Olga reached out and took his hand. They walked away. Ivan was like a little kid being led to school for the first time.

"I hate to break this to you, Ivan, but I'm the lady Mikhail told you about. The one who will be working with you and the American. I guess Yakov forgot to tell him my name."

Ivan finally found his tongue, but he still didn't know what to say. Here was the most beautiful lady he had ever seen in the world, and she was KGB. This was a cruel trick, and he wasn't sure how he should respond to this after he made such a fool of himself.

"I'm glad I made such a great impression on you, but you better deflate that thing in your pants and get it all under control before you go back to Mickey." She led him around the corner and into the bedroom at the end of the hallway where she had just been with Petra.

Before he knew what was going on, his pants were down, and she was on him. After they were finished, she fixed her hair, smiled at him, and left the room. He stood there for a few minutes, trying to figure out what had just happened, shook his head, and went back to find Mickey.

The drive back to the airport with Dmitri took under an hour. The British Airways flight to London was scheduled for a five-ten departure and due to arrive in London at six-twenty for the connecting flight to JFK.

"Ivan, is something bothering you?" Mickey asked.

"No, I'm just thinking about all we need to do to pull this off."

"Well, in two weeks I'll be back to present the proposal to Boris and Mikhail. In the meantime I'll keep you updated on the progress. Don't get too nervous. We'll work things out."

"I feel pretty good about the football project, but we need to do a lot of work on the cars."

"As soon as I get home, I'll work on the cars first. How do you think it'll be handled on this end?"

"Mikhail thinks we'll need to bring them in through Leningrad. He has a partner up there who knows how to get things done. The port is wide open, and this guy has the people in place to pull it off. I'll see if I can find out more." Ivan wasn't exactly sure how it would work.

"Well, I must say the first trip was interesting, and we seem to be headed in the right direction. Be sure to say my good-byes to Mika and Sasha. I would hate to have them think that I've forgotten them."

They got to the airport, and as Mickey got to immigration, after checking in, they were put to the head of the line.

Ivan looked at Mickey and gave him a bear hug. "It's time we start to make some money, bring cars into Russia, and become famous for American football. Boris and Mikhail are like family to me, so I won't let them down. I'll set up the company with their help and open up the bank accounts. Call me next week, and I'll let you know what is going on here. Hopefully you will have good news from your end. Have a safe flight home."

They shook hands, and Mickey proceeded through immigrations and to the gate for the flight to Heathrow.

# CHAPTER 8

The flight was a little bumpy, but the drinks helped. When Mickey landed in London, he picked up his bag from the claim area and walked out through customs. He immediately headed for the Aer Lingus counter for his flight to Shannon, not to JFK as the Russians thought. After a little wait and a few pints of bitters, he boarded and took off for Ireland. Passing through customs was a breeze, and as instructed he walked out to the curbside and found the black Mercedes. Sitting in the backseat was a guy he had never met before, but he was sure he was going to get to know. Pete had told him they would be there, and what Pete said was going to happen always did.

"Hi, I'm Padraig Doyle, your controller for the next few weeks. Pete told me what happened so we don't need to discuss that. Honestly I could care less about it. What matters is what happens from this point on. We need to discuss who you met with, what was discussed, and what the next steps are in regards to Moscow. When you return to Moscow, we'll set you up with your contact and how you communicate. Sit back and enjoy the ride. We'll begin as soon as we get to your home for the next two weeks. I hope you're up to it."

The countryside was amazing, and the shade of green was a shade Mickey had never seen before. It was a soft day with a light rain, but he guessed that was why it was so green. The house was between the towns of Listowel and Ballybunion in the southwestern part of the country, and the drive took a couple hours from the airport.

Mickey thought about the pub life in the smaller towns. He had spent a little time in Ireland, and the people were fantastic. They were polite and hospitable and always made him feel at home. He wished he could've stopped for a few pints, but he was sure Padraig would have just laughed at him. Things needed to be done.

The house consisted of a kitchen, an oversized living room where they would be spending most of their time, and three bedrooms. Stella Moore, the housekeeper, occupied the third bedroom, and she was there simply to clean up after them and prepare their meals.

After a quick dinner, they got down to business.

"Mickey, I need to know who you met with in Moscow."

"Most of the meetings were with Ivan's contacts. The two main people are Boris and Mikhail Vladikoff who run a business that I'm sure is somehow tied into the mob."

"Don't be surprised if the KGB or the government has its hand in there somewhere. What did you discuss?" Pete and Padraig already knew, but they wanted to be sure Mickey was being up front with everything that happened in Moscow.

"We talked about cars we would work through Leningrad and another contact they have up there, but the cars would eventually be sold in Moscow. They're very interested in American football through the EFL, which is set up already, and maybe the NFL."

This went on for three days. Padraig took notes, and then each night sent a dispatch that was answered the following morning with questions and instructions. It was startling how quickly things were set up on all fronts. On the fourth day, the business plan was unfolding.

"We'll bring in the cars with the help of your dad's old friend, Bill Reilly from Stamford Toyota. You'll need to work with Ivan on getting them in, but I'm sure that's what the Leningrad contact will do. As soon as you get his name, please let us know so we can check him out," Padraig said.

"In four days we have set up an automobile smuggling ring, and we're looking at other businesses in Moscow. Someone must be putting a lot of pressure on you to get this done so quickly?"

"Pete said you were no dummy. Look, Mickey, in time you will be told what is happening, but right now there's no need for you to know. Just concentrate on what we're doing and be ready to meet with Boris and Mikhail."

"What about the EFL and our contact base in the NFL?" Mickey asked.

"The business you and Tommy set up recently will spearhead the effort for American football. We'll clear the way for equipment shipments and start a dialogue with the NFL. Pete will work on that with your dad's contacts, and all of it will be run under Rossetti Enterprises and EFL Clinics Inc. We'll take advantage of what has already been set up."

"Who's going to be my handling agent in Moscow?

"You'll never meet your handling agent, but for messages we'll use four drop areas in succession around Moscow and then start from the back to the front. On every eighth drop, a message will outline the next four drops. Some of the drop areas might be used again, but never in the same sequence as before. Pete will give you a contact, but your handling agent will be kept secret. He'll handle getting your information to the right people."

*I hope this is going to work,* Mickey wondered.

"Training while at rehab" was what Padraig called it. In reality it was just that. Mickey hadn't had the chance to get any coke so the withdrawal process wasn't so bad. *If something isn't around, you just can't do it.*

For the next week, Mickey was put through a comprehensive training regimen based on the program that all CIA agents get. Padraig was in charge, but there were also a few guest trainers. They went through the surveillance and counter surveillance sessions in a few days but spent a little more time on the psychological aspect of the job. Padraig specialized in bombs of all types and detonation devices so Mickey got a crash course on this. Basically it came down to having the balls to put himself in positions that could sometimes be difficult to get out of.

Mickey could only recall what Pete had said to him as he boarded the plane for Russia. "Mickey, you screwed up big time, and I called in a favor. You're a good kid, but you need to get straight and figure this all out. You're smart, resourceful, and full of life, but you need to start channeling it all in the right direction. I put my balls on the line for you because I have faith that you will do the right thing. Few people get another start so take advantage of this opportunity."

Mickey knew the risks going in, and based on why he was there, he had no choice but to learn. "Am I strong enough to handle this shit, Padraig?"

"It's not so much that you have to be ready to kill. It's more of a feeling that you know what is going on around you and to make the right move at the right time."

Mickey thought about getting the hell out of town. *But I got myself into this mess, and I'm the only one who could make thing right.*

The day he left for London, they reviewed the plan in detail to be sure there were no questions.

Mickey asked Padraig, "Do you think it will all work out?"

"Look, Mickey, you tested well here, and you grasped the concepts quickly. On top of that, you have what it takes to be a good agent. Pete saw something in you and decided he could take the chance. Don't let him down."

"Thanks, Padraig."

"Pete will meet you in London before you head back to Russia and fill you in on the rest. And by the way, the NFL is sending a few teams over next fall." Padraig had a glint of Irish in his eyes.

The possibility that the NFL might get involved just blew Mickey away. Just the idea of two teams coming to Moscow would make him a celebrity. "You're not serious, are you?"

"Talk to Pete."

London was one of Mickey's favorite cities, and the electricity in the air always regenerated his soul. Mickey decided to walk to dinner through Green Park to St. James Park and see Buckingham Palace on the way. Reservations for dinner with Pete were at eight at a little Italian restaurant called Dasario's right up from the Sheraton Park Lane Hotel near Piccadilly. He wandered through the parks and hoped Padraig and Pete were right about him. *I'm a little in over my head with all that's happening, but I'm a little tired of messing up all the time. What the fuck am I doing with my life?*

He got close to the restaurant and figured out that it was quite simple. *I don't have too many choices at this point. Maybe something good would happen.*

Pete and a familiar-looking lady sat at the table. *I know her from somewhere.* He kissed Pete on the cheek, as Italians often do, and said hello to the mysterious lady.

"You're looking good. Ireland must have agreed with you." Pete was in a good mood.

*I'm surprised Pete would talk about that in front of this woman, but Pete must know what he's doing.*

"Sit down, and we can get started. We've ordered a few appetizers and some wine. I suggest you get the veal rollatini for the main course. Best you'll ever have. This is Petra from Moscow. You might have run into her at a party?"

*He is unreal. What the hell is happening?*

Pete sat there like everything was under control.

"Hello, Petra. Did I meet you at the Vladikoff party at the Intourist? Weren't you with Olga?"

"Well, we never actually met, but I was there and did see your Russian pal Ivan go gaga over her. Some party, huh?"

"It was great. The people were just amazing. I mean the politicians, the sports people and the—"

It hit him. *This isn't some casual dinner. It's a well-planned meeting. They're finally going to let me in on what's happening.* "What's going on, Pete?"

"I met Petra last week in Crete at a house of an old friend. You don't need to know everything, but let's just say that she's on our side. It fits right in our plan, and she'll be one of your contacts in Moscow if you need her," said Pete. "Don't be surprised if she shows up somewhere and is around Ivan and the Vladikoffs. She has been there before, as you know, and will continue in her KGB role in Russia. When we leave tonight, she'll give you her contact information, but you must memorize it and then dispose of any evidence. You understand? The whole point of this exercise is to get you in place with the Russians. We needed another agent in Moscow that the KGB knows nothing about. In time you will learn the game and play it well."

"I'm not sure I'm ready yet."

"Padraig seems to think you have done all right for us in Moscow. Do you agree?"

"Yes, but I'd like to know more about what's going on. We set up a decent deal with Tommy on the football end, but I feel something is happening."

"Tommy will be over in a week to work with Boris, and you'll both handle the football end. Relax and go with the flow. The cars are being set up, and we're working on a few other things."

"That's great."

"Mickey, it's time you got this all under control and grow up. You have what it takes, and I know that. Now you need to know it and move on so we can get the job done. Things will start moving quickly."

After dessert Pete paid the check and said his good-byes. Mickey and Petra sat for a while and then walked to Shepperd's Market, a three-block area of pubs and small restaurants not far from Mickey's hotel. Petra and Mickey sat at the Ye Grapes pub and finished the night off with a pint.

"Mickey, I know this is happening fast, but maybe that's better. I've worked for the KGB for years, and it takes time to learn the game. Be yourself, and it will work out. If what Pete told me about you is true, it'll be fine."

*I hope so. This is getting pretty crazy, but it's the real thing.* They walked back to the hotel, and Petra slipped her hand in Mickey's as they turned the corner and headed to the hotel. *Am I going to get lucky?* When they got in the elevator, Mickey was surprised to see she hit the same floor button as his. *This is too good to be true.* They got off the elevator and headed toward the rooms.

Petra looked at him. "You might think you are getting something tonight but not with me. I'll see you in Moscow. Sleep tight." She kissed him on the forehead.

*It's going to be a long and lonely night.*

Mickey would have a few more days in London to get things settled, call Ivan, and have his last meeting with Pete. *This is really happening. I just might be able to handle it.*

# CHAPTER 9

Soviet President Vladimir Vasilyev had some very hard choices to make, and it basically came down to giving in to the military commanders or trying to open up Russia to the West. Russia in the eighties was going through a state of flux.

"Alexei, we're in a mess. The whole country is run-down, and the people feel the pains of being a communist country for over sixty years. The concept in principle is a lovely thought, but in reality the system doesn't work. Food is scarce, there are hardly any products, and the products we do have aren't worth crap."

"We've known this for some time now."

"I know that, but I'm concerned with the nuclear arsenal and the status of the armed forces."

Being a reform-minded leader, the president instituted the idea of openness and the restructuring of the Soviet empire when it was mired in domestic problems and engulfed in an escalating cold war with the United States. Roger Reed, the current American president, wouldn't back down from confrontation, and in the years prior to Vasilyev's Russia, the leaders had escalated the nuclear threat.

"We must open dialogue with the United States and see where it goes," the president said to his second-in-command. "The Soviet Union can no longer exist with the problems we're facing. I'm not sure about this new U.S. president, but we'll never know until we meet. We need to reach out to them quietly without the military knowing. If this ever leaks out, we're doomed."

Alexei was no stranger to espionage and how to go about getting things done in Russia. He had been second-in-command at the KGB for many years and now found himself with the president, handling the problems of the nation as prime minister. He had never lost the contacts he made while in the spy business, and he welcomed this challenge. He also realized that his country was doomed if they didn't make a move, but he didn't underestimate the reach of the military or, for that matter, the KGB in having a say in what direction the government should take. This was very serious business, and he knew it.

"We must not go to the senior levels of our intelligence agency to get this done, Mr. President. We must work the middle agents and bypass the top so they're not aware of what is going on," Alexei said. "Too many of them are still tied in with the military, and we can't chance that. Give me a few days to figure out who is best to trust with this project. If we choose wrong, we could both be dead."

Vasilyev walked around the desk and stood directly in front of Alexei. "This friggin' President Reed is putting a lot of pressure on us. We can't fold, but we need to open dialogue. We lost fourteen nuke cases from Odessa, and the ministry isn't sure what happened to them."

"You're fuckin' kidding me?"

"I wish I were, but we just got word last night. I've ordered a complete lockdown of all arsenals until we can figure this out. How it happened and who did it, we're not sure, but we sure as hell better find out."

"That's great. It has to be a renegade KGB agent or the military that has access to the bases. Who else could it be?"

"We don't have any leads at this point, but if it gets out to the world, I'm not sure if we can hide it for very long. I would rather, for once, try to work with our enemy to see what our options are."

"If you open up dialogue with the U.S. president, you'll need to follow it through. Are you ready to do this?" Alexei knew that, once the U.S. learned the Soviets had lost some nuclear cases, all bets were off. This type of confession changed the rules of the game.

"I think it's time we confront our problems and discuss this cold war we have created with the United States. Please start the process, and together we'll see this through."

It didn't take long for Alexei to determine that Yakov should be the lead agent on this. Yakov Passov knew that, when Alexei called to see him, this wasn't a regular assignment.

They met at Alexei's *dacha*, thirty-five miles outside of the city. Security was tight, and Yakov was patted down twice prior to entering. Alexei was seated by the fireplace with his back to Yakov, who noticed a chair to the right. He slowly walked behind his old boss and took the seat.

"Ah, my good friend Yakov, how have you been? The years have been kind to you."

"I've been well, thank you, but I think that will change after our meeting. Your wife is fine?"

"Unfortunately no, but that was to be expected once she got sick. She has been fighting cancer for the past two years, and our Russian doctors have done all they can. How I wish I could get her to the States for treatment. But that is not to be. Are you at all curious why we have invited you here?"

"When my old mentor calls me, I only come to serve. This must be most critical, so if you are ready to tell me, I'm ready to listen."

Alexei sipped the cognac and began the most important meeting of his career. "We're in terrible way, Yakov. The Soviet economy is near collapse, and we can't do much about it. Our military is splintered into two groups, and our capabilities are limited.

Our society is crumbling, and some very hard choices face the president."

"What type of choices?"

"Choices that might change the Russia we know forever. President Reed from the U.S. has approved a massive arms buildup and proposed what he's calling the Strategic Defense System, which could possibly put nukes in outer space to shoot down our attack missiles."

"But that is all rumors." Yakov had heard this story many times before.

"Maybe so, but we're in bad shape, and it's time we reach out to the United States and see if we could start negotiations with them secretly. I don't want to do this on a normal diplomatic agenda because, if the military became aware of the underlying need to restructure the country, there might be civil war."

"Then how do you want to handle it?"

"We want to show diplomatic concerns on the nuclear situation with the United States. During these meetings we want to handle the nuclear threat above board at the summits but also work together on the greater problems of the Soviet Union." Alexei paused. "The truth is that we have lost fourteen suitcase nukes from the Ukraine arsenal, and we believe General Asimov and his renegade army have control of them. If this ever gets out, the whole world would be in turmoil, and we can't allow this."

Yakov had heard rumors of the Odessa arsenal being depleted, but he was unaware of the total dismay within the upper echelons of the government.

"We need to get the threat of nuclear war under control. The arms buildup has always been a concern, and now someone has stolen some nukes?"

"That's basically the situation, and the president wants us to handle it." Alexei was glad he chose Yakov for this assignment.

"The problem is the stolen nukes can actually be used. The damage could be great, but the psychological effect could be overwhelming. What do you want me to do, Alexei?"

"It's time we find peace with the West, and we need to be very careful how we go about it. We must not let this be handled at the diplomatic level. We must go through an American intelligence man we know, someone we can trust. I do have someone in mind, but I wanted to get your thoughts on it also."

Yakov needed to be sure he was hearing it correctly. "Alexei, this is pretty fuckin' crazy. You're talking about possibly changing the structure of world power. Are we ready for this?"

"President Vasilyev thinks it's time, and he's had many sleepless nights trying to figure this out. I'm glad he came to me with the problem rather than others in the government. If this isn't handled correctly, there can be major problems."

"Can we not find the nuke cases on our own and handle the economic crises we are in? Why do we need to reach out to our enemy?" Yakov poured Alexei another cognac and topped off his own.

"Our structure is falling apart. Shit, we have all this oil, and we don't have the technology or can't afford it to get the stuff out of the ground. We need new partners. We're near collapse, and the nuke cases are a major concern."

Yakov understood the situation but wanted to hear it from Alexei. "Who do you think has them?"

"It has to be Leonid Drygin or General Asimov. If they are in this together, we'll need every resource we have to stop them. What would you do, Yakov?"

"If I had the nukes, I'm not really sure, but it doesn't matter because I'm not insane. Anyone who would steal nuclear bombs is fuckin' nuts, and we'll never be able to guess what he'll do with them. How the hell did we lose fourteen nuclear suitcase bombs and have no idea where they are? Are we that fucked up, Alexei?"

"Yes, I think we are, and so does the president. Who do we contact in the U.S.?"

"My guess is that we're thinking about our good friend who helped us through the problem we had with the Israelis and Palestinians. I haven't heard from him in over five years, but I know how to contact him. How do you want to handle it, Alexei?"

"I think it's best if you go see him as soon as possible. Here's the plan we have worked out, which we hope to get to President Reed."

When Yakov left the *dacha* with his driver, he couldn't help but notice the car following them out to the main highway. Something looked familiar about it, but he wasn't sure what it was. It wasn't unusual for the KGB to be spying on their own people, and Yakov hoped this wasn't the case.

After meeting with Petra and Mickey at dinner, Pete walked across Piccadilly, up the street, and into the Ritz. He entered the lobby and thought about going to his room but instead went into the bar for a nightcap. While he was sitting there, the bellman came up to him and handed him a note:

*I am staying at the Mayfair Hotel in Room 432. Need to speak with you. Urgent, your friend from Leningrad.*

He looked around the bar but noticed nothing unusual and finished his drink. He went to the concierge, asked directions to the Mayfair, and left from the hotel's side entrance. The directions were easy, and the Mayfair was near, but he decided to take a little walk to see if someone were following him. If he were right in his thinking, this was a very serious matter and would probably keep him involved in what was happening in Moscow. He planned to get Mickey slowly involved and let him take over his contact base. Once that was accomplished in a couple years, he could bow out of the service and live the rest of his life in the little farmhouse in Rouen. Something told him to disregard the message, but he knew better than that.

He knocked on the door, and his stomach got that old familiar jump to it. He knew this was it. The door opened, and his old comrade, Yakov Passov, stood there.

"Hello, Mr. Martin. I knew you would come. Please take a seat and make yourself comfortable. I'm afraid we have a lot to discuss."

Pete walked through the door, and his mind drifted back to the circumstances where he first met Yakov.

Captain Bolder looked forward to an easy flight over Europe and a quick return trip with his passenger. His F-4 Phantom lifted off from RAF Lakenheath well after midnight into a clear September sky. Flight time to Jordan would be a couple hours. Based on how long the meeting went, he hoped to get back to England before sunup.

The plane started its descent. The captain said, "If you need anything, Mr. Martin, please let me know. We should be landing at Zarqa in about fifty-five minutes."

Pete knew Zarqa well. The town was to the northeast of Amman, which then housed the Popular Front for the Liberation of Palestine (PFLP) and three hijacked airplanes from different countries. The PFLP chose Zarqa as its home base for this act of terrorism based on the land they had captured in Jordan the last few years. There were numerous skirmishes between the Palestinian guerillas and the Jordanian security forces after the 1968 Six Days War, and the PFLP thought they owned the country.

*This is becoming a bad habit. Since 1968 there have been at least five hijackings with many people of all nationalities killed. No longer an Israeli-Palestinian conflict, it's now an international problem as well.* As the plane banked into the evening sky, Pete reflected on his last meeting with Joe Shaw, the U.S. director of defense, before Pete left for the Middle East.

"This shit's gotta stop," Pete said to no one in particular.

Joe was in no mood for anyone's bullshit. "Pete, you got something to say? Let's hear it. You ain't doing anybody any favors by keeping your thoughts to yourself. We need all the input we can get on this thing."

Pete, never one to hold back, let it all hang out. "Joe, ever since the end of the Six Years War, the PLFP has been running roughshod through Jordon. Hussein's been trying to stop it, but it just keeps getting worse. They've gone too far this time. Five planes hijacked in one day with over seven hundred people from nine different nations. Three planes are sitting on an airfield north of Amman and the remaining are in Cairo." Pete knew it was no longer a Palestinian-Israeli problem but a much bigger international conflict about to explode with terrorists establishing new rules.

"I know, Pete, and they've made Jordan a central base for their conflict with Israel for several years now ever since they were displaced from the West Bank. There have been meetings among the Jordanians, Americans, and Egyptians at the highest levels, but nothing has stopped the raids. The situation is worse than you think. It's much more than just the hijacking. To make things worse, in the last several days, there have been two assassination attempts on King Hussein. He survived both, but the last one was really close." Joe continued, "We've been in discussions with London and Cairo for some time on the situation in Jordan, but this latest hijacking takes it to another level." Joe paused. "Prime Minister Baldwin from England wants to negotiate with the terrorists for the release of the hostages, and as you know the U.S. won't take that stance. President Moore is against it and has asked the Joint Chiefs of Staff to prepare a plan for military action to go in and get the hostages. But there are more than American hostages on the planes, and we can't act alone to rescue them."

"What are the Israelis up to?" Pete knew the Israelis would be a big player in the game.

"At the moment they're almost ready to attack. They have planned a response for this sort of scenario for some time now, so it's only a matter of getting all the pieces together. They can be ready in less than forty-eight hours."

Pete had worked with the Mossad, the Israeli secret service, a few times. They would undoubtedly be ready if called on.

"We need to watch the Russians and Egyptians. Egyptian President Najib is in bed with the PLO, although we can never be sure what's going on there, and the Russians will be working with the Syrians and Iraqis to start causing problems along the Jordanian border."

"Have any Russian agents been seen with the Syrians?" Pete asked.

"No, but we have intelligence that one of their agents has been seen with Jordanian Prime Minister Hassan Majali, if you can believe that? Do you think they're trying to play both sides?"

"You never know, but if they are we'll find out and see what we can do about it."

Pete figured the timing was right for his idea. "What if the Jordanians, with the backing of the U.S. and the Israelis, attempted to squash the PFLP and scare the Syrian allies? Do you think King Hussein would have the balls to go along with it? I would guess the Syrians are amassing troops along the border at this very moment. If the Russians are playing both sides, maybe we can convince them to play along with us for once. I know it's a long shot, but you never know."

"Pete, I'm not sure where you get your information, but it's pretty damn good. There's a tank division almost in place as we speak. Hussein is mobilizing whatever forces he can to combat the Syrian tank division, but we don't think it will be enough to hold them off."

"What if we could get Hussein to request assistance from the Israeli air force and do a few flyovers near the Syrian border? I'm sure we could get to General Shalev for Israeli approval, and we could talk to the Jordanians. I have a great relationship with Majali, and you know there's no way they can handle this themselves. And if the Russians will just stay out of the way, it could work."

Joe liked the idea. "Not a bad idea. Maybe we could talk Hussein into an all-out conflict to get rid of the PFLP and PLO all together. Attack them in Amman and hopefully get rid of them for good. It's worth a try. Let me talk to the president and see what he thinks."

"We're on our final approach into Dawson's Field, Mr. Martin," the pilot said. "Please be sure you are still buckled in. You never know what we might run into on landing. Once we land we'll taxi to the far end of the runway where the prime minister's party will meet us."

Pete knew General Majali would be there, and he was looking forward to seeing him again.

Hassan Majali, a short man with a bushy mustache and a full head of hair, had come up through the ranks with King Abdullah, and he was a trusted official in Jordan. He was well respected and greatly feared within the hierarchy of the kingdom of Jordan. Being a leader of the Transjordian Frontier Force prior to the Israeli-Jordan conflict in 1948, he was well known for his fierce loyalty to King Abdullah and later to the Arab Legion. He and Pete had met during this time and formed a mutual respect.

"Nice to see you again, Pete. It's been many years. Lost a bit of hair I see."

"Yeah, lost a bit, but everything else is still working."

Standing behind Hassan was a man Pete had never seen before.

"I'd like you to meet Yakov Passov from Russia." Hassan had a slight grin on his face.

Pete knew that it was rare to see a Soviet agent standing beside a Jordanian general.

"Nice to meet you. A little far from Moscow, aren't you?"

"A little closer than Washington, wouldn't you say, Mr. Martin?"

Pete thought he might like this Russian guy just by his first remark, but he knew they both still had a lot to prove to each other. If he were here with General Majali, then Pete had to figure he was working toward the same goal. *Only time would tell.*

"Tell me, Hassan. Does King Hussein have any idea what he's going to do about the planes up in Zarqa now that most of the hostages have been moved in and around Amman? We would sure like to know where the American hostages are being kept."

Hassan looked at Pete and then to the Russian. "With the help of the Russians, we have identified where your people are, and they are under complete surveillance. All are safe. But how do we handle the PFLP up at Dawson's Field and the Syrians on our border?"

"I think we can help on the Syrian issue," Yakov said. "It's in our best interest to work with you on this case to resolve what is going on. I know you might not believe that, but the offer is there."

"Are you willing to let him assist us in our quest to get this hijacking resolved, Hassan?" Pete asked.

Being this was uncharted territory, no one was sure what to do. Hassan had to make the choice as the world was watching his country. The Russian and Pete were just pawns in a world chess game.

"Yakov, it would be best if the Syrians stood down at the borders and let the Jordanians handle the PLFP in this case. They have crossed the line, and the Jordanian government needs to be the winner. Do what you can with the Syrians, and we can hopefully get this situation handled very quickly."

The Russian nodded in agreement, shook their hands, and walked out of the tent. *The Russians have an ulterior motive, but now isn't the time. I'm supposed to settle the problem and get back home.*

"What do you know about our Russian friend, Hassan?"

"He's been working behind the scenes with the Syrians and making some progress. I'm not sure of his final intention, but let's see where it plays out."

Following his meeting with the king the following day, Hassan reported to Pete. "After transferring most of the hostages to the city of Amman, the PFLP took the unprecedented step of blowing up the three planes on the runway. Forty of the hostages are secured near the airfield, and the remaining hostages are in Amman. The king thinks your idea might work, but he wants to be sure the Israelis and Americans are definitely on board for the entire plan. This whole thing could back-fire, but he realizes it's time to get the PFLP off Jordanian soil."

"Everything is in place as we discussed, and both governments are determined to stop this threat from going any further. Hopefully the Russian can handle the Syrians and make the job a little easier. We would love nothing more than to displace this bunch of terror-ists and hopefully keep them off balance for a while."

The plan was put into full effect. The Israeli planes did a few flyovers near the Syria border, and the troops amassed there stood down, as Hassan requested. Yakov did as he said he would, and the Syrians backed off, leaving the opening for the Jordanians to com-mence their assault on the PFLP.

An all-out attack was launched in Amman and the other cities under PFLP control. The fighting lasted for a few weeks, but the Jordanians immediately recaptured the cities, and the hostages were released. When the crisis ended, an American CIA agent and his Russian counterpart had assisted the Jordanians in get-ting their country back. When Pete's jet taxied down the runway, they happened to pass a Soviet MIG off to the right side. When his plane passed Yakov turned and saluted Pete with a big grin on his face. Pete wasn't sure what it meant, but he was sure it wouldn't be the last time he saw this man.

# CHAPTER 10

General Asimov had no question in his mind that what he was doing was best for his beloved country. There had been rumblings lately from the weak government about *glasnost* (openness) and *perestroika* (restructuring), and he had never heard such things. *Lenin and Stalin would turn over in their graves, and I'd be damned if my country would open up to the West and restructure the way of life in my Russia. I've fought too long and hard for my country to let this happen.*

It had been quite easy stealing the weapons from the arsenal outside of Odessa. Once he had all his men in place, the plan had worked better than he had expected. Director Drygin's plans were very accurate. There was even a question whether the Defense Ministry even knew they were missing. The controls they had over the nukes had been so outdated for so long that he bet they didn't even know the total number of tactical warheads in the Odessa arsenal, never mind in the entire country.

"Leonid, they still haven't found out about the passageway from the kitchen to the basement of the headquarters, have they? This secret must be over fifty years old. Unbelievable."

"When you are the best intelligence agency in the world, there are many kept secrets. Tell me, do you still have that little honey you met at the Metropole Hotel last month?" asked the director.

Drygin found it unbelievable that the general didn't even know she was from the KGB. The remark surprised the general, but he didn't let it show. Drygin knew everything.

Drygin was the director of the Second Chief Directorate of the Soviet Union, which ran the KGB. At thirteen he was shipped out to live with an uncle in the town of Gori in the Soviet state of Georgia. Gori was the birthplace of Joseph Stalin, and young Drygin was absorbed into the Stalinist doctrine of Russian rule. Everything was for all the people and not a special few.

When he was old enough to leave Gori, he made his way to Moscow and immediately fell in with the right people. The director of the KGB at that time, Vladimir Vasilyev, saw Leonid as a threat and decided to keep him close so he could monitor him. As time went by, Drygin was promoted through the ranks, but Vasilyev was too connected for an underling to oust him. All Drygin could do was wait for his chance, no matter how long it took.

"Our plan seems to be taking shape, General. Do you think Alexei or President Vasilyev has any idea what we're up to?"

Asimov shifted in his chair. He knew the hatred that the director had for Alexei and President Vasilyev. "I don't think they have any idea, Director."

"I hope not. It's time we caught them off guard and beat them at their own game. I can't wait to see the look on their faces before they both die. Are the suitcases safely stowed in Odessa, General?"

"The last time I talked to Colonel Marisova, they were, and he was putting the final security measures into place. The next part of the plan will take a little while to get going, but it should all be done within a few months. I'll finalize the locations and set up the teams."

They had decided that ten agents from the KGB would pick up the nuke cases and bring them to their own embassies in ten world cities. By blowing up their own embassies, it would show they weren't connected with the current Soviet government. By hitting these cities, they would show they were fed up with the West and its politics.

"Finalize them and let me know so I can give you final approval on the sites," Drygin demanded. "The key now is to get the scientists that we need to figure out the remote detonation. If we're going to put pressure on Vasilyev in the next eighteen months, this needs to be done now."

The tone of his voice and what sounded like a demand took the general aback. *Were they not equal partners in this game?*

"The scientists need to finalize the firing mechanisms, as they are very sensitive due to the size of the warhead." The general had contempt in his voice. There were times when the director micromanaged. This was one of them. "We need to be sure the impact is sufficient to explode the nuclear material. We know what scientists will be working for us, so we're in pretty good shape."

"Pretty good shape isn't good enough. We need to get it done and get it done now. Do you understand?"

"Yes, I understand, Director, but it'll take time," Asimov retorted. "If we move too fast, we may make mistakes." Asimov wanted to tell him to go fuck himself.

"You may make mistakes, but I don't. The last piece of the puzzle will be the military plan to take over the White House and the Dumas. I'll take care of that myself with the other generals." He noticed the look of anger in the general's eyes but could care less.

"I can assure you that my men won't make mistakes." The general waited for a response. *The director is up to something. If he's going to handle the plans for the military takeover, then my days might be numbered.*

"I hope we never need to put the plan in motion, but if we do I won't back down from taking over this government, General. We can't sit around and let President Vasilyev give our country away. How do you think it will feel to be in charge of all the Soviet forces?"

Drygin's twisted smile said it all. He was a man to be reckoned with, and he was on a mission.

# CHAPTER 11

President Reed was running a little late when Pete and Donald Smith arrived. Donald, the secretary of state, was a personal friend of the president's. He was a no-nonsense guy, and the president liked that about him. He had known him for over thirty years, and he had always been the same. Smith grew up in Eadsworth, a little town in Ohio west of Akron, and he was as American as they came. He got into politics first as the mayor of his hometown and then won the congressional seat six years later at the age of thirty-two. Both he and the president were Republicans, and neither trusted the Russians one little bit. Donald was about to get his chance to deal with them on matters he couldn't have imagined.

Smith was a little apprehensive about the situation with the agents in place, but Pete assured him that everything was in order. The president would be asking the same questions so Smith needed to have all the angles covered. That was his job.

"Mickey Rossetti will be able to handle what is thrown his way. I know he's new at it but he'll be okay."

"I'm not too sure about that, Pete. We might have a big opportunity here , and I'd feel better if we had more experienced agents in place."

"Mickey is just one of the players on the field. The rest of the team has been in place for years, and will handle their end. There's not much we can do. It just worked out this way."

"Pete, if you say it's okay, I'll go along, but we'll need to be up front with the president. We don't need any surprises on this one. This is critical, and we need to play this correctly. We have a chance to change the world, but we need to handle the threat of the nuke cases. What are your thoughts on that?"

"We need to find out who the hell has them and what they plan to do with them. Nothing has been confirmed, and we need this confirmation to be able to act. Hopefully Yakov and Prime Minister Popov will be able to update us on the status of the situation and where the hell these things are."

"Do you think they'll use them?" Donald asked.

"If Yakov has brought this to our attention, I'm sure there's a good chance they will. He feels that General Asimov might have them and he might be working with Leonid Drygin, who as you know is one bad character. If these two are in this together, we're going to need good intelligence and a heck of a lot of luck. This will all have to be confirmed at diplomatic levels when you meet with the Russians, but it's something we must take seriously," Pete said. "We'll have to work with them above board at the summits to look at the nuclear arms and the strategic warhead situation, but the nuke cases scenario will need to be played out in the intelligence community. This can't go public. We need to get the approval on the pre-summit and then schedule the first summit with President Vasilyev."

The door opened, and the president invited them into the Oval Office.

"Hello, gentlemen. I guess we have some serious business to discuss. Let's sit down and get started."

"Mr. President, we received information from very reliable sources. The state of the Russian economy is terrible, and they need help. They also want to open up discussions on nuclear arms," Pete reported. There was no time for small talk.

"And why is that, Pete?" President Reed knew there had to be something else. "Do you think the Strategic Defense Initiative might have something to do with it?"

"It may, Mr. President, but as they've approached us first, this might be a time to start talks with them. They've lost fourteen nuke cases from the Odessa arsenal, and they don't know who has them, but all leads point to General Asimov."

"Fourteen nuke cases are stolen and they want our help to find them? This must have put President Vasilyev in an awkward position. I can see him squirming now!" President Reed couldn't believe what he was hearing.

"Also a few of the satellite countries are starting to rumble with the talk of secession from Mother Russia," Donald said. "Maybe this is a good time to see what we can accomplish and try to come to terms on the nuclear race?"

"I'm not sure we can trust them. The track record hasn't been favorable, and we're never sure what they're up to. Do you think this is legitimate?" the president asked.

"Maybe the Strategic Defense System and the evil empire speech hit the mark," he thought.

Pete sat on the edge of his chair and looked the president straight in the eyes. "Mr. President, we need to do whatever we can to engage them in conversation. If Yakov has come to us with this information, then we can be assured it has come down from the top. My guess would be that Alexei Popov got the request directly from President Vasilyev."

"You have this much faith in a Russian agent, Pete?"

"He has been a double agent for many years, and although he's loyal to the Soviet Union, we've had an understanding for a long time. We have both worked for peace within the system, and he has proven himself to me many times. Yes, Mr. President, I have faith in this man."

President Reed looked at them both. "Who do we have in place over in Moscow to follow through on the nuke cases and ensure we get the right intelligence? I know you were there, Pete, but it has been a while since you retired. Are you comfortable with the people we have there now?"

"The network is still in place with Yakov inside the KGB. Our main task now is to get close to the general, and we think that is possible. One of Yakov's agents is the general's new mistress, and we have someone close to her," said Pete. "The key is finding out the plan and when they will put it into effect. The immediate intelligence is that it will be at least a year to eighteen months until they could have everything in place as far as the nuke cases are concerned. We think we also have someone who is tied in with the military so that may provide us with some information." Pete knew it was a long answer, but the president needed to be keyed in on all issues.

"I'm sure you two have discussed a plan, so let's hear it."

Donald took the cue. "The nukes were just stolen, and they'll need to figure out a firing mechanism for them. We can monitor the areas where we think they'll work on them. However we feel we need to push the process along and make them work faster than they want to. Hopefully they'll make a mistake, and we'll be able to get a lead on the cases."

"If we can start the economic progress between the two countries, that would put a little extra pressure on the bad boys. We'll need to control the process and be sure Yakov and President Vasilyev are on board," Pete added.

"And you both think we have the players in place and the wherewithal to pull this off?" The president knew the opportunity was great but had to ensure Pete and Donald could make it work.

"Yes, we do, Mr. President. I'm scheduled to meet with Pasha Titov, my counterpart in the Russian government next week to get the information directly from him. They usually stall, but let's see how they handle this situation. If everything seems above board, I'll approve an initial summit meeting between yourself and President Vasilyev." Donald paused. *We just might pull this off.*

Without hesitation, the president responded, "If what you tell me today is confirmed, set it up, and let's get this going. We have no time to waste. You both report directly to me on this one, and no one else knows what is happening. Do we understand each other?"

They both nodded yes and left the Oval Office.

# CHAPTER 12

*Dmitri must be my personal chauffeur,* Mickey thought.

The flight from London was a little early, but he was waiting for him outside customs, and Mickey wasn't surprised to see him. He was surprised that Ivan wasn't there, but as Dmitri spoke no English, there was no way he was going to find out what was happening. Mickey sat in the back of the black Cadillac with a thousand thoughts running through his head. When they pulled up to the Europa Hotel, he was pleased to see Ivan standing at the front door waiting for him. He was also pleased that he was at the Europa, one of the newest hotels in Moscow.

"Sorry I couldn't meet you at the airport, but I figured Dmitiri could handle it. Like the hotel?"

"Not a problem. Yes, the hotel looks nice. I just read how they opened in Moscow a few months ago and it was the most Western-style hotel in the city. It will be nice to have real bar of soap."

"Get yourself settled. Then we need to talk about where we are with everything." Ivan was all business. "Mikhail wants to know about the cars, and Boris wants to know when Tommy will arrive. Boris has already picked out twenty men from the wrestling and weightlifting federations to be the first offensive and defensive linemen. These guys are going nuts over this football thing. He has also selected twenty men to be the first coaches from all different federations."

*That's good to hear. This would be the easiest thing to get going.*

"Tommy's all set to start work on the clinics, and I told him about Boris' enthusiasm. I can't wait to see them working together." Mickey knew they were going to be some show. "We also need to make the Vladikoffs realize that this isn't going to be as easy as they think. It's a very complicated game."

"If I were you, I'd let Tommy handle that with Boris. Mikhail will have enough to do with the government and the federation. They're the ones who are going to want to see progress immediately."

"Then we'll need to be sure Tommy starts to work with the receivers and quarterbacks so they can see some action."

"That's up to Tommy and Boris. I'll be back to get you in an hour to meet the boys. See you later."

Up in the room, Mickey had a chance to collect his thoughts for the meeting with Boris and Mikhail. He looked over the notes and presentation they had made on both businesses and then took a shower. *It's sure nice to take a shower with hot water when I'm in Moscow.* His first drop wasn't until the following day so he would have enough time to write the report after the meeting. *I'm fuckin' James Bond. This is getting pretty crazy.*

Ivan and Dmitri picked him up for the short drive to the Intourist and the meeting with the brothers Vladikoff. He wasn't as nervous this time around, but Pete had told him to act a little jumpy. Pete advised that being cocky was the worst thing because they would suspect that something was up. When they got off the elevator, they saw Boris in a new workout suit and new pair of sneakers.

"Welcome back, Mr. Football. And you are how? Does Coach Amendola come to Moscow?" Boris asked.

"I'm fine, Boris. Tommy will be here in two days. He wants you to review this report before he arrives. If you have any questions, let me know." Mickey handed him the report and Boris went into office.

They waited a while and then Mikhail's' assistant showed them into his office.

"Nice to see you back, Mickey. I guess Boris already saw you on the football. He has thought or talked about nothing else since you left. Please tell Tommy that he's to work with him as he will get what he needs from all the federations of sport in Moscow. He'll be invaluable to him."

"I'll do that, Mikhail. I'm sure that Tommy and Boris will get along just fine. How've you been?"

"I'm fine, and Ivan tells me you have some information on the cars, yes?"

"We have contacted Bill Reilly, a friend who owns a Toyota dealership, and he's very interested in working with us. We'll need Ivan to come to the States to pick out the first cars and follow the first shipment through."

"That isn't a problem, but what about payment for the cars?" Mikhail asked.

"Once we secure the cars, Ivan will fax an invoice to you, and you can wire the payment to the bank."

Mikhail looked up at Mickey. "How much will the cars cost me, and where do we send the money?"

"The fax will provide the type of cars and cost of each one. The first shipment will be fifteen cars, and you'll need to wire the money to the bank. The account number has been provided. American dollars only. We think the average cost of the car will be sixteen thousand, and that includes shipping and everything."

"That's two hundred forty thousand American, which isn't a problem. We can sell them over here on the black market for double what they cost. Not a bad markup. When do you think we can expect the first shipment to arrive?"

"If Ivan comes back with me next week, we should be able to get the first shipment here within six weeks once the money is in the Toyota account." Pete had worked out the shipping and customs arrangement with the government so there would be no problem there.

"Bill has contacts in shipping and customs, so we should be all set there. We only need to pick out the cars and send over payment from Moscow. Bill will advise us on the boat's arrival date into Leningrad."

"That sounds fair."

"I think Ivan should follow the first shipment from Stamford, to the docks, and onto the boat. Then he can report when all is in order."

Mikhail was pleased to see that Ivan had stayed silent. "Okay. Ivan, you go back with Mickey next week and pick out the cars. Tomorrow you both take the train to Leningrad and meet with my people up there. Here's a packet with everything you need, and see me before you go to America. I want you to pick up some blue jeans and shirts while you're there."

On the way out, Boris just looked at Mickey and gave him the thumbs-up. "I look forward to meeting Amendola."

Mickey and Ivan entered the elevator. *Is that Petra?* But Mickey wasn't sure. He didn't know why but he found himself hoping that she was all right.

The drop and pickup, scheduled for six that night, was to take place at the Arbatskaya Station, where the number one and three lines intersected in the Metro. Because this was Mickey's first drop, he was a little nervous but figured no one was probably watching him at this point. *But everyone is watched in the USSR.* He thought about where he was to sit and where the drop was supposed to be made. As soon as this was done, he was to leave the station, walk around town awhile, and then return to the station for his pickup.

He arrived at the station and looked out the windows of the train. The beauty of the station struck him. When Mickey left the train he found the designated spot, sat there for a few minutes as instructed, got up, and placed the drop behind the garbage can. He immediately left the station and returned thirty minutes later. He went back to the garbage can and picked up the return drop. He slid it into the book he was carrying and boarded the train for the trip back to the hotel.

Back in his room, he locked the door and went over to the desk by the window. His hands were shaking as he looked at the note. For the first time, he noticed he was sweating. He calmed himself down and opened the note.

He couldn't believe his eyes. *Could this shit really be happening? What the hell did I get myself into? I'm not sure if I can handle all of this.* The note read:

- Get to Petra when you get back from Leningrad. President Reed is on board with the prime minister's plan.
- Summit approved by President Reed.
- Prime minister to set date and time of summit, but it will need to be approved by President Reed.
- Donald Smith will set up a pre-summit with Pasha Titov.
- Get information back from Petra and proceed as normal.

*Who the hell am I to be passing on this information? I thought I was selling cars and starting an American football league? Drugs, partying, Mexico…now I'm going to die in Russia all by myself. Who else knew about all of this, and what am I supposed to do? This is more than I bargained for. Now I'm a fuckin' spy!*

The tickets that Mikhail gave Mickey and Ivan were for the night train that left at ten-thirty and arrived in Leningrad Moskovski Station at seven twenty-eight the following morning. Mickey would have liked to have seen the countryside, but Ivan advised him that there wasn't much to see between the city of Tver and Novgorod. The compartment was small, and the train jostled from side to side. If the seats had cushions, it might have been okay, but they were hard wood with little pillows that served as seats.

Besides Ivan and Mickey, four other people were in the compartment, which wasn't big enough for six people in total. The babushka in charge of the compartment served tea and brown bread with butter at one in the morning, and then they all tried to sleep. Mickey was almost there when the man across from them was snoring louder than the train. *It's going to be some kind of night.*

When they arrived, much to Ivan's delight, Olga, who had a car waiting, met them. They hadn't seen each other since the party. *What is going on?* When Ivan, Mickey, and Olga all got to the hotel, they were already checked in to their rooms so they gave their bags to the bellman and went to get some breakfast.

"I'm not sure if Ivan told you, Mickey, but I'm going to be with you setting up this business in Leningrad. I work with the Vladikoffs and have been part of the Leningrad operations for four years now. I grew up here and know the city well. I hope you're not disappointed," said Olga.

*How could I be disappointed? At least Ivan is happy.*

Before their meetings they took a little tour of the city, also called the Venice of the North, with Olga giving information on the points of interest.

"Unlike Moscow the city of Leningrad has no high-rise buildings. The ones we have are styled in the Baroque and neoclassical design. The highest building in Leningrad is the Peter and Paul Cathedral, which is on Zayachy Island. The structure takes up a large part of the right bank on the Neva River. The Hermitage Museum is the best-known heritage site and is located in the Winter Palace."

The Hermitage simply mesmerized Mickey. It was the residence of the Russian tsars in olden times. There was a much different feeling in this city than any of the other in Russian cities he had seen.

*Maybe it's the location, or maybe it's the history that makes it so different.* Whatever the reason there was a stark difference between here and Moscow.

Olga walked them through the museum's back entrance. The meeting took place in an underground room below the Hermitage. Going through the basement was quite an experience. There were more treasure and artworks in the bowels of the museum than those presented to the public upstairs. When they actually walked into the room, Mickey realized immediately where they were and what he was seeing.

"It's not completely finished, but parts of the room are done in amber and a baroque design, which was re-created off pictures from the original Amber Room," Olga explained. "Reportedly the Germans looted it in World War II. The whereabouts of the original room are still being searched for today, but this re-creation is quite impressive."

Only one man was present, and he was seated at the ornate table in the center of the room. He looked to be rather young, tall, and good looking.

"Please have a seat. How are you, Olga?"

"I'm fine, Stephan, and I hope you're also well?" She blushed.

Stephan Petrov ran the Nosova Bratva . The group was stronger than ever and still ran the waterfront in Leningrad. The brotherhood had grown over the years, and their reach was felt all over Russia, but Leningrad was still their strongest port. Anything and everything that went on at the waterfront was under Stephan's control, and if there were any way that the cars were going to enter this port, he would have the final say on the matter. There weren't any negotiations on the deal but rather getting the approval to work through the port and how much each car would cost to bring in. The amount was already set, so the meeting wasn't going to take that long.

Ivan and Mickey were sent up so Stephan could see who he was dealing with and to get a feel for the American. There still wasn't a great deal of trust between the cultures. A face-to-face meeting was a must as far as the Russians were concerned.

Stephan took immediate control of the meeting. "We can get the cars in, get them through customs, and have them shipped to any location in the city for one thousand two hundred fifty American dollars per car. This isn't negotiable, and if you think it is, you can try to make another deal somewhere else. If that deal doesn't work and you come back to me, we won't let you bring in the cars. Olga, do we understand each other so far?"

It was like Ivan and Mickey weren't there, so Mickey figured it was time he spoke up. "Would it be okay if I said something and become part of the discussion? I'm not trying to get out of line, but it's my reputation."

Both Stephan and Olga looked at him and then at each other.

"So the American has some balls, I see. What about our Russian friend?" Stephan didn't even look at Ivan.

This remark caught Ivan off guard a little bit. He looked right at Stephan. "I'm here to do business with you on behalf of Mikhail and Boris Vladikoff. They said Olga would get us the meeting and we should work with whomever she recommended. We'll do so out of respect, but we won't be treated like shit." He continued, "We'll accept your deal. Tell me how you want to handle the paperwork and who we should work through from this point on. I'm confident we can bring in a steady stream of cars and handle our end of the bargain. Will you be able to handle yours?"

"Don't try to pull any shit with me, Ivan. You're on my turf now, and the Vladikoffs can't do much for you up here. In Leningrad I'm the boss so watch how you handle yourself."

Ivan leapt at Stephan, but Mickey was a bit quicker and got in Ivan's way before he could do any damage. It was probably a good thing because Mickey wasn't too sure that Stephan was a pushover. *I might have saved Ivan from being killed.*

Stephan laughed. "Mikhail said you were both all right, and I guess he knows what he's talking about. But Ivan, if you ever come at me like that again, you won't know what hit you. But to answer your initial question, yes, we can handle our end of the deal, and we have also located a small warehouse where you can keep the cars. The price of the rent includes security, which you will need in this part of town. From this point on, if anyone asks, you tell him you are dealing with me and all will go well. Should we go and get something to eat?"

That evening Olga reported back to Yakov from her hotel room. She only had a few minutes so the call was a quick one.

"Mickey and Ivan both held their end up today. Mickey's got some balls, and Ivan didn't back down from Stephan. It was good to see. Maybe they both have some guts.'"

"Guts are good, but you need brains to go along with it. After you get back to Moscow in the afternoon come right into the office. There's something big happening."

Olga hung up the phone. There was no way Yakov could let her know what was happening over the phone. She'd have to wait until tomorrow to find out.

# CHAPTER 13

Tommy arrived in Moscow the following morning, and Dmitri met him at the airport. Mickey wished he could have been there when Tommy met Boris, but he was off with Ivan at a meeting. Dmitri whisked him right up to the suites at the Intourist, and he had his first meeting with Boris.

After the meeting Dmitri dropped him off at the hotel, and Mickey met him in the lobby. Mickey was certainly happy to see Tommy. *They don't get any better than Tommy and Pete.*

"What the fuck are you up to, you old bastard?" Tommy's grin was worth the wait to see him.

"That friggin' Boris could play tackle for the Giants. I've never seen anyone so put together in my whole life. When he opened his mouth, I almost died. What have you been up to? Before I forget here's a letter from Pete.

Mickey put the letter in his briefcase. He'd have to wait until later to read it. He wasn't sure but guessed that Tommy knew nothing. *It's probably better that way.*

"Are you comfortable with Boris and the way things are progressing? We need to be sure to keep him in the loop with everything that goes on. You handle Boris, and I'll stay with Mikhail."

"That'll work, but do you think they have the means to get all this done?"

"The first deposit came in as planned, and it seems they've got things in order. We'll need to watch them carefully, but Pete has given us the all clear to start moving forward with both the cars and the football program." Mickey looked at his friend and had to smile.

*In all my years, I've never met anyone like Tommy.*

"Is Ivan doing well?" Tommy asked.

"I was just with him. We're working with one of our contacts on setting up some accounts at the bank. I tell you, until you have seen this system, you would never believe it works. I mean it's fuckin' crazy. Without Mikhail and Boris, there would be no way we would get things done. The paperwork is unreal, and if you don't know someone, there's no way you're getting what you need. Did you meet any of the other coaches or players yet?"

"No, that's supposed to happen tonight at dinner. We're getting picked up at eight, and they're taking us to some restaurant to meet everyone. How's the food?"

"Like shit but tonight we'll probably do vodka and caviar. That usually happens the first night someone arrives. Go get some rest, and see you down here at seven. We'll meet Ivan for a drink."

When Mickey got upstairs, he sat down and looked at the letter before he opened it. *It's Pete's handwriting all right.* But he was surprised to see that it was on stationary from the St. James Court Hotel in London. *When I left Pete a few days ago, he said he was going back to the States to get some things in order. He said I would see him on his return home later that week.* Mickey opened the letter:

Mickey, Hope you are well? Be sure that Ivan comes to the States with you on this trip, we need to get the car operation started as things are moving a little faster than we had anticipated. Everything is set up, so once Ivan selects the cars, they will be transported to Leningrad within five weeks. We've set up a company called Trans Atlantic Enterprises Inc. in Stamford with the bank account at First Federal. I expect that once we get in the first legitimate payment there will be illegal payments following. That is usually the pattern. We'll discuss this when I see you. Tommy is up to speed on the football program so be sure to discuss it with him. Let Tommy know the clinics are all set when he brings the teams over with Boris. Lastly, get to Petra to finalize the date and place for the pre-summit. Take care of yourself.

Ivan was happy to see Tommy, and the talk was nonstop. The last time they were together was in Rimini with the Italian federation from the EFL where Tommy, Mickey, and Ivan had all first met.

The bar at the Europa was full, and to their great surprise, Olga and Petra came over to say hello. Tommy hadn't met the women yet so he was quite impressed that Ivan knew them. As usual they were both dressed impressively, and Ivan was speechless as usual. When he was alone with Olga, he was fine, but in mixed company he was quite shy. *It's fun to see this self-assured Russian humbled a little bit.*

"Hello, boys. And how are we this fine evening?" Petra asked.

Tommy looked at Mickey, who looked at Ivan. Ivan looked at the floor.

"We're fine. How are you ladies?" Mickey finally said.

"Good. We just stopped in to have a quick drink before going out tonight. Mikhail has promised to show us a little bit of the nightlife. Maybe we'll run into you later. Have a nice evening."

After they walked out, Ivan looked forlorn. Mickey just looked at him and shook his head.

"What was that all about?" Tommy asked Mickey.

"Oh, Ivan is a little lovesick over Olga. We met her at a party that Mikhail and Boris gave, and Ivan hasn't been the same since."

"That's all? He'll get over it."

On the way out, he looked at them again and said with his gap-toothed grin, "They were almost as nice as the Chesterfield girls from Italy."

Dmitri was waiting for them in the car outside the hotel. As always they were never sure where they were going, but they always made it to the place they were supposed to be. Mickey somewhat liked Dmitri. *He's kinda growing on me!*

The restaurant was near the Kremlin, and all the Russians were there to meet them. Boris gave Tommy a big bear hug. The look on Tommy's face was precious. They were best buds already, and Boris couldn't wait to introduce him to the other coaches and the selected players.

"This is new favorite coach, Tommy Amendola," boasted Boris. "He teach us American football."

As Mickey had predicted, they started with the vodka and caviar, but after a while actually had a bite to eat. It was a little borscht and some meat, but it wasn't exactly delicious. When the borscht was served, Tommy was stunned. He had never seen anything like it before. It was a putrid red color, and the texture was rough. The meat was dry, and it was served with cabbage and some brown bread. *What else?* Mickey wasn't sitting near Tommy, but he could just imagine what he was thinking. When he lit his fourth cigarette in minutes, Mickey knew that was about it. Tommy looked at Mickey with a "save me" look so Mickey had to rescue him.

"I can't understand a single word they say. Even when they try English, I have no idea what's going on. This is going to be something."

"Don't worry. There will be translators at practice tomorrow, and when you take them to the U.S., we'll be sure to have enough translators around to make it work. Just be patient, and everything will work out."

Ivan came over with a bottle of vodka and sat down with them. "All the passports are in order, and the team has been finalized. It was actually easier than I thought."

*Is it the Vladikoff brothers on the Russian side or Pete in the States? Whoever it is we're playing with the big boys now.*

Ivan took the bottle and topped off the three glasses on the table.

Tommy lit a cigarette and coughed. "To Russian football. May they learn the game quickly but not quick enough to beat the New York Giants." He gave Ivan his infamous grin and polished off the shot.

Gorky Park was easy to find, and it was a lot bigger than Mickey imagined it would be. Mickey got off the Metro at the Park Kultury stop and proceeded in through the gates. He was told to find the Cosmic Experience, a mock-up of the Buran space shuttle located in the east end of the park. The amount of rides and the giant Ferris wheel along the river amazed him, and he got lost in his thoughts for a while. This whole thing was spinning out of control, and he needed to get it in perspective.

*Here I am in Moscow, acting as an agent for the CIA. I could actually get killed but can't think about that. What had started as a minor role in Russian- America relations had become very serious business.* When he snapped out of it, he was in the wrong part of the park and had to retrace his steps. In the end he found the park bench and took a seat a few minutes late.

Mickey looked around and felt that something wasn't right. The first shot rang out and hit the bench two inches to the right of his elbow. He wasn't sure where the next shot hit or if it were even directed at him, but he heard it. It seemed to come from another area altogether. He was immediately up and running, trying to get as far away as he could. He noticed someone running off to the left. Someone was chasing him. Mickey didn't stop to try to figure it out but just kept going away from the way he entered the park.

He finally stopped and hid behind a kiosk to look around, catch his breath, and decide what he should do. He waited for another ten minutes and couldn't see any activity. He slowly walked through the park and exited from the northern end. He dared not take the Metro from the Park Kultury stop, so he kept walking and picked it up at the Bibleotika Lenina stop. *What the heck is going on?*

When he made it back to the hotel, he went right to the bar and got a drink. After the third one he went back to the room and just sat there with the lights on. *Maybe it was random. Maybe it wasn't.* In either case he needed to find out, and he needed to be able to handle it. In the basic training he got, the handlers said, the first time you get shot at, it scares the living shit out of you. So far the training was right on target. The little training he had would have to carry him through this. With the help of Pete and his handlers, he had no choice but to get tough. *Maybe it's about time I did something and acted like a man.*

An excited Tommy was knocking at his door a few hours later. He was geared up about the first practice. Mickey had decided on the Metro on the way back from Gorky Park not to tell anyone about the shooting. It didn't make any sense to get the others up tight, and if this is what it were going to be, he had to figure out how to handle it. *"It is what it is!"*

"You should have seen the size of these guys. I thought Boris was big. These fellas are bigger, and they can run. The talented positions, as always, are going to need work, but the wide receivers can run and have pretty good hands. We need to concentrate on the quarterback, but that's always the case when you start a football team from scratch. This is going to be interesting. These are the best athletes I have seen so far outside of the United States. What's the matter? You look a little pale." Tommy lit a cigarette.

Tommy loved this country for the fact that anyone could light up wherever he liked.

"No, I'm fine. Just a little tired. I think I need to get back home. What do you have for the rest of today?"

"I have a meeting with the coaches in two hours and then practice later this evening. After that we prepare for the trip to the States. Everybody is all set and excited. I'll see you later tonight." Tommy left the room, leaving Mickey with his thoughts.

Mickey had to laugh. *Here Tommy is doing what he did best; here I'm doing something I know nothing about and learning on the job.* Mickey knew he had to get a message to Petra and talk to her before he left for America. He couldn't wait to see Pete.

"What happened at Gorky Park the other day?" Petra asked.

They met at their usual spot. The question took Mickey aback. He knew she was a double agent from their dinner in London and his handler internally within the KGB.

"Nothing really. Just a little encounter with someone I didn't know." *I'm not gonna get into what happened with her. Shit, Pete doesn't even know.*

It was crazy how some agents worked both sides, but he guessed they had their own agenda. He wasn't sure who was looking out for him on the U.S. side and probably didn't need to know. He only knew it was probably the person running through Gorky Park the other day. If he ever found out, he would have to thank him.

"We need to set up a pre-summit with the State Department to get this process started. Secretary of State Donald Smith will be the U.S. representative, and his people want to have something in place prior to the summit, like a good faith document prepared beforehand that will show that your President Vasilyev is serious about this whole matter. This isn't the first time the Soviets have tried to open discussions. This time the U.S. government wants to know that strategic arms control can begin. We both need to show that we're serious about this threat." *Are we ready to have the pre-summit?* But it was the one thing that President Reed had demanded.

He couldn't afford to be shown up by any country, especially the Russians.

"I'll get the message to my people and the answer to Pete before you leave for the States tomorrow. Mikhail told me that everything should be set to start bringing the cars in, as he has spoken to Stephan Petrov. I suggest you get them started as soon as possible when you get back to the States."

*What type of lady is she to be putting herself in the situation she has with Mikhail? It probably isn't easy, but she must be committed to giving herself up for what she thought was best for her country.* When he sat back, he realized he was getting to this point and hoped the commitment was worth the sacrifice. He had no choice initially and realized that maybe this was where he belonged. Petra, on the other hand, had chosen this life from the beginning and then realized she needed to work with the other side to get things done.

Before Mickey left the next day, the bellman had hand-delivered a note from Petra. *Does anyone really know what is going on in this country?*

# CHAPTER 14

Mickey, Ivan, Tommy, and the team flew back to New York with a stop in Shannon to refuel. The Irish had granted the Russians this right of stoppage years ago and were the only Western country to work with them. The group consisted of forty-three travelers on the way to New York; forty had never been out of the Soviet Union. The amount of alcohol consumed on the way to Shannon was unreal. Mickey hoped the rest of the flight would be peaceful and the Russian contingent would sleep.

After the short stop, they took off again and headed for America. Boris wouldn't leave Tommy alone, and they only talked football the whole way over. Ivan and Mickey discussed the cars, and the rest of the group finally caught some sleep. When they landed at JFK, some of Tommy's staff met them. They boarded the buses for the ride to Shelton, Connecticut. These Russians would never be the same.

After getting settled in the hotel, Mickey and Ivan went to Stamford Toyota to start the cars rolling in Russia. Billy Reilly met them at the door.

Ivan wasted no time. "Billy, can we get the Celicas in blue and black? I don't want to send too many red cars over to Russia. When do you think they can get the cars ready in Newark to ship to Leningrad?"

*I need to give Ivan a lesson on how to do business in the U.S. Why did this Russian always need to be in control?*

"The mechanics can get them ready and out to Newark in a few days if all goes well," Billy said. "Toyota's agents in New Jersey will work closely with us to be sure all is handled properly. We have contacted our shipping company, and they're ready to take delivery and get them shipped to Leningrad. The brokers and customs officials have been advised, so we only need the money to be deposited in our account. If you come back later today, I'll have all the paperwork ready for you to get to Moscow."

"That will be great, and I'll advise you tomorrow when the money should hit the bank. Can you start getting the cars ready so we can start the shipment when the money does come in?"

"That works for me, Ivan. Nice doing business with you. See you later today."

Billy was excited about the prospect of sending cars to Russia. Pete had made sure that any of the inquiries he made to the government were handled quickly and with no problems.

Mickey and Ivan left the Toyota dealership and went to Derek's Bar and Grill to see the boys. After not having access to coke for a few months, Mickey found he could go back into the bar and not need it. They respected that and left him alone. *There are more important things in life, and I'm finding that out pretty quickly.* He still enjoyed a few beers with the gang, and the talk was always great.

Mickey asked Ivan for his birth date and that of his father's. A convenience store was next to the bar, so he played the numbers and gave them to Ivan to hold. Later that night they hit, and Ivan won two thousand dollars. Ivan thought America was one hell of a country!

The money was transferred the following day and would get to the U.S. bank in three working days. Once the money hit, the cars would be ready, and they would be in business.

Pete and Mickey were having lunch at Al's Dog House in Stamford, a city favorite with some of the best chili in town.

"Tommy and Boris seem to be doing fine over at the academy," Mickey said. "If you didn't know them, you'd think they were brothers. They're always together."

"That's the way it's supposed to be when you do what you like. Where is Ivan?" asked Pete in between bites of his chili dog.

"He had some business in New York, so I sent him on the train. I thought it was time he saw another aspect of American life."

"Was that a good idea?"

"He came on a little strong at Stamford Toyota earlier today, and I thought he might need a little lesson in being humble. He needs to know that not everything over here is apple pie. Since we have known him, he's only seen the good things. Let him see a little poverty and realize how we work for what we get. He'll be all right."

Pete was amazed that it was Mickey who was talking to him. *Maybe the kid is growing up after all.* "You may be right, Mickey, but watch him. Don't let him get out of control. Be sure you know what he's doing at all times. Remember that." Pete held Mickey's eyes to be sure he understood.

Mickey knew what needed to be done. His mind was set on handling the job. "Right before I left, Petra got to me and told me everything was all set for the pre-summit. They want to hold it two weeks from today in a little town in Ireland called Adare at Adare Manor. Here are the details, signed by Alexei Popov with his seal. They expect Mr. Smith to be there with as few agents as possible, as there is a major need to keep this secret."

"That's fine. We'll be sure he's there. Now tell me is there anything else we may need to know?"

This question threw Mickey off, but decided to keep the little shooting incident to himself.

"No, Pete, that's about it, but tell me what to expect down the road. A lot of things are happening, and I just want to be sure I'm on top of as much as I can."

Pete thought for a moment. "The car operation is going as planned. The money hit the Toyota account this morning. The cars will be shipped to Leningrad and arrive in five weeks as planned. Petra has advised me that Stephan Petrov has approved the cars in Leningrad so Mikhail and his team will be able to pick up this first load and make a nice little profit. This should make you look good in their eyes and get you a little more trust. I expect they will try to start laundering money a few weeks after they receive the cars."

"That's great. What about the NFL game in Moscow? Do I need to do anything on that?"

"Not yet. We've had initial talks with them. They're interested in possibly having an exhibition game over there in August, but a lot of work needs to be done. We have a meeting with them later today to discuss sending someone over to the EFL meeting, so I'll keep you posted. We're also working on getting a Russian representative there from the government."

"Thanks for everything, Pete. I'm going to go back to Europe with Ivan to attend the EFL meeting in Bern and then head back to Moscow as we discussed. I should be back in Moscow in a week and will be sure to meet Boris and the gang when they return with Tommy."

Pete shook his hand and kissed him on the cheek. "Take care of yourself, and call me from Bern. If you think someone is watching you, you can always go to the embassy and get a message to me. Padraig Doyle will be in Bern and make contact with you. Safe travels."

Boris was having the time of his life. He was learning American football from one of the best there was, and he was eating and drinking anything he wanted. He put on five pounds in the first week. He and Tommy were getting along just fine. The other coaches were doing what they came here for and were good students of the game. The players were getting the basics down and wanted to start hitting already. That would come later. The plan was to let them work out with the Stamford Academy to see what they could do. They would be here for a few more weeks and then travel back to Moscow to start training the rest of the selected players.

"When we get back to Moscow, Boris, I think we need to select three teams the first year and then add more the following year. The best team will come back here and play a few exhibition games," Tommy said. "The EFL has invited us to play in the Euro Bowl so we can also point to that as an incentive for the teams."

"Whatever you say, Tommy, but pass the mashed potatoes. We can discuss this later. You don't get food like this in Moscow!"

# CHAPTER 15

The flight from New York to Geneva took a little over six hours. Mickey and Ivan were excited about meeting with the EFL to promote football throughout Europe and Russia. The added aspect of having contacts within the NFL was a bonus, but Mickey had to be sure they played that hand correctly. *The worst thing I could do was come on too strong with the federations.* There were still infighting throughout the committees that went way back, but with the plan Rossetti Enterprises had, Mickey felt the timing was right.

"Ivan, the train station is right over there," Mickey said after the all-night flight. "I wish traveling was this easy back home."

"Do you notice how clean the trains are? Remember the train ride from hell to Leningrad when we first went up to meet Stephan. That train was a mess."

The train from Geneva to Bern went through the mountains and valleys on the way. It was a beautiful day full of sunshine. The mountains against the blue sky were magnificent.

As they approached Bern, Ivan woke up and looked out the window. *What is he thinking?* He didn't think Ivan had ever seen anything like these mountains. Ivan didn't speak for a while but just looked out the window. He finally uttered, "Beautiful. I have never seen anything like them."

When they pulled up to the Bellevue Palace Hotel, both were in for a little shock. Not only was the hotel's front entrance grand, but the two ladies waiting for them were just as striking. This business was full of surprises.

"Hello, Ivan. How I have missed you since you have been away," Olga said. "I bet you never expected to see me here in Bern."

Much to Mickey's amazement, Ivan looked directly at her as if no one else were around. "Hello, my dear. No, I didn't, but I'm glad you're here."

He took her in his arms and gave her a big kiss. *So much for the shy Russian guy! Is Ivan's new attitude a good one? Could he be getting a little too arrogant?*

Mickey and Petra just laughed and left them at the front door in each other's arms.

"Did Pete get the message? Are we all set for Adare?" she asked.

"Everything is in order. The Secretary of State will be there ready to meet your people."

They checked in, but before going to the rooms, they headed to the bar for a drink. There was Mikhail, like a Cheshire cat waiting for them.

"Shock number two," he said. "While you were gone, we set up the Russian Football Federation or RFF, and I'm the president so we thought it best that I accompany you on the first meeting with the EFL. Ivan Sakolov, you are the new vice president in charge of operations. How do you like that?"

Ivan had a wide smile. Mickey was grinning just as broadly.

"When do the meetings start?"Mikhail asked.

"We meet with the board tomorrow morning for breakfast at eight. Then we meet the full committee at ten. Will you be at both of them?" Ivan was thrilled to be a major player in the new federation.

"Just the first one, as I have another appointment later in the morning," Mikhail answered. "I want you to introduce me to the board and then handle the business as VP of operations. I'll be the figurehead for the government."

"How do you want me to proceed after you leave the board meeting?"

"Don't say too much, but let them know that you think the EFL will be too small for the RFF in a few years and we're setting our sights on the NFL."

*What am I hearing?* But Mickey didn't have a say in how they approached the EFL. His job was to teach them American football and sell cars. The rest was up to them.

They sat with the ladies for a while and had a few drinks. Mickey was feeling the jet lag. "I think I'll head up to my room."

"See you in the morning," Mikhail said. "I'm sure you are both tired, so ladies, if you will accompany me to an early dinner, we can let these gentlemen get some rest."

Mickey saw some disappointment in Ivan's eyes, but he couldn't do much. Olga winked at him so he left happy. Mickey and Ivan went up to their rooms.

When Mickey opened the door to his room, he saw Padraig sitting on the couch watching CNN. He looked up at him and then went back to watching the TV like he belonged there. Mickey waited for a while.

"What up, Padraig?"

When he was with him in Ireland, Mickey knew he'd see him again but wasn't sure where or when. He knew it would be unexpected, but he also knew it would mean something important was brewing.

"Pete sent me over to be with you and to give you some updates on what was happening in the world. It seems the pre-summit is all set. You are to tell Petra so she can relax a bit. It will take place as scheduled next Tuesday in Adare. Also the NFL is sending a representative to the EFL meeting, and you are to introduce the Russians to him to start discussion on the game in Moscow. His name is John Duddie, and he reports directly to the commissioner of the league."

"Do you think they're serious about the game, or is he over for another reason?"

"No, the main reason for the trip is to meet with the Russians to discuss the game. It would be a good idea to take him out to dinner with Ivan and Mikhail, away from the rest of the committee. The less they know, the better. Did you meet with the contact in Leningrad for the cars?"

"Yes, his name is Stephan Petrov, and we seem to be all set. The agreement was reached, and we're all set to get the first fifteen cars over to Leningrad."

"Good job. We thought it would be him, and it verifies what we were told."

"Is there anything I need to know about what was set up with the NFL prior to the meeting?"

Padraig handed him an envelope. "What you need to know is in the packet."

There was also a letter from Benny, as well as a communiqué from Pete on a few other things that were going on in Russia. They talked for a few more minutes about the meeting. Then Padraig got up to leave.

"Just be sure to be careful and remember what you were taught in Ireland. One last thing, Pete said you need to tell us when something happens that puts you in danger. We know about the shooting in Gorky Park. Take care of yourself." He smiled at Mickey and left him alone in the room.

*How the hell did they find out about the shooting? A lot more players are in this scenario than I know about.*

Mickey thought about all that had happened up to this point, and at times he was secure with where he was, but there was always that nagging doubt that he might not be able to pull it off when it counted most. In sports he knew he had it in him to get the job done, and most of the times, it went his way. *Shit, if you complete 60 percent of your passes, you were way ahead of the game, but you always need to make that final pass to win the game. This crap is the same except, at the end, if my pass is incomplete, I might die.*

Mickey was about to open the envelope. The phone rang.

"Is there anything you need, Mr. Rossetti?" asked the front desk manager.

"Can you give me a wake-up call in two hours, please? I seem to have a little jet lag." He slid the envelope under the mattress and fell into a deep sleep.

In his dream Mickey was back in Mexico City, but he had no idea how he got there. All the Mexicans were there, as well as all of the people he knew from Russia. They were all looking down at something, and the conversation was all garbled like he was underwater. The Russians were pulling him toward them, and the Mexicans were trying to pull him back. Off in the distance, he saw Pete, Padraig, Petra, and his dad. Two other people were with them, but he couldn't tell who they were. They were all just standing there, waiting to see what would happen. He woke up in a cold sweat a few minutes before the wake-up call rang.

He took a shower and watched CNN. When he felt refreshed, he finished dressing, drank the rest of his beer, and went downstairs.

Ivan was waiting at the bar.

"Let's just have a few drinks and get a little something to eat. I need a good night's rest," Mickey said.

"Sounds good to me. I never know how these pilots and stewardesses do this all the time. This trip has kicked the crap out of me."

As far as plans go, it was a good one, but they ran into Peter and Ari from the Swedish and Finnish federations. After a few drinks and a few laughs, they had something to eat. They were walking back to the hotel when police cars passed them with the sirens blasting. They were going away from the hotel. They thought nothing about it.

In a few minutes, they were back at the hotel and walking through the front door. Mikhail and the ladies pulled up in the limousine. They introduced them to their friends from Scandinavia and then went in for a nightcap to the lobby bar. Mikhail, as usual, was a little shitfaced, and Petra wasn't far behind, which was a little unusual. Olga, on the other hand, was all the way there.

She and Ivan sat at the end of the bar. Mickey found himself with Petra and Mikhail. They sat for a few minutes before he decided it was time to get some sleep. Mickey said his good nights and went to his room. In the confusion of his dream and going out for dinner, he had forgotten all about the envelope.

While Petra lay with Olga, she was aware that something was bothering her. She knew she had to find out what it was. It had been a while since they had been together, and there was always the slight chance that they would be caught. As far as they knew, no one was on to their relationship. They rarely worked together anymore unless the case was a big one. There was more going on here than cars and football, but Petra wasn't sure what it was all about at this stage or if she would find out.

"Something is bothering you, Olga. Would you like to talk about it?" She looked into Olga's eyes.

Olga could never lie to her, and Petra knew it.

"So much is going on that I haven't told you. I'm scared that, if you know and it gets out, you will be in grave danger. Our country isn't what it once was, and there are people who aren't in line with the current government thinking."

"Can you tell me who they are?" Petra asked. She knew that, once Olga started, she would get most of the story.

"People you don't know have a plan that will make Russia what it once was and should be today. We need to be strong and take our rightful place in the world. We have been beaten up in too many ways and have given in to Western pressure. We can't survive as we are now."

Petra had never heard her speak like this before. Olga was now rambling.

"The world must know we're still strong and do not need anyone else to help us out with our affairs. We are Russia. We are the bear. Don't mess with us." She cried.

Petra held her tight, and she went to sleep, like a baby in her arms. A weight was taken off Olga's shoulders. Soon Petra would have to find out the rest and get the information to Yakov.

The reading was good material. It wasn't until two in the morning when Mickey had finished all the reports. His dad's letter just told him what was going on at home with the family, the grandkids, and other family news. His mom was a little anxious with him being gone so long, but Benny had explained what had happened and the circumstances that led to his being away. He would have to make it a point to call her in the next few days and let her know he was doing fine. Pete's communiqué was mostly about the meeting with John Duddie from the NFL on the proposed game in Moscow. Pete knew that Mikhail was over since the newly formed federation was part of the discussions. *How the hell did he know that? Is Mikhail in on the deal with Pete, or are his contacts so good within the Soviet Union that he found these things out?*

After the meeting with the EFL and the NFL, he was to write a report and drop it off at the Savoy Hotel for a John Lowe in Room 145. The last page of the report was about the pre-summit, as well as the scheduled summit with a slight twist. Part of the initial discussions at the pre-summit would be about fourteen nuke cases that had gone missing from the Odessa arsenal about month ago. It would also be discussed at the summit, but the public would never be made aware of this threat. Mickey was to keep an ear open and see if there were any talks about this in Moscow or Leningrad. If anything came up, he was to be sure to get the information to Petra. It only took a while to get tired again, but as he drifted off to sleep, he thought, *Pete is the man for the U.S. in Russia. It seems unreal, but it must be true. How else could Pete know what was going on?*

Mickey woke feeling better, and while having his coffee, he picked up the local English paper. The lead story was about a corner suite of the Bern Park Hotel that was blown up the evening before. Such a thing hadn't occurred in Bern before, and the public was quite concerned. There had been killings and robberies, but even these were scarce. The police had few leads but were in the process of gathering as much information as they could, although not much was left to that side of the building. The suite was registered to a Russian oligarch named Aleksandr Federov from Leningrad who was in Switzerland meeting with the government on unknown business. Or at least that was the story.

Mickey found it funny that Mikhail was in town when this happened and wondered if he had anything to do with it. Again Mickey wasn't sure who he knew or what was going on, but part of the training was that there are no coincidences. *Things happen for a reason. Go with your initial gut reaction, and watch all that is going on around you.*

The meetings began as scheduled with the director of the EFL, Paolo Schneider, leading it off with his yearly report followed by the budget, which all the federations always scrutinized. Mickey learned one thing very quickly in dealing with the Europeans. They truly don't trust anyone. Grudges go back for centuries, and certain countries get along with each other while others never really will or even try to. *How the hell a German is in charge, I'll never know.* But those were the bylaws they were working with, and everyone seemed to be going along. They had established an EFL Marketing Group, which a Jewish American, Ronald Seinfeld, who happened to live in Britain, ran. Ronald was giving a presentation on what they planned for the following year. Mickey and Tommy had met him a few months back when they were discussing some possible deals with the NFL and an American equipment provider called AllPro.

*Imagine that. A German running an American football league with a Jewish American marketing rep from Britain. It's too good to be true!*

"In closing," said Ronald, "I would like to thank you all for letting us present our ideas and hopefully gain approval on them at the next committee meeting. If you should have any questions, please let us know."

"Can someone explain how the deal with AllPro will work based on getting the equipment to each country?" The question was asked by the Danish federation.

Mickey, having provided the same service in Mexico, took the question. "Each country will get samples of the equipment with which to make sales calls on the different clubs. There will be a new set of equipment and a restored set so clubs can choose which ones they want to go with. Naturally the newer seats will cost more, and all prices will differ per country based on custom charges and VAT. Each federation will handle the ordering and money transfer as well as distribution once the equipment gets to your country." He continued, "For this each federation will make two percent of the total revenue for use to fund their organizations. We did look at bringing the equipment into one country, but if we did we'd get hit with two sets of custom charges and country taxes."

Peter with the Swedish federation asked, "We hear a representative from the NFL is here, and we were wondering why it wasn't on the agenda."

Ronald looked at Paolo. They both looked at Mickey.

"John Duddie, an old friend from the NFL, used to work for the New York Giants. He has graciously consented to come over to meet you all, and it was planned as a surprise for tonight's reception. There's no real agenda for him, but the NFL is interested in finding out what we're all about. You'll get a chance to meet him tonight."

Paolo took his cue and closed the meeting. For the first day, things had gone rather well. John would placate all of them tonight at the reception. John was rather short and a little round in the belly.

A dinner was planned after the reception with just Mickey, Ivan, and Mikhail. Although he knew that alienating the rest of the federations from the dinner might cause some problems, Mickey didn't care as John was the contact for the NFL and his charge at this time was to start discussion on the game in Moscow.

After the reception with the EFL delegations, Mickey, the Russians, and John headed out to dinner. Mickey picked a little café on the other side of the bridge, a short walk from the hotel. They didn't have a reason to take a car as the nights were beautiful and Bern was a great walking city. Not as good as Amsterdam but pretty close. John and Mickey lagged behind the rest of the group.

"You and Tommy seem to have a good relationship with most of the federations."

"Yes, I think we do, John. We've been working with them for a few years now, and the programs we've set up seem to be working. We're not the NFL, but we try."

They walked on a little farther over the bridge to the restaurant.

"Mickey, you know the NFL isn't interested in the grass roots approach. We want to get some games over here to see how the Europeans take to the game. If they like it, we might try to open up a European Football League. Kind of like a farm system to the pros."

"That might work for you, but for the sport to take off they need to learn to play the game. That's all we're trying to promote."

*I'm not sure which is the better approach, but at least this way Rossetti Enterprises is involved in both.*

Once they were seated, Mikhail opened the discussion. "John, I have a commitment from the government of the USSR to stage a game in Moscow at the Luzhniki Stadium, the host stadium for the 1980 Olympics. We're most interested in hosting such an event."

Mickey wasn't sure how he could make such a statement, but he just did. The one thing about Mikhail was that, once he had an idea in his head that was going to work, he'd pursue it to the end. There was never a moment that he let up, and this was going to be no different.

"Let's step back a bit and start from the beginning if we can," John said. "There's more than just the game. We need to be sure on protocol, transportation, hotels for the teams and the management, practice facilities, media, and, most of all, security, just to name a few items. There's a tender list and proposal request that the host country and venue need to fill out. The NFL then approves that. I have a copy back at the hotel that I'll leave with you in the morning."

"Why do we need to go through all that bullshit to get the game? If the Russian government has approved it, what else do you need?" Ivan asked.

*I'm glad I coached John on what he might expect from Ivan.*

Mikhail gave Ivan a look that all the participants around the dining table understood. The stare scared the crap out of Mickey, and it wasn't directed at him. "I'd be glad to look at the tender, and Ivan will be more than happy to assist you and Mickey with anything else you may need."

Ivan slumped into his chair, like a little boy whose father had just scolded him.

"That's great, Mikhail, and our usual procedure is that, once the tender has been approved, a site visit will be set up. It'll be a party of three with me being one. I look forward to visiting your country. Mickey tells me the RFF is going well, and he seems to think there has been a lot of progress. Do you agree?"

"I think the league and the teams are where they should be based on the time they've been at it. When you visit Moscow, I'll be sure to introduce you to my brother Boris, who's working with Coach Amendola. I think you'll like him." Mikhail couldn't keep the smirk of his face. Boris had a strange affect on people sometimes.

"How long does the process take to get approval prior to the site visit?" Mickey asked.

"In this case I think it'll move along pretty fast. The NFL has been looking for a place to showcase the sport in Europe, and what better place than Moscow."

Mikhail never paused. "Whatever you need done, we'll do. Security will be the tightest you have ever seen, and the money guarantee is no problem. I'll have the document back to you as soon as we can get it done and will advise Mickey here on the progress. If that is all of the business matters, let's enjoy ourselves."

Once the business was done, no one was more charming than Mikhail was. He was a madman with style.

Mikhail and Padraig's meeting was brief. "Pete asks that you keep your eye on Mickey for him. This is getting a little more involved than we wanted, but nothing can stop it now. We need to keep moving forward."

"I understand, Padraig, and please tell Pete that I'll do all I can to keep him safe. He's actually a pretty good kid."

"Yeah, we know. We want to keep it that way. See you in Moscow some time."

# CHAPTER 16

Mickey, Ivan, Petra, and Olga flew back to Leningrad in Mikhail's private jet. Ivan was seated with Olga in the back of the plane while Petra was up front with Mikhail. Mickey wasn't real sure about their relationship as he knew that Mikhail was never tied down to one woman. At times they seemed to be together; at other times they were worlds apart.

Mickey slept most of the way or faked it as he needed a little time to himself to collect his thoughts. Before they left Bern, he had left the report for John Lowe, as Pete requested. Mickey was sure John Lowe was Padraig. *But who am I to question these things?*

Mikhail and the women headed for the hotel to check-in after the plane touched down at Leningrad Airport. Olga and Petra had time to relax, and planned to do a little shopping. Mikhail had a few appointments set up.

Mickey and Ivan were headed for a meeting with Stephan Petrov to finalize the cars and then meet with Mikhail at the Conservatory for Russian Music after he was finished with his other meetings. Their meeting with Stephan was to take place in the same room as the first time, right in the basement of the Hermitage. Waiting for him outside the museum, Mickey and Ivan just watched the people as they walked across the square.

Stephan pulled up in his black limo and got out. "Nice to see you boys. Was the trip to the States successful?"

Everyone shook hands and headed into the museum from the front entrance this time. The crowd was big, but they just walked right through, down the stairs, and into the Amber Room.

Ivan, not too fond of Stephan, wasted no time.

"The fifteen cars will arrive in Leningrad in three weeks. And here is all the paperwork you will need for customs to get the cars through. Please deliver them to the warehouse as soon as possible, and advise this man at this number when they will be there. He'll be our main person here in Leningrad, and he'll contact us."

The way Ivan came at him so abruptly amused Stephan, but he let it go. "The cars will be delivered as we discussed within three days after arrival. I'll expect to get paid two weeks prior to the arrival as I'll need to spread a little of the money around. When do you expect the next shipment?"

"The procedure will take place every six weeks after the arrival of the first cars. We have them already selected, so that isn't a problem. If all goes well with this shipment, we'll give them the go-ahead to start sending the rest over according to the schedule."

"Ivan, do you think there will be any problems on the U.S. side?" Ivan looked at Mickey.

Mickey took the lead on this one. "We should be all set, Stephan, our contacts have guaranteed that all will go as planned. We met with them when we were in the States, so everything is a go. As long as they get paid and the paperwork is in order, there won't be any problems."

"Good, then that concludes our business. I'll be in touch with your man once the cars get in. Have a good day, gentlemen."

Mickey and Ivan took their leave and headed up the stairs out of the Hermitage and into the square. The palace housing the Hermitage was one of the most beautiful buildings Mickey had ever seen. While they were standing there admiring it, they looked off to their left just in time to see the Soviet police handling a little commotion. Someone had pick pocketed a tourist, and the police had apprehended the thief as he was trying to get away. While the police hauled the antagonist off into the car, a huge explosion happened right behind them.

Mickey turned around and saw Stephan's driver running from the car with his pants on fire. The whole square was in a panic, and people were running in all directions. While Mickey and Ivan stood there unsure of what to do, Mikhail came around the corner, grabbed them both, and threw them into the waiting car. They heard gunshots. As they sped out of the square, Mickey looked back and saw the driver on the ground next to his car. He wasn't moving.

"I'm glad you two are all right," said Mikhail. "We got word while we were at the last meeting that something might happen, and we rushed right out to get to you. Stephan has been targeted, and anyone with him today was in possible danger. Was he still downstairs?"

"Yes, we left him a few minutes ago. He was finishing up some work. I would doubt he was even near the square at the time of the explosion," Ivan answered.

"That's good. The competition has been trying to get to him for a few years now ever since he took over for his father. He isn't my favorite rival, but at least we know who we're dealing with. These new gangs are out of control. Once he finds out who blew up his car and killed his driver, there will be hell to pay. I'd hate to be them. If you are going to kill someone, you better be sure you do the job."

*That must be lesson number one in gangster school. If you're going to kill them, just do it right.*

Mikhail's driver dropped them off at the Conservatory, where they were scheduled to see the final rehearsals for the school's next performance. Mikhail had an idea to bring the kids to the United States on a musical tour to the East Coast cities if they were any good.

While the group waited for the rehearsal to begin, Mikhail leaned over and whispered, "Mickey, if they are any good, do you

know anyone in the entertainment business who might be interested in signing them up for a tour?"

*I don't, but I'm sure Pete does.*

"Mikhail, I'm sure we can set this up through our contacts if
you want us to."

"Good. Here they come. Let's see if they are any good."

Not only were they good, they were amazing. It was like watching angels sing. Mickey looked over at Mikhail and saw this gangster with tears rolling down his face. On the way out, Mikhail gave
the director a wad of rubles. He was still drying his eyes.

# CHAPTER 17

Dmitri was there with another driver when the group arrived back in Moscow on the final leg of the journey from Leningrad. Before anyone started directing them to the cars, Mickey jumped in the front seat of Dmitri's Cadillac to be sure he rode back with him. He never said a word to him, but after all this time, he felt comfortable with Dmitri in the driver seat. Petra went with Mickey and Mikhail while Ivan and Olga went with the other car. They dropped Mikhail off at his place first and then proceeded to Mickey's hotel. Petra got out with him at the hotel and told Dmitri that she was meeting an old friend so he could leave her. He seemed to pay no mind to the change and left. Petra and Mickey made their way to the bar after leaving the bags with the bellmen and sat for a few drinks. Olga was by far the better looking of the two friends, but Petra had an air about her that let everyone know she was something special.

"Something is bothering Olga. I'm not sure what it is yet, but she was a little strange the last time we were together. Did Pete tell you anything?" she asked.

Mickey wasn't sure how much she knew, but he needed a confidant in this affair. *She might as well be it.* Pete had introduced them so; he guessed it was all right.

"He did mention something in my last communiqué, but it hasn't been confirmed yet. It had something to do with warheads missing from an arsenal in Odessa. He didn't have confirmation, but it's going to be part of the discussion in Ireland."

She sat there for a minute and sipped her martini. "I sure wish we knew what was going on here. I only know that I'll need to get it out of Olga. This thing is getting way out of control, and we have somehow found ourselves in the middle of it."

"I know, and I think it'll only get worse. We need to get a handle on it."

"I think you should know that Olga and I have been lovers for a few years. I love her and all, but I'm not sure if it'll be forever. No one makes me feel the way she does, and I'm not sure anyone else ever will."

"I know this may sound crazy, but what about us?"

"I'm not sure there is us at this point with all that is going on. It's been a long time since I loved a man."

"What about you and Mikhail?"

"That's only business, and I'll keep that up as long as I need to. Our jobs aren't easy, and at times you just have to do what needs to be done in order to stay on top of everything. It's just that it all seems so important this time. I mean nuke cases, military coups, and world destruction."

They sat there for a long time, lost in their own thoughts.

Mickey finally spoke, "Petra, I'm not sure I should know all of this, but now that you have told me, there isn't much I can do."

"I know that, but sometimes we all need to trust someone. I guess that someone in my case is you." She took his hand and looked into his eyes with a look that made his heart melt.

He could tell she was a little scared so he held her hand tightly and didn't say anything for a while. *Shit, I'm scared myself.* "If this is what it is going to be, then I think it best that we confide in each other and keep it at that. This isn't a time to become intimate with each other and put added pressure on the whole thing. Shit, it's confusing enough as it is."

"Mickey, I'm in love with Olga, and I'm sleeping with Mikhail to keep close to his business. Do you think I need another partner in this game?" She kissed him on his cheek and left him at the bar.

*This espionage crap is something else!*

Boris took over the logistical part of the league and left the coaching to Tommy, the way it should have been handled. When the coaches and the twenty players returned to Moscow, the RFF immediately got the teams and the leagues in order. While Boris was in the States, he left his staff behind to handpick the three teams so that, when they returned, they would be ready to go and not waste much time.

The teams would compete against each other for a few months, and then the best team would be selected to play some friendly games with teams from the EFL. Tommy and Boris would eventually select the best team to play a few games in the States and then in the Euro Bowl at the end of the season. Tommy advised them not to expect too much, but the Russians weren't used to losing.

The marketing committee headed by Mickey named the teams the Moscow Giants, the Moscow Tsars, and the Moscow Dynamos. No one was sure where the last name came from, but everyone guessed Boris had something to do with it. Boris was into it big time and almost forgot his other duties with Mikhail, which was fine as long as Mikhail didn't need him.

The call from General Asimov forced Boris to face reality. Someone who is part of the Dynamo sports club was part of an underground network that never let members go. Either the KGB or the military could call on members at any time, and it was their duty to respond. In this case, both were calling, and Boris had no choice. He would just have to balance football, the general's request, and his responsibilities to Mikhail.

"Boris, I need you to work with Colonel Marsilov for a few days in Odessa if you don't mind. We need help with this little project to be sure a few people stay in line and understand we're serious. I'll make the proper arrangements, so please be ready to leave day after next. You'll be back in a few days so don't bring too much. Do you have any questions?"

There were never any questions when General Asimov called. Members simply did what they were told and got on with it.

General Asimov was the only one who knew the exact location of the secret laboratory, as he had moved it a few months ago right in front of the Atomic Defense Ministry. The ministry was outraged, but they couldn't do much except try to figure out what had happened. The ministry had picked Odessa because it was the home to the Black Sea Fleet of the Russian navy and very well guarded. Its history went back to the 1700s, and it was an established base for the Russians during WWII. It was also home to an arsenal of nuclear warheads and, in particular, a top-secret program for nuke cases, the smallest tactical weapons ever made. General Asimov had control of these weapons, and they would help him rule the world. They were designed to be used at close range to deliver an immediate impact but also a psychological advantage to the Soviets. The closest things the Americans had were a backpack version called the Mk-54 SADM, which weighed about fifty-one pounds. The Soviets version, however, was small enough to fit in a medium-sized suitcase and was five times as powerful.

General Asimov had assembled a crack team of scientists to complete the project. The scientists were working on the final wiring component for the remote control detonation of the case. When this was in place, the tactical warhead would be ready for use if needed by the Soviets.

Boris arrived as scheduled and then reported directly to Colonel Marsilov for his orders. "We've had a little problem with the two scientists working on a project for the general. He wants us to go over to their rooms to have a little talk with them. You are to say nothing. Just stand there and look mean."

"That's fine with me, Colonel. Anything else?"

"No, that'll be all. But you'll need to stay around for a few days to be sure it works. After that you will be free to go back home to your Russian NFL."

Boris had no idea what the project was and didn't care. He and the colonel called on the scientists that afternoon, and there was no problem. Just to be sure they understood, Boris hit the door on the way out and shattered it into a thousand pieces. The next day they went back to see them before they went to work. All seemed to be in order. Word came back to the colonel that everything was fine so Boris could go back to Moscow. While boarding the military plane to go back home, he swore he saw Olga getting off a private military craft. *What the hell would she be doing in the Black Sea?*

Olga wasn't sure if Boris saw her but realized it didn't matter in the end. She was on assignment and aware she needed to start finding out as much as she could. As it was she wasn't sure what was going on or whose side she was on.

"Did anyone see you get off my plane?" The general appeared a little tense to Olga.

"No, I don't think so. Is there a problem?"

He seemed not to hear her. "How are things back at the office in Moscow?"

"I don't think Yakov or Alexei have any idea what is going on. There doesn't seem to be anything different than usual, and work seems very normal. Are you sure you saw Yakov leaving the *dacha?*"

Olga hadn't seen anything out of the ordinary, so she was a little confused when General Asimov requested her presence in Odessa. She had been working with him for some time now and knew most of what was going on. She wasn't aware of the magnitude of the cases or the numbers, but she did know that a few KGB agents were being screened for a special assignment.

"Director Drygin knows about us, but that isn't my concern. He remarked in passing the last time I met with him, so I just wanted you to be aware of it. On the nuke front, Yakov knows something is up, and you need to be on the lookout. Has Petra said anything to you?"

"No, she hasn't said a thing, and if she knew I think she'd let me know. Are the scientists back in line with the program?"

"Colonel Marsilov had a little talk with them the other day, and everything is fine. It's amazing how touchy these guys get. They know what the cases can do and what they will be used for. If they were going to have a conscience, they should have never signed on for the project. We're still waiting to work out the final firing mechanism, which may take up to six months. These are the smallest atomic weapons out there, and this part is very tricky. We need to be sure it's handled properly so there are no mishaps. That's all we need to happen. Hopefully the president won't do anything foolish by then, like giving our country away."

"What do you think our next steps will be?"

"Once we test the firing mechanism to be sure all is set, we'll meet with Drygin to finalize the plan. In the meantime you need to get back to Moscow and stay as close to Yakov as you can. We need to know what they know and move accordingly."

"Do you still think the plan is a good one?"

Asimov watched her for a moment to see if she were getting skittish, but her expression didn't give her away. "It's best that we get our motherland back where it belongs. Do you not agree with that?"

"Oh, I agree, but do we need to kill our own people? Is there a better way?" Inside she was torn, but her appearance was one of genuine concern for her people.

"I didn't realize you had such a tender side, Olga. In this game we'll do what we need to do. The final decision will be up to the director. Now let's get out of here and go to dinner. We have a little time to waste before you fly back home."

# CHAPTER 18

The first shipment of cars arrived as planned to the docks in Leningrad. Stephan had greased all the right people so they didn't have a problem getting the cars through custom. Once the cars were through, the brotherhood that Stephan led got the cars to the designated warehouse as planned. Stephan decided to wait to call Ivan's contact, as he wasn't that fond of Ivan either. Ivan and Stephan still seemed to have a little problem with each other, and Stephan would have to talk to Mikhail about it. Stephan owed Mikhail one for the call he received right before his car blew up outside the Hermitage. He tried to get to his driver, Pavel, in time, but it wasn't to be. Federov's gang tried to get him. He would miss Pavel, but he couldn't do anything about it.

Stephan saw Pavel's wife after the shooting to let her know he was sorry and to be sure she knew that he would take care of her kids in the future. The Nosava Bratava made sure to take care of its own in time of need. It went a long way to securing the loyalty that was needed in the brotherhood. The newer gangs didn't have this loyalty, so there was always the possibility of turning one of the members to the other side for revenge. Aleksandr Federov had been one such case. One of his bodyguards, Konstantin, had turned to Mikhail's team.

Anyone who thought people made it on their own in Russia didn't know how the system worked. If someone got too big, he was simply killed. People made it because the system wanted them to make it. If the mafia or KGB wanted someone dead, it was that simple, especially for the KGB or the government. Throughout the history of the USSR, people disappeared. That was it. There were no questions and never any answers. If someone made it, then he made it for a reason, usually because the system needed him to make it. People also really never knew who was working with whom, as the system was so paranoid that everyone spied on everyone else. That was why the KGB was so good in the international intelligence game. They had been doing it forever.

Stephan looked at the big Armenian and asked him a simple question, "Konstantin, why did you turn on Aleksandr and help us out when they tried to assassinate me?"

"He wasn't a good man. He had changed and was only out for himself. He wasn't the person I knew for five years anymore. The others within the Bratava are no different."

Konstantin had been with Federov as a driver first and then a bodyguard, so he saw a lot of what went on.

"I know you helped us out a few times, but we need you to do more. You'll be in charge of dismantling the Oksana Bratava from the bottom up. We have gotten the word to take them all out anyway we see fit and to do it fast. Are you willing to take this on for us?"

The Armenian had been waiting a long time for a chance to become part of the Nosova Bratava, and here was his chance. "I'll do whatever you want, Stephan."

Plans were devised for the elimination of the Oksana Bratava that Konstantin and a handful of loyal gang members would carry out. Stephan had just made the move to take over Leningrad for Alexei.

# CHAPTER 19

Donald Smith and Pasha Titov had met once before, and were well schooled on each other. The pre-summit was to be held at the Adare Manor, one of the grand manors in Ireland, a perfect selection for a meeting between these two superpowers.

The late-afternoon sun was slowly sinking over the emerald green hills in Adare as the meeting began. Because the Russians had requested the summit, it was up to them to start the meeting and to let the U.S. know what was going on. When Secretary of State Donald Smith heard from Pasha what was happening, he knew this was for real.

"So what you are telling me is that you think one of your renegade generals has a bunch of nuke cases and may be shipping them around the world, your nuclear arsenal is in bad shape, and, on top of that, your country has no money. Things in general—no pun intended—are falling apart."

Donald couldn't believe what he'd just heard. *Could this Russian be telling me the truth? It's a helluva way to start. Usually the Russians never let anyone know what is going on, but in this case there is no question that things are serious and above board.* It had been the first time in his long career that Donald Smith believed what his Russian counterpart had told him.

"Yeah, that's about it," replied Soviet Secretary Pasha Titov. "I think we can open up conversations now, no?"

"I thank you for your honesty, and I think we need to start working together. Are you with me?"

"That is why we are here, Mr. Smith. We know we need to work together to solve this situation. But we need to be very careful as we really don't know who is on the side of General Asimov. We think it might be Director Drygin, but we can't be sure, and we can't call him out. Even if we're right, we don't know who else may be working with them. If we're wrong, we'll lose whatever edge we have on the general. We think that, if we work it together, we might be able to draw them out not only through diplomatic negotiations but also espionage. First, we must find these nuke cases and stop the general. Then we can concentrate on getting the Soviet Union back in shape."

"That's a good idea, but first we need confirmation that Director Drygin is the main culprit. We definitely need to let the public know what is going on with the nuclear arms race, but the secret nuke cases is a different story. Would your president be willing to move fast on an arms treaty deal to put pressure on General Asimov and his people so maybe they'll make a bad move?"

"I think he would, but we would need guarantees on loans to help out the economy. We would need assurances that your government will back us up on getting through this dilemma. We're a very proud people, so we need to be sure we can save face with the rest of the world in these negotiations. Do you think President Reed will go along with this request?"

"I think the president will work very closely with President Vasilyev on this whole program. If we can agree on dismantling the nuclear arms race, end communism as we know it today, and help the Soviet Union out of economic disaster, I think he'll work very closely with you."

Pasha looked a little glum. "That sounds terrible to a man who grew up believing in his country and system. But I need to understand and acknowledge that this is the current climate in which we find our nation. This isn't an easy thing for any of us to do. We're negotiating the collapse of the Soviet Union. It's a sad day for all of us."

"It may be a sad day for you, but an end to the Cold War as we know it can't be a bad thing. Shall we get on with it, Pasha?"

The first summit was scheduled for January 8, 1986, at the Hotel des Bergues in Geneva. It would be announced several days before taking place, so the Soviet military and whomever else they were working with on the nuke cases plan would be kept off guard.

# CHAPTER 20

Mikhail was pleased with what Boris had done with the new RFF. The first five weeks were a huge success in Moscow. It was just the type of game the Soviets would love with the hitting and strategy behind each play. The games were held in smaller stadiums with a capacity of twenty thousand people, and they were at least halfway full, which was good according to EFL standards. Tommy was head coach of the Moscow Giants, the best team in the league. It might have been the coaching, but it was probably because Boris, who was in charge of operations, put the most talented athletes on that team.

The league was running as smoothly as it could for an upstart. One of the main problems was the referees, as no Russian knew enough about football yet or the rules to work the games. The solution was to bring in referees from the Scandinavian countries each week. Tommy set up clinics for the Russian referees during the week, and they worked side by side with the Scandinavians to learn the game. Tommy was in his glory, as he lived for football. Nothing was better than starting a league from scratch. Mickey and Mikhail worked together on the league setup and merchandising of the product, which was quite interesting. They were basing the organization on the NFL model while trying to keep it within the confines of the Soviet business structure. The situation called for Boris and Tommy to finalize the teams for the two

EFL tournaments the Russians would be playing in. For the Euro Championship, they would have to send the Moscow Giants, as they were the team that won the season in Moscow. The Euro Bowl was another story as it was more an all-star team that would need to be picked. This would also be the team that would be sent to the States to play the first ever Russian versus United States teams in Shelton, Connecticut, and Plattsburg, New York. Tommy would coach both of them the first year. A completely Russian coaching staff would take over in the years to come.

"I think we need to take another quarterback to the States, Boris. If something happens to the first two, we'll be up the creek."

Boris didn't understand the whole concept yet, so at times Tommy needed to get what he wanted. But he needed to be sure that Boris thought it was his idea.

"Okay, Tommy, if that is what you need, but we can only take forty players and five coaches. I need to get the final list tonight so we can get passports and visas for the team. Do you think we can get it done?"

"I'm sure we can. I'm almost ready with the forty. Would you like to approve it before we let it go? We'll have to advise the team so they can start to prepare for the travel and to get all their personal matters in order."

"What personal matters? These guys only have to play football and win games. They will be ready to go, believe me. I need to finalize the rest of the traveling party as the RFF has agreed we can take another five people in the party. This will give us a total of fifty people traveling to America. Is there anyone special you think we need to take?"

"I would take Viktor, the head referee, so we can get him some training over there. We'll need to make that a priority soon. We need to get your own people refereeing the games here. Outside of that the other four should be whoever you want to take."

Boris was playing the boss, and he loved it. "I'll decide soon on the other four. Please be sure to have the list to me tonight by eight. I'll see you tomorrow."

After Boris left Tommy came to see Mickey to discuss what was going on so he could be updated on the process of the league operations. Tommy was in a good mood, which had something to do with knowing he was going home for a while. Life in Moscow wasn't that easy, even with the contacts they had made through the football and car business. They took little things they had in the States for granted, like heat, good food, and gasoline. Everything they needed to survive was a problem to get, which took a lot of energy and time. Tommy couldn't wait to get a good steak and a bottle of good red wine.

"This Boris thinks he's the king pin of American football," Tommy said. "You should see him giving orders to everyone, including me." He lit a cigarette and blew the smoke at Mickey, who wasn't paying attention.

"I'm sorry, Tommy. My mind is on Ivan and what's going on with the cars. I'm not sure, but I think Ivan needs to be cut down to size. I've been thinking about it the last two weeks. Ever since we left America, he's changed."

"There's really no difference between Boris and Ivan. All Russians come on strong until you put them in their place. Something will happen to straighten them out."

"Are you ready to go home?"

"I'll tell you, Mickey. It will sure be nice to get back to home."

"You'll be home in a few days with a Russian team who plays American football. It'll be the first team ever from the Soviet Union to play a game on American soil. Can you imagine that? With everything that is going on in the world, we're in Russia working with them on a game."

Do you think Mikhail is tied in big time, Mickey?"

Tommy only knew what they wanted him to, but in the past few weeks, Mickey had learnt a lot more from Petra and Pete. But Tommy didn't have a need to know what was happening.

"He probably has some connection with the Mafia, as most businesspeople do here, but I don't want to know too much. I figure that, once we get the football program in place with the EFL and get the cars rolling off the boats, we can start to slowly move away from being so involved. I know I don't want to stay here forever."

Mickey had always thought that, at some point, when all this business was done, they could get away from there. He knew it was going to take a little time for the governments to work out the nuclear situation and these nuke cases would have to be found, but Mickey, not Tommy, was involved with those problems. Tommy was here to get the game of football ingrained in the Soviet culture with the help of the RFF and the EFL. Once that was done, Tommy was out of there.

"I think you are right, Mickey. Let's take this a step at a time, win some games, and teach them the right way to play. If it all works out, we can be back home for good after this season ends."

Mickey's final drop and pickup before going back to the States went off without any problems. After the incident at Gorky Park, there had been a few other drops as well, and things went off as planned. He hoped the Gorky Park problem was a one-off and had nothing to do with what was going on in the world. He had seen Petra and Olga off and on for the last few weeks, but nothing crazy seemed to be happening. However, all that was going to change when they got to America based on this last communiqué.

Mickey was amazed at how well Pete knew the game, and the communiqué backed this up. The money was showing up in the American banking account a week after the second sets of cars were delivered to Leningrad, just as Pete had suspected it would. The amounts were small, but then every few days, there would be another transfer that was larger, just as Pete had said. They never reached the single ten thousand-dollar max deposit that the banks looked out for, but the total amount was getting too high, just as Pete had said. When the total hit fifty thousand, Pete knew this was more than just a small little businessman sending money to America. It was the start of a money laundering operation that was either tied to the Mafia, KGB, or the government. *Who knew? It could probably be all three.*

Pete was thrown off. There wasn't anything to back up the money. It just showed up in the account periodically, as if it were supposed to. Things were falling Pete's way, and he knew he would have another player in place to help find out what was going on. Maybe even two. He advised the bank to just let the money keep coming in as he would handle it from his end. He didn't want the parties in Moscow to know anything was up. Pete knew that Ivan's father and Boris were close and both were probably in with the military in some aspect based on their earlier involvement with the weightlifting federation and Dynamo sports club. If he got lucky and Boris was involved, he might be able to turn him based on what he had on Ivan. It was worth a shot, and it was good one.

Ivan and Boris would finally get the chance to meet Pete.

Olga couldn't believe how much she yearned for Petra's touch. Even as she lay with the general, she constantly thought about Petra and the way she made her feel. No one did to her what Petra did. She wasn't sure why she was even with Asimov, but she always felt she needed to take advantage of a situation when it arose. It was just pure luck that she had bumped into the general that night at the Metropole, but that confident look in his eyes immediately told her that he was important. She didn't know how important, but once she got to know him, she figured out he was one of the most influential men in Moscow. *Did Yakov set them up on purpose?* He had also let her in on what he was working on, so she just played along. She wasn't sure how it got this far in this short a time, but she knew they were playing a very dangerous game. *How could he actually think he could take over the government with Drygin by a*

*military coup? Why did he need to blow up ten cities in the Western world to make his point?* She was a communist as well, but she wasn't sure this was the right thing to do.

The general was stirring, so she made her way quietly out of the bed, got dressed, and left by the side door. She needed to report to work as usual this morning to see if anyone had any idea on what was going on. Plus she needed to see Petra again to see that smile so she would know everything was right in the world. *Why couldn't life just be that simple?*

# CHAPTER 21

The Russian team arrived in New York on the Wednesday before the Giants were scheduled to play the Eagles at Giant Stadium. The excitement it created for the city was unreal and everyone got into it.

Pete was there to meet the team and accompany them to their hotel in Connecticut. The talk on the bus was all about the Russian football team, the games they had scheduled, and the NFL. Pete had known Tommy in another life, and they got along well. Ivan was a little taken back with Pete and the way he took charge, but that was Pete's way of doing things. *Shit, I've been doing it this way for many years in many countries. That isn't going to change now because the Russians are in town.*

Pete made his way over the empty seat by Ivan and put his plan into motion. "Ivan, I think this is your second time to the States, correct? Are you glad to be back?"

Mickey, who overheard the question, could see Ivan's wary expression. *What is he going to say?*

"Yes, it is, and I'm glad to be back. Your country is so different than ours, but then I would guess that you know that?"

It was a direct hit, but Pete had handled people better than Ivan. "You're correct, and I probably know your country better than you think. I lived there for a few years back in the sixties? It was a tough time to be an American in Moscow, but we made it through."

Mickey had never seen Pete taken off his game. Pete made his point with Ivan and turned his attention back to Boris and Tommy. Ivan stared at him for a while with that defiant Russian stare, but Pete never saw it. After a while Ivan just closed his eyes and slept the rest of the way to the hotel.

Mickey and Tommy had selected Shelton, Connecticut, as the first stop for the Russian games. They stayed at the Marriott right off the Merritt Parkway. Because colleges couldn't play the Russians and high school teams were too young, they got a semi-pro team from Stamford, the Golden Bears, to play them. The team was a mix of ballplayers from area colleges who never made it to the pros but still loved to play. Their great quarterback, Mickey Lione, almost made it to the NFL with the San Diego Chargers in 1981. Tommy knew the coach, so they were sure the guys were upright and would not embarrass the Russians. Times were still tense between the United States and the Soviet Union, so they needed to be sure the teams understood that this was an exhibition and not WWIII.

The game was played on a Saturday night at the high school in front of nine thousand people. The Russians lost twenty-seven to seven, but they scored on an eighty-two-yard pass up the right sideline in the fourth quarter with two minutes left to play. The place went wild. It was the first time a Russian team had scored a touchdown on American soil. After the game both teams went to a joint called Pellicci's for pizza and beer. If the two governments could have seen the camaraderie between the players and the coaches, the Cold War might have been something in the past. Sports had a way of bringing people together that no other activity could. It was just the pure competition, man on man, team on team, that made it so special.

That night at the hotel, after a few more drinks, the Russian team finally gave up and went to bed. On the way back to his room, Ivan was surprised to see Pete following him.

"I think we should have a little talk, Ivan. Best if we do it in private."

Pete opened the door to his hotel room, which was right next to Ivan's, and they sat on the couch. Ivan wasn't sure what was up, but he figured it was probably not good. Pete reached into his briefcase and removed a manila folder, which had Ivan's name on it. He shuffled through the papers and finally found what he was looking for.

"Can you explain this to me?" Pete handed over a stack of papers to Ivan.

Ivan looked at the papers and noticed the final amount at the bottom of the page was $72,500. He knew exactly what it was, but he wasn't sure what Pete intended to do with the information. Boris had told him this was normal procedure for business with the West and Mickey would have no problem with it. The account was the joint account that had been set up for Ivan and Mickey.

He decided to be straightforward and tough with Pete, the way he always acted when he felt he was being put in the corner. "It's the profit from the cars we are bringing to the States so we can further our business on this side of the ocean. Is there a problem with that, Pete?"

"Don't fuck with me, Ivan! You may think you can fuck with a lot of people, but I'm not one of them. The sooner you understand that, the better off we'll all be."

"What are you talking about? We've done nothing wrong." A line of sweat appeared on Ivan's upper lip.

"You've done nothing wrong? Shit, this is so blatant that it's ridiculous. Should we get Mickey and Boris so they can tell me what's going on?"

"No, no, don't do that. I don't know what you mean."

"Ivan, there's no fuckin' way that much money was made on three shipments of cars, and there's no backup paperwork. Do you think we don't know what's going on and who you work for? And by the way, don't think we don't know about the relationship between Boris and your father."

It was the first time anyone had made that connection outside the family. It frightened Ivan.

"Do you think we just let Russian businessmen do what they want over here on this side of the ocean as you say? Do you think we don't know who the Vladikoffs are and what their game is? Do you think we're fuckin' stupid, Ivan?"

Pete wasn't asking questions. They were pointed facts that Ivan wasn't supposed to have answers to. Ivan just sat there, unable to speak.

Pete let him sit there and squirm for a few minutes. Then he hit him with the final blow. "As you can tell, this isn't a discussion. We need to get to Boris, let's say, to have a heart-to-heart talk. You are going to get to him for us, or you will never see Russia again. We have your passport, so there's no way you can get out of this country. Boris is involved in something we need to know about, so we would talk to him while he was here anyway. This just gives us a little more leverage. You have until we get to Plattsburg to talk to him, or we'll take you down. Do you understand me? Now get the hell out of here. This discussion never took place."

On the bus the next morning, Ivan looked like he hadn't slept for a few days. He had bags under his eyes, and his hair was unkempt. Mickey wasn't sure what had happened but figured Ivan would tell him if he wanted. It usually took him a little time to figure out what to do, so he just left him alone in his own thoughts.

The team arrived at the Holiday Inn in Plattsburg, New York, in the late afternoon and went to their rooms. The game wasn't for a few days. As Mickey was the son of a Hall of Famer, there were interviews and social events to attend. On the way over to the radio station, Ivan told Mickey about the meeting with Pete.

Mickey pretended to be caught off guard. "Shit, Ivan, why the hell didn't you tell me they were going to try to launder some money through the account in Stamford? There's no way that would get through with the banking regulations we have in place. Mikhail should have known this."

"Look, Mickey, I just take orders and do as I'm told. You know how it works in Russia. What the hell am I supposed to do now?"

The plan was for Mickey to confide in Ivan and let him know about the presidential summits and the dire state of the current Soviet economy. He was not to mention the nuke cases or the possible role that Boris was playing with General Asimov.

"Ivan, this is more complicated than you think. Pete is a big-time player and has been for some time. I'm not sure if he's telling me everything, but I know there are rumblings about the nuclear arms race and the state of the Soviet economy. Your country has been making secret diplomatic overtures to have our two presidents meet in Geneva soon. What this has to do with Boris, I have no idea, but I suggest you tell him the truth and let him deal directly with Pete. If I were you, I'd try to get out of Pete's way and let Boris handle it."

"That's easy for you to say. Boris is like a son to my dad, and I don't want to put him in a tough situation if I don't have to. But I don't think I have any other choice."

After the interview they went back to the hotel. Mickey left Ivan who made his way to Boris' room. For the first time in his life, he felt a little sorry for the guy.

The Plattsburg Wolves beat the Russians forty-five to fourteen in front of a crowd of four thousand screaming fans. They played better than they did in Shelton, but the competition wasn't as good. The people were very gracious to them. When the game was over, the town threw the team one of the biggest cookouts the people had ever seen. The Russians had never seen anything like it either with all the beer, along with the steaks, hot dogs, hamburgers, and ribs being roasted over charcoal fires. When dinner was over and the townspeople brought out the marshmallows, the Russians had no idea what to do with them. All in all it was a great time and a good finish to the first ever Russian football team in America.

On the way back to Moscow, Boris and Ivan constantly talked on the matters that were at hand. They were both faced with dilemmas on how to handle the situation, and they weren't sure what they were going to do.

"Boris, what the fuck are we going to do? If Pete follows through with these threats, we'll both be in trouble. Should I tell my dad?"

"We need to think this through and then decide on our own. I'll have to decide what to do with Mikhail, but I don't want you telling him anything. That's up to me."

Ivan reclined his seat a little and looked directly at Boris. "Did Pete say anything to you about the money?"

"He advised me they would let the money be sent to the Stamford account, but the amounts had to be cut in half. I think I can get this past Mikhail."

Boris didn't tell Ivan that, if he played the intelligence game with the U.S. and won, the money could possibly be his if he needed it…if he survived.

A confused Boris would have to tell the general about the proposed summit that was scheduled for January in Geneva, but he wasn't sure how to handle things with Mikhail. Mikhail wasn't aware of his working relationship with the military, although he had suspected it. The businesses they were involved in, especially the RFF, EFL, and NFL, were all in good shape. There was to be another meeting with the NFL soon on the proposed game in Moscow. This wasn't a weak man's game, and the stakes were getting rather high. He wasn't sure how much of what Ivan told him was true. He knew the men he had scared in Odessa were scientists. *But were they really there to arm nuclear suitcases to be used in the Western world? Am I working with madmen who are bent on destroying people and cities to take the Soviet Union back to where it was in the fifties?*

It was a little too much for him to put in perspective, but he knew some quick decisions would be needed on what he was going to do. Maybe Olga knew something, as he was almost sure he saw her when he left Odessa. He would have to follow that up just in case. But how was he going to find out the truth? He did know he would protect Ivan like a big brother. He had to figure this out.

# CHAPTER 22

With everyone in the United States except Mikhail, Petra and Olga, the girls were able to spend a little time together. This was the last night they would be together before everyone returned, so they went to the Bolshoi to catch Tchaikovsky's *Sleeping Beauty*. Then they had a simple dinner at Petra's apartment. The ballet was beautiful, but the night at Petra's was wonderful. The dinner was a simple one, and the wine never stopped flowing. As the evening wore on, Petra realized Olga was finally going to open up to her. Olga never could handle her wine, so after their second round of lovemaking, she was sobbing. Petra knew this was it.

"Do you think it's time you let me know what's been bothering you? If you can't tell me, then who can you tell?"

"They're going to take over the government and blow up ten cities. My God, I said it." Olga had been waiting for this opening. Not only was it the part about the general's plan that held her back, but also the fact she had been sleeping with him.

"Slow down. What cities and what government?"

While they sat naked in bed, Olga told her the whole story from the time she met the general to the last time they had been together.

"They're the two scariest people I've ever been around. I think they're both insane, but there's a logic about them that makes you think they might be able to pull it off. They have nuke cases they're going to place at our embassies, and if the military coup fails, they'll detonate the cases."

*I can't believe what I'm hearing.*

Petra finally asked, "Do you know where the cases are now?"

"No. He hasn't told me, but maybe I'll be able to find out the next time I'm in Odessa. He sometimes leaves for a day, and I stay at the villa with only the waitstaff. Next time I'll need to see what I can find out. He has a little office in the annex, and maybe something is there that will let us know the whole truth."

"I think you're right, but please be careful. We don't know how much he knows about you. Remember, if Drygin is involved, he may know more than you think."

"I think Boris might be involved somehow, but I'm not sure. I've never seen him, but I felt his presence a few times in Odessa."

"Boris was part of the Dynamo family, so that might be possible. We'll just need to be very careful."

Petra sat there deep in thought. *Who else knows about this, and is Olga telling me the truth?* Olga didn't have a reason to lie, so Petra had to figure most of it was right. She now needed to be sure that Olga wouldn't let anyone know that she had told Petra her story.

"Olga, as far as anyone knows, you never told me this. If they ever find out, they'll kill you. There's no doubt about that. You must play along, as you have for the last six months, until I tell you what to do, and then we must act quickly. I don't want to lose you."

Petra knew something was up when she met with Mickey the last time, but there was no way anyone knew Olga was involved. This was going to be tricky, and she had to be sure she handled this correctly. Olga was still sobbing, but Petra knew she had to put her mind in the right place or she would lose it. She was a big girl and had been in many tight places. This was no different, so she would have to face up to it and do what needed to be done.

She took Olga's face in her hands and kissed her gently. "We've been through worse than this, and we'll do the right thing as we always do. We can't let the general get away with this. Because you're already involved with him, you'll remain so and learn as much as you can about the plan. You'll always tell him that no one knows about it at headquarters because this, my darling, is why he's using you. We won't even let Yakov know until we're sure what the final plan is."

Olga nodded that she understood and held Petra tightly. They fell asleep that way. In the morning Petra made sure that Olga understood what needed to be done one more time. Olga was happy she had told Petra and was no longer the only one who knew. She realized that together they would have to face this problem for the good of Russia.

# CHAPTER 23

The general wasn't quite sure what happened. The first test in the small factory at the military base outside Odessa was a catastrophe. He only knew that he lost one of his nuke cases, and that was all he cared about. *I could find other scientists.* They were now down to thirteen nuke cases and couldn't afford to lose anymore as they needed one more to be sure the mechanism worked properly, ten for the different cities and two as backup in case the whole plan fell apart. The explosion rocked that northern side of Odessa, and the fallout was terrible. The number that died immediately was in the thousands, but the real problem was the aftermath and effect the radiation would have on those who were exposed to it.

"General, we took out a whole section of Odessa. How are we going to cover this up?" asked Colonel Marisova.

"I don't think we need to worry about that. Nothing is left of the building we were using, so no one will have any idea what happened. I'm just glad we only had one of the cases there."

The nuclear case that exploded was high yield, and they weren't sure what impact the others would have when they detonated. The Western world never got hold of the story, as this was probably what the Russians were best at, hiding what was happening behind the Wall in the world of communism.

"Colonel Marisova, we need to find another scientist to complete the job. I don't care if he's with the cause or not, but we need to get him in here to finish the job. Here are two names given to me by a friend from the KGB who is sympathetic with us but knows how to remain discreet. Take Boris with you to find them, and bring one of them back to me so we can advise him on what he'll be doing for the next few months. I want no more mishaps." General Asimov turned to leave as the Colonel was dialing Boris.

Boris met the colonel at the entrance of the Old Metropole Hotel, where they were driven to the home of Alexandre Putinov, the second scientist on the list. The first scientist hadn't been too excited about the chance to work for the general, so the colonel just shot him. They left him in the bathroom of his house in the tub with the water running. Someone would find him. The usually quiet colonel was in a talkative mood on the way to the house. *Maybe because he had just killed a man. Killing does funny things to some men.*

"You know, Boris, it's time to get all this done so we can move on and get our country back into shape. Enough of this *glasnost* bullshit that's bringing our country down. We've had enough. In a year or so after the general has worked his plan, we'll be back on course and show the Western world what we're all about."

"Tell me, Colonel, do you think the plan will work?" Boris knew it was important to keep the colonel talking, as he might not ever get this chance again. *What could the plan be?*

"It has to Boris or President Vasilyev and Alexei Popov will make a deal with the United States, and all will be lost. Timing is crucial, and we need this scientist so we won't take no for an answer. This time we'll simply tell him to pack a bag and that he's coming with us. If he starts to complain, just knock him out and drag him to the car."

"What does this scientist have to do with the plan?"

"Ah, Boris, I have spoken too much already. Just be sure he does what I want him to."

Alexendre Putinov wasn't excited to see Boris either. "Get the hell away from me, you madman!" The scientist held his hands over his head. "Just tell me what you want, and get the hell away from me."

The colonel whispered something into the scientist's ear, and the scientist went to pack a few things. On the way to the car, Putinov kept looking over his shoulder at Boris.

"Keep him away from me, Colonel, and I'll do what you say."

The colonel was glad he had one of the scientists he was sent to get, and Boris made the decision that had been bothering him since he spoke with Pete. When the colonel got out of the car to board the military transport, Boris handed him the envelope addressed to the general with the message about the summit. He wasn't sure if the colonel would read it, but he didn't care. The message would get to the general either way, as it was that important. He had done what he needed to do. Now he had to figure out whose side he was on. He was military, but he wasn't up for a military coup even though he wasn't really sure what the final plan was. He only knew there was a plan and the general was going to see it through.

# CHAPTER 24

Mickey was glad to be home. The 1985 NFL season ended on December 23 with the playoffs starting the following week. The Giants beat the San Francisco 49ers seventeen to three in one of the wild card games so all the bars in the New York area were happy. It meant another weekend at least for partying while they watched the next game. Every city in the U.S. thought they had the best fans, but in reality there was nowhere like New York for sports. It had been a while since they were in the Super Bowl, and this year was going to be no different. Chicago beat the Giants the following week at Soldier Field. Mickey watched the game at his dad's house as he had promised his mom he would spend a little time at home during the holiday season. Mickey felt it was good to be home, especially since his dad had finally forgiven him for what he had done. When he thought about the way the papers would have read, "Benny Rossetti's Kid BUSTED for Cocaine," it would have been the worst thing that could have happened. Mickey's name would have been brought into it eventually, but his father's reputation would have taken the hit. He wasn't even sure what he was thinking about at this point, but whatever it was, it wasn't the right thing to do.

When Mickey was younger, he thought nothing could ever happen to him. He didn't always think what the consequences could be for the family and the people he loved. He went through life thinking he was the only one with problems. He drank too much, did the wrong things, and made the wrong decisions. It was time to turn things around.

Ivan was back in Moscow with his family, and the rest of the Russians were where they belonged at this time of the year. No one was sure if Boris or Mikhail had a family, but Petra and Olga were at Petra's *dacha* in the countryside for a few days but would be back in Moscow for New Year's Day. The world was still revolving, and the presents were under the trees for those fortunate enough to have them. The new year was around the corner, and the world was hoping it would be a better place. The only two working on this weekend were Pete and Yakov at Pete's farmhouse outside Paris.

"Yakov, you're sure the plan is to set off ten nuke cases in different cities in your own embassies and, at the same time, stage a military coup in Moscow to take over the government? The general and Director Drygin don't think small."

Pete had just heard the story for the first time but was sure that Yakov wasn't mistaken in what he had been told. Petra had been responsible for getting the information to Yakov. Pete and Yakov knew there were missing nuke cases, but now they knew how they were going to be used and why. The two countries needed to come up with a game plan now that they knew the general's motive. But what should be done and by whom? Arresting the leading general of the Soviet army and the head of the KGB without concrete evidence wasn't an option.

"That's what our intelligence tells us."

Pete was sure what needed to be done, but he needed Yakov to agree with the plan. "I think the original plan to force the summits on Director Drygin is still a good plan, and we should proceed as planned. When the press gets a hold of the story, it will be all over the world and should get in Drygin's ear."

"That's great, Pete, and I agree, but we need to come up with a few different scenarios. The best would be if we could find the nukes before they're moved. Then we could devise a plan to capture them and secure them. This is optimum, and the USSR needs to handle it, as it would take place within its boundaries. If Olga can find this out, we'll be able to move on it." Yakov explained, "However, if we can't find them before they're moved, we'll need the resources of the Soviet KGB as well as every other intelligence agency in the Western countries to apprehend the cases or the agents involved."

Pete agreed with Yakov except he also realized that Boris might be able to clarify the subject.

"We have another person in place who's close to the general. I'll get into the specifics later, but Boris Vladikoff might be able to find out what is going on and will get the information directly to Mickey through Ivan. Mickey can then pass on the information to both of us, directly to me though his drops and through Petra to get to you. I know it seems a long way around, but I think it's important that only you and me know who the players are. Do you agree?" Pete asked.

"Good move on Boris. We knew he was close to the military, but we weren't sure how close. Based on this information, we'll keep an extra eye on Asimov and see if he can lead us to something else just based on who he's hanging out with these days. Is there anything else we need to know? We're in this together, Pete, with a chance to change the world for the better."

Pete paused. "I think it's important that you stay with Petra, and I'll work the angles with Boris and Mickey. We know Olga is close to the general, so maybe more will be coming from her. We seem to have the people in place, but we need to get lucky. We got a drift of a little explosion in the Odessa area that was never made public. Anything on that?"

"We know it was one of the nukes, but we don't know where the others are now. Once we investigated the explosion, we knew what it was, and we figured that something probably went wrong with the tests for the firing mechanism. These cases are very sensitive because of their size, but they still need to figure out a way to set them off without being near them. We're thinking either timer or remote, and our best guess now is remote. We guessed that one of their scientists working on the mechanism was killed, so they would need to get another one pretty quickly." Yakov paused. "Our guess was right. We found one of them in a tub with a hole in his head, but Alexandre Putinov has gone missing. We think he was kidnapped to work on the nukes. Maybe Boris can verify this, so we at least know where he is."

"Do you think all the stolen nuke cases are in the same place?" Pete asked.

"At this point there's no way to tell. If I were the general, I would keep a few to work on. I would keep the others in a very safe place, far away from the experiments."

"I think you're right. Let's see what we can find out from Olga and Boris and then decide what our plan of action should be. I don't want to alert anyone else until we know where the cases are hidden or when they're being moved. There's still time to work on the intelligence as the nuke cases won't be ready to be moved for some time. They still have the firing problem, and they need to work on all ten and move them to the cities throughout the world. We have time but not that much."

"Is everything all set for the presidential summit next week in Geneva?"

"Yes. The whole plan needs to be worked out in unison so all the parts are handled properly and orchestrated by both of us. We pull the strings on the operation, so we need to be sure that everything is in order. Is Alexei okay with the initial briefs?""

"Alexei has looked at the briefs that Mr. Smith provided. These should set the stage for signing an initial agreement on arms control. President Vasilyev is eager to meet with President Reed to start the process. He's aware that we need to show good faith in our dealings with the United States."

"Good." The progress they had made pleased Pete. "We think it best if we hold off on signing any agreements until the second summit, as it may look orchestrated. We can release a document that states we have agreed to the following points and will work toward the next summit, which we'll announce in a few weeks. Are you okay with this scenario?"

Yakov nodded his head in agreement. "I think you're correct, so we'll proceed along this format. I'll see you in Geneva then, and hopefully we'll both have more news."

"Can you believe this shit, General? I thought it was possible, but I didn't think they would get together this fast. How far are we from being ready to move the nuke cases to the designated cities?"

Based on new information Director Drygin had just received, he needed to know where they were in their planning stages. The presidential summit had made the headlines in all the world papers the following morning. The fact the two countries were even willing to talk was something that the rest of the world was ready for. Drygin and the general were not. With a week until the presidents of the Soviet Union and the United States were scheduled to appear together, the world would be wondering what this was all about. No doubt it had to do with the nuclear arms race, but was there anything else?

Asimov saw the concern on Drygin's face. "We should have the firing mechanism finished within a few months. Then we can work on all thirteen cases that are left. I would think this could be done by the end of May if there are no more mishaps."

"General, there better be no more problems. It took all my diplomacy to hide the little problem in Odessa. How is the new scientist working out?"

"He knows what he's doing and has solved the problem we were having. Now it's just a matter of time until he can fine-tune the remotes to coincide with the codes. Too bad we'll need to kill him after he gets it all done. It would be nice to keep him around, but that's the price of world dominance. Once the nuke cases are ready, they'll be put in diplomatic pouches, and the KGB agents will fly them in person to the designated sites. Until that time we'll keep the remaining twelve cases at the Odessa naval base control-led by the forces loyal to us."

The only people who knew the whereabouts of the cases were the director, the general, and Colonel Marisova.

"What about getting the military ready to take over the Dumas and the Russian White House on the day we blow up the embas-sies? Do you think there will be any backlash from the rest of the generals?" Drygin asked.

"At this time, Director, I think it would be safe to say we have about forty percent of them with us. After the outcome of the first summit, based on what transpires, we could get a lot more. If it seems that the president is giving in to the U.S., there's a good chance they will come with us."

"Good. I would guess that the only reason for these summits is to discuss nuclear arms. If Vasilyev is stupid enough to talk about the economy and our other problems, then we'll need to move faster than we thought. Do you think they know about the nuke cases?"

"I doubt it, Director, but we should proceed very cautiously and then move based on what we see out of the first summit. If there seems to be a deal or if they announce another summit is in the future, I think we'll need to move our plans up. As long as we can get the things to go off when we want, I have no problem moving them earlier."

"Good, General. I think we need to move along as planned with the thought that, if we need to speed things up, we do so. Let's see how the first summit goes?"

"And if things start to move quickly, we'll make the moves we need to. I'll look at this scenario and get back to you with the plan."

*Too bad you might not be around to see it in action.* The director paused. "Good idea, General. I look forward to getting it."

# CHAPTER 25

Olga and Ivan were with each other on New Year's Eve. After the party at the Intourist, in Boris' and Mikhail's suite, they decided to take a room at the Europa Hotel away from everyone else. Petra was home with her family for the holiday and would return in a few days. The party wasn't a big affair, just some of the friends of the Vladikoffs who were invited year after year. On the walk over to the Europa, Ivan was so drunk that a car almost hit him, so Olga had to be sure to hold on to him the rest of the way. She wasn't feeling well about what was happening with the general, and the news of the summit just made things worse.

*What if the two superpowers could work something out to at least start getting along and working on nuclear disarmament? Wouldn't the world have a chance to maybe get it right for once? All this Cold War crap was enough to make you crazy.*

She knew she had to get back to the general to try to find out what the heck was going on and when it was to come down. As far as she knew, she was the only one who had any chance to get the right information.

Boris left the party with some Russian actress he had just met that night. She wasn't too good-looking, but she was a lot of fun and made him laugh. He hadn't been laughing much lately. The two teams the RFF sent to Europe both got their butts kicked in the EFL tournaments. Tommy had warned him not to expect too much, but as always, he thought there was no way the Russians could get beat. They had a lot of work to do, but he was up for it, and they would start planning in the next few months for the 1986 EFL season. The situation with the colonel was bothering Boris. He knew what he had to do, but he felt like he was a traitor to the people who had helped him out through his whole career. He had served the mandatory military service, but he was part of the great Dynamo Club that was like a brotherhood. The thought of turning over a secret plan to the enemy wasn't sitting right, but he didn't believe in blowing up innocent people either. *I know what I have to do, but now I need to figure out how to do it.*

Pete met with Mickey a few days after his meeting with Yakov. Mickey was scheduled to return to Moscow on January 20, so it was important that Pete update him with all the new information and plans that were being put in place. The summit would undoubtedly put pressure on the director and the general, but the intelligence gathering needed from within Russia was most important. Boris and Olga were in the best places to get this information, but it would be Mickey's responsibility to get it back to the States through his drops, which would be every week once he got back into the USSR. Boris would pass whatever he got through Ivan while Olga would pass her information on to Petra. Yakov would need to stay out of it as Director Drygin was probably watching him. It was up to Mickey and his counterpart in Moscow to get the intelligence to Pete. The plan from the start was to work through middle-level agents rather than at the top.

Pete explained, "Mickey, we think we know what is going on, but we need to get the final details out of Russia. We think Boris and Olga will help us out, but you can never be sure where their loyalties will end. Whatever information that Petra or Ivan gives you, just be sure to pass on through your drops every week. Don't make any judgments on what you think needs to be sent out. Just send what is given you."

"Whatever you say, Pete, but when will I start to get this information?"Mickey figured it wouldn't be soon, but he wanted to get a feel on when he could expect something.

"As soon as either one finds something out, it will be passed on. But we won't know when that will be, so if you get something urgent, you will call this number in Moscow. Once it's picked up, simply hang up and go to your next drop point, and your contact will be there. Only use this number in case of an emergency because it will only be answered once and you won't be able to use it again." Pete gave Mickey a list of four drop points that would be used upon his return to Moscow.

*Gorky Park is back on the list.* But he didn't say anything to Pete. "Can you tell me what's going on with the summit, or is that off the record?"

"The summits will move along as planned, and there should be a signing at the second one with regard to arms reduction. The whole point of the summits is to get this under control but, at the same time, let the Soviet president save face on the economy and the disintegration of the USSR. The strategy is to have three summits to get this in order and then to move and assist the Soviets with what they need to shore up their country and get it working again," said Pete. "That isn't going to be easy, but we'll need to work with them to make it happen."

"Thanks, Pete. I'll do whatever I can back in Moscow to help the situation. When will Tommy be back to Russia to work with Boris?"

"There will be another meeting with the NFL in Moscow the week of February 2, right after the Pro Bowl, to finalize the game in Moscow. All the players will be there, so it will be a good time for us to catch up on what is happening within the USSR. Our regular channels will advise you of the meeting once you get back to Moscow."

"So the NFL is seriously thinking of staging a game in Russia?"

"We hope the game coincides with the news of the arms treaty and the financial package that the Western world will provide to the Soviets. Hopefully by then we'll be on the third summit so it all falls in together. If not at least it will show the commitment of the US on opening its doors and products to the Russians. It should be some show."

*Boris will be pleased with this announcement. And it would be great for Mikhail in his business relationships in Moscow?* If the game was a success, Mikhail had the most to gain, as he would be the promoter and marketing arm in Moscow.

Mickey had been wondering about Mikhail lately, as he had taken a different approach to a lot of the things he was working on. He had let Ivan become more involved with the RFF and Boris. Although he was on top of the situation, he was letting Ivan take over the sponsorship of the league. This was a big responsibility, as the sponsorships kept the federation going in the early stages. As it progressed, the sponsorships became the main moneymaker for the league. Mikhail was doing the same with the cars into Leningrad, as Ivan was also becoming the main player among the brotherhoods.

*It would be interesting to see the way Ivan and Stephan worked when they were together the next time.*

"Getting the NFL to Moscow before anywhere on continental Europe would be a feather in Mikhail's cap," Mickey replied.

"Mikhail will be the focal point for the program, so stay close to him throughout the process. The NFL has been asked to let you be the liaison among NFL properties, the stadium, and the retail outlets in Moscow. This way we can keep you close to him. Learn how things are done in Moscow," said Pete. "This may change a little in the coming years, but the system they have in place has been there for centuries. It won't change that much."

The day before Mickey left, he made sure he saw his parents once more before he took off for Moscow. Part of the deal with Pete was that the cars or, for that matter, any business they did would be run through Rossetti Enterprises. Although he never said it, he knew his dad knew what was going on, and he made sure to keep it from his mom. As far as she knew, they were doing business in Europe and Russia and Mickey was the representative for the family business. It had come a long way from the cocaine distribution ring, and they had a lot more to do. *How life has changed.*

# CHAPTER 26

On his way back to Moscow, Mickey had the whole flight to reflect on what was happening. He was glad to be alone and felt pretty good about how his life was going. *A few months ago, if anyone told me I would be in Moscow as a spy, I would have laughed my ass off and had another drink.* But here he was in the middle of who knew what. He only knew the time had come to stand up and be counted. So much was going on around him.

In the middle of January, two of the most powerful people in the world sat down for the first time to discuss the nuclear arms race, the state of the Soviet economy, and fourteen nuke cases that had gone missing. Also during that time, the Chicago Bears beat the New England Patriots 46–10 at the Louisiana Super Dome. It was never a close contest, but millions of people still had a good time watching it. Most spectators were hammered by halftime. But the most important development during that time period never made the headlines of any paper or newscast: somewhere on the Eurasian Steppes, in the southwestern part of the USSR, two scientists and a colonel detonated a nuke suitcase by remote control.

Director Drygin looked up from his desk at General Asimov. He was excited about the news but was getting a little bored with the general. *His game is getting a little old.*

"So we have figured out how to detonate the cases from three miles away, General. That's good news, but tell me. What do you plan to do now?" Director Drygin knew what was going to happen from this point, but he wanted to hear what the general had to say.

"I think it best if we do as we had discussed earlier and move the remaining twelve cases to our base outside Moscow. We can bring Dr. Guliyev up here with them to work on getting all the cases compatible with the remote. I think we should let Colonel Marisova handle that detail with Boris Vladikoff. I'll stay with Putinov in Odessa to work on the actual remote control devices. It's best if we separate them now, and it will be better to have the cases up here as we will be transferring them from Moscow anyway."

"Do you think the colonel will have any problem getting the cases to Moscow?"

"We've built special traveling cases into the back of the truck so we should be able to move them without a problem. It will take a few days to get them here as the travel will be slow and we don't want to advertise what we're doing. When the colonel gets everything settled, I'll have him get in touch with you."

The plan was coming together just in time, as they still needed a few more months to get all the cases ready. It was work that took time as well as patience. If the nuke cases weren't structured correctly, they could possibly implode on their own. The general couldn't let that happen. So far Putinov had done what he was told to do, which was in his best interest if he wanted to stay alive. Dr. Guliyev would finish what he was told to do, as they had his wife and daughter hidden away and wouldn't release them until after the mission. Guliyev would never see them again, but he had figured that from the onset.

"Good work, General. Now tell me about Olga?" Drygin would use whatever he needed to keep his adversaries as well as his associates off balance. But he didn't know that the general didn't really care for Olga. He was just using her to get as much information as he could.

"She's fine, but I'm getting a little tired of her. The only good thing is that she's close to Yakov so I might as well keep her around. She might prove useful yet, and she does believe in our cause."

The director was impressed that the general had found this out. It was a little late as his time was almost at an end.

"That's good, General. Just be sure she doesn't know too much, or we'll have to get rid of her. I would hate to see a lovely creature like that get hurt. Wouldn't you?"

*I don't really want to kill her. What I do on my own time is up to me.* He finally spoke,

"I'll take care of that when and if the situation arises. Right now she's providing me with very useful information." He lied.

"That's all well and good, General Asimov, but when the time comes, be sure you handle it. Do you understand me? No loose ends!"

"I'll take care of what needs to be done." Asimov answered. "Did you give any thoughts to the secondary targets just in case we have a problem with the initial nuke cases?"

"Not yet, but something will come up. I think we shall wait on that decision until later. It's time we put the final touches on this plan. When do you think we would be able to get the cases to the ten embassies?"

The general had to think a few minutes, as time was needed to make the preparations for the final movement once the cases were all ready and the remotes all set to work. "I would think we should be set to move around June if everything goes all right. The hardest part was creating the mechanism. Now that this is done, we need to arm them properly and be sure the remotes are all set. It's a slow process, but with luck we should be all set."

"Then all we'll need to do is pick a date and time to detonate them once they are in place. I think the best time would be after the summer when everything starts to get back to normal. Let's start to look at mid-September as the timetable to put the plan in motion. That will give us a few more months to be sure we're all set, and Vasilyev won't be able to give away the USSR by then. With luck we'll have the old Soviet Union back by Christmas."

At an undisclosed CIA bunker back in the U.S., the soldier at the satellite monitoring desk couldn't believe what he was seeing. The American spy satellite picked up the detonation of the nuke case, although not huge, as the device flew over that part of Russia. It had always picked up the larger ones during testing, but it was pure luck that they noticed this one. It was undoubtedly nuclear, but the size of the blast was smaller than what they were used to seeing. In the end, the captain in charge that evening was just going to log it in his report, but he decided to get it up to the attention of Assistant Defense Director James Gelfand.

"Mr. Gelfand, I have something here that I'm going to send over to you in the morning. If you need us to follow up on it, please let me know, and we'll get right on it."

"Captain, can you have someone bring it over now? I'll be here for a few more hours so I might as well look at it. Thanks for following through on this."

When the report, with the photos, came through, Gelfand knew what it was immediately. He just sat there and shook his head, trying to figure out how the Russians had figured out how to pack nuclear weapons in a case small enough to carry and then detonate from miles away with a remote control device. *What were they going to do with this knowledge and when?*

He got on the phone to Donald Smith and told him what he had just seen.

# CHAPTER 27

Donald had been to the Oval Office a thousand times before, but this time it was different. Most times he'd be one of the direct reports present at the morning meeting, but this time it was past midnight on a Saturday night.

"Mr. President, they have figured out how to detonate the cases with a remote device. We just received confirmation from Assistant Defense Director Gelfand. We aren't sure yet how they figured it out."

Donald's stomach churned. He had seen the explosion himself on satellite video, and there was no way it could have been anything else.

"That makes the stakes a little higher, doesn't it, Donald? Do you think President Vasilyev is playing this above board, or does he have an ulterior motive?" President Reed took another sip of his coffee. He knew this was going to be a long night.

"I think it is what they say it is. It would make sense that the explosion happened nowhere near any of the confirmed laboratories that we know about. Whoever has the cases has figured out how to make them go boom, Mr. President."

"Does Pete know anything yet?"

"Not yet, but I planned to see him as soon as I'm finished here."

"I think that's wise. Do you feel secure with the team he has in place in Moscow?"

Donald needed to think this one out before he answered. He got up and walked to the window looking out over the White House lawn. "Yes, I do, Mr. President. I know it's a mixture in terms of experience, but as a team I think they can accomplish what we need."

"How do you think we should proceed?"

"I'd like to turn the heat up on Asimov and Drygin. We might need to push the team to get the information a little faster."

"Donald, do what you need to, but keep the Russians involved also. We'll need their assistance on this if we're going to pull it off. Keep me updated. Get back to Gelfand, and tell him 'Good job.' If you need anything, let me know. Have a good flight."

After meeting with the president, Donald called a few people before he headed to the airport. He couldn't get to Pete, but he knew where he was and left his assistant the instructions for tracking him down. The plane was ready when he got to the airport, and before he knew it, he was headed to France.

Pete picked up Donald at the airport. Pete's farmhouse was outside of Rouen, about a ninety-minute drive outside Paris. It was a nice ride through the countryside, but Donald didn't even notice. Deep in thought and in constant conversation with Pete, he was startled when the car stopped at the farmhouse.

"Pete, we need to get Yakov involved with this and up-to-date. I would think he knows what they have accomplished, but we need to be sure."

"I know, and if we can get to the American embassy to get a message to Mickey, we might be able to get to Yakov soon, but we need to get Yakov to Helsinki so we can discuss this face-to-face. The game has just been elevated to crisis mode."

Pete knew what had to be done and wasted little time. The message reached Moscow, and Mickey received it the same day. He and Petra met at their usual spot. No one ever paid attention to them because they looked like lovers on a leisurely stroll.

"Pete says we need to get Yakov to Helsinki the day after tomorrow for a meeting and it's most urgent. Can you get a message to him immediately?"

"Not a problem. I think it's best if he flies into Tallin and takes the Silja Line ferry over to meet them. Can you advise Pete that he'll be on the ferry?

"I'll get to Pete, but I think we need to give Yakov some backup to be sure he isn't followed." Mickey was learning the game fast.

"I'll be on the flight just in case to check and will be the watch-dog. We need to know what Drygin is up to and if Yakov has a tail. No question."

"Pete also told me we need to get to Olga and Boris to put a little pressure on them. You'll need to get to her and I'll get to Ivan so he can talk to Boris. Please be safe, Petra. I'd hate to have something happen to you. Call me when you get back."

The flight the following morning was oversold, but that was typical. Yakov simply went behind the counter and into the ticket office. Within a few minutes, he was back with two boarding passes. Petra was seated at the back of the plane so she could see what was going on around Yakov. The flight left at seven in the morning and, as usual, was late. It landed in Tallinn at ten-thirty, which was better than usual. On the way out of the terminal, she noticed a man who seemed to be keeping pace with Yakov. Because he didn't have any bags, Yakov had simply walked through the baggage claim and out to curbside to look for a cab. The man was right inside the terminal, talking into his lapel and watching what Yakov was doing.

When Yakov got in the cab, the man ran outside, jumped into a waiting car, and sped off following Yakov's cab. That was all Petra needed to know, so at this point she turned around and caught the

next flight back to Moscow. She would make her report directly to
Alexei, in Yakov's absence, and Alexei would pass on the information to Pete in Helsinki.

*When Drygin's man got to the Silja Terminal for the ferryboat cross-
ing, there would be so many Yakov lookalikes that he would be so confused
he wouldn't know which way to turn. He would give up and report to his
commander, and they would have to pick up Yakov again when he returned
to Moscow.*

The meeting among Pete, Donald, and Yakov was something to
behold. Here were two men who had known each other or of each
other their whole adult lives, now working together to achieve the
same goal. Donald was new to the group, but he had the attention
of the president of the United States. Pete had turned Yakov years
ago when they were small players in this game of espionage during
the Jordanian conflict. Together they had figured out how to communicate and keep each other safe for all these years. They were
now trying to pass this on to Petra and Mickey as they both realized
this was their last hurrah. It wasn't the worst circumstances to be
ending their careers on. The chance to end the Cold War as everyone knew it and to open the USSR to the Western world was a
pretty good way to go out. Now if they could just pull it off.

"The president thinks we need to get a nuclear arms treaty in
place for the next summit." Donald looked directly at Yakov. "This
will make Drygin move a lot faster, and hopefully we can get this
all over with soon."

Yakov would have to handle this with Alexei, but he was sure
President Vasilyev would agree to the terms.

"I don't think that will be a problem, Donald, but we'll need
assurances that your government will assist with our economic
problems in the way of loans and opening up trade agreements
with my country."

"President Reed has already agreed to that part of the plan and has talked to our closest allies into assisting with it. We need to finalize this and get it signed at the April summit. At the same time, we'll announce an economics summit with the U.S., Russia, and a few European countries that will be held in the summer months as soon as we can get it all together. Do you think that will please President Vasilyev?"

"I'm sure it will, but it will need to be productive so our economy starts to move in the right direction. We'd like to be sure that the Scandinavian countries are included as that will provide the fastest relief to our people," said Yakov. "For many years there had been basic trade among Russia and these countries, but if it could be supplemented with goods from Europe and America, that would work. We mainly need to get the infrastructure up to working levels as the roads and the basic facilities needed are in total disrepair. The Scandinavians could assist with this immediately."

"We'll do our best, and I'm sure your neighbors will help with rebuilding your roads. Is there anything else we need to discuss with regard to the economy, or are you fine with the direction we're taking?"

Naturally, more needed to be discussed, but that was for the state departments of the countries invited to the economic summit. These three men were here to stop a few madmen from destroying the world.

"What about security at the presidential summit in April?" Donald asked.

"Pete and me have gone over the plan, and we think it's fine. The Swiss know how to handle these things." Yakov said.

Pete had been quiet as he was only concerned with the nuke cases and how this part of the agreement would be handled. When he was sure they were satisfied with the summit situation, he spoke up. "Yakov, I'm not sure about you, but Donald has told me that my balls are on the line with this situation. Are you getting any heat?" Pete smiled.

"No, just the usual from Alexei. Hope you figure this out, or you'll be on the next transport to Siberia on an unheated train!"

They all laughed, but they knew what was at stake.

"They've figured out how to get the signal to the cases so the devices implode internally to start the nuclear reaction to detonate the bomb," Pete said. "It will take them a while to get all the other cases ready, but it won't be an eternity. Summer is our best guess when they could be ready."

Donald reached into his briefcase and took out the photos of the nuke case exploding somewhere in southwestern Russia.

Yakov looked at it and just nodded his head. "We had been aware of an explosion in that general area, but our satellites weren't over the vicinity so we couldn't verify it. Our best guess now is that they will probably move the cases from the Odessa area. We think two scientists are still working on the project and they'll split them to have them work separately on getting everything ready. That is what we would do anyway."

Pete and Donald had discussed the same scenario on the way to the meeting, and that's how they saw it.

"How do you think they will move the remaining twelve nuke cases?" Pete asked Yakov.

"No matter where the cases are, they will most likely move them by truck up to Moscow. Once they arrive there, they will work on the internal schematic of the bombs to get them ready for the remote signal. Once completed it will just be a matter of when they make the final move, whatever that is? Tell me, Pete, what would you do with the cases?"

"If I were a madman and Russian and thought my country was falling apart, I'm not sure. We know twelve cases are left, which are small enough to get to different locations. I'd put them in different parts of the world and threaten to blow something up. It's anyone's guess what this is, and it doesn't matter at this point. We need to find those cases to try to get them back, but I guess they will be heavily guarded. If that's the case, then we need to watch them intently until they are moved. Then we make our move if we can. They'll also need to work on the remote controls so maybe there's another way to stop them. It's time we put the pressure on our agents to come up with some real intelligence. Do you agree, Yakov?"

Unquestionably, they needed someone to get them more substantial knowledge on where this was all taking place. They knew they were close, but close wasn't good enough unless the game was horseshoes. And this was no game.

"Olga could be getting close, and maybe Boris will be coming through with something soon. We have verified that Drygin is indeed in charge, so we've been watching him, but we don't think that will lead us anywhere. The general is another story, so we'll stay with him and Olga."

Pete looked at Donald and then to Yakov. "As you know, the NFL has scheduled another meeting with Mikhail in Moscow for Friday, February 21, to finalize the game. The meeting will be an all-day affair, starting at eight for breakfast at the Europa. The NFL wants to see the facilities, stadium, and hotels that will be utilized for the program. Along with John Duddie, two other representatives from the NFL will give Mikhail the approval to have a regularly scheduled game on Sunday, September 21, 1986, between the Miami Dolphins and New York Giants. The league has been toying with the idea for a while, so they figured this would be as good a place as any. Plus President Reed asked them to do him a favor as part of his plan to help open up the Russian economy. The formal announcement of the game will take place at a reception during the meeting in February with the NFL."

Yakov liked what he heard and couldn't stop smiling. *If the president were telling the NFL to bring a game to Moscow, then he was serious about the whole affair.*

Pete looked at his Russian friend. "Yakov, we've been through a lot together, and hopefully this will be our last mission. Let's be sure we don't fuck this one up and be known as the two agents who blew up the world."

Yakov stood up and walked over to his comrade. "Together with our teams we'll handle this as we have handled all the others. We've come a long way." He hugged his friend and left the room for his journey back to Moscow.

On the way back, Yakov realized he needed to talk to Petra about the state of affairs in Russia and let her in on the whole story. *She'd need to get to Olga to pressure her into getting as much information as she could out of the general. Pete, on the other hand, had to get to Mickey to advise him on the meeting with the NFL and how to handle his end. Donald had to report back to President Reed. The game is on!!!*

The city of Geneva was a great backdrop for this summit as it stood for neutrality in a world where everyone thought he still needed to choose a side, everyone but Pete and Yakov. The Russians had just gotten out of the Afghan War, not unlike the war the Americans fought in Vietnam some years before. Both countries had learned that war wasn't as popular as it had been in the past and fighting an enemy with an unknown strategy on their home turf wasn't real smart. The history books might never tell it this way, but both got their butts kicked. Everyone in both countries felt the loss, and when the boys came home from these wars, they weren't heroes.

Pete pondered on the situation. *That was probably the saddest part of the whole thing. The countries no longer felt the patriotism that was needed most during the tough times after a war. The public was against the war, and there were many protests, especially in the U.S. This might have also occurred in Russia, but no one would ever know. It's just the way it was.*

Pete and Yakov had orchestrated the first arms summit, as it was being heralded, that was a huge success for both countries.

When President Reed welcomed President Vasilyev on the steps of the hotel wearing a large smile, the world knew this was going to be something special. It was a historic beginning to a historic meeting that could possibly change the world forever…or at least for a while.

Two days into the summit, it was leaked that both sides were very interested in reducing the total number of warheads on their intermediate arsenal, but there was a stalemate over President Reed's insistence on keeping the Strategic Defense Initiative, or Star Wars, as the press had named it. Only one day was left in the summit, and it was important that something good come out of this first meeting.

At the end of the third day, both presidents agreed to look into the finalization of an INF (Intermediate Range Nuclear Forces) treaty at the next summit, which was scheduled for April 7, 1986, in Reykjavik, Iceland. Both governments had decided to move as fast as possible on the treaty to make this a priority but also realized that, the faster they moved, the faster Director Drygin had to move.

# CHAPTER 28

Every time the truck hit a bump, Boris farted. "Better than shittin' in my pants!"

The colonel, who was sitting next to him in the passenger's seat, just laughed every time it happened. "When we stop you better check your pants anyway, Boris. Who knows what you got down there?"

No one really knew what would happen if the nuke cases got jarred or if the truck ran off the road. Heck, for all they knew, if they fell out of the padded racks, they could go off and blow a hole in the earth a few miles wide.

The distance from Odessa to Moscow was eight-hundred miles. They figured it would take them three full days to make the trip, but they had enough provisions to last them a week. In any case the vodka would not run out, and they would need to take their time and hit as few bumps as possible. Boris only wanted to get back to Moscow and sleep in his own bed.

Ivan had seen Boris just before he left and passed on the messages from Mickey. He had made it a point to see Ivan as soon as he read the note from Pete on getting as much information as they could. Everyone wanted Boris to get back as soon as possible as the meeting with the NFL was a week off and he was scheduled to be there with Mikhail, Ivan, and Mickey. Boris didn't want to miss that meeting. After he got the call from the colonel, he figured it had something to do with the nuke cases, but he wasn't sure what needed to be done. He simply followed orders and took the military flight down to Odessa to meet the colonel. When he found out he was driving a truck up to Moscow, he figured it was the cases, but it was never mentioned. It was only said that he was to be very careful and to take the route through Kiev to the military base outside Moscow, the one near Istra off M-9.

When they were near Moscow on the outskirts by the town of Podol'sk, Boris figured it was time to see what he could find out. The colonel had a few vodkas in him, so he gave it a try. "Colonel, do you think you could finally let me know what is going on?" Boris believed in what he was doing. *I don't have much to lose. I can't let the general get away with whatever he was planning.*

The colonel looked out the window but said quietly. "We plan to take over the government as soon as we can get all the bombs ready. We aren't going to let Vasilyev give Russia to America because we have a few problems. Marx, Lenin, and Stalin are turning over in their graves. We'll get this done by Christmas. Does America think it's messing with a Third World country in the desert who can't feed its own people? We'll never be beholding to them, and if they think we will, they're crazy. We'll show them and the rest of the world that Russia will never fall. We have more resources, and we'll bring them to their knees."

Boris couldn't even think about what the colonel was saying. "But where will the bombs be put?"

"The general has told me they'll put ten of them in various embassies throughout the world. When we march on the Dumas, if we're defeated, the ten bombs will be detonated and destroy parts of the Western and Arab worlds. You won't tell a soul, Boris." He was silent the rest of the way.

Boris didn't talk either as his mind was racing with what he now knew. *I have to get to Mikhail as soon as this job is done and let him know the madness that was happening all around us. This shit is crazy!*

They pulled up to the military base and were escorted through gates. After a brief stop at the commandant's office, Boris drove the truck, alone with the colonel, to the warehouse at the far northern end of the base. No one else was there to help them, so Boris and the colonel stored seven of the cases in the back of the warehouse and locked the doors. The other five, already wired, were left in the truck to be transported to another spot that only the colonel knew about.

While they were walking back to the truck, Boris only heard a gunshot and felt a pain at the base of his head.

The colonel was sad for a few moments as he actually liked the big guy. He went to the cab of the truck and finished the bottle of vodka. He then took Boris' body and dragged it back into the warehouse. Someone would dispose of it in the morning.

# CHAPTER 29

No one had heard from Boris in a week, causing concern for Mikhail. He knew his brother was part of the Dynamo military sports deal and that usually was a protection rather than a detriment to one's life. But, like always, when Boris had to leave, he'd never tell anyone where he was going or what he was doing. He would only say when he would be back. Sometimes he came back when he said he would, but he would be delayed other times. MIkhail just took it for granted that he would return. If they ask too many questions, it wouldn't look good. Mikhail could only get a message to Yakov and hope someone had seen Boris.

The meeting with the NFL went on as scheduled without Boris. The NFL couldn't have been more gracious, and Mickey was excited about the prospects. Mikhail made sure they were treated like VIPs and a lot of press coverage was there. The traveling party included John and Larry Nussbaum and George Buck from the commissioner's office. The men had the authority to start the deal if they liked what they saw in Moscow. Mickey already knew this was a done deal from the note Pete had gotten to him. *John looks like a nice guy who won't bullshit us*, pondered Mickey. *Not your usual NFL type of guy. Larry and George, on the other hand, look like they walked out of the NFL magazine*

When the NFL staff, Mickey, and Ivan left Mikhail's business suites, two lovely ladies who would accompany them throughout the day escorted them down the elevator. Two Zil limousines were waiting for them in front of the hotel, and one of the drivers was none other than Dmitri. Mickey hadn't seen him for a while, but there was no question he was riding with him. The two girls and the two guys from the commissioner's office went with Mikhail while John and Ivan came with Mickey in the car driven by Dmitri.

"I think Larry and George are impressed so far. Mikhail's presentation was very professional, and the numbers added up. If the facilities are up to par with what we Americans are used to, they should get the deal," John said.

Ivan was all smiles but stayed silent. *If we could all pull this off, Mikhail and I would be heroes forever.*

"John, the venues should be fine as I have seen all of them already. Are they really going to bring the third game of the season here? We thought it would be one of the exhibition games?" Mickey asked.

"Word came down from Commissioner White that, if all were in order, Larry could commit to a regularly scheduled game. We thought the Giants versus Dolphins would be a good one."

When they turned the corner, John noticed they were in front of Luzhniki Stadium, where the game would be played. It was the biggest stadium in Russia, holding seventy-eight thousand people, and used mostly for soccer. The pitch was in good shape, and the locker rooms, media section, and a few of the suites had just been renovated. The public areas needed work, but the presentation had shown what was intended in these areas.

"The field looks in pretty good shape. Do you think the work can get done on the suites in time?" John needed a few assurances.

"They'll get it done on time. Mickey and Ivan will work with me to be sure," Mikhail answered. "They'll also be responsible for the TV contracts we'll be working on for the rest of Europe. How do you want to handle CBS?"

"We'll have our contacts at the station work with you all, and you can use the same basic contract for the Europeans and any other country that wants the rights." John had been advised by the commissioner's office to make the process as easy as possible. "What about security?"

Mikhail walked John and the rest of the NFL team through the stadium. The security teams were all in place, as they would be on game day. Mikhail also took them into the control room on top of the stadium to meet with the boss.

On the way down to the cars, John pulled Mickey aside. "The NFL has already approved the game based on this fact-finding trip being positive."

Mickey just looked at him like he knew nothing. "Thanks for letting me know." *John's a pretty good guy. He didn't need to tell me.*

They left the stadium for the ride to the hotels the teams would be using, the best in Moscow. At the last one, the Europa, there would be a cocktail reception for a few selected Russian VIPs and media, which Alexei would host.

When they got to the reception room, one hundred people were already in attendance. There were a few men in military uniforms, the media, and others from various sport federations and the government. It was hard to tell who was who except for one general in uniform who was walking around like a prize peacock. Mickey had seen his picture in the *Ivestia* newspaper but had no idea who he really was and how important he might be within the military.

He walked over to Ivan to see what he knew. "Who's the general with the big head over by the bar. The one just watching everything?"

"That would be General Asimov, one of the most ruthless military men we have. He has been honored many times and even survived the mistakes he made in the Afghan War. They say he blamed the miscalculations on his staff and had most of them shot."

"Nice guy."

*This place is scary at times. Everyone mingled as if all of them were best friends, but in reality you never knew who was Mafia, KGB, or the government. Thank God the military has to wear uniforms.*

"Ladies and gentlemen, may I introduce Prime Minister Alexei Popov," Mikhail announced.

Yakov had briefed Alexei on the NFL program. Yakov had gotten all he needed from Pete.

*It's amazing how high up all this is already, but you can always tell the people who didn't know by the initial look on their faces.*

After the usual small talk of thanking everyone for coming, he unveiled the secret. "The NFL has opened up discussions with Vladikoff Enterprise to hold the first NFL game on European soil in Moscow. Discussions have centered on a scheduled game being played here in September of this year, and we're in final preparation with them. As soon as we have any more information, we'll pass it on to you. Thank you, and have a nice day." He looked directly at the general and left the podium.

"Are you kidding me?" the general asked himself. He wasn't in the routine of talking to himself, but this was all too much. "How the hell did this happen so fast. What the fuck is going on?"

While he was leaving the reception, someone handed him a note, but he didn't even have to read it. He knew Drygin was summoning him.

Alexei was quite pleased with himself, especially when he saw the look on Asimov's face. He knew they had him, but it was a matter of cracking the final details. Yakov was in a back room, monitoring the people who had attended. He was surprised that Director Drygin hadn't shown up. It wasn't like him. *Does he know what's going on?* He probably did, but that wouldn't surprise Yakov.

After the general rushed out into the hallway, Yakov saw the note passed to him so he decided to follow him. When he entered the lobby of the Metropole and went directly to the kitchen, there was no question about who he was going to see. Alexei had told him about the secret passage from the kitchen up to the director's office years ago. They had just confirmed the players. Now they needed to confirm the plan.

The walk over to the Metropole was a little faster than Asimov would have wanted. He needed time to get his thoughts together. *First, the summit and now they just announce an NFL game in Moscow.* The whole process was moving too fast, and he needed to get up to speed.

While he walked through the kitchen and headed to the secret door, he knew it was a matter of getting everything done now. He also had figured out what his final plan would be. He decided to only use five nuke cases at the embassies. He would hold two as backup, and he knew where he would place the remaining five. Hopefully the director would sign off on it.

# CHAPTER 30

When Olga arrived early at work a few days after the NFL announcement, Yakov was waiting for her. He was concerned that she knew what was at stake after the announcement but more concerned about her welfare and state of mind.

"When were you going to tell me about your relationship with General Asimov? It makes me question whose side you're on." Yakov knew a direct approach was best.

"It just started one day, and I never knew who he was until we got further into the affair." After the announcement she hadn't seen Asimov.

"We've known about it for some time now. You should know that there isn't too much we don't know. However you didn't answer my question. Do you believe in what he's doing, or are still on our side?"

"I must tell you I wasn't sure at first, but as time went on, I realized the insanity behind the scheme. I'm not worried about our relationship but more concerned with his plans of mass destruction. The nuke cases are moving along, and I'm sure he has worked out his final plan."

While she told him the story, she felt relieved, but she knew it was now part of her job to get Yakov and Alexei what they needed. She had known this from the start, but the general was quite convincing when she heard his side. She was glad she had Yakov to confide in and to work for. *There's no way I could let him down.*

"He has asked me to join him for a few days at the mansion in Odessa. We plan to leave tomorrow and be back for the weekend."

"You know how important all this is, but you need to act as if nothing has changed between you two. If he suspects anything, he'll kill you before you know it. I hate to keep you involved, but we don't have too many options open to us."

"I'll keep acting as if nothing is wrong, and he'll never know. Hopefully he'll divulge what the overall plan is or at least more."

"If he has an office or someplace he keeps any secret files, see what you can find. Hopefully he's vain enough to keep records and is stupid enough to write things down. You never know?"

"He does have a small office at the mansion, and I'll snoop around as soon as we get down there. He'll probably be away for a day, so I'll do what I have to."

"Be careful. The staff is probably well-trained agents even if they don't look it. If you can find something and get it out, that would be best, but if you can't just photograph what you find."

"I will and hope I can find something. Do you think they killed Boris?"

"There's no way to know for sure, but chances are that they did. He was last seen outside of Istra with Colonel Marisova on the way to the military base. No one ever saw him come out."

"Are you going to tell Mikhail?"

"Not yet. It wouldn't do any good to get Mikhail all riled up and on a personal vendetta. As much as I hate keeping it secret, it will have to wait. Plus we have no proof that he's dead. When you are in Odessa, see if you can find out where the two scientists are who are working with the general. We believe one is at the base in Istra with the nuke cases, but we need to find out where the other one is. Chances are he's working on the remote control devices in Odessa."

Olga looked at Yakov for a long time before she gave him a big hug. He had been like a dad to her, and she would not let him down. Yakov watched her walk away and hoped it wasn't the last time he would see her.

"Be careful in Odessa."

Petra woke up in a sweat and realized she was crying. Olga had left four days before, but she felt as if it had been forever. They had been together the night before she left for Odessa. Olga had told Petra about her talk with Yakov. Too much was going on, and she wasn't sure if it were going the right way. Boris hadn't been seen, so they just figured he was dead. Mikhail was in a foul mood, so she couldn't hang out there for security. There was always Yakov, but then that would remind her of Olga. She called Mickey to see if she could come over to the hotel to talk to him. He wasn't in, so she just sat there and cried.

The phone rang. When she answered it, she was surprised to hear the voice on the other end tell her what was happening. After a few minutes on the phone, she hung up, got dressed, and left the apartment.

# CHAPTER 31

The satellite technology the U.S. had was unbelievable. It actually could spot a truck moving along a road and follow it to its final destination. It could zoom in so close that someone could see the faces of the people in the truck. And that was what happened on the night that Boris got shot. When the photos were shown to Pete, he knew he had to get them to Yakov and he wasn't going to let anyone else handle the situation. He also knew he had to see for himself what was going on with his people to be sure they were on top of the situation. It would be a quick in and out to meet with a few of them, and then he would get back out the way he came in.

*I'm getting too old for this, but I need to make one last trip to the USSR.*

Petra was waiting on the bench when an old man sat next to her. She was ready to ask him to leave as she was waiting for someone, but when she was about to speak, the old man gently held her hand and said, "Now, Petra, would it be nice to ask an old man to leave? I'm only waiting for you."

A big smile came over his face, and Petra realized who she was looking at. Pete got into Russia as he always did in the past. The contacts the Americans had in Finland had been there for years and would always be there. They first set up the run about thirty years ago. It was actually easier in the winter as everything was frozen. If he dressed properly, which the Finnish knew how to do, the cold really never bothered him. It was a journey from Helsinki to Kesalahti, a few miles from the Russian border over frozen tundra. Kesalahti was small with a population of around twenty-one hundred people, but they all hated the Russians. The next part of the trip was by dogsled over the frozen lakes where they crossed into Russia. An American who lived in Sortavaia picked them up. He hadn't seen Pete for some time. After that, it was a longer dogsled ride over the frozen Lake Ladoga and into Leningrad. The contacts were all still in place, and the trip took eighteen hours, but it still worked.

Pete and Petra had met outside the Church of the Ascension of the Lord in the village of Kolomenskoe located on the outskirts of the city on the Moscova River.

"Pete, in a million years I would never known that was you. How are you?"

"I've been better. It isn't easy for an old man to get into your country any more without being noticed. That's for the younger generation. How's Mickey?"

"I think he's fine. I tried reaching him before I came, but he wasn't in. I think he understands what this is all about. He looks more confident but not overly, and he blends into the background when needed. He knows his place and is beginning to play it right. Does he know you are here?"

"No, but if you see him, please tell him I am here and I'll contact him. I have a few errands to run, and then I am back to Leningrad. Please take these pictures to Yakov for me, and tell him to do what he thinks with them. We have located the nuke cases at a military base outside of Moscow, but we aren't sure yet where the remote devices are being worked on. You should have someone watch the base just in case they move them again, but my best guess is that, the next time they move them, it will be to their final destinations. All the information is in the packet." Pete paused.

"Oh, watch Olga. She's getting too close to the general, and he might just kill her." Pete noticed the concern on Petra's face.

"I will."

"How's Ivan doing? Is he still as cocky as ever?"

"No, I think Mikhail had a discussion with him once they returned from the meeting with the EFL in Bern. I'm not sure what he said, but since then Ivan has been businesslike and humble. It's a nice change, and they all are working toward one goal."

Pete sat there for a few minutes and looked at the surroundings. It was a beautiful day, and he wished he was back in Rouen at the farmhouse, sitting with his family on the patio sipping some red wine.

"Is that all, Pete?"

"No, one last thing. Did you notice anything funny in Tallin when Yakov boarded the ferry to Helsinki?"

"No, nothing out of the ordinary. Someone was following him, but we knew that would be the case. We took the correct steps to alleviate the problem."

"That's what I thought. Please tell Yakov I'll see him in Iceland at the summit, and we should sneak off for a few hours to talk things over. He'll know where to meet me. The time and date are also in the packet. Take care of yourself." He patted her leg and got up from the bench.

She sat there for a few minutes to be sure no one was watching. When she felt safe, she got up to go back to her office to see Yakov.

After Pete left the bench, he walked through the church, which was under renovation, through the vestibule, and out the side door. He was sure someone was following him and needed to get away as getting caught in Moscow wasn't part of the plan. While he ran through the ancient graveyard into the Church of the Beheading of St. John the Baptist, he knew his only escape was down the bank to the boat he had waiting there. He stopped to catch his breath and to see if he could get a glimpse or shot at his pursuer. He looked around the column and saw two men he hadn't seen before but was sure they were KGB.

*Getting old is tough, but having to run at this age is even tougher. I need to get to the boat and get out of here to finish what I've come to Moscow for.*

He watched the two men leave the north side of the church and bolted out the back and down the riverbank. When he was close to the river, he tripped on a tree branch and went sailing past the vessel. His companion reached out and caught his back leg as he was sailing past and then dragged him into the boat. While the boat sped out of there, Pete looked back to the river bank to see the two men with guns drawn watching him speed away. They went a mile up the river to the spot where the car was waiting. He got into the car and felt a little twinge in his left side. It wasn't the first time he cracked a few ribs. It was part of the job.

Petra got back to the office as soon as possible and was glad that Yakov was still there. Yakov knew Pete was in town, but it was too dangerous for them to meet in Moscow. In all these years together, they had used intermediaries for drops and messages. The few times they had to meet, they made sure it was far away from Moscow. Petra handed Yakov the packet and then sat there and waited for him to speak. It was a while, as a lot of material was in the packet.

But he finally shook his head. "The American technology is fantastic. As advanced as we think we are, they're years ahead of us. Take a look at these photos." Yakov rarely let Petra, or anyone for that matter, see classified photos, but under these circumstances he had decided that Petra needed to know everything that was going on.

She took the photos and couldn't believe what she was look-ing at. Boris was walking from what looked like a warehouse with a military man behind him. In the next photo, this same man was dragging Boris back into the warehouse. She could see their faces, but Petra had no idea who the other man was.

"Do you know who the military man is?"

"Colonel Marisova, the henchman for General Asimov. I need to let Mikhail know so there can be some type of closure on Boris. I also know he's going to want to get back at Marisova, so I need to figure something out there. Look at the other three photos and tell me what you think."

The other photos were of the military compound, which showed how the area was being guarded. "I would think that there is no way into this compound and trying to shoot our way in is almost impossible. It might be best to just keep an eye on it from a distance to see when these cases are moved."

"I totally agree with you, Petra. I would have liked to be able to go after them, but at least we know where they are. Maybe we'll still be able to figure something out, but the question is whether all twelve of the cases are in the warehouse. The other photos are unclear with regard to the number of cases that were moved."

"How do you want me to handle this intelligence? Is there anyone else I should tell?"

"No, Petra, for the time being, it'll be only for us to know. In time we'll advise the others but not until we've worked out a plan. No one knows but us."

When Petra left Yakov got his senior team in place to watch the Istra military compound and the warehouse housing the nuke cases. They noticed that a lone scientist entered the warehouse in the morning, stayed there all day, and then left in the evening. Colonel Marisova, who got him in the door and then locked it, drove him to the building. No one else went near the place until later that day when the colonel went back to pick him up. Based on the reports, the scientist wasn't Professor Putinov, so Yakov figured he was still with the remote devices, wherever they were being worked on.

*If only I knew how many of the cases were in the building?*

The colonel never left the compound, so Yakov decided he could let Mikhail know that the military had killed Boris. He wouldn't be able to let Mikhail know what was happening, but at least he could stop worrying about his brother and bury him...at least in his mind. As there was no body, they would never be able to prove anything, but at this point that didn't matter. Yakov had to keep his team alert so they would be able to follow the cases when they were moved. But no one knew when that would be. It could be tomorrow or five months from now. But whatever the timing, he knew he could only keep an eye on the compound.

Mickey was getting chills as he walked up to the park bench in Gorky Park. The bullet holes were still in the top left corner and would probably be there for quite some time. He sat there, looked around, and thought about the last time he was here and how close he had come to death. He still didn't know who had shot at the agent who tried to kill him. *I'd never find out, but that's probably for the best.*

He reached under the bench. The packet was right where it was supposed to be, except the packet had an envelope on the outside. Written in handwriting he had seen before was the note, "Meet me at the bench across from the Ferris wheel."

There was no mistaking the handwriting. On the way over to the fun park, Mickey kept looking around, surprised to see that no one was following him. *Is it possible that Pete is here, or is someone playing a trick on me?*

When he got to the area, he looked across to the Ferris wheel. There on the park bench sat Pete. He had a smug smile on his face, and when Mickey was close, he stood up and hugged him. It was like he was with him the whole time.

Pete got right to the point. "That's from your mom. I saw them last week and promised I would give you the hug when I saw you. How are things going, Mickey?"

"I'm good. Thanks for asking. The meeting with the NFL and John went well, and I think they were impressed with Mikhail's organization and security. The stadium and hotels were a little under their standards, but they were okay."

"That's to be expected. You should have seen them five years ago."

"The cars are coming in fine, and Stephan is a good partner in Leningrad."

It started to drizzle, but it didn't bother them. They sat there with their own thoughts for a while and stayed silent. Pete thought it was time to give Mickey a little reassurance, but he wasn't totally sure. As Petra told him, he was confident but not being cocky. That was important, but he needed Mickey now, and there was no way around that. *The game has gone too far.*

"Are you sure you're okay?" Pete asked.

Mickey held his gaze and responded with sincerity, "I have my moments of doubt, but they've become less and less as time goes by. I know I might be in a little over my head, but what can I do? I've been given a crash course and training in espionage 101 by the best the world has to offer, and I need to do the best I can. That's all I can do, and I'm almost sure I can get it done."

"That all sounds great. I'm glad you feel that way, but remember to expect the unexpected and to just react. Don't think too much, okay?" Pete handed Mickey a manila envelope. On the outside was written "BORIS."

Mickey wasn't sure if he wanted to open it, but he did. He closed the envelope. "Do you think we'll ever find the body?"

Pete just shook his head. "I want you to share what you know with Ivan. Hold nothing back, and advise him that you saw the pictures confirming Boris' death. Among you, Ivan, and Petra, we need to keep things together down the road, as things are going to happen quickly. We aren't sure what Olga is up to, but you should also tell Ivan about her involvement with the general. He needs to know all of it now so we can keep things together. I won't be back again, so if you have any questions or need anything, now is the time to ask."

Mickey thought about it for a while. He leaned over and kissed Pete on the cheek. "Give that to my mom the next time you see her."

They said their good-byes and left the park. Mickey had a lonely ride back to the hotel on the Metro.

# CHAPTER 32

General Asimov had picked a good spot, and he was sure it was still a secret. The mansion sat at the end of the dirt path that lead from E-105 west from the resort of Yalta on the westernmost point of the peninsula. No one knew much about it except a wall that ran from coast to coast surrounded it and a Soviet Navy vessel patrolled its water out in the Black Sea. The locals only knew that, every once in a while, a black Zil limousine passed through Yalta on the way to the mansion. The windows were tinted so no one could see who was in the car. The limo, however, usually came back through Yalta the same day, so whoever was in the car was just a visitor, if there were ever anyone really in the car. The general had been using the mansion for some time as a safe haven away from the rest of the world.

A Russian whose name nobody actually knew built the mansion itself in the fifties. It wasn't an expansive area and only covered an acre, but on the northern point, there was a small bathhouse and an adjoining building that was currently being used as a workshop. In the workshop was Alexandre Putinov, working on the remote control devices. Sitting at the pool was Olga, trying to figure out her next move.

The general had left the evening before and said he would return in a few days. In the meantime, Olga was told to stay put and enjoy the mansion until he returned. She wasn't used to being

told what to do, but she was a prisoner with little choice. She figured she might as well snoop around and see what she could find.
The sleeping rooms were on the top floor of the mansion, on the
southern side of the building, while the lower level housed the
kitchen, the formal dining room, recreation room, and terraces
that overlooked the pool and the sea. Off to the left was a beautiful
small annex that was the general's working office. She knew where
she needed to look.

Breaking into the room was easier than Olga had thought, but
finding anything of importance the first time wasn't easy. On the
third go-around, she noticed a little nook in the upper right por-
tion of the wall. It was a tiny buttonhole that was almost invisible.
She almost didn't see it but as she turned to survey the other side
of the room the light hit the hole just right. She was about to put
a bobby pin into the hole to see what would happen but heard a
noise outside the room. She scrambled under the desk and waited
there a few minutes until the noise subsided. She went back to the
pinhole, but her hand was shaking as she knew this was what she
was looking for.

The bobby pin hit something hard but would not enter, but
she gave it one more push. *Bingo!* A little door up in the ceiling slid
back, revealing a small space. Among the different denominations
of hard currency, guns, and files, she saw a small leather-bound
notebook with the general's name embossed on it. *This is my only
chance.* She took the notebook from the vault and slid it into her
pants. When she slid the pin out of the hole, the door slid back
over the opening, concealing the general's hiding place. It took
her a while to be sure she left everything as she had found it. She
slipped out the door and back to her room.

When she was finished undressing, she took out the book and
read. It was a diary, in the general's own hand, laying out his career
as well as foreseeing his future. His gall and audacity in where he
saw himself going in the future appalled her. The plan was all laid
out in front of her, and she knew she was the only one beside the

general and Director Drygin who knew the magnitude of it. There was no way she would be able to fall asleep. She decided immediately that she needed to memorize the whole plan and then try to get the book out to Petra, but she knew that was almost impossible. She dared not go back into the office as she was lucky to not get caught the last time she was there. The book would need to be hidden, and if she ever got the chance, she would get it out of the mansion. *No one will believe what these guys were up to.*

The room was in Kirvosk, a little village on the outskirts of Leningrad off the M-18. It was a safe house the CIA had used for many years for the crossing of the lake. Yakov was amazed that the KGB didn't know about it. *Pete never ceases to amaze me.* Yakov had taken the train up to Leningrad to meet with Pete before he went back over the border.

"I wish we knew about Boris and the military base with the nuke cases before I let Olga go to Odessa with Asimov. I have a bad feeling about it. I hope she takes care of herself," Yakov said.

"There was no way you could have known, Yakov. We needed her down there anyway as that might be the place where the scientists are working on the remotes. We'll need to try to get to her in the next few days to see what she's found out. By the time we meet with the presidents next week in Iceland, we need to have our final plan worked out and be ready to put it into motion. Is Alexei okay with the way things are preceding?"

"Alexei just wants to get his hands on the nuke cases. He's convinced our two countries need to work out the arms situation as well as Russia's economic problems. He's ready to implement whatever strategy President Vasilyev's team works out with the US. We now need to find Olga and the general in the hope they can lead us to the remotes. That's the missing piece at the moment."

"Did you tell Mikhail about Boris?" Pete asked. *It wouldn't have been an easy thing to do.*

"Yes, he took it in stride, but I'm sure it just killed him inside. We'll need to keep him busy and watch him at the same time. We can't afford to let Mikhail go nuts and want revenge. I think he's professional enough to handle it properly."

Pete shook his friend's hand. "Then we're all set. Together we'll brief the two leaders on the nuke cases while they work their magic with the press and the rest of the world. I'll sure be glad when this is over."

Pete made it across the lake and back into Finland about the same time Yakov got back to Moscow. In a few days they would be back together, saving the world in Iceland.

# CHAPTER 33

Donald was looking forward to the coming events. Because it was the beginning of April, the whole world was anticipating the next presidential summit to be held in Iceland in which he had a major role. *Is it really possible that these two countries could work something out and start an end to the Cold War?*

Behind the scenes Pasha was finalizing the first strategic arms treaty that would be signed at the opening of the summit so everyone would know that these two presidents were going to get this done. He and Donald had worked most of it out after the first summit. They had become good friends in the last few days and looked forward to the upcoming summit. They had been in Reykjavik for the last few days reviewing the final drafts before the presidents arrived on Monday. After the signing in the afternoon, there would be a simple dinner that night. Then the presidents would return to the meeting the following morning to discuss the next steps in curtailing the Cold War, finalizing the agenda for the economic summit and discuss Director Drygin and the missing nuke cases. This was indeed an historic time in the relations between their two countries, if everything went according to plan.

The presidents arrived on schedule for the first session of the summit, which was being held at the winter palace on the outskirts of the city. The meeting went as planned, and the two presidents signed the arms treaty limiting the number of nuclear warheads in their arsenals. When they made the announcement on the treaty, they also discussed the plans for the economic summit, which was to take place in Paris during the third week in July. After they moved on to other business, they concluded the summit with a dinner with dignitaries from Iceland. The following morning, prior to their final press conference before leaving Reykjavik, there was a secret breakfast meeting among Presidents Vasilyev and Reed, Yakov Popov, and Pete Martin. The interpreter was given the morning off as Yakov would take over that duty.

"Yakov, has anyone seen or heard from General Asimov since his last meeting with Director Drygin?" Pete asked. "It would be nice to know where he is and what he's up to."

"The last we know is that he went to Odessa with Olga. If he knows we're on to him, I doubt very much he'd surface until he's ready to put his plan into motion."

"I think you're right, Yakov," President Vasilyev remarked. "If Asimov is underground, we need to get her to find out where he is, but we should also keep a close eye on Drygin. If, as you say, he's part of this game, maybe he'll lead us somewhere."

"Are we sure that some of the nuke cases are at the military base in Istra outside of Moscow where Boris was killed?" Pete asked. "The key may be to get to that warehouse to see what they have in there."

"Pete, we have a force watching the base as we speak. It will be tough, but we could pull it off. We have Captain Bodkin working on a plan now."

"Once the plan is approved, let me see it before we give the final go-ahead," President Vasilyev said. "I'm still not sure if I want to raid my own base that close to Moscow. What if the cases have been moved?"

President Reed looked directly at Vasilyev as if nobody else were in the room. "If we don't move on that base, all bets are off. We didn't agree to this to have Russia back out. If we're not in this together, let's end it now and move on so the world can know that

Moscow has lost nuclear warheads. I have no time for this bullshit." Yakov looked at Reed before he translated. "Interpret it just as I said it, Yakov."

President Vasilyev reacted as Reed thought he would. Strength versus strength was the only way. "Yakov, are you sure the nuke cases are at the base?"

"We're sure that at least seven of them are there and we might be able to get to them."

Vasilyev looked at Reed and nodded to Yakov. "Then let's set it up."

"Pete, is there any more information coming from Rossetti or any of the other agents we have in place?" Reed asked.

"There's nothing new that we know of. Ivan and Mickey have both been updated on their part, but as far as I know, nothing has changed. Our best bet is to try to take the base and hope we can find it all there."

"Then I guess we're all set," Yakov said. "I'll work with the Spetsnaz units to organize an attack on the military base at Istra. Hopefully this will be all we'll need to do, but chances are it won't. If I were them, I'd not keep all the cases in the same place. After the raid we'll need to reconnoiter to decide what to do next, but that will be up to me and Pete with approval from both of you." Yakov paused. "At the same time, we'll keep a close eye on Drygin and keep a lookout for the general. Pete, I suggest we use Mickey and Petra for all correspondence as it is critical that we work this together."

They all nodded, shook hands, and left by different exits.

At the conclusion of the breakfast meeting, the presidents held the final press conference as planned. The final joint communiqué read:

*The Soviet Union and the United States of America have taken the first steps in reducing the amount of nuclear warheads. Along with this first historic step, we have also initiated the first economic summit to be held shortly in Paris. We both hope this is the start of a relationship to end the Cold War as we know it and to bring the world closer to global peace. On August 18 of this year, we'll hold another summit to further discuss these initiatives and to discuss other programs that are currently in the works. We look forward to getting together again as friends in pursuit of world peace.*

Somewhere in the inner sanctums of the KGB headquarters, a madman staring at the walls was vowing that such a thing would never happen.

# CHAPTER 34

On April 26, 1986, at one twenty-three in the morning, a part of the Chernobyl Nuclear Power Plant exploded in what would become the worst nuclear power plant disaster. The explosion sent a plume of nuclear fallout throughout the whole area that spread as far away as the eastern section of North America.

Several days later, in the early evening, as the world was made aware of a minor explosion in the Ukraine near Kiev, a Spetsnaz special forces unit headed by Captain Vladimir Bodkin began their assault on a military base outside the town of Istra. Bodkin had been in charge of this unit for five years, and they were the best. Much like the rest of the Soviet Union, this base was in complete disarray as far as the structure of the facility was concerned, but elite forces of the Russian army guarded it. Colonel Marisova was in charge of these troops, which all the other forces in the army held in high regard. That is all except the Spetsnaz special forces unit and Captain Bodkin. The Spetsnaz were by the far the best trained of the Russian military and for good reason. It was their job to move in and out of covert operations when the KGB instructed them with direct approval from the Russian president. Very few people even knew of their existence, but they had been around ever since the KGB needed this type of secret force many years earlier.

Twelve men from the special forces were well hidden in the woods outside the northern end of the camp just after dusk. The night was overcast with a slight mist, which was perfect for the mis-sion. They waited for a few hours to be sure all was going according to their reconnaissance and then made the move into the camp through the base of the wire fence one hundred meters from the warehouse. Intelligence had shown the base to be heavily guarded at the front of the base, by the entrance, rather than at the ware-house, as it was believed no one knew where the cases were being held. The only people on the base privy to this information were the colonel and the lone scientist. No one on the base really knew what was going on inside that particular building. They only knew that their orders were to let no one in the base unless the colonel advised that it was okay.

As the night became darker, the time for the force to move was near. Bodkin had briefed his forces, and the plan was to sneak in through the fence, take out the guards closest to the warehouse, enter the warehouse as fast as possible, gather up the cases that were there, and get out the same way they came in. A military transport helicopter would be synchronized to pick them up on the outside of the fence and fly them out of there. The first part of the plan worked well, and they were about to assault the guards by the doors when a jeep pulled up to the warehouse with Colonel Marisov driving and the scientist in the jump seat. The guards moved aside when they recognized the colonel, who headed to the door with the scientist right behind him. At that point Captain Bodkin launched the assault and took out the four guards. He was on the colonel before he knew what hit him. The colonel turned to see what was happening, drew his gun, and shot the scientist between the eyes. Bodkin was too late to stop this, but he was able to get a good shot at the colonel and hit him just below the heart. The colonel gazed at him for a long time and then hit the ground dead.

While the commotion unfolded, the other guards from the base heard the shots from the direction of the warehouse and rushed to protect the colonel.

With the nuke cases set in the back of the warehouse, Bodkin decided to keep the fighting to the front of the building. The men were on the ground, standing behind whatever they could find, holding off the guards who at this point numbered a few dozen. Bodkin knew he had to make a move, or he would be caught between the guards and the cases. The men he had left at the back of the building near the fence were holding the guards back. In a split second, Bodkin grabbed four of his men, ran back to get the cases, and headed out the back door. While the number of guards increased at the front of the building, the men he had left to defend it were overrun and killed. He ran for the fence with the other three men in tow, carrying the cases. The men he had left at the back of the building shielded him.

*If one of the cases took a bullet, who knows what would happen?*

At that very moment, the helicopter descended from behind the trees and landed twenty yards from the men. He made sure all three got in with the seven cases and watched it ascend over the woods and out of sight. When he turned the guards were overrunning the men who had his back. He knew he couldn't be taken alive, so he randomly fired into the crowd. The burst of bullets that came back his way were overwhelming. When Bodkin died he could hear the rotors from the helicopter and knew the mission had been a success.

Yakov thought it would be a good idea to meet with Ivan and Mickey to see what was happening in the lives of the two youngest agents working on the case. Pete had told Mickey about Yakov, but they had never met in person. Mickey and Ivan had been instrumental in creating the front they were putting on for the business end of the NFL and the cars, an important part of the overall plan. Mickey was also very active in the movement of information to Pete from everyone inside Russia, as he was the conduit from his biweekly drops to his contact, whoever that might be. Yakov had gotten the okay to use Alexei's *dacha* for the meeting, and he was waiting for them to arrive.

Dmitri picked them up outside the hotel for the drive to the *dacha*. Ivan was in a foul mood so Mickey left him alone.

About twenty minutes into the ride, Ivan opened his mouth. "Fuckin' Olga dropped me, Mickey. She ended it last week, and I feel like shit. She told me to forget her and to never contact her again."

"The world is falling apart, and you're feeling sorry for yourself. What the fuck! There's more than just what you want. We're caught up in the middle of the biggest game being played in the universe, and you can only think of yourself."

"Look, Mickey, I didn't ask to be put in this situation. I wish it were all over and we could get back to normal. Do you think that'll ever happen?"

"Something is going to happen, and it'll probably be real soon. We need to suck it up and do what they want. No time to pull out now."

"But what about Olga. I'm worried about her."

"We're all worried about her, but it's part of the game. Maybe it's for the best."

"What do you know? After we talked last, no one has seen her for over three weeks. I hope she's all right. With Boris dead this is getting scary."

"Don't crack on me now. We started this together, and we'll finish it together, even if I need to kick your butt. If we get through this, who knows what'll happen to us. Maybe we'll get a few medals."

Ivan laughed, but Mickey wasn't convinced he'd be okay. *I need to talk to Mikhail.*

Mickey had been busy with the NFL, setting up conference calls and meetings with the hotel, the stadium, and all the vendors involved in the catering for the stadium. The entertainment contract had been given to a Swedish company who had done a lot in Moscow so Mickey didn't need to worry about that. He had been working with Mikhail on the details, which wasn't a lot of fun. Mikhail wasn't the same since the day Yakov had told him about Boris, but he went on with his daily routine, especially now that the NFL had approved the game. Boris would have been in his glory.

"We need to do this for Boris, Ivan. He was like a brother to you, and you can't let him down. Mikhail is having a few problems with it, and we don't need you causing problems. Hang in there, and we'll be all right." Mickey hoped Ivan believed what he was saying. *We need to work this out together.*

"All right, Mickey, let's work on it together as we have, and see where it takes us. Lord knows what's happening, and we're better off together."

When they got out of the car, Yakov met them at the door to the *dacha* and invited them in. Sitting at the kitchen table was a man that neither one of them knew but would soon learn that he was second-in-command to President Vasilyev. Alexei wanted to see what the next generation of agents looked like but also ask them a few questions to get a feel for how things were going from another perspective. It wasn't unusual for him to do this, as he liked to know what was happening with his recruits, both Russian and American, so he didn't get too far from the game.

The meeting took place in the same room as the one where Alexei first told Yakov about the problems facing the USSR. Since that time they had accomplished a lot, but there was still a fair amount to settle.

When everyone sat down, Alexei was the first to speak. "Gentlemen, I don't usually let meetings take place here unless they're very important. I have watched you two through Yakov and like what I have seen so far. After tonight you will probably never see me again, and that is just as well. Yakov will give you a full update on where things stand. Starting on Monday you'll both spend the morning hours learning the finer points of this business. Be careful."

When he got up to leave, Yakov walked him to the door and then returned to Ivan and Mickey.

"Ivan, Olga is on an assignment and is somewhere with General Asimov at the moment. We know they're in Odessa, but we haven't heard from her in a few days." He looked at Ivan, who just nodded. "You'll still be involved in the NFL game and the cars with Mikhail, and he has approved working with you both. Mikhail is a bigger player than you both know, so be sure to heed what he says."

"Yakov, Mr. Popov said we would undertake some new training. How long and where will it take place?" Mickey asked.

"Due to the situation we're in, you will have two months, as that is all we can spare. Just do what is asked of you and learn. It'll take place just outside Moscow, and Dmitri will pick you up at the Intourist each day after work. He'll also get you back to where you need to go after the sessions, which will end at midnight. You have a long two months ahead of you, so take care of yourselves, stop drinking, and get some sleep."

On the ride back, Ivan was in a better mood, although he was concerned about Olga. After the meeting, he had understood what was needed to get the job done. He was thankful for the chance and glad he'd be working with Mickey and Mikhail.

# CHAPTER 35

Mikhail made sure the boat hit the beach on the inside of the fence that separated the property from the rest of the peninsula. In the distance, as dawn approached, Mikhail could see the mansion silhouetted against the little hill. Petra was sure that Olga was still inside the building. To stop Mikhail from going crazy over wanting revenge on Colonel Marisova, the solution had been quite simple. They let him go with Petra to find Olga and the general. After all the general had to be the one who gave the order to kill Boris, so he might as well use that to his advantage. After leaving prison as a youth, Mikhail had been part of the most dangerous clandestine naval unit in the Russian military. He had run many covert missions for them in the past. When he retired Yakov recruited him to be part of his team. Alexei had been in charge of that unit, so he was well aware of the special talents that Mikhail had acquired over those years.

Russian intelligence agents had spotted the general when he was boarding his yacht in Odessa, so they had followed him at a distance but needed to veer off course when they got close to the mansion. The reconnaissance on the property was given to them, by the agents, once they reported the spot to Yakov, who had also sent along a few other members of Mikhail's old team to help with this assignment. The grounds weren't overly guarded, as the general felt no one could get through the naval barrier that they had set up to guard the entrance by sea. The general had grossly underestimated what a crack unit of the navy's best could do to their own kind. Two men were left to guard the boat, as they didn't plan to stay around that long. Petra, Mikhail, and the remaining three men slowly made their way up the hill at the back of the mansion. When they approached the buildings, two guards were stationed at the entrance by the end of the pool. Mikhail and one of the other men crept slowly up behind them, slit their throats, and threw them in the bushes. One man was posted there to watch for any unforeseen intruders while the rest of the party went upstairs to find the master bedroom.

"Olga, your mistake was getting involved with me in the first place. I may have let you live, but stealing my diary shows who you are. What am I supposed to do with you now? You leave me no choice, my dear."

"You're going to kill me just like that?" She felt another presence in the room.

"I've killed many and some much prettier than you."

The general was standing naked over Olga as Mikhail entered the room silently. Olga tilted her head and saw Mikhail. Before he knew what hit him Olga kicked the general right between the balls, and he landed head over heels at Mikhail's feet.

"Good evening, General. You seem to have fallen out of bed." Mikhail smirked.

Petra came into the room as Olga was putting on her robe. She rushed over to her and hugged her. That was all she could do at the moment. They needed to get out of there as soon as possible.

Olga looked at her. "Wait here. I need to get something. Then we can leave."

While she walked away, Petra saw Mikhail kick the general in the balls again and heard a slow moan. She didn't need to watch Mikhail take care of the general, so she said her good-byes and left to find Olga.

When she turned, Mikhail said, "If I'm not back to the boat in five minutes, you are to leave without me."

She shook her head, indicating she understood, and left. When she found Olga, she was almost dressed and ready to go. Olga reached under her mattress for the general's diary and then led Petra back out the door. While they were headed past the master bedroom door, they heard some words being spoken but didn't stop to find out what was going on. Petra's job was to get Olga out of the mansion and to the boat. Mikhail was in charge of the general.

While running past the pool, Petra looked up and saw Mikhail's silhouette with the gun in his hand. There was one crisp shot, and it was over. When they got to the boat, they waited for Mikhail, but he never showed up. The four remaining members of the team motioned her and Olga into the boat and sped away. They were back aboard the naval vessel and safe fifteen minutes later.

Mikhail needed to find Putinov and the remotes, but he didn't know where to look. He had taken care of everyone who was guarding the mansion, but the scientist was nowhere to be found. Thinking back over the material on the compound, he remembered a little house on the coast by the sea. He knew he was alone, so he took his time walking over to the area where the house was located. He had enjoyed killing the general, but he still had his sights on Colonel Marisova. One day he would be face to face with him, and this could all end. His job right now was to try to find Dr. Putinov and the remotes and then get back to Moscow as soon as possible.

The door to the little house was open, and the light inside was flickering on and off. A slight smell was coming out of the door, and Mikhail knew immediately what it was. As he slowly approached the house, a bird flew out of the door and scared the crap out of him. The scientist was sitting in a chair by the desk. His neck was broken with pieces of flesh hanging out where the bird had been enjoying a snack. Mikhail saw a bunch of remotes, wires, and other paraphernalia that the scientist must have been working on, but he couldn't see any intact remote controls. Chances were that General Asimov had taken care of the scientist and sent the finished remotes to whoever he was working with on the plan. Mikhail couldn't wait to get his hands on Drygin.

# CHAPTER 36

The general's book was extremely valuable as it not only described Asimov's personal path to glory but also outlined in detail the plan he had set in motion. While Petra read it on the way back to Moscow, she was amazed at the players who were part of the plan. She knew there was no way to prove what was going to happen, but at least they now had a good idea on what the general was setting up.

*There were some missing parts, but maybe Yakov he could fill in the pieces.*

She also realized that they would need to reduce the material as much as possible to get a copy to Mickey, who would need to get the information to Pete. Maybe together they could fill in the blanks. There was also a good chance that, with the general dead, Director Drygin might make changes to the plan as he would have full control now. Chances were that Drygin was the man, and although they were a bit closer to proving that, they still didn't have enough to go after him. After all he was in charge of the biggest spy ring in the whole world, and his reach was as far as that of the President.

After the naval vessel docked in Odessa, a car was waiting to take them to the airport for their transport back to Moscow. Yakov had made sure that everything was ready as he knew that, if they made it out alive, they would need to get back to Moscow as soon as possible. He was aware that Mikhail wouldn't be with them as he had sent Mikhail on another little mission if this one were a success. He was waiting at the base in Moscow when the plane landed.

He noticed that Olga looked worn out from the ordeal and would need some time off. Petra, however, looked as if she were energized with a new passion deep within her. He would need to be sure to keep her more involved at a higher level, as she had proved herself at Yalta.

"Olga, I'm glad you're safe and this part of the mission is over. I hear you were able to get some good information on the general."

Olga handed him the leather-bound book. "A lot is in there, but I'm not sure how much of it will be useful as he is dead. The director will probably change a few things, but there's enough in there to be useful although not enough to get Drygin. I also doubt very much if Mikhail found the good Dr. Putinov alive. I think General Asimov might have taken care of him a few days earlier before he went up to Odessa."

"Do you think they finished wiring the cases and finalized the remote control mechanism?"

"I can't verify that, but he was overly confident the night he died. He'd made plans to fly back to Moscow early the next morning for a meeting with the director. My guess is, if they're not finished, they're very close to it."

"Was anyone else at the mansion?"

"Not that I know of, Yakov. He usually had his meeting in Odessa and then came back later to check on Putinov. Before he died he was in Odessa for a few days. The general told me about Boris. When he did I realized I was probably next."

"You're probably right, and I'm glad we decided to get down there when we did. You did well, Olga. Go home, and take a few weeks off to rest. If I need you, I'll get in touch." He looked at Petra and smiled at her. Then he closed the door as he watched the car speed off into the night.

He realized the papers he had in his hands would provide a good reading on what the plan had been, but the director would be influencing it as he saw it. After he had been through the papers, he would need to get to Alexei to see how he wanted to handle the rest of the situation. They were getting close, but they had lost a few good men, which, although not hard to replace, still made him think a little about what this was all about. As always it came down to figuring out what the bad guys were up to and stopping them before they killed innocent people. The only problem with this case was that some very important and coldhearted people were involved in the plot.

*I can't believe what I'm reading. This is all madness, but at the same time, it's possible that someone could pull it all off.*

The first part was an egotistical summary on General Asimov that was part fictional and part reality. The early part of his life was real enough with his heroics in WWII and then his later bravery in Afghanistan. There was no mention of Afghanistan being a failure and a lost war but rather a triumph of a man on his way to becoming a major player in the resurrection of the Old Soviet guard. His ramblings about the Soviet Union and the teachings of Marx, Lenin, and Stalin made Yakov shudder with the knowledge that death of innocent people was of no consequence. Nowhere in the report was there a mention of anyone helping the general, just broad descriptions of the other players who had a part in the overall plan. When he read further, Yakov realized this was the rambling of a madman bent on destruction. The military coup was a massive undertaking with a battalion of men, tanks, and other weapons of destruction marching on the Dumas and the Russian White House in a coordinated effort to take over the government and its buildings. The plan incorporated taking over various media outlets on the way into the central point and other strategic buildings that the general felt they needed to control. It was a well-thought-out plan, but there also needed to be a parallel component from someone in the government or within the walls of the KGB to orchestrate an internal takeover. Only one man could be strong enough to pull this off, and Yakov knew he had to get to Alexei on this.

The other part, which was even scarier, was the placement of the nuke cases not only outside the Russian borders but within its own territories. *Was it rare that someone would kill his own people on such a massive scale while trying to take over his country?* The list included the ten cities that were selected as well as the proposed NFL game if the government approved it. Since they had captured seven cases at the military base and two had been blown up, five were left. The plan would have to be changed.

*Those five cases could do a lot of damage.*

Yakov noticed the final pages were the schematic diagrams of the nuke cases and the remotes that would detonate them. *Why are these part of the general's diary?* But he was thankful that Asimov had decided to incorporate them even though they seemed so out of place. It would be important to get these diagrams to anyone who might be connected with the case, as the information might prove vital in dismantling the remotes. He would have to be sure to get a copy of this to Pete.

The vessel picked up Mikhail at the designated spot, which wasn't far from the house where the dead scientist lay. Yakov had told Mikhail that Putinov was on their side, and hopefully he'd be alive when he was found. If not, he had, with any luck, sabotaged some of the remotes so they wouldn't work if anyone ever tried to use them. But even if the remote didn't set off the device, someone with knowledge of the nuke cases could detonate them. Naturally they would be blown to bits, but some martyrs were out there who wouldn't care if they believed in the cause.

Mikhail decided to lie down to get a few hours of sleep before his next stop. The captain of the vessel advised him it would be a few hours before they were near the mouth of the northern section of the Bosphorus near the town of Cayagzi. Once they were near the mouth of the Bosphorus, it would be another few hours before they got to Istanbul and the meeting, so in all he would have four hours to rest. He needed more sleep, but that would have to do.

The yacht the vessel pulled up to was one of the most elegant that Mikhail had ever seen. He wasn't sure who he was going to meet, but he had to be one of the richest people on earth. When he was escorted to the living area, he heard a voice with an Irish brogue that he was sure he knew. Sitting with Padraig at the bar enjoying a cold beer was Pete. Mikhail just stood there, amazed at what he was seeing.

Padraig smiled. "Want a beer?"

"That would be great. Thanks."

"Did it go as planned at the mansion?" Pete was a stickler for information.

"The general is dead, but so is Putinov, the scientist working on the remotes. Olga seems to be all right, and she's probably on her way back to Moscow with Petra. I'm so glad we got her out of there. My guess is the general was about to kill her."

"Timing is everything," Pete said. "Now we need to be ready for the rest of what they throw at us. If Putinov is dead, I would guess they've got the nuke cases and the remotes figured out, wouldn't you?"

"I think so, but they still need to deploy them. Only five cases are left so that cuts down the odds a bit, but we still need to know where they'll place them. As much as a control freak that he is, I bet Drygin is sitting right on top of them," Padraig said.

"What if we watched him? Would it be possible to see when he moved them?" Pete looked at Mikhail, who was in deep thought.

"No, I don't think that'll matter. First of all we aren't positive where he has them. Even if there're in the offices, there are so many ways to get them out that I doubt we could cover all the exits."

*I'll have to figure this out,* Mikhail thought to himself.

"Then the best you can do is keep a cover on him and any of his associates who are close to him. Chances are we'll need to find them when they're about ready to use them. Maybe we'll get lucky," Pete concluded.

Yakov and Pete had already guessed about a few of the cases being sent to the NFL game at Luzhniki Stadium. They had a plan in place to handle that part of the dead general's scheme. Pete had also looked into and finalized a procedure with all the U.S. embassies in the cities where they thought they might deploy some of the nuke cases.

"Mikhail, you'll need to get final approval from Yakov on the plan we've worked out for the US and Russian embassies. Because it's a joint effort, Yakov will need to get security information to them as soon as possible."

"Okay, Pete. I'll get the approval back to you through Mickey."

"We don't know when the military plans to take over the government," Padraig said.

"Yakov will need to handle that with Alexei, but I'm sure they're working on something," Mikhail replied. "Olga had a book that was the general's, so maybe they found something that will help."

"It might provide some background information that'll be useful, but Drygin will probably change the plan to suit his needs now that the general is dead. Shit, I bet he was going to kill him anyway and do as he pleased. Not like Drygin to share the power." Pete looked at Padraig.

"You're probably right about that."

"One last thing, Mikhail, we're awful sorry about Boris. He was a good man, and we know there'll be hell to pay when you get your chance," Pete said.

"I've taken care of the general, and the director will be next."

# CHAPTER 37

After the meeting with Alexei, it seemed that Mickey and Ivan's lives had changed. There was new urgency to everything they did from working with the NFL in the morning and then going to KGB training school for the rest of the day and into the night. They had their own instructor so they could be flexible with the time they trained, but it was mandatory they get at least six hours in each day. It wasn't only training on new espionage techniques but also mental and physical training. Mickey had never been in better shape, and his mind was the sharpest it had ever been.

*It's amazing what a controlled environment could do.*

The training also seemed to help Ivan through some of the mental pain he was dealing with in regard to Olga and Boris. Something important was about to happen, and they were right in the middle of it. The last two years, they had become close, and this helped them through this ordeal. It was strenuous but good for them, and they knew and appreciated what Pete, Alexei, and Yakov had done for them.

*Training for anything had never been this hard.*

Plus, he actually didn't know where they were. Just that they were with ten other men learning the innermost secrets of espionage. Nuclear detonation as well as placement was part of the schooling but also the psychological aspect of someone who would use these types of weapons. Weapons training, mental alertness training, physical training, and any type of training someone could imagine, they went through all of it. Ivan was one tough character, but Mickey seemed to stand out. It was the first time in his life he was clean from drugs and alcohol, and it was a special feeling. Although it had been only two months since he started, the training in the last few weeks made him realize at times that it was good to be clearheaded. His mind and body had never been sharper, and the change in lifestyle made an enormous impact on his daily life and routine.

*I miss the buzz, but in the morning life sure looks a lot brighter. No hangover, just a feeling I can handle whatever the world throws at me. And it's about to throw a lot.*

"You know they don't just train anyone like this?" Ivan remarked.

"I know, and as much as it scares me, we seem to fit into this type of work. It isn't what we set out to do, but it's the way things seem to be going. We've found ourselves in the middle of the biggest spy game in the world that is going to play out soon. I know we're on the right side, but we need to be sure we hold up our part."

"Do you think the NFL game is the target for these nuke cases?" Ivan asked.

Mickey hadn't been totally sure before, but after getting Pete's last note, there wasn't any doubt.

"I think it is, and I think we better be ready to do whatever they want us to do. As part of the marketing mechanism in Moscow, we'll have access to all parts of the stadium. I'm glad that Mikhail will be with us on game day, but there may come a time when we need to put some of this training to use. Are you ready to do that?"

"No question in my mind. All I ever do when I question myself is think of Boris and I get strength. He'll be watching over us."

They didn't talk for a while, but then a thought occurred to Mickey. "When I was younger, we used to go to Yankee Stadium all the time with my dad. Part of the fun was starting at the top of the stands and seeing who could get to the locker rooms on the field level the fastest. There were so many different routes to take that it was like a maze, but, if you were familiar with them, you knew which shortcuts to take. I think it might be a good idea if we do the same at Luzhniki Stadium, just in case we need to work the stadium at some point."

He wasn't sure if Ivan was impressed, but he brought it up to Yakov the next day.

# CHAPTER 38

With the confirmation of General Asimov's death, Director Drygin needed to be sure the next person he put in charge would be more capable than the general. The general couldn't keep his pecker in his pants, and in the end he got it right where he had his problems. It was an ugly scene in the bedroom, and no one knew who had accomplished such a feat. Every single guard watching the mansion had been killed, the mansion had been ransacked. Whoever the perpetrators were had escaped without a single sign. This was definitely a professional job, and the director knew only a few units could pull this off. Only one was Russian.

*I've underestimated Alexei, but I won't make the same mistake twice.*

They had recovered seven of the nuke cases at the military base. The remaining five were under his care, and he knew just how he was going to use them. With both the general and the colonel dead, he needed to put someone in charge who he could trust with his life.

*Only one man fit the bill.*

Assistant Director Anton Demidov had been a trusted agent and assistant to the director for many years. He was a short, bald man with wire-rimmed glasses who looked like he taught engineering at Leningrad University. Drygin knew all along that Anton would be the man to carry out his final orders. No one knew who he was as he was never out front in anything that had to do with the KGB. He was a ruthless ambassador for the director and had taken on many cases for Drygin when no other could be trusted.

Director Drygin knew he could trust this man. "Anton, this is the biggest challenge we've had yet, and I know you're up to it. Have you reviewed my final plan on the nuke cases?" The director wanted to be sure he and Anton were thinking similarly before they met with the generals.

"I have and agree with the placements. The hard part will be getting them into the stadium, but we'll figure that out. What can you tell me about the coup?"

"We'll discuss that at our next meeting, but you and I will decide the final plan."

The meeting took place in the lower level of the KGB building. Present at the meeting was the director, Anton Demidov, and two of the generals loyal to Drygin who would now be in charge of the coup. The date had been set for the military coup, and that date coincided very nicely with the first-ever NFL game to be played in Moscow, Sunday, September 21. If all went as planned with the takeover of the government buildings, there would be no need to set off the nuke cases at the game. But if the coup was stopped, the director knew he and Anton would hit the right buttons.

*Too bad General Asimov and Colonel Marisova wouldn't be around for the finale.*

"Anton, I want you to review the final plans that General Asimov submitted with Comrades Yachenko and Lenevski for the military coup to be sure we have all the bases covered. These two will be in charge of the operation, but I want you to oversee the movement.

Once you are satisfied with the plan, get back to me so we can also review it one more time."

"Yes, Director. Is there anything else you will need from me during this time?"

"We'll discuss that after the Generals Lenevski and Yachenko depart. Do either of you have any questions?"

General Lenevski asked, "During the takeover we'll be poised to do it without firing a shot, but if they become aware of the plan for some reason, do we use force to break our way in?"

The director looked at all three. "We'll take the buildings at all cost for our motherland and won't back down to anyone once we make the initial move. Is that understood?"

The generals left, and the director went over some minor details with Anton. "Be sure the two generals are killed if the coup fails. We don't need them around if it doesn't work. On second thought kill them even if we are successful. It'll send a message to the remaining men." He turned and walked back to his office.

When Drygin put on the light, he was aware someone was sitting at his desk. He walked around the table and took his seat as if there wasn't anything wrong. Amazed this meeting hadn't taken place sooner, he was glad it had finally come. They had been enemies within the KGB for many years now and had basically mirrored each other's rise through the party. The respect was there on both accounts, as they knew each other well, but the hostility that had been bred throughout the years had blinded them to each other. They knew at some point that one of them would lose, and the time for that conclusion was near. The game was ending for one of them, and neither wanted to lose.

Not really wanting an answer, Alexei was the first to speak. "So you still think you are bigger than the system, Leonid? I would've thought that after all these years you would've figured out that no one is bigger than the state."

"Oh, how I've missed you, Alexei. Ever since you've been kissing the ass of Vasilyev, you've almost risen to the top of the party. Too bad that's as far as you'll go."

"And why is that, Leonid? Have you decided to take over the government? That would be a major mistake."

"As far as I'm concerned, there isn't much to take over, even if that were my mission. You and the president have screwed things up so badly that the nation has no idea what is going on. The American president is blowing so much smoke up your ass that your eyes are all clouded over."

"And your head is still up your ass!" Alexei chuckled.

Drygin didn't think the remark was that funny. "Alexei, you never seemed to have realized that the path you and Vasilyev have led us down is a path of total destruction for our country. We can never be part of the West but should always remain the communist bloc that we are. There is no *glasnost* or *perestroika*. There is only Mother Russia and our belief in our socialist system."

"Oh, the path is correct, but people like you and the deceased General Asimov can't see what's going on. Smoke up my ass? Not really. Just the thought of a world at peace and the hope we can save our country from ruin."

"Mother Russia needs no one and will always be able to stand on her own two feet. It's time the world learned this lesson one last time."

"We can't prove it yet, Leonid, but we know something is on the horizon that you have a very heavy hand in that will disrupt the summit process and the possible peace between us and the world. I won't allow you to do this, and we'll figure out what the final plan is, no matter what you say."

"I have no idea of what you are speaking about, and if I did I'm sure I wouldn't tell you. Do you think I would confide anything in you after all these years? Our paths have always collided and always will. The only difference is that, some day, one of us won't be alive to see the final outcome. My hope is that someone will be you." Drygin felt sorry for his old adversary.

"For a madman you speak with feeling of your motherland, but like other madmen you'll fail at your delusional mission. Leonid, you can hate me forever, but when it's possible that innocent Russian lives may be at stake, we'll do all we can to stop you. We'll watch you; you will watch us. In the end we'll prevail because we're the better people. We'll look to do what we think is best for our country based on the situation we're in and what is best for our system. We'll figure out your plan and stop you, or we'll die trying."

"If you're finished, Alexei, I have, as always, enjoyed our little chat. Please go out the way you came in as I don't want anyone to know you were in my office."

On the way back through the tunnel to the kitchen of the Metropole, Alexei for the first time felt that whatever was being planned was going to happen in the next few months. Things were coming to a climax with the presidential and economic summits so they would need to be on the lookout for any telltale signs that might give anything away. The general's diary had been very helpful. They knew a military coup was imminent, but they didn't know when. The nuke cases were also a major problem as they had to be part of the overall plan. *But where would they place them?* The NFL game was the most obvious, but the diary mentioned the embassies in ten cities throughout the world. With only five cases left, there was no way they could place them in all those locations. His best bet was the game and maybe two or three embassies in the West. Pete and Yakov had been right so he needed, at this point, to shore up the defenses within the Dumas and White House as well as any strategic points within the city of Moscow without Director Drygin knowing. They also had to step up security at the stadium to be on the lookout for anything suspicious that could hold something the size of a suitcase.

There was a lot to do. As he exited the hotel, where his driver picked him up, he headed to his next meeting. On the way over, Alexei recalled his last meeting with Pete and Yakov.

"We need to find these damn nuke cases," Yakov had said.

It wasn't the only problem but definitely the biggest. *The destruction these cases were capable of? It scares the crap out of me.*

"No question about that, but where do you think Drygin will place them?" asked Alexei.

"The obvious place would be the NFL game. Is he mad enough to try to blow up seventy thousand people with a nuke?" Pete asked disbelievingly. "I mean you have to be bent on destruction to approve that."

"We aren't dealing with a sane man. What about the embassies mentioned in Asimov's diary?" Alexei knew Drygin would do anything to accomplish his goal at this point, but they needed to figure out where they might be placed.

"My best guess, at this point, is the game and various options in and around Moscow. We know only five are left as we have accounted for the other nine," Pete said. "We only have a few months left. Hopefully we'll get a break."

Everyone was waiting for Alexei when he entered the meeting room on the fourth floor. They had been discussing various aspects of their counter plan and all agreed on when they thought the coup would take place. They also thought there might be another location where a nuke case could be placed. The purpose of the meeting was to report to Alexei what each unit had decided and how they were going to implement their part.

General Titonov , the commander of the 3rd Shock Army, was the first to provide his report, along with General Alekseev. "As we see it, we can't let the director's forces get into Moscow. Based on the timing of the movement, they will need to start preparation about a month prior to the initial move. Our surveillance will keep an eye on the bases and report any movement within the camps that look like preparation is underway. In the meantime we have infiltrated his forces with some of our own spies to see what we can find out." The general paused. "Once the date is confirmed, we have two ways we can stop them. First, we could meet them at the gates and stop them from ever leaving the bases with their forces intact. Second, we would let them start the maneuver but cut them off at various strategic junctions on their way into the city." The general looked at Alexei. "We like the second option. It will get them away from any reinforcements they have at the base that they can call on if we move too quickly. Once they leave their respective bases, we'll cut them off from any supply line and their bases so the troops can't reinforce them. By doing this we'll only have to deal with the troops that have left their bases."

"Good plan, General. I agree with the second option. Be sure you have enough men on hand not only at the cutoff points but also at the bases as no reinforcements can be allowed to get through once we cut them off. The coup has to be put down before it reaches the city, and the generals in charge must be held accountable for their actions as well as the person who gave them the orders."

The next to report was Georgi Cherlin, who was responsible for all the security at Luzhinki Stadium and the surrounding area. His résumé read like a who's who in world of espionage. Alexei was glad he was the lead person at the stadium.

"We have doubled the guards at all entrances and stepped up the security patrols in and around the stadium to three a day. Our dogs are trained in explosives as well as nuclear components so they should be able to detect anything that seems out of order. We also have some new technology coming in that will detect any trace of nuclear material as small as one-cent ruble coin. It should be here within two weeks from our friends in East Germany. We'll change our routine every two days and then randomly go back and forth to old patterns. I'll be in charge of that daily so only I'll know what the schedule will be. We'll keep this procedure up to seven days before game day. After that we'll rework the patterns and staff to ensure we aren't getting complacent. No one will be allowed in without a pass that our security firm will control. There will be individual codes for each person. We're working with Mikhail and Mickey Rossetti right now on who will have access prior to game day."

"That will be pretty hard to enforce, don't you think?" asked Alexei.

"Only if we let it get out of hand. We're using the NFL guidelines for game day security along with our own to minimize the numbers and the risk. We've also decided that the teams will only get access two days before the game to practice on the field. We'll use two other soccer pitches for their other two practice days."

"I want you to be sure to get Mickey and Ivan involved with the teams so they're around if we need them. They will be finishing their training, and all reports have been favorable," Alexei added. "What about game day, Georgi?"

"Gates will open to the public three hours before the game starts. We'll be sure to sweep the entire stadium twice with the dogs and the nuke sniffers before anyone gets in. We'll also place our agents in the hallways, locker room areas, and maintenance facilities throughout the building."

"Sounds good. Please continue."

"Access to the stadium for all food items, press, and entertainment will be through Gate 1 and only Gate 1. All items will be checked at this point, and we'll have more staff than needed to handle any problems that may occur. The public will enter through the other five gates, where they'll also be checked. They won't be able to carry in any bottles, food, or large containers past this point. Throughout the stadium there will be agents who will be part of the crowd who will be ready to assist at any moment."

"Thank you, Georgi. It's nice to have you working this with us," Alexei said. "Yakov, what have you worked out for the stadium?"

"We have worked through the plan with Georgi and decided we'll have ten teams of three agents each in various parts of the stadium. I'll be in charge of five teams, and Mikhail will handle the other five. We'll be troubleshooters based on what Georgi and I see happening during the day. With Georgi's teams in place throughout the stadium and our ten teams inside, we feel comfortable that we'll have it all covered," Yakov answered. "We'll also do numerous walkthroughs with Georgi's team, Mikhail, Ivan, and Mickey. It's important that we know every nook and cranny in the stadium."

"And what will Pete be doing on September 21?" Alexei questioned.

"He'll be monitoring the game outside of Russia. We aren't sure where the other nuke cases might show up, but we suspect they will show up on this day. We're betting on Berlin as one of the cities. The strategy of watching all the Russian and American embassies in major cities has been accomplished, so if any agents show up with the nuke cases, we'll be ready to apprehend them. Pete also has his best agents stationed in the ten most likely cities that were in the general's report."

Alexei sat back in his chair with his eyes closed to visualize if they had missed anything. When he opened them, he simply said. "God help us if we have missed anything. Good day, gentlemen."

# CHAPTER 39

Mikhail had made sure that, with the coming of summer, the Russian division of the EFL was in full swing. Although they were beaten pretty badly on their last games through Europe, it didn't dampen their appetite for the game. It finally sunk in that it would take a few years to get even par with Europe and it was going to take hard work and a lot of money. The money would come from the government as well as from Mikhail's companies, as he had made it a point to take over the whole program after Boris had died. He had promised himself that he would make it a success and, in the end, name a stadium, a trophy, or something after his brother.

Tommy was still involved, and Mickey was glad for that. He had a soft spot for Tommy, fifteen years his senior. There weren't many people like Tommy when it came to sincerity, and he was just an all-around nice guy. When they were both working the EFL a few years back, which seemed like a lifetime ago, they had forged a great relationship with Tommy handling the football strategy and Mickey marketing the product. If Mikhail could rely on anyone, it would be Tommy.

Practice started the first week in August, and everyone knew about the sport. Because they only needed one hundred and sixty players to field the four teams, the competition was cutthroat. An added bonus was that the top eighty players would be invited to a one-day clinic before the NFL game in September.

# CHAPTER 40

Pasha and Donald had done their regular good job of setting up the procedures and being sure all treaties were in order prior to the signings for the summit of August 18. Negotiations were done way ahead of time, and the two presidents used the time to look at further business opportunities and how they could get the two countries closer together, not only through the arms agreements, but also through the economic guidelines the two countries had agreed on in Paris a month earlier. An example of this business opportunity would be the NFL game scheduled for September, only five weeks away. The excitement the game had generated in the U.S., Russia, and worldwide was more than either of them could have anticipated.

Yakov and Pete's plan to draw out Director Drygin had seemed to work, and the information they were gathering was showing some dividends. All the players in this secret game had arrived on time for a final get togther. A meeting like this had never been done before, but both Pete and Yakov had persuaded the presidents to be at this gathering after their summit had ended. The meeting, which was being held in Orlando at the Grand Floridian Resort in Disney World, was the real summit that would hopefully stop the world from self-destruction.

None of the players knew the others were attending, as they had all been told to make their way to the side room separately or in pairs to the restaurant by two o'clock on Wednesday, August 23. Naturally Mickey and Pete knew the hotel and the area well, but the other participants weren't aware of the Magical Kingdom and all it had to offer. Petra and Olga had come together and were like little kids when they finally got to the hotel. Mikhail was all business as usual and was a little apprehensive as to the meeting's agenda. Ivan was his usual self, aloof and seemingly in charge, but inside his stomach was churning. Padraig was settled in, as he had come a day early with Pete, but wanted to get down to business. He and Mikhail were of the same mold and only cared about the business at hand.

This group of ten was all the world had between it and the possible start of a war that would have both the West and the East at each other's throats. It was anyone's guess what side the Arab countries would end up on, but the smart money was on the Russians. Nuke cases, military coups, and destruction were the ingredients that Director Drygin was mixing, and the outcome would be catastrophic.

"Mr. Presidents, we're at the final stage, and we know now that Drygin is the player we're after. We can't, however, just go in and take him, as our main objective needs to be the five nuke cases that are left," Pete said.

"Does anyone else in the world have any idea what is going on?" President Reed asked.

"Not to our knowledge, sir, and based on that we need to be as secretive as we can with our next steps and all we think may be happening," answered Pete. "Our satellites have shown the military buildup outside Moscow, and there's no doubt they're going to move."

"Do we have any idea when that may be?" President Vasilyev asked.

"Not definitely," Yakov answered. "But we think it will be a coordinated effort controlled from one point. Alexei has looked at the photos and decided the precision work being done on the tanks and the regiment status can only mean they'll move soon."

"Yakov, there is no way we can assist you with the military coup," Pete stated.

"Pete, we're fully aware that you can't assist with interference of the military machine that will try to take over our country. We need constant and real-time information from you on the troop movement. Alexei has been working with the generals loyal to the president and has a plan in place. We can assure you that these are the only two renegade bases in the area and our plan will work."

"Can you please tell me what that plan is, Yakov?" President Vasilyev asked.

"Once we get confirmation that the troops are moving, we'll cut them off fifteen miles from the base. It's far enough from the city so there should be no public knowledge of the movement in the inner city of Moscow. We'll have massed troops and tanks along the routes we're sure they will take and surprise them as they make the turn on to the main roads."

"What if they have reinforcements at the bases ready to assist?" Mikhail asked.

"At the same time, we'll surprise them at the main roads with a helicopter force that'll fly down and bomb the exit gates at both military bases, cutting off any help they might be waiting on," Yakov replied.

President Reed nodded, and President Vasilyev seemed content with the answers.

"What about the nuke cases?" President Reed asked.

"With the announcement of your speech at the Berlin Wall on the same day that the NFL game will take place in Moscow, we think they might try to make a statement and bring a few to the Wall. This is only a guess, but we feel we may be right," Pete answered. "Our next best guess is the NFL game itself, somewhere else in the Moscow area, and possibly Russian embassies in foreign countries. This last piece of information came direct from General Asimov's diary."

"That's a lot of area to cover," Padraig put in.

They all knew the US wouldn't be able to help in Russia.

"I know, but you'll be with me at the Berlin Wall," Pete answered. "Yakov will be with the rest of the group covering the NFL game and Moscow. Agents from both our countries are watching the other embassies, and so far they are clean. Chances are Drygin will want to keep the cases close to him or in the hands of people he trusts."

The fact of the matter was that they needed to watch as many places as they could and they had the personnel to carry it out. But what would they do if they found the cases? The key would be to capture the remotes, but if that wasn't possible, they would need to disarm them immediately and take their chances.

"We have set up training over the next two days on nuclear disarmament as well as diffusing any remote control devices that we might find. Thanks to General Asimov and his diary," Pete continued. "Padraig and Mikhail will run the courses, as they have already been trained. I advise all of you to learn and ask any questions you have while you are here in Orlando. Once we leave here, there won't be any more chances to acquire the knowledge you need to handle this situation."

The meeting broke up, and the entire group, except the presidents, boarded a van and drove fifteen minutes to a little restaurant called Christini's. Pete always knew the great places to eat in any city he was in, and Christini's was no exception. The eggplant and garlic spread that melted on the warm Italian bread was quite delicious. They didn't talk much about what was going on, and they were all glad as they needed a chance to unwind. They all knew that, once they left Orlando, it was crunch time and Director Drygin was the enemy.

# CHAPTER 41

Drygin needed to figure out his final plan for Sunday, September 21. He was always in charge, but with the death of the general, things had changed, and he needed to rely on other people. He had a few choices with regard to where the nuke cases could be placed, but after the last summit, he knew he would have to place one in Berlin during President Reed's address to the German people. The final choice would be where to place the last four.

*The NFL game is a natural but maybe too easy to guess. Security would be tight, and getting the cases in could be a problem.*

He knew the answer would come to him, and he knew Anton would handle the plan to its conclusion.

*I'm glad Asimov isn't around. He'd try to advise me on what to do.*

At this point Drygin needed little help. Everyone was his pawn to do with as he pleased. He was the man in charge, and in a month or so, he would be ruling Russia.

*Who would ever have thought that a poor boy from the hills of Azerbaijan could rise to be the dictator of the world's most feared country? I will avenge the death of Stalin and all the bad things that had been said about my hero.*

"Well, it took a while, but the time has come." Drygin said to himself.

He heard a knock at the door. He got up to open the door but thought twice and went back to his desk to get the gun he kept in the upper right-hand drawer. He made sure the safety was off.

"Door's open."

When it swung open, the lights and shadows made it look like an ambush. Drygin didn't like what he saw, so he dove to his left behind the couch, rolled on his left side, and came up ready to fire. Anton was startled and couldn't believe the director was still this sharp. He gathered himself and held up his hands.

"You still got it." Anton said.

"Shit, Anton! What the hell are you doing here so late at night? I almost shot you through the eyes."

Drygin got off his knees, went to the desk, and placed the gun back where it belonged. He motioned Anton to take a seat opposite him on the couch. "Anton, I have decided to place one of the cases at the Berlin Wall while the president of the United States is speaking on the twenty-first. As far as the rest are concerned, we'll need to get some agents into the stadium as workers to check on what the security will be like prior to and during the game. In any case we'll use the NFL game as a target or at least a decoy once we establish if we can, in fact, get them into the stadium."

"We can have a few agents in place on the crews that will be working on the suites, which won't be finished until almost game time. We should know in a few days if it's possible, but as you said, if we need a decoy, that would be a good one. Do you have any other ideas on where to place the remaining four?"

"We could always get them out to a few of our embassies as we initially planned with the general, but I think we might need a bigger bang than that so we'll need to keep thinking," Drygin said.

"We could always keep them in Moscow or maybe look at a few places in Leningrad." Anton realized the director was getting a little strung out. He was concerned he might not be thinking clearly. "Our personnel is getting limited, and we don't want to stretch them out too much."

"I've thought about that, and if we can come up with a site that shows we're getting rid of the current government and going back to the times of Stalin, that would be great. Give me a few more days, and I'll come up with the something. We have enough people in place to get the job done. If I need to get the nukes in place myself, I will. Just take care of what I tell you to do, and it'll be fine."

"Whatever you say, Director. Just let me know when and where, and the cases will be placed properly."

Anton was about to leave but thought better of it. "Is there anything else?"

"Now that mention it, I think I'm going to have you place an explosive inside Lenin's tomb. I don't want to put a nuke there, but I do want to knock the shit out of the tomb."

"When should we place it?" Anton knew better than to question the director.

"I'll make sure the guards are absent at two o'clock on Sunday morning. Be sure to set the timer to go off at three o'clock on Sunday afternoon. I may need a diversion, and that should work."

When they left for the night, Drygin couldn't help but feel elated. The final plans for the coup were in place, he had figured out where to place one case, and had a pretty good idea on the other four. Stalin would be proud of him.

# CHAPTER 42

*Wednesday, September 17*

The teams left for Moscow on Tuesday so they could arrive on Wednesday morning and get used to the time difference by Sunday game time. It wasn't unusual for them to travel, but they weren't used to the distance and time change in Moscow. The Giants were the first to arrive, and the media crunch at the airport was unbelievable.

Head Coach Roger Fox was the first to talk to the media and, as always, said the right things. "The flight was long, and we're a little tired, but we're in Moscow, one of the great cities in the world. We look forward to playing on Sunday at Luzhinki Stadium. It's going to be a show that we hope you'll all enjoy, and hopefully the Giants will come out on top."

Olga, the government liaison, just stood in the background and watched the proceedings with Petra. Standing next to her was Dmitri, who was there to chauffer the owner of the Giants to his hotel.

"Olga, will you take a look at some of those bodies? I know we like girls, but that could make you think." The size of the men amazed Petra.

Olga just looked at her and smiled. She was well aware that Petra went both ways as she was sure Petra knew the same about

her. "We can always try a few out and see what we think." She patted Petra's ass. "I actually think Coach Fox is rather cute."

After the short press conference, the Giants boarded their
buses for the ride to the Europa in downtown Moscow. The team
would get a few hours to relax and then go through a simple walkthrough practice to get their legs back under them. Because it was
the beginning of the season, the teams weren't prepared for each
other as there wasn't a lot of film to watch and it was only the third
game of the season.

On the ride over, Olga had a chance to sit with Coach Fox. She
was amazed at how friendly he was to her and the other staff members. The coach seemed to single her out in conversation, and she
was quite pleased.

"Are you going to be with us the whole time, Olga?" the coach
asked.

His smile made Olga weak at the knees. *If he's flirting with me,
he's doing a pretty good job.*

"I'll be with you most of the time, working the schedule and
making sure our security is in place. Would you like to see anything
special?" Olga smiled, trying to be as businesslike as she could.

"I'd love to see the non-tourist side of Moscow before we leave,
but I'm not sure if we'll have the time. I'm sure I'll need someone
to show me the sights."

"What would you like to see?" Olga could feel herself blushing.

"I'd like to see how the people live, where they eat, what they
do at night, and where they go. I'm sure we'll see Red Square and
St. Basil's Cathedral along with the other tourist areas. I want to
see what the people see and feel. I'd like you to show me if you
would."

She was all tingles inside and knew immediately that she wanted
to do nothing else. "I'd like that, so we'll need to be sure we work
it out and put it into your schedule. Let me look at the program
again, and I'll figure something out." She felt like a young girl who
was going to get her first kiss.

"Thank you, Olga. I'm looking forward to it."

After getting to the hotel, Olga reported to Yakov that all was fine and she was going to take a few hours off before her team's next movement. It had been a while since she had some time off, so she walked around the Kremlin and St. Basil's Cathedral. She was always amazed at the vastness of the square and the beauty of it all. There wasn't anything as gracious or as beautiful as the three domes that were seen as soon as she approached the cathedral. She walked past Lenin's tomb.

*Where is this all going?*

She was involved with Petra, but she knew it would have to come to some type of conclusion. She realized it would be for the best and always wanted to stay close to her but realized she wanted a man and a family.

*Could this Coach Fox be the one I've been waiting for all these years?*

She was sure Petra would understand and she couldn't wait to tell her.

Olga was getting a little jumpy as they still were guessing at what the director would do. With the general dead, no one was sure where the remaining five nukes were located and what was going to be done with them. It was common knowledge that Drygin probably had them, but they didn't know what his plan would be. At least with Asimov they had an idea based on the records he had kept, but now it was a different game. Olga would need to stay close to the team to be sure nothing happened to them but also to work with all her partners to be sure this threat from within was handled.

*There isn't anything worse than a madman in a powerful position with powerful weapons who thought what he was doing was for the best of his beloved country.*

It was a long way from the old days in Leningrad. How she yearned for those simpler times. But she had chosen this life, and she wouldn't let her people down. Russia would survive this, as it had survived many uprisings in the past.

Yakov made sure he met with Mickey and Ivan in a secured space where there would be no interruptions. He brought in a light lunch of vegetables, a little fresh meat, and some fruit. There wasn't any alcohol. He wanted to be sure his two hotshot agents were sober for the next four days.

"Alexei decided to assign you both to my team at the stadium."

"Do you think any of the nuke cases could be placed at the field Yakov?" Mickey asked.

He had followed this for so long that his instinct was saying he'd have a role in this saga. What it would be and how it would end up was anybody's guess, but he felt he was ready for the challenge. After Boris' death was confirmed, they all felt a little different as to the objective of the game. Mikhail had been convinced to stay out front on the business end and to allow Mickey and Ivan to become part of the security teams. They would be involved in normal security functions prior to the game, but on game day they would be more focused on the suites where the owners of the two teams would be seated.

"My immediate guess is that they will show up there, but how many and where in the stadium is anyone's guess."

"Yakov, I'd like to get a hold of the diagrams of the stadium to see where all the tunnels lead and where the secret rooms are hidden. All stadiums have some secret areas, and if I were to place the cases, that is where I'd put them. When my dad played for the Giants, I knew every nook and cranny in the stadium."

"I think you're right, Mickey, but how do we cover all those areas?" Ivan asked.

"That will be up to Georgi and your team as surveillance has already begun. It will be twenty-four hours a day until the last person leaves the stadium after the game," Yakov remarked.

The time had come to get Ivan and Mickey in step with the program and turn them over to Georgi so he could put them to work. They had both done well during training and were ready for whatever came next. Pete, Yakov, or Alexei couldn't do much else for them.

"Yakov, what do you know about Georgi Cherlin?" Ivan had heard a few things, but they wanted to know more.

"He's a favorite of Alexei's, and that's saying a lot. In the old days, he worked the streets for him and did all the little jobs no one else wanted to do."

"Are you saying he was undercover most of the time, or did he go in, get the job done, and then get out?"

"He did both, but his main job was to infiltrate organizations that were in conflict with the government and report to the KGB. He was stationed in Prague for many years and was instrumental in keeping them an Eastern Bloc country."

"Was he an assassin for the government?"

"Not to my knowledge, and if he were I'd never tell you anyway. The Soviet Union did what it had to do in the fifties and sixties to combat the risk from the Western world after WWII. There was a threat to our way of life, and we weren't going to let anyone change us. We felt our system was the right one."

"Are you saying that now we were wrong?" Ivan asked.

"I'm not sure yet, but I know what is happening now isn't what we expected. There's a need to open up Russia to the world and work together on certain issues. Having a madman with nukes isn't the way it should be. I'm not sure what Georgi believes, and it doesn't matter. He's the man for the job."

Mickey and Ivan met Georgi that evening at KGB headquarters on the fourth floor. They were given their immediate workload and responsibilities and were glad they were posted for the same assignments. Because they had trained together, they were aware of each other's habits and patterns. Hopefully in time of danger, this would help them both get through. They would report in the morning to the stadium, get their first look at the areas they would be working, and meet the other team members.

When Mickey thought about the meetings the next day, he was glad he had met with Petra and the security plans were on the way to Pete. He had a way of finding that missing piece that sometimes proved to be the one they needed. Hopefully they had a plan in place to keep the stadium safe, but in the end it would all come down to the final planning and a lot of luck.

Georgi was in charge, and there was no mistaking who was the boss. He had the look of experience, but there was an air of superiority that was felt as soon as opened his mouth. The meeting took place outside the stadium in a large set of truck trailers that were actually the security headquarters for the team. From the outside they looked like a bunch of trailers waiting to be moved to their next location, but the monitors and wiring inside were the latest in surveillance equipment, which the CIA gave to the Russians.

"Based on the nukes being the size of a large suitcase, it's important that we be able to detect any trace of a nuclear substance or pick out anything that is the size of a can of beer." Georgi said.

It was always a problem as so many things were going in and out of the stadium that it was almost impossible to search them all.

"With the game a few days away, there will be a lot of movement setting up the stadium for food concessions, team equipment, TV, and final construction. We need to be sure we check everything that goes into the stadium."

"How are we going to handle that? Mickey asked.

"The plan is quite simple. As we discussed everything will be going through Gate 1. Each team will have Geiger counter devices to check all packages going into the stadium. After their shift each team will have the chance to go through the entire stadium at their own pace to get a feel for the layout of the place."

*This is probably the most important surveillance method we would undertake.*

"I think we need to look at the shortcuts we can take advantage of in case we need to get to a particular location in the stadium. At Yankee Stadium there were ways to get to the locker room that we found after checking out the stadium so I'm sure it will be the same here," Mickey said.

"I agree with Mickey," Yakov commented. "Let's be sure we go through the entire stadium and come up with different routes just in case."

"Do you have the plan laid out for the teams and the owners for game day?" Ivan asked.

"Not completely yet, but I think we need to be more concerned with the days leading up to the game. Security is in place for this, and we'll finalize the game day shortly. Because the owners may pop in and out, we'll need to monitor that, but that's someone else's responsibility, not yours," Georgi answered.

"What about the press and media for the practice days?" Mickey asked.

"That's all under control, and when we do the stadium run through, you'll be able to see it. Mickey and Ivan, I need you to concentrate on Gate 1 and then be sure you know the stadium inside and out from the owner s suites to the locker rooms and back."

Georgi concluded the meeting and handed out the schedules for all the teams. Yakov had briefed them on his style of leadership, and he had been precise. Although he was mild mannered, he undoubtedly knew what he was doing. At the conclusion of the meeting, Mickey and Ivan went off to their first assignment.

They finished their first shift at Gate 1, and not much happened in the way of deliveries. The two teams, however, did come in for their practice times, and their size amazed Ivan. They only had their personal items as all the equipment had been delivered the day before and the devices and trained dogs had checked it. The manifests were all in order, and all went smoothly.

When they ended their shift, they had a chance to see the end of the Dolphins practice while they were doing their final two-minute drill. The precision between the quarterbacks and receivers was something Ivan had never seen, and they sat to watch the conclusion.

"That was awesome," Ivan remarked. "I've never seen anything like it, and to be able to do it under pressure would be something else."

Mickey gave Ivan a shot to the arm. "They do it all the time, Ivan. That's why they're the best in the world. Let's get on with the walkthrough and see what we can find out about this grand ol' stadium.

Mickey realized Luzhinki Stadium was a maze as soon as they entered the tunnels. With so many ramps and secret passageways, it would take a long time to get this all down to memory, but it had to be done. There was no question that, if the moment arose, there would be a need to get somewhere quickly to handle a situation, whatever that situation might be.

The immediate security showed nothing out of the ordinary, and as they reported in to close out the day, the other teams said the same. The night shift would be coming on. Though there would be no deliveries until the next day, they needed to secure the stadium for the night. Work was being done on the luxury suites to finish them in time for the game, but all credentials had already been approved.

When they left the stadium, Mickey was satisfied with his first day on the job and was looking forward to the weekend festivities. The game was four days away, and they had a lot to look out for to be sure all went as planned. It was a huge undertaking, but he felt they could all handle it.

*Only time would tell if my instincts are correct.*

She was sitting at the hotel bar looking better than he had ever seen her. It seemed as if she had a peace over her that he hadn't seen before. Mickey knew he had some feelings for her, but at present he wasn't sure how much.

*It's probably better that way.*

Pete had gotten to her with a few items that needed work, and Mickey had some difficult work ahead. Pete was concerned with security during the game and wanted Mickey's input as to what was going on. He trusted Yakov and the boys, but he always wanted to know what was going on and to lend any advice he could. The faster Mickey learned, the quicker Pete could get to that farmhouse in France.

"You're looking lovely tonight, Petra."

She looked at him with that lovely smile. "I feel good, Mickey. To tell you the truth, I'm really not sure why. I like it though."

"Well, it suits you well, and I hope you can bottle it and give me some."

Petra took his hand and squeezed it.

"Pete wants to know what's going on with the security at the game. He's aware that Yakov and Georgi are in charge but wanted your input as soon as possible. Do you think you can get me a report within the next twenty-four hours?"

"Tell Pete that I'm learning how he works, and I just happen to have a condensed briefing on the plan setup for the game."

"Boy, he's going to love this. I wish I could see his face when he gets it."

With the business concluded, she asked, "You seem to be at peace. Do you feel it also?"

"I'm not sure, but I have an inner strength I never felt before. It's all still crazy, but we've been trained in a short time, and I feel

I can handle it. It might also be that this whole game will soon be ending. I know bad things can still happen, but we all seem to have it under control."

"I feel the same, but I still worry that all of us might not be here when this over. Someone could get hurt, and it could be you, me, or Olga. It's all part of it, and even with that thought, I'm still at peace with it."

"How is Olga?"

"Oh, she'll be fine. She's a tough bitch, and we've been through a lot together. We'll come out okay. I just hope Mikhail gets to some closure about Boris."

"He will. Take care of yourself. I'll see you around."

Petra kissed him on the cheek. "Please be careful."

Anton knew that getting the credentials forged would be the easy part. The hard part would be getting the cases into the stadium, and that was up to him. The director had decided to let him handle the stadium and to let him figure out the best way to get things done. His assistant Timor secured the passes, but trying to figure out how to get the cases into the stadium was another matter.

"Anton, do you think we can get to a few of the guards and pay them off? I don't see how else we can get them into the stadium," Timor asked.

"I checked with my man inside, and he told me that we could probably get to some, but the problem is the KGB and the other agents they have in place. Even if we got to some of them, it wouldn't help because the security is so tight and we couldn't be sure it would work."

"Fuckin' Russian mentality. Why can't this be like it always is? How do they expect us to get our job done?"

Timor was an idiot sometimes, but Anton had to agree with him on this.

*How the hell are we going to get the nuke cases in?*

Graft was the usual way, or he figured he could at least count on the inefficiency of the Russian workers. The director was going to have a shit fit, but he couldn't do much about it.

On the way over to the director's office, Anton figured he might as well be up front with Drygin. He didn't have a reason to bullshit him, as they needed a way to get them in.

Maybe the director has a better idea.

"Director Drygin, I'm telling you that security is tight and getting a few of these cases into the stadium may be futile. I'd hate to lose another one, and we may need to use plan B."

Drygin didn't say anything for a few seconds as he needed time to think. "We can't even pay off the staff at the stadium to get them in?"

"I don't think so, the KGB under Yakov and Georgi Cherlin from the stadium are inspecting all boxes that go into the stadium through Gate 1. All the other gates are closed up solid, and the agents are watching them. The gates won't open up until three hours before game time so it will be tough to get them in through there."

Drygin had no direct command over the stadium staff or extra KGB security that Alexei authorized. He couldn't do much about the situation. His pal Alexei had gotten there first on the game security, but there were other ways to get done what he needed. The five remaining cases could be put in a few other selected areas on game day, and he knew where.

*I might need to use the game as a decoy to keep Alexei off guard.*

"Anton, I'll instruct you on where we will place the cases soon. The stadium isn't out of the question yet, as I'm sure we'll be able to find a loophole or pay someone off on game day. Let's be patient and play our hand at the last moment. Please have Oleg

Koslov report to me as soon as we finish our business here so we can start moving some of the cases."

"If we can get them in, is there any special area you want them placed?"

"I think we should put one in the Dolphins owner's suite and one in the lower basement area near the Giants locker room."

"Anything else?"

"Not on this matter, but get to Oleg Koslov so we can finalize the plan on the cases that will be headed to the Wall. You can tell him most of it, but leave the placement and date to me."

Oleg was Drygin's special agent in East Germany. He had been working the zone for many years and crossed in between the East and the West with ease. The director never asked him how he did it and didn't care as long as he got the job done. So far Oleg hadn't let him down.

After Anton left, the director knew just what he was going to do, but that was for him alone to know.

*I'm the big player in this game and no one…not even my team…would know what the final destination for the five active nuke cases would be. Power…is a beautiful thing!*

Anton had worked with Oleg on many occasions, and he knew he was a renegade agent but one who always got things done. He located Oleg, and they met for a drink at Anton's local bar.

"It's nice to see you again, Anton, after our last time together."

Anton would rather forget that time. He and Anton had been working together in East Germany five years earlier, and things got a little out of hand. In the end Oleg, had to save Anton's ass, but he never said anything to anyone as far as Anton knew.

"Director Drygin has a job for you and needs to meet with you in the morning. He asked me to give you a little background on the job."

"Then tell me what's going on. Will you be part of my team again?" The sarcasm was very evident.

"No, I won't, Oleg. You'll be on your own, and the operation is probably the biggest you'll ever have. Look, there's no point in busting each other's balls here so let's just get on with the business at hand and forget the past."

Oleg sat back in his chair and took a sip of vodka. "Does this have anything to do with the missing nuke cases?"

There had been rumors that Drygin held the cases, and with the deaths of Asimov and Marisova, it made sense. By the look on Anton's face, Oleg knew he was right. Anton could never hide anything from Oleg.

"Yes, it does, and the director wants you to get two of them into West Berlin. Do you think you can handle that?"

"Why are we going to West Berlin and not East Berlin? What does he plan on blowing up?"

*This is crazy shit! I love it.* Oleg had been dreaming of something like this for a long time.

"The director will fill you in on the date and placement of the case when you meet him in the morning." Anton knew Oleg was a poor choice for this mission as he was too much of a renegade, but it was Drygin's decision.

"You're telling me we're going to detonate a nuke case in West Berlin in the near future?"

Anton could see the excitement in his eyes, and he was a little concerned. "That's what I'm telling you, and try to control yourself. If it were up to me, you wouldn't be the one I'd be sending."

Oleg couldn't wait to meet with the director in the morning. He ordered another vodka and gulped it down. *Tomorrow is going to be something special.*

"I realize that, but it's not up to you. Pay for the drinks before you leave," Oleg said.

Sunday was the day Drygin selected to put his full plan into motion as the streets would be mostly empty and most of the citizens' attention would be on resting or watching the game between the Dolphins and Giants. The coup plan was quite simple. The regiments of tanks, convoys, and personnel would approach Moscow Centre from the east and the north, as the stadium was to the south, and converge on the Russian White House and the Dumas, which was the adjacent building. Because everyone from the government would be at the game, the only resistance they might incur would be from the military guarding both of the buildings. When the guards saw the regiments approaching from both sides, there would be no question as to what was happening. The only question would be if they chose to fight or join the coup. Chances were they would join, but if not they would simply be killed.

Drygin had handpicked the regiments, and each man knew the mission he was undertaking. Each general was in charge of his regiment and would safeguard against any mutinous behavior within his ranks. As far as they were concerned, they had their orders and would do whatever was needed to get the mission accomplished. As far as Drygin was concerned, they were dead men either way.

"Where will you be when we start to move the troops, Director?" asked General Yachenko.

"I'll be right here monitoring everything that's going on. I'll make my excuses to the president early Sunday morning that, unfortunately, I won't be able to attend the game. Do you think the troops are up to the mission?"

"I think they are, and they can't wait to get started. They've been through so many dry runs that they could do it in their sleep," Yachenko answered.

"I want to be sure that we knock out any communications we can on the way into Moscow. Once we hit the five-mile radius from the Dumas, we need to start that course of action. I don't want word getting out that something is happening."

"We understand, Director, and we've set up a group of special-ists to handle that. We also have backup troops ready to assist if we should encounter any problems on the way in."

The director sat back and closed his eyes for a few seconds. "Be sure we leave at exactly noon as we planned. It's imperative we get to Moscow on time and take the two sites as soon as possible. It has to be done before the game is over."

"It will be," the generals replied in unison.

"That is good. May we take the targets for the resurgence of Mother Russia. Whatever happens in the next few days, we'll be remembered forever. Good night, Generals, and good luck."

# CHAPTER 43

*Thursday, September 18*

The nuke cases left for Berlin on a military transport plane with Oleg aboard and in charge. After his meeting with Drygin, all the cases had been changed to look nondescript so they could be moved anywhere they needed. Oleg had noticed a few other cases that looked the same, but he was only concerned with the two under his care.

*Were both nukes?*

The choice of East Berlin was a no-brainer as the East Germans were still under the Russian control. Getting the cases planted and into West Germany would not be a problem. The Wall was porous as hell if someone knew where to go to, and the East German police knew the exact spots where they could get the two cases across and placed during the speeches scheduled for Sunday, September 21. The president of the United States, as agreed upon during the August 18 summit, would be delivering his speech as planned.

Oleg was pleased to see that Stanislav, his East German counterpart, was meeting him and all was in order as his plane touched down. Stanislav usually delivered on his promises to Oleg, so he hoped this would be no different. Standing with him was Konrad Bauer, the nuclear physicist that Oleg had asked for. For all their faults, the East Germans still knew how to handle covert operations, and for this Oleg was glad.

"Konrad, so nice to see you again," Oleg said. "I see you have the two cases, and they look just about right."

The scientist couldn't tell one from the other. Oleg put his two cases in the back of Bauer's car and made the switch with the other two.

"I'm not sure if they're both nuclear, but we need to find out tonight. Please let Stanislav know, and he'll handle the rest."

Oleg handed Konrad an envelope, and the scientist drove off.

Stanislav was waiting next to the car. "The meeting is all set with the commissioner, and as soon as I hear from Konrad, I'll let you know. Is there anything else you'll need done?"

"Yes, but first be sure to get at least a half-million American dollars for each case. My guess is that only one is a nuke. Why would we need two to get the job done? Here's the account the money should be transferred to." He made sure that Stanislav understood.

"I want you to place a bomb in the munitions factory we have set up, and be sure there's enough power to blast the building to bits. I need it to go off at exactly four-thirty in the afternoon on Sunday. Can you handle that?" The timing was critical to Oleg's overall plan.

"One of my comrades will be able to make the bomb. Gerhardt and I will be sure to place it in the basement with the rest of the ammunition. We'll sneak it into the building on Saturday night. There's a big football match against our archrival so not too many people should be around the building."

"I don't give a fuck what you do. Just be sure it goes off at the right time, and don't let Gerhardt know what it is. Be sure it is timed for exactly four-thirty on Sunday."

The drive to the Wall would take about forty-five minutes, and once he was in West Berlin, the safe house would be a few blocks away from the part of the city where the ceremonies would take place. He knew he had to play the West Berlin plan as Drygin had written it, whether the cases were real or not. Drygin had eyes everywhere. If all went well, Oleg would be watching Western television, drinking a few beers, and having a decent meal by the end of the day. He was looking forward to the evening, especially the time he would have with Gertrude Volker, his West German contact. Little did he know that, at that very moment, she was meeting with Pete in the café of the Annabel Hotel for a late afternoon lunch.

"Pete, if Oleg is here, it must be something big. If it were just an intelligence-gathering operation, he would be nowhere near Berlin. I'm meeting him tonight at my apartment and will advise you on what I find out when we meet tomorrow afternoon."

"That's what we need, but be careful and find out as much as you can. It makes sense that something big is going to happen if Oleg is here."

"Do you have any idea what is possibly going on?"

"I may, but until I get something from you, I don't want to push any panic buttons. Just do what needs to be done."

Bribes work almost everywhere in the world, and Oleg knew it. He had been working in Berlin for more years than he wanted to admit. Before he left for Berlin, his meeting with the director was brisk and to the point.

"Oleg, I'm giving you the most important operation we've ever had in the USSR. Do you think you're up to it?"

"You know I am, Director, so let me know what needs to be done."

"In a day or so, I'll trust you with two nuke cases that you'll transport to Berlin with you. These cases are to be used to blow up the Brandenburg Gate during the festivities on September 21. How you handle it is up to you, but I want no mistakes. When the president of the United States starts his speech, make sure he doesn't end it."

"I'll get it done, Director, and long live Mother Russia."

They went through the final preparations to get the nukes to Berlin, and the meeting was over.

After the meeting Oleg knew immediately what he was going to do with the two nuke cases. He was a renegade, and he loved it. He had trained all these years for this type of opportunity, and he wasn't going to let it slip by. If they all lived, the director would be proud of him.

Sitting in the apartment, Oleg needed to figure out where he was going to place the cases and how he was going to get it done. He had scoped out the stage area earlier in the day, and he knew there was no way he was going to get the cases near it. The only place that might work was the trash canisters that would be placed away from the stage but in the general area of some buildings. He called his agent in the West Berlin government to see what could be done.

About an hour later, the agent called back. "Oleg, this is going to cost you a lot, but it can be done. As always please don't tell me what's going on. Just leave the money at the regular drop, and make it three times what it usually is. I'll take care of the sanitation workers."

Oleg knew the German agent would hardly pay the workers anything, but he didn't care. "What time, and where do I meet them?"

"Be at the Victory Column Circle on the Altonaer Strasse in the Tiergarten at ten in the morning on Saturday. The truck will be there with two canisters on the back. Simply place what you need in the canisters and move on. The workers know where those two canisters are supposed to be placed. The bin numbers will be #1435 and #2641. It's a pleasure doing business with you." He hung up.

Pete and Padraig had been in Berlin over a week now on the hunch that all wasn't what it seemed to be. Pete realized, after he got his report from Mickey, that getting any nuke cases into the game could be difficult. If Drygin couldn't get the cases into the game, he would have to place them somewhere else, and Pete's hunch was the Berlin Wall.

*What better place than where the president of the United States would be giving a speech on communism?*

Pete was very rarely wrong, and in this case he knew he was right on the mark. He needed to be sure Gertrude got as much information as possible, but the key was that Padraig follow Oleg to determine when and where the cases would be placed.

Olga and Petra were actually having a lot of fun being the liaison for the two NFL teams. Not only did they go everywhere with the teams, they were getting to know a few of the ballplayers. Although their paths crossed, they weren't together at the end of the evening. This seemed to be fine with both of them and Coach Fox and Dan Pascarini, the quarterback from the Dolphins, didn't seem to mind either. Olga wasn't the only one having a little fun.

Mikhail, the president of the RFF, had a major part in the daily schedule of the teams and was coordinating it all with his staff on the top floor of the Intourist. With Boris dead he had no choice but to take over and be sure that all went as planned. Olga and Petra were instrumental in helping plan the events for the week, and as they were working with the teams, they also acted as coordinators for these events. It was a load off Mikhail's mind, and as the days passed, he couldn't get his mind off the photos of Boris and Colonel Marisova that somehow came across his desk with one word written on the back, "Drygin."

*I'll get that bastard no matter how long it takes.*

He figured it wouldn't be that long before he could confront the director. The meeting that morning with his staff and the two girls was productive, and it seemed all the details had been handled.

"What time do the teams get to the orphanages for the photo shoot?" Mikhail asked.

"Practice should be over by noon. After showers and lunch, they should be there by one-thirty as planned. Both teams should be back to the hotel by three-thirty for their meetings," Olga said. "After that they're on their own until tomorrow morning."

"What about game day. Are we all set with the buses and trucks to move the luggage and other containers of equipment?"

"Buses will be leaving to get the teams to the stadium two hours before game time. The trucks will be separated between equipment for the stadium and luggage for the plane. The truck with the luggage is scheduled to go immediately to the airport to load on the chartered planes," Petra said.

"And the truck with the equipment will be reloaded after the game and follow the team to the plane."

"That's the plan, Mikhail, and if all goes right, we'll have the teams out of here three hours after the game ends." Petra looked at Olga and could see she was in a little pain about her man flying home. She squeezed her hand, and Olga relaxed.

"Is that about it for today, Olga?"

"Yes, it is."

"That 's great, Olga. Anything else?"

Olga shook her head, and Mikhail dismissed the meeting. The two girls stayed behind, as was their habit, to talk to Mikhail.

Petra was the first to speak. "Mikhail, you seem to have something on your mind?"

"Nothing really. I just want to kill Director Drygin."

Dmitri left Alexei's office by the passageway that only he and Yakov knew about. Dmitri was Alexei's trump card, and no one knew about him. *Not Pete, not Yakov, and not even Drygin.* He had been with Alexei through thick and thin and was as loyal as they came. He knew more than any of them did and was always placed at a lower level of surveillance…or so it seemed.

*How much could Mikhail Vladikoff's driver know?*

Ivan and Mickey had been at it for five hours already, and there was no end in sight. The equipment and supplies would be coming in for the rest of their watch and probably through half of the next one. The amount of materials and supplies that came in for a game was unimaginable. Along with the foodstuffs, the construction was going on to finish the suites as well as other jobs. The amount was double what it would usually be. By moving all this material only through Gate 1, the backup and security measures added to the time it took to get the materials through.

"Will this shit ever stop coming in?" Mickey asked.

"Take a look at the line, and you tell me. I've never seen anything like this in my life. The food items are easy enough, but that construction equipment takes forever to go through."

"I didn't know we would be check-in clerks for the stadium when we accepted this assignment. I can't wait to get off and get back to walking the stadium. I think I've found a shortcut from the suites down to the lower levels."

At the end of the shift, they were going to meet with Georgi and Yakov to see if they could work out some routes through the stadium to get to different areas in good time. Chances were they'd be using these routes when the people were still watching the game so they could have free passes. But if the alarm went off during halftime or at the conclusion of the game, they needed to have alternates routes just in case.

Mickey led the way to the suites on the upper level and stopped at the one where the Giants VIPs would be seated. During the game Olga and Mikhail would be stationed up here along with Yakov to keep an eye on this part of the stadium. Ivan and Mickey would be stationed with Petra across the way in the Dolphins suite. Georgi with his team would handle the locker rooms and field. In total, two hundred and fifty agents would be assigned to various gates, suites, rooms, and locations throughout the stadium.

For this practice run, they were all stationed at their posts, and the object was to get to the referees' locker room on the lower level first. The locker room was in the middle of the lower level so they would meet there first if there were any trouble on that level.

At the selected time, the four of them left their posts for the run down to the ref's room. Out of the gate Mickey went left out of the suite. Ivan thought he was nuts but didn't say anything. The object, after studying the stadium charts, was to find the quickest way down. On the initial trial runs together, it had taken them three minutes and thirty seconds to get to the locker room. When they went their separate ways, Mickey knew he'd be the first to get down to the room and would be there within two and a half minutes, taking a full minute off the original time.

Yakov came around the bend and noticed it had been three minutes since he began. He was sure he'd be there first but didn't let up until he got to the door.

When he opened it, Mickey was sitting there, smirking. "Stop to take a piss?"

At that moment Georgi and Ivan came through the door out of breath.

Yakov had a look of disbelief on his face. "How the hell did you get here so fast?"

"It's my old training from when I was a kid. At the two-minute warning, we'd leave the seats to see who would be the first to the locker room. I never got beat."

After reviewing the routes, all four knew about the secret ramps that Mickey found at the far end on the stadium. A little door led to a set of ramps that went straight down to the lower level with no access from any other point. Yakov decided to keep this information with the four of them and a few other specific agents who would be patrolling the upper suite level.

"Good job, Mickey. If we need to get to the lower level quickly, we now know it can be done."

That night Oleg got what he needed from Gertrude and then slit her throat. When he left the apartment, he wasn't aware that Padraig was following him. But Padraig was also not aware that Gertrude was dead.

# CHAPTER 44

*Friday, September 19*

Padraig was surprised that Oleg was using this particular safe house. He was never very careful upon leaving the place and never noticed he was being followed. This wasn't the first time Padraig had followed him, so he was well aware of his moves. This time, however, things seemed to be a little different.

Oleg walked out of the apartment building and went directly to the metro and headed north on the green line. He got off at the Brandenburg stop and walked up the stairs into the square. He stopped at a little café on the Dorotheenstrasse area and sat at a table in the corner with two men who Padraig had never seen before. He sat with them for a while, and they were in a discussion that, at times, got very animated.

"I'll push the remote a few seconds into the president's speech. If the remote doesn't work, you will shoot the trash canister with the bazooka, as you have been ordered," Oleg said. "The explosion won't be big enough to get to you, so you won't be in trouble."

The two agents looked at each other.

"You're bullshitting us, Oleg, and we know it. How the fuck do you expect us to sit there knowing we could be blown up?" said agent number one.

"You won't be blown up. I have placed the bombs in the back of the canister closest to the stage area so the blast will impact that way."

*These fuckin' idiots have no idea the bombs are nuclear, and never will. Shit, they'll be vaporized before they know it.*

"What about our money?" Agent number two asked.

"The money will deposited in the banks later this evening. Look, if you two want to pull out, do it now so I can shoot you before you go back to East Berlin. I'm tired of all this. Are you in or out?"

*They're both dead if they leave, and they know it.*

"We're in. Just be sure the money is deposited as you said."

Oleg wanted to shoot them right there.

Padraig made it a point to call his backups who were at the café in fifteen minutes and arrived just before the three men left. Each man took one of the Russian agents and followed him the rest of the night. In the morning they would touch base, and hopefully Pete would be aware of where all three men were and what they were up to.

Padraig stayed with Oleg and followed him back to the Brandenburg Gate, and as Oleg surveyed the area, Padraig knew he was looking for a few spots to place the cases and to be able to detonate them both from the same area.

The remote control waves from these devices were only good from three miles out, and Oleg needed a direct line of sight to be able to complete the task. When Oleg looked to the west with his binoculars, he was able to pick out a spot on a small hill, overlooking the Gate, where he would be able to do the job. Satisfied he found the spot and checking one more time on the line of sight, he grabbed a cab for the ride back to his apartment.

Padraig watched. Oleg's brazenness amazed him. When they both got out of their cabs, Padraig watched Oleg walk into the corner market, get something to eat and drink, and then disappear into the apartment building for the rest of the evening.

Padraig called Pete.

"Padraig, Oleg killed Gertrude last night in her apartment."

"Pete, he acted as if he didn't have a care in the world. Shit, he just killed a girl and plotted where he was going to kill thousands more. He's a real cool character."

"He's a top KGB operative reporting to Director Drygin. He's the best they have, and we'll need to watch him closely. They're definitely plotting something for Sunday, and my guess would be a few nuke cases. Do you agree?"

"Yes. It scares the crap out of me. We also need to keep tabs on the other two men he met as I'm sure they're part of his plan."

"Me, too, Padraig, but this is why we get paid the big bucks. Stay on him and his two friends, and let me know when they move."

"Sure thing, Pete. Whatever you want me to do." He stood there for a while and then turned and left.

After he hung up the phone, Pete sat there and put all the pieces together. There was no doubt that a case or two would end up at the Gate during President Reed's speech on Sunday. There was also the possibility that the remaining cases could be anywhere in Russia, but Pete guessed they would be in Moscow at the NFL game or elsewhere in the city. Yakov was almost sure they would be at the game, but Pete suspected they might be located somewhere else. Mikhail agreed with this assessment. The NFL game was too easy to figure out.

*But then again what better way to make an impact on society than to blow up a stadium with seventy thousand people in attendance. Would a madman risk killing this many people to make a point, and what else could he have in mind?*

The file on Drygin was full and very complicated. He was a shrewd man without any scruples who would do whatever was needed to keep himself in power. Killing people was an easy thing as long as the final goal was accomplished.

The phone rang and startled Pete out of this thought pattern. "Hello."

"Pete, it's Yakov. I'm glad I caught you. Mikhail seems to be going off the deep end. Petra and Olga reported that he wants to kill Drygin."

"He would be doing us a favor. Have the girls keep an eye on him and report to you. How are Ivan and Mickey doing?"

"They're fine and fitting in with the other agents and Georgi's staff. They actually are pretty good and know what they're doing. I'll watch out for them. Anything on Oleg?"

"He's as brazen as ever, but in this case he's showing us the way. I must let you know he killed Gertrude last night. I'll be sure to take care of her family. She was a good girl."

Yakov had worked with her many times and knew she would be missed. He could only think how he would feel if it were Olga or Petra.

Pete continued, "We think he'll place a couple cases near the Brandenburg Gate for the speeches on Sunday. Padraig is on it so we should be able to handle them. Thanks for that nuke scientist you sent to defuse the bombs when we locate them. Anything else happening we should know about?"

"That's about it, but let's stay in touch. I'll tell Mickey you were asking for him. Take care of yourself, Pete, and maybe this will be the last one we need to work on. I'm getting too old for all this."

*Me, too,* Pete pondered as they both hung up the phone.

Ivan picked Mickey up at the hotel for the drive out to the stadium. After this was all over, Mickey needed to find a small place of his own, as his cover would need to be that of an American doing business in Russia. In fact that's what he was doing with his working relationship with Mikhail and Ivan. As far as anyone knew, he was the person responsible for getting the NFL to Moscow through the EFL but more so through his American contacts through his father.

The cars were still coming into Leningrad, and they had just brought in food from Sweden and Italy through their EFL contact base. Stefan up in Leningrad was still in charge, and business was booming.

Ivan said, "Mikhail seems a little strange lately. He's been hitting the vodka awfully hard. He was so drunk last night that we put him to bed and all he kept mumbling was, 'I'll get that bastard.'"

"I'm sure the girls have told Yakov what's going on, but it might be a good idea if you mention it to him the next time you see him."

"I was going to do just that later today. Do you think there will be a lot of action at the stadium today?" Ivan asked.

"There might be as I would think today would be the last day to get everything in except for any perishable foods. We're going to lock it down pretty good tonight and only allow the builders to finish the suites. It should all close down after the clinics today, and then we can do the final walkthrough tonight and get ready for the trial runs tomorrow. I can't wait to see the scenarios they come up with."

"Yeah, they should be something."

When they got closer to the field, both fell silent and reflected. It would be good to get these next two days over with and get to game day. On Sunday, they would be up in the owner's suites with Petra, Olga, and Yakov monitoring the suite level. If anything was going to happen, they figured it would be here or near the team locker rooms.

When the shift ended they were glad nothing unforeseen had happened, and they were looking forward to watching the clinic that the NFL ran. A handful of Giants and Dolphin players, along with the coaches, would put the Russians through a few drills. Ivan was excited to see the Russians standing on the sidelines warming up and looking good in their new RFF warm-up suits. They started to descend down to the field, and Mickey saw Tommy.

"Hey, you old bastard, how the heck are you doing?"

Tommy just laughed and waved at them to come on over. They saw Tommy had a wide grin.

"Is this great or what? You should see how excited the Russian boys are. It's unbelievable," Tommy said.

Ivan looked at the players and nodded to a few, as he had been with them for over a year now. He was about to say something to them when everything got quiet all of a sudden. From the far end zone, a bunch of the Giants players started running toward the Russians.

"Look at the size and the speed." Ivan said.

"That's the big difference between any league and the NFL. The players have more speed and size. It sets them apart from the other leagues," Mickey replied.

"I'm beginning to see what you mean. When you see them up close, it's just an awesome sight. After watching them practice, you also get a better understanding of how complicated this game is."

"You're finally getting it, Ivan. See, Mickey, I told you he wasn't that stupid." Tommy laughed.

After some speeches from the coaches, the players were split into positions to begin the clinic. The talented positions were where the Russians needed to make the biggest leap if they were going to be competitive in the game. While Tommy watched the whole thing, he knew exactly what needed to be done. They needed to get down to simple basics and learn from the bottom up. He went over to the coach in charge and explained what needed to be done. Everyone thought it was easy, but not everyone played in the NFL. After a while the quarterbacks were holding and throwing the ball properly, and the wide receivers were actually catching the ball routinely.

They had a long way to go, but at least it was a start. The clinic went on for another ninety minutes. Then the NFL contingent needed to return to the hotel for meetings.

Mickey made sure the press coverage made the two countries look like they were working toward the same goal. The press enjoyed the clinic and the pictures, and the PR would go over well in the world papers.

"What better way to have people with different philosophies come together than through sports," Coach Fox said. "The world has been doing that for years now, but recently we boycotted the Olympics because of politics. We need to keep it together."

While the teams were leaving the field, Ivan and Mickey went back up to the suites and were surprised to find Olga and Petra there with a few of the VIPs who had come in to watch the clinics.

"That was awesome," Petra said. A sportswoman herself, she knew what it took to be a player and be part of something special. The size and agility of the Americans also amazed her, but she felt the Russians, with practice and years of coaching, could be just as good. "Mickey, how long do you think it will be before we can be competitive with the NFL?"

Mickey didn't want to disappoint her. "If they stay focused, work hard, and learn the game, they could be close to the Americans in ten years. You need to remember the skilled positions need to be taught, and that will be the tough part."

She looked skeptical. "You Americans always think no one can compete with you."

Ivan suppressed a smile.

At that moment the door to the suite opened, and Yakov walked in. He looked at everyone and smiled. "Mickey and Ivan, join me outside."

Mickey and Ivan said good-bye to the girls and the VIPs and followed Yakov out to the hallway.

"We have uncovered more about the plot that I think you two need to know about. Drygin plans on putting at least two of the cases here at the game. We aren't sure where they will be placed, but we have increased the number of agents and dogs for the game. You two will now be in charge of this whole level as I'll need to be working more closely with Georgi on the overall surveillance plan during the game."

"So then the best guess is that the remaining cases will be in Berlin with Pete?" Mickey asked.

"That's what we think, and that's the plan we're going with on Sunday. Pete has been advised, and I'm sure he'll be ready. One last thing, be here a little early tomorrow, as I want to go through that route to the locker rooms with you before anyone gets here. I have a feeling it may come in handy."

Olga and Petra spent the night together, and both felt it might be their last. So many things had happened over the last years that they had trouble keeping things straight. They only knew that, no matter what happened, they would be friends to the end. They recognized that things had a way of changing, life goes on, and the time they had spent together was very special.

"Roger has asked me to come over to visit him in New York after the game is completed," Olga said. "I would like to go. Does that bother you?"

"No, not really. I knew we would get to this point one day, and I have set myself up to handle it. I always knew it would be you who left, and I knew I could never stop you. We've had enough for a lifetime of love and fun for eight years, and for that I'm very thankful. Are you sure you'll be all right?"

"No one is ever sure, but I feel it's the right thing to do. We've had a good time together, but I want a family, and I think he might be the right man. We're never sure, but I feel it's something I must do. Who knows, but it feels right."

"Then it is what you must do." Petra smiled even though her heart was aching. She agreed with Olga's assessment. "Just because we will no longer be lovers, there's no reason for us not to be friends. I'll always love you and be there for you whenever you need me."

"I know that, Petra. I'll always remember you."

In the morning Olga woke up early showered, dressed, and kissed Petra gently on the head before she walked out of the bedroom.

*Life is never going to be the same.*

She sighed, opened the front door, and left.

"Anton, are you all set with getting the cases into the game?" Drygin asked.

"The cases will be going in with the band equipment on Sunday morning. I have them all set up now, and they're with the truck that will be moving in the morning. One of my men has a brother who is handling the trucks, so we paid them off. There is always a way."

"You've done well, Anton. Let's be sure we get them into place and ready to blow at the time we discussed. Have you had any problem getting into the stadium?"

"Not at all. The forged papers work, and the construction on the suites won't be finished until right before the owners get to the stadium. Thank God for Russian incompetence."

"What about the bomb in Lenin's tomb?"

"We're all set to move it in as we discussed, and it will go off at three."

The director seemed happy. For the first time in months he seemed to relax.

# CHAPTER 45

*Saturday, September 20*

Mickey was tired, but he knew he needed forty-eight more hours of energy, and he knew he would find it. The past few months had been nonstop work, and it was all finally going to end. With only one more day before the game, he felt that, if they weren't ready by now, they never would be. Yakov, being a perfectionist, wanted one more walkthrough before game day.

"Yakov, you okay?" Ivan asked.

Yakov was still surprised that Mickey had beaten them all down to the locker room by more than a minute. The route he had found wasn't even on the plans for the stadium, but somehow he had found it. The problem, as Yakov saw it, was that only a few agents could actually disarm a nuclear device. He would need to be sure they were all stationed close to where he thought the nuke cases would be placed. When Mickey and Ivan approached him, he was in deep thought.

"I'm fine. Just running a few last-minute details through my head. I have to think the cases will be near the locker rooms or in one of the suites. Where else could they hide a case?"

"We've been through all the scenarios, and we can only hope we have them all covered and we handle them when the time comes. What do you want us to do?" Mickey asked.

Yakov had all the team members assigned to the game at the stadium for a final review of everyone's responsibilities. After the meeting and the actual run through, they all felt they had done what they could to get ready for the game on Sunday. Mickey still had the best time, and no other routes could get them downstairs any faster. In the end Yakov knew he and the boys would handle the cases if any were placed at the game.

When they left the field, Yakov said, "Be sure you get some sleep and stay away from the girls tonight. We need to be ready in the morning."

They just looked at him and laughed. On the way to the hotel, Mickey and Ivan decided to have a few drinks at the lobby bar as they knew they might not get this chance again after tomorrow.

"Ivan, do you remember the first time I landed and we sat at the hotel bar and got totally shitfaced? I know I'll never forget it. I wish the two sisters were around tonight!"

"Do you want me to make a call?" Ivan asked with that Russian smirk.

"No, not tonight. Maybe tomorrow night when this is all over and we can relax a bit. Ivan, can you imagine how far we have come in such a short time?"

"I know…cars, football, and the NFL game tomorrow. It seems like it has been ten years since we began all of this. And all the places we have been! The people we have met: Olga, Petra, Mikhail, and poor Boris. I know we're supposed to become cold to our feelings in order to handle this, but do you think we'll ever be that way?"

"I hope not. I don't think we're capable of that, but I do know we'll need to handle whatever happens tomorrow. Chances are someone we know will probably not make it out alive."

Ivan took a sip of his beer, and they ordered two more. They weren't going to get blasted, but a little buzz was definitely in order. They had been through a lot in a short time, and they would be through a lot more tomorrow.

"Do you think Mikhail will be all right?" Ivan asked.

"I'm sure he will be, but he and Boris were close. We know the general ordered the kill. But it all leads back to Director Drygin. I would hate to be the director if Mikhail ever gets him alone."

"Me, too, Mickey. Something is scary about Mikhail. I mean, Boris was big, and you could tell he was mean. Mikhail never lets it show, but you just get the feeling a madman might be in there somewhere."

On his way up to the room, Mickey decided that he was where he needed to be based on what had happened in his life so far.

*You never know what it will bring, and you only hope you are up to it.* Mickey would soon find out.

Something was wrong, and Padraig knew it right away. He had been watching Oleg for a few days now, and the pattern was pretty regular. Oleg should have left the safe house by now, and Padraig was concerned that he hadn't seen him.

Oleg had seen Padraig from the start, and he was glad it was Padraig and not someone else who had been assigned to watch him while he was in West Berlin. Because Padraig knew Oleg's moves, he knew the same about Padraig. For three days, after he had killed Gertrude, he had kept to his usual routine that he thought Padraig would get used to. Except for the stop at the Gate and the rendezvous with his two associates, it had all been quite simple.

Early this morning Oleg took the secret passageway through the alley and slipped out on Padraig. As in all safe houses, there was a secret passageway used only one time when it was most needed. Oleg's strategy was to keep his enemy agents close to him when he was doing nothing and to get rid of them when he made his move. Today was the day he needed to start getting everything ready, and it was almost seven in the morning. He needed to get the cases and be sure he was at the Victory column by nine forty-five, but first he wanted to do some quick surveillance on the spot. He met up with his agents, and they scoped out the area. It was important that Oleg keep up the ruse.

"It looks okay to me, but we need to be sure no police are around when we make our move. We'll park the car over there and move the cases when I give the all clear," Oleg said.

Both nodded and got back in the car. They drove to another safe house where the cases were stored, picked them up, and headed straight back for the meet. Oleg parked the car and got out to take a walk around the column, leaving the other two agents in the car.

On his return he caught a glimpse of the car, and his heart stopped. Two policemen were questioning the agents, and they were about to get out of the car.

He got to the car just in time. "Sorry about that, but I wanted to look at the column. I left my friends in the car. I hope they didn't cause any problems."

"The car is parked in a no parking zone, and these two wouldn't move. Or they stupid or just dumb?"

"They're out-of-towners and not too smart, but if it's okay with you, we'll be on our way." Oleg slid into the driver's seat.

"Just be sure you watch where you park the car next time."

*I can't believe how close that was.* He couldn't wait to get the cases into the trash canisters. They moved the car and watched for the sanitation truck and the cops. At five minutes after ten, the truck pulled up, and the workers got out for a break and sat on the park bench. Oleg pulled the car up behind the truck, popped the trunk, and put one nuke case in each canister after he checked the bin numbers. Then he drove off with the two agents.

Oleg went back later that afternoon to check on the trash bins. Police security was tight around the Gate, but the trash canisters were right where they were supposed to be, and nobody moved them. The bin numbers matched. He walked around and felt good about the spot he had selected. He had all his bases covered and was ready to call it a day. He would return to the safe house, have dinner, and then get a good night's sleep. In the morning he would chance using the secret passage one more time and hide out near the spot he had chosen. A huge crowd would probably be in the park and at the Gate for the speeches in the early afternoon. He felt the odds were in his favor, and that was all he could ask for. His plan had to work, and Drygin would be proud of him. The two agents would die, but he didn't have a second thought about them.

Padraig couldn't believe that Oleg was coming back to stay at the house.

*How cocky can you get? Once you have lost a tail, you usually hide out, but here he was walking back into the corner food market like he owned the world. We need to get a small tracking device on him and hope the device stays on him in the morning.*

Oleg lingered in the store, waiting for his meal. When he looked around, he couldn't see Padraig, but he knew he was there. He put the change in his pocket without looking at it. Even if he had, he wouldn't have noticed the device in the coin center, as it looked simply like a normal coin.

Padraig, who was in the apartment above the store, heard the beep as soon as he activated the control device and smiled to himself. *Oleg isn't escaping this time.*

Oleg's two associates weren't too smart. As soon as they got settled into their low-rent rooms near the gate, they went out to the local bars and had a night of it. They probably figured they were dead any way so they might as well have a good time. When they retired to their rooms early in the morning, Pete's agents reported that all was status quo and took turns watching the room. Padraig, on the other hand, after reporting to Pete, stayed up all night to be sure he would be aware of it when Oleg moved.

*It's going to be a long day.*

When Petra went through the front door of her apartment, she was glad to be home and to be alone. She knew Olga was with Coach Fox, and that was just fine. The realization that their relationship was ending wasn't as hard as she thought it would be. She had cried for a while, but after that she knew it would be okay. Olga was where she wanted to be, and Petra was actually happy for her. Roger Fox was an accomplished coach, and everyone who met him liked him. Olga mesmerized him. Petra hoped things would work out for them.

*Life changes fast, and you better be ready for the change!*

Petra's main concern at this point was being ready for tomorrow and for what the day would bring. The Dolphins were at the hotel, and she would need to be there early in the morning to be sure the team's breakfast and meeting rooms were in order as well as being sure the travel people were there to handle the team luggage and transfers. Immediately following the game, both teams would go directly to the airport for their charter flights back to the States. During the game she would be stationed at the owner's suite and would be in constant contact with Yakov. She was prepared for what might need to be done and ready to take any action needed to assist in the apprehension of the cases.

She thought about Mikhail and was concerned that he would make himself crazy with this notion that he needed to avenge his brother's death. Drygin didn't get to where he was because he was a nice guy.

*Who knew how many men he had killed to get there and stay there? This is Russia, and strength is the only thing that matters...And who you knew. People got killed in this game, and there was never any time to figure out how until it was all over. Life went on, and bad guys were bad guys. The good guys needed to kill the bad guys.*

When she drifted off to sleep, she was content with where she was and who she had become. After tomorrow, life would be different, and who knew what it held for her?

Drygin's palms were clammy, but he knew this was a good thing. His palms always sweated before he killed someone, and he was going to kill many tomorrow if all went as planned. The U.S. and the Russian governments needed to be stopped, and only one person could do this. General Asimov and Colonel Marislov had been pawns from the start, and he was glad he didn't have to kill them. They were weak and not very smart, and they let their physical needs get in the way. The general got it right where he deserved to get it.

Drygin's main concern now was that the remotes the general had dropped off in Odessa the day before his death still worked and, when the time came, the charge set off was strong enough to accelerate the nuclear material at the speed needed for an explosion. The amount of nuclear material needed wasn't that much, but the force of the explosion was the key. Without this speed the cases would be useless and would not explode. He rested all his hopes on the dead general and the scientist who had worked on the remotes. His name escaped Drygin, but it didn't matter anyhow.

One nuke case would be given to Anton, who had worked out a way to get it into the stadium on Sunday morning. Everything was falling in place for the director. His hands were still sweating. Soon many would be killed. When they had finished their business, Anton left as he had come in to finalize the plans with his agents.

Generals Levenski and Yachenko entered and took their seats in front of the director's desk.

He looked at them and just smiled as he wiped his hands on his handkerchief. "And how are we tonight, my generals?"

They both nodded but stayed silent as they knew he wasn't finished.

"I hope everything is in order and the tanks and men are ready to take over the government. We have been planning this for a long time, and if it goes wrong, we'll all be dead. Do you understand me?"

Again they nodded but didn't say a word.

The director still wiped his hands. "The coup will start to roll at noon, an hour before the NFL games start at the stadium. As our plan has dictated, we should be at the White House and the Dumas at three fifteen. As few people will be there, we should have control of both of them by four. After that we'll march on the Kremlin and take over the final piece of the puzzle. Am I understood?"

Both stood, saluted, and then exited the way they had come in.

After they departed, Anton came out from behind the secret door, smirking. "You have them right where you want them, Director."

"If they don't do their job, we're finished. I want to be sure we have everything else in place so let's review what you are going to do."

After they finished Drygin took out a bottle of vodka and two glasses, filled them halfway, and gave one to Anton.

He stood and faced the flag. "To Mother Russia, may she live forever!"

The satellite photos that Alexei and Yakov saw showed the final preparations for the Russian army's military coup. Pete had gotten the photos to them through one of his channels that only Alexei knew about. It was rare for two enemies to get along, but the three of them figured out years ago, when they were together in Israel, that someday there would be a need for friendship between the intelligence agencies of the United States and the USSR. They didn't always agree, but they worked together for what they thought was right. From the start they knew nuclear war or even nuclear battles could never take place as they represented total destruction.

"Do you think we have enough firepower to stop both armies when they leave the compounds?" Yakov asked.

"I'm sure we do, but why not put a few more men with the regiments we already have in place? I'm amazed they haven't detected us in the areas around their bases. Maybe they're too busy getting ready themselves?"

"That might be the case, but let's hope we get through tonight, and then when they move tomorrow, we can cut them off and stop any replacements they might have ready. With any luck it would be an easy one."

While Alexei pondered the whole scenario, he was pleased with what they had designed. They had orchestrated everything from the cars, to football, to the summits, and finally to the NFL game to lure out the director before he was ready. He knew all about the cases and what needed to be done to make them ready, and he was hoping that, if they couldn't find them fast enough, with luck, they might not have had time to get the job done.

*Only time would tell.*

Yakov was also prepared for what tomorrow would bring and knew they had done all they could. There were three fronts, and good people were at all of them. They wouldn't have direct control over stopping the coup, as they would at the stadium and in Berlin, but he was sure the generals in place would handle the situation.

"Yakov, you've been a good comrade, and I wish you well tomorrow. I can't be out front, but I'll be here monitoring and updating the situation. I'll have a direct link to you, General Titonov, and Pete, so I'll be able to let you know what is happening. Be careful, my friend."

"I will, Alexei, and may we have a drink of vodka together when this is all done?" Yakov left the office and realized the game was about to start.

Mikhail knew he would have his chance soon. The vodka tasted like crap, but he needed it to get some sleep. Ever since he knew that Boris was dead, he couldn't help but feel he needed to defend his honor and that of his brothers. There were many late nights, just like this, since that day sitting by himself in his office with the bottle and his thoughts.

Mikhail had monitored Boris all through their life and was glad that Boris had found Ivan's father to also help him along. Not many people knew it, but Viktor Sakalov was a connected man, not only in the Dynamo sports club but also in the military juggernaut that the USSR had at that time. He had also recruited Mikhail without anyone knowing it and was responsible for his being part of the covert units in the Russian army. The businesses were taking off. With the help of Mickey's U.S. contacts and connections, it had gone a lot faster than anyone had guessed

Mikhail knew Drygin was the main player, and he knew that bad guys really never won.

*Payback is a bitch, and Drygin's time was coming. It would be over soon...one way or another.*

Mikhail put away the bottle and walked into the bedroom to pass out for the night. Waiting for him, as she had been for most of the nights after they found out about Boris, was Petra. Since Mikhail had confided in her about the pictures, she had stayed with him through the nights. They never made love. She just held him until he fell asleep, and then she left. Dmitri would wait for her in the lobby of the office with the other bodyguards and then drive her home.

After Dmitri dropped off Petra, he headed back to check in with Alexei, as was his usual habit. He knew Alexei was concerned about tomorrow because he had to worry about too many fronts. It wasn't just the game, just the gate, or just the coup.

"Good evening, my good friend, and how was Mikhail tonight?" Alexei asked.

"I'm worried, but we can't do much. He knows what needs to be done tomorrow, and hopefully something will happen that will get him out of this mood."

"I hope so, but that isn't our main problem. I need you to stay close to Ivan and Mickey tomorrow. Yakov and the girls will be fine, but the two boys need to be watched. Will you do that for me?"

"Of course I will." Dmitri kissed the old man on his cheek. "I'll do whatever is necessary, Alexei." Alexei smiled as he left the office.

*Dmitri is a good man.*

Alexei was concerned, but it wasn't about himself. It was about all of them and the out-of-control madman he had known for many years. It would have been easier to just arrest him, but in Mother Russia this wasn't how it was done. Leaders tried to overthrow each other in various ways to take control. Alexei was sure that Drygin was one of the last followers of Stalin, and this bothered him the most. Like Stalin he would do anything to stay in power. Killing his own countrymen wasn't out of the question.

Olga was never happier than she was at this very moment. She would never have guessed that a man could do this to her, but here it was. Petra was okay with what was going on, and Olga was happy that she had understood. She knew she would.

After practice and the public relations tour through the government and the Dumas, the team was back at the hotel for their final meetings and meal prior to lights out at eleven. As the coach instructed, Olga wasn't around the team during this time but hid away in his room and waited for him to show up afterward. It had been this way from the first night, and she still felt like a little schoolgirl in love for the first time. She watched her behavior as she realized that Coach Fox needed to concentrate on winning the game, but he had a unique way of separating work and pleasure. She hoped it would never change.

When she heard the key in the door, she felt the moistness between her legs and was initially embarrassed that a man could do this to her. When the door opened, Roger flicked on the light to see her naked on the coach waiting for him. He kicked off his shoes, laid his jacket on the chair, and sat down next to her.

When he kissed her, he looked into her eyes. "After tomorrow I'll have to fly home, but we'll be together forever, if that is what you want?"

She cried so he just held her tight.

*If only it could be?*

The stadium butted up against the Wall. No grass was on the pitch, and the goals had holes in them. The players' uniforms were worn out, and so were the players. This wasn't the Premier League in Europe, but it was the best the East Germans could come up with. It kept their minds off their problems, and it was a little entertainment for the sparsely crowded spectators scattered on the old wooden bleachers.

"Where the hell did you get this vodka?" Stanislav took another sip. "Smells like the crap my wife pours down the drain to clean it. Tastes even worse!"

"You're always complaining, but you're always drinking," answered Gerhardt.

It was the boys' night out, and drinking while watching the soccer match was the entertainment for the evening. After the match they'd usually go to Stanislav's house for some beers before going home, but tonight they had to take care of a little errand. The money was okay, but they'd never spend it on getting better vodka even if they could find it.

At halftime a comrade of Stanislav stopped by.

"I'm telling you that only one of the cases is a nuke. The other is a decoy, as Oleg had thought it might be. What do you want me to do now?" Konrad asked.

"Take the nuke to the hiding place we discussed, and I'll get to Oleg tonight after I meet with the commissioner. I'll get back to you in a day or so and let you know where we need to move it. Until then sit tight and wait for my call."

"What should I do with the other case?"

"Just throw it out on the highway somewhere on the outskirts of town. No one will know what it is, and if they do they won't go near it."

"Okay, but get back to me as soon as you can, Stanislav. I don't want to sit on the case for too long. Who knows what might happen?" He shook Stanislav's hand and left the stadium.

Stanislav watched him walk away and returned to the bleachers.

"Who was that?" Gerhardt asked.

"Just a friend, but that reminds me that we have to run that errand we discussed earlier."

The game ended in a tie, but the boys decided to leave before they started the overtime period. They walked past their homes and went into a warehouse close to the munitions factory. Stanislav had a little office in the back, and they picked up two suitcases that needed to be moved. Gerhardt was pleased to be making a little extra money, so when they snuck into the munitions factory, he didn't really care or think anything of it.

"Gerhardt, place the suitcases over there by the door leading into that other room. I'll let the manager know they're here in the morning, and he can take it from there."

They left the way they came in and called it a night.

After walking Gerhardt to his house, Stanislav waited a few minutes, returned to the factory, and set the timer. *At four-thirty the manager wouldn't know what hit him.*

"Yakov, I hope everything is all right in Moscow?" said Pete. "We're okay over here, but Oleg is playing a tough game. We're not sure where the cases are yet."

"Just stay with Oleg, and he'll lead you to them. He's got big balls so chances are he just placed them and they need to be somewhere near the stage. Is Padraig on him?"

"No question about that, and knowing Padraig he'll stay up all night and watch for his next move. I talked to Donald today, and President Reed wants to be updated constantly so let's try to stay in touch."

"Okay, Pete, and before you ask Mickey is doing well and seems to be on top of his game. Tough spot to put him and Ivan in on their first mission, but what the fuck could we do?"

"After this one anything else we throw at them will be a cinch. Talk to you tomorrow, and get some sleep." Pete knew a lot of people wouldn't be sleeping much tonight. Tomorrow was game day in many ways. One team would win, and hopefully together two countries would stop a madman and save the world.

# CHAPTER 46

*Sunday, September 21*

The morning of Sunday, September 21, was glorious, in the mid-fifties with bright sunlight. The city of Moscow was getting up slowly as any early risers were trying to find food or just walking off a hangover. It would be nice to say they were on their way to church services, but religion wasn't part of the Russian strong suit, as it wasn't well tolerated in the USSR.

In West Berlin the people were hustling off to services and having a quick breakfast in the cafés on the cobbled streets. Being west of Moscow, it was a little warmer, and people were already gathering in the Tiergarten District near the Brandenburg Gate for the afternoon festivities. Hawkers were trying to sell their wares, and food concessionaries were setting up for the afternoon of speeches from the dignitaries. The mood of the people was also different, as the Muscovites went about their business in a cloud of gloom while the Berliners seemed happy and upbeat.

Oleg woke up early, as was his custom, showered, and dressed for the day. Before he left, he called his East Berlin agent. "Stanislav, is the bomb in place, and are you set up?"

Oleg needed the blast to happen as planned to divert the crowd's attention from the stage.

"I'm all set, and the bomb will go off at exactly four-thirty as we discussed. We placed it last night, and the timer is set. It's hidden near the ammunition as you suggested, and the explosion should be enormous."

"Be sure it happens at four-thirty," Oleg knew Stanislav would get the job done. "What did Konrad find out?"

"As you suspected there was only one nuke case, and the deal has been set with the commissioner. The money should be in your account within a few days."

"Good job, Stanislav. I'll be in touch." Oleg hung up the phone.

When he was about to leave the apartment, he grabbed his money and loose pocket change off the dresser and went on his way. He was sure he wasn't being followed but decided to wait until he was on the other side of Tiergarten before grabbing a breakfast and reading the morning papers.

Padraig felt his heart jump when he heard the beep acknowledging that Oleg was on the move. He hurried out of the room and headed south to intercept Oleg as he emerged onto the street through the butcher shop around a quarter mile from his safe house.

*A tunnel had to connect both buildings,* Padraig pondered.

He made a mental note to let Pete know this as it might be useful eventually. While Padraig followed Oleg at a distance, he realized his mark was walking right past the spot on the little incline where he intended to sit with the remote to detonate the nuke case. He could see that, from that vantage point, Oleg would be able to look down on the crowds and the stage area where the speeches would be made. It was less than a half-mile, and Padraig wasn't sure if this distance were far enough away from the blast if it occurred. All reports were that the immediate field of danger with the nuke cases would be in the range of two to seven miles based on the amount of nuclear material being exploded. If it were a low yield force, then the distances would be much less.

When Oleg reached the café, Padraig took a seat on the park bench across and at a right angle from Oleg so he could watch him. Even if he lost sight of him, the tracking device in the coin would alert him to any movement. While Oleg ate Padraig contacted his two other agents to be sure they were still in contact with Oleg's two friends and checked in with Pete. Everything was okay so he sat back and kept watching the storefront. It was about a half hour before Oleg came out of the café. He headed back into the park. Padraig thought about taking him out now, but if he did he realized they might not find the cases.

"Pete, no idea where the cases are yet, so we'll have to stay on plan," Padraig reported.

"Okay, Padraig, and good luck. I'll keep you posted on any news from Moscow."

After a few minutes of thought, Pete made a few calls and then left the hotel for his next meeting.

Security was tight at the hotel, but that was to be expected. President Reed was waiting for him and Donald in the conference room of his hotel suite. When they entered the room, Donald gave Pete the high sign that all was well.

"Hello, Pete. It has been a few months since we last saw each other. I hope you're well." President Reed asked.

Pete was amazed at how cool the man was. Here they were meeting on the possible destruction of the Soviet culture as they knew it, and he was sitting there cool and calm, reading a newspaper and sipping coffee.

"I'm fine, Mr. President."

*If he could be cool, so could I.*

"Tell me, do we have things in order, or will I have to let the world know that the Soviets have had a major coup during my speech this afternoon? I would hate to have to tell our people that the main target was the game between the Giants and the Dolphins."

Pete looked at the president. "We're all set, and you can be assured that Moscow will be handled properly. My main concern at this point is what will happen here in Berlin and your safety."

"That's nice of you, Pete, but my main concern is that, by the end of the day when I get on Air Force 1 to fly back home, President Vasilyev is still in power, and we have located the five nuke cases. We have discussed my safety at length, and there's no way I'll back down from terrorist threats."

"I fully understand, Mr. President. I'll get to Donald as soon as we get confirmation that everything is settled in Moscow."

"Pete, do you think there can be any other motives for this dilemma we find ourselves in?" President Reed asked.

"I'm not sure I follow what you're asking, Mr. President."

"Things have gone rather smoothly with the Soviets, haven't they? In the past this was never the case, but since we first met in my office, the process has been pretty seamless. Do you find this odd?" The president looked over his paper.

"Maybe a little, but we're in unprecedented territory. Nuke cases, a bad economy, and a renegade KGB director. I'm not sure what we should expect, but I trust the people we have in place."

"Just be sure we have all the bases covered. We're out on a limb with this one."

"I will, sir. Have a good day."

The president looked over his glasses. "Thanks, Pete."

Coach Fox was up early and pacing the suite. Game day in the NFL is a mixture of emotions for the players and the coaches. They all knew that, by the end of the game, their bodies would be bruised and they would be mentally exhausted. Both teams had been away from home for days now, and all of them were looking forward to playing the game and then getting on the charter for the flight back to the States, all but Coach Fox who had fallen in love with a girl from Moscow.

They had room service in the early morning. When he was about to leave for the team breakfast, he looked at Olga. "There is no way this will be our last day together. After the game I'll have to fly home, but I want you to follow me in a few days. Is that all right with you?"

She simply smiled and nodded her head.

"Then I'll see you after the game, and we'll make plans then." He left the room.

Olga sat there for a while and finished her coffee. She was elated with the way things had turned out over the last five days. This would be her last assignment, and she would need to talk to Yakov sometime tomorrow to let him know what she was going to do.

She took her time getting ready and then met the staff in the breakfast room to get ready for the rest of the day. The buses were scheduled to arrive in two hours, and immediately following their last meeting, the team would board the buses for the trip to the stadium.

*What a beautiful day.*

Petra didn't like the way the day started out. Her alarm went off late because the electricity in her building went off for a few hours during the night. There wasn't a lot of hot water, and she spilled her tea while she was trying to work on the heater. It started out as one of those days where nothing went right. Hopefully it wasn't a harbinger of things to come. She usually wrote it off as just everyday life in Moscow, but for some reason she had a bad feeling that she couldn't get rid of.

After finally getting everything in order, Petra took the bus to the hotel and waited for the team to come down for breakfast. She was just a little late, but it worked out as the rest of her crew was also late. They went over the day's activities, and Petra decided to let the other crewmembers handle the team this morning while she went to the stadium. The feeling of doom hadn't left her, so she thought it best to get to the suites and check everything out. Upon arriving she went to the security trailers to see if Yakov needed anything. On the way to the trailer, she walked past Gate 1 and noticed the military marching band. They had a lot of equipment and several people hanging around. It was mayhem, but they expected that this morning as all the suppliers, performers, and construction people would be there early to get all their materials in as well as the food and equipment.

"Good morning, Yakov. How long have you been here?"

"I never left, as you knew I wouldn't. Are you all set for the day?"

"I think I am. But I thought it best to get here a little early to check on the suites and walk around. Something is bothering me, and I felt it more when I got here."

Yakov looked at his agent. "That's normal. Just go about your business, and be careful. It will all end up fine. Go check the suites and report to me." She left the trailer and headed back to Gate 1.

*Hopefully the band would be through the gate with all their instruments.*

The two electricians waited patiently in the line at Gate 1. The carts they pushed were filled with equipment they needed to finish the work in the suites on the top level. In front of them was the military band that would play during the game. There were over one hundred and fifty instruments and various-sized boxes that were being pushed through the gate to be stored in the lower-level storage rooms by the team locker rooms. When they were checked one by one, the two electricians watched very carefully as the guards inspected two large bass drum containers and passed them through. They weren't sure if the bribe had done the trick or if the special padding they had placed around the nuke cases had worked. They only knew they had accomplished this part of the mission and they were through the gates.

"Anything is possible as long as we're in Moscow, Timor," Anton remarked. "Now we need to secure the two cases and put them where Drygin ordered."

*How many hangovers was this in a row?*
Mikhail couldn't even imagine the answer, but he knew it was getting out of hand. Ever since Boris had died, he had been on a binge. The bad part about the whole thing was that they didn't even have a body to bury. He was undoubtedly dead, but knowing his body was dumped somewhere and would not get a proper burial caused him pain. He missed his brother.

He was thankful that Petra was there last night when he finally decided it was time to sleep, but as always it was a blur. He remembered the meeting the evening before with the whole staff, and he was glad that part was over. They all knew what had to be done, and all the logistical parts of the program were in order. It was up to them to make sure the game was a success, and he couldn't do much more. Throughout the game he would oversee the program and monitor the suites along with Yakov. He wouldn't drink. He took a long shower, ate breakfast, and got ready for the day ahead.

Today he would get his revenge. He had thought of nothing else for the last four weeks and was glad he had good people under him to run the game. This revenge was all consuming because he knew the disregard that people like Drygin had for their fellow human beings. Yes, Mikhail himself was a killer, but he had been trained to do that. He only killed enemies of the state, but he had never lost respect for life. Drygin killed because he liked it and because he had to.

*It's easy to justify anything you want to, and Drygin is a master at that, all in the name of Russia. How many had he killed? How many would he kill today? If his plan worked today, how many would he kill to keep his dream alive?*

The last thing he did, before he left the suites on the top floor of the Intourist, was to phone Dmitri, who would pick him up in front of the hotel.

When he got out of the car at the stadium near the security area, he said to Dmitri, "Stay close to the car when you return. I have a feeling we'll need to get out of here quickly at some point today. After you pick up Mickey and Ivan, let me know that you are back here."

Dmitri just nodded and went to get the boys at the Europa.

Ivan woke up in a bed he knew wasn't his. After Mickey had left, he had stayed and had a few more drinks at the hotel. He couldn't remember how much he had paid for the evening, but the lady next to him looked rather pretty. It was early in the morning, and he had a lot to do before he met Mickey. He got up, dressed in the dark, and left the building.

*Where the hell am I?*

When he left the apartment, he was glad to see he was only a few blocks from his pad so he hustled off in the dark and got to his door a few minutes later. Everything seemed okay, and the little piece of paper in the doorjamb was still in place so the apartment was secure. He didn't have time to shower so he just changed clothes and returned to the little street stall down the corner for his morning cup of tea and Khrusty, a Ukrainian finger pastry that he had loved since he was a kid.

"Going to the American football game today?" Nakita, the proprietor of the kiosk that Ivan frequented almost every morning, asked.

"Yes, I'm looking forward to it. Do you want me to get you a souvenir or something?"

"A Dolphin hat would be good. I like the way the fish looks."

"Okay, I'll see what I can do." Ivan paid and said his good-byes.

On his way to the hotel to meet Mickey, his thoughts returned to the early days with his father Viktor. He knew his dad had been connected, and he thanked him every day for leaving him Mikhail to look after him. Ivan had grown up with Boris and Mikhail, and now Boris was gone.

*It's hard losing people close to you, but you need to keep going. You could be sad for a while, but you have to know deep down inside that you need to bounce back and handle death.*

He had cried over Boris when he was alone and was at peace. He was worried about Mikhail, but he knew that, in the end, he had to avenge Boris' death, or Mikhail would never be the same. Hopefully by the end of the day, things would be back to normal.

When he turned the corner, Mickey was out front, bullshitting with the front doorman. He could only hear Mickey saying, "You friggin' Russians are nuts!"

*He's something else.*

Mickey had turned into a good friend but also a good partner in their current employment. They had come a long way from the two guys who wanted to introduce football and maybe bring some products into Russia.

*If we got through today, who knew what we could do together?*

Mickey was up and ready early this morning. Having gone to bed when he left Ivan last night, he was actually able to get a few hours of sleep. He knew the stadium inside and out and was sure he'd be put to the test at some point this afternoon. He had spoken to Pete, and he was aware of what was going on in Berlin, but his main concern was the game and the NFL. If they could get through today and if everything was handled in Moscow, as well as in Berlin, he would be able to step back for a few months and decide what he wanted to do with the rest of his life. It was the two-minute warning, and the outcome of the game was on the line.

Director Drygin sat at his desk and knew he had planned the takeover to the best of his capabilities. He had been training for this moment for his whole life. In all four cases had been placed, and only he knew which two were the decoys. It had been a long and grueling process, but he was sure that, by the end of the day, he would be the new Joseph Stalin in Russia.

*How dare they move Stalin's body from Lenin's tomb! How dare they say he was a tyrant and a killer of the Soviet people! How dare they say he was evil and paranoid?* Lenin's tomb was selected simply because Stalin was no longer buried there.

The troops would be moving within a few hours, and the anticipation was driving him crazy. His hands were sweating again, and he was aware of a slight feeling of euphoria that he had never felt before. He was glad he was alone, as he couldn't think of anyone to share this moment with. He would monitor it all from here and make the decisions based on gut feelings as the day unfolded. As always he had a sense of total control, and he felt secure that Anton and Oleg would do their jobs. But the remote controls bothered him. In Berlin there was direct line of sight, but in Moscow a few of the nuke cases would be hidden. Hopefully the controls worked. He couldn't do much now.

The generals were in constant contact with Alexei as they waited for the coup to start. Based on the last satellite photos they had, more than enough troops were in place to stop it. On top of that, they had decided to put more troops at the White House and the Dumas for extra protection in case the first attempt to stop the renegade forces failed. The helicopter gunships were ready. They had all flown to their designated assembly point by five in the morning and were well hidden. In all sixteen gunships were ready to cut off any reinforcement plan that the coup might have had in place.

Earlier that morning Alexei had taken breakfast with President Vasilyev. The president would be in the Giants owner's suite, and Yakov would keep him apprised of what was going on.

"And how will we know what is going on in Berlin?" the president asked.

"I'll be in constant contact with Pete, who will have direct access to Donald Smith and President Reed. As you know Yakov will be with you in the suite, and I'll be on the line with the generals. Once the coup has been crushed, I'll let you know immediately."

"What do you think the timing will be for all the events?"

"The game will begin at one in the afternoon, and we're constantly monitoring the stadium and have been for the last week. President Reed is scheduled to speak at five-thirty, Moscow time at the Wall, if all goes as scheduled. Our best guess is that the coup will take place before these events as it will take time to get the troops in place. We think they'll start to move around noon or earlier. We'll intercept them about two hours after they move at the allocated sites."

The president was well aware of the scope of the plan they had put in place, and he hoped they had calculated correctly. He was sure they had forced Drygin's hand, but they still needed luck to pull it off.

"Do you think the Americans will handle the situation in Berlin?" the president asked.

"After speaking with Pete this morning, I have no doubt. They have the main agent in sight as well as his accomplices so we should be all right. Pete has his best people on it."

"It will be a pleasure to finally get rid of Drygin."

"Yes, it will. We've been waiting for this for many years now, as we knew he would make a move sometime. It's time to put this to rest finally. I won't miss him."

Yakov realized there would be a lot of fan excitement for the game later in the afternoon as he walked through the parking lot. When the time came near to open the gates, he walked around the perimeter of the stadium to be sure everything was in place. Four hours before game time, he had reviewed the plans for the last time and still wasn't satisfied, but that was his nature. The stadium was abuzz with electricity that only a sporting match could bring. The fans came into the stadium two hours before game time, a half hour before security wanted, but he couldn't do anything about it. Agents who were searching everyone staffed the five gates that were the entryway into the seats. It was an old stadium but had seen many great sporting events in its time, like the finals of the World Cup matches as well as the Olympics in 1980. Yakov hoped it would still be standing when the day was over.

Mikhail, Petra, Ivan, and Mickey were already there so Yakov's team would be complete when Olga arrived with the Giants owners. The security teams were still doing the final sweep of the stadium before they let in the spectators. Nothing had been found. That didn't mean they were in the clear. Just that they hadn't found anything. When they reached the Dolphins owner's suite, the electricians were just finishing their work on the wall outlets.

"Are you almost finished?" Ivan asked.

The head guy turned around and gave him the thumbs-up sign. "We'll be finished in a few minutes. Just tightening the last screws, and we'll be out of your way."

Mickey thought there was something funny about the two guys, but he couldn't figure it out. He did notice the putrid green color of the coveralls, the guy's name, and the company name on the shirt, but they were almost finished so he just let it go. Mickey didn't know these same two electricians had just moved two big cases from the storage room on the lower level to each team's locker room before the teams arrived.

The teams arrived at the stadium a couple hours before the game, which was unusual, but the facilities at the stadium weren't conducive to forty-four-man teams with all the equipment. All of the pregame preparations were done at the hotel so the teams would only dress at the stadium. The locker rooms were small, but rooms off the main one could be used for offices and training rooms for last-minute taping of ankles and minor injuries. The teams were in the locker room, and the coaches were going over the last-minute details prior to the game. Coach Fox was meeting with his offensive coordinator, looking at the first twenty plays they would call. Naturally they would adapt to game circumstances, but he always made a habit of orchestrating the play calling for the games.

When the teams arrived, Olga went immediately to the Giants suite to check in with Yakov. It had been an uneventful morning as far as she was concerned, and she longed for this day to be over.

Yakov saw the look of concern on her face. "Is something bothering you, my dear?"

"Not really. It's something we'll need to talk about in the next few days, but for now all's fine. Anything happening I should know about?"

"Everything seems to be okay, and everyone is in place now that you are here. The families should be up here in a minute, so stay here and wait for them. Mikhail is finishing something he needed to do and will be back in a few minutes. I'll be back in a half hour. I need to check on a few things."

A few minutes after Yakov left, the team owner and his family made their way into the suite. The food was all laid out, and the drinks were on the console. Not what the Americans were used to, but it would have to do. Olga had checked in with Petra, and everything was fine in the Dolphins suite. Mikhail had made his way back to the suite, and he was standing guard outside the room so Olga felt safe.

An hour before game time, the teams took the field for warm-up and calisthenics. The cheer that went up was deafening, and everyone knew at that moment that the NFL had arrived in Moscow. The crowd was going crazy chanting cheers and singing songs. They were mostly rooting for the Giants, but there was a bunch of Dolphin fans as well.

While the teams went through the early warm-ups, Mikhail came up to Olga. "Olga, I wish Boris were here. I could just see his face as the teams came out on the field."

"I know you miss him, and we all do, but it'll be all right."

Mikhail just smiled sadly and walked back outside. It was the first time he had mentioned his feelings to anyone, and he was glad he did. He wished Petra was here to be with him, but he knew she was on the other side of the stadium. He wanted to thank her and to tell everything would be all right soon. He had come to get closure, and it would now end, one way or another.

About the same time the teams took the field, the gates at two different military posts on different sides of Moscow opened, and the tanks were rolling. The first unit under the command of General Lenevski was coming into Moscow from the east and slowly making its way down the M-7 through the outskirts of the city. General Yachenko's battalion was taking the M-8 highway from the north and would head into Moscow from that direction. Both were supposed to get to the city at the same time to take over the targets, as Director Drygin had instructed. Both units consisted of thirty tanks, three hundred men, and other vehicles to round out the unit. The tanks were first, and they were some sight. While they made their way to the city, the Muscovites who saw them just looked at them in amazement and waved. They weren't sure what the hell was going on, but they figured it was just a military parade. They went about their business as if nothing were happening.

But Alexei knew otherwise. Monitoring the whole coup by satellite and communication with his generals, he was waiting to make his move. Pete had his intelligence men set up a satellite hookup in Alexei's office the week before so he would have firsthand knowledge of every move that Drygin was making. It was understood that, if they came out of this, the unit would be dismantled and shelved in a secret room in the KGB headquarters for further use. The timing of his move was critical as they needed to get the units far enough away from the bases before they stopped them but at the same time not to let them get too close to the city center. There was no way they could break the perimeter into the city because, once that happened, they would be in a very populated area. Alexei didn't want to fight it out in front of all of Moscow.

Alexei punched the button on his control. "They're on the move. Action plan begins now."

The generals on the other end knew the coup had started.

Drygin, for his part, was sitting at his desk listening to radio reports from his commanders. He was also in contact with Anton at the stadium and looking forward to coordinating the whole plan. His hands were shaking, and he was strung out and tight as a drum as a result of lack of sleep and a lot of vodka, not to mention that he was sitting on a nuke case that made him a little jumpy anyway. In a last-minute change, he decided to keep one of the cases with him in his office under his desk and put the other two nearby, tucked away safely in his closet behind him.

"Anton, have you set the bomb at the tomb as we talked about?"

"All done and went smoothly just as you planned it, Director."

He sipped his vodka and surveyed his desk to be sure everything was in place. It was all there.

In Berlin the crowds were getting dense, and security was becoming a problem close to the Gate. The German police were in the process of moving the stanchions closest to the stage back a hundred yards so there would be room in front of the podium. When they did so, they needed to move back other items that were in the way so they could have a bigger buffer zone in front of the Gate. While Oleg was watching from the hill with his binoculars, a little panic showed in his face when they rolled the trash canisters away from the stage. He wasn't sure if they were going to remove them completely, but in the end they repositioned them further back from their original position. His line of sight no longer worked so he needed to relocate fifty yards further into the park in order to get access for the remote. His two agents were in a panic when the trash canisters started to roll, but in the end they still had a clear shot. It was even closer than it would have been if the canisters remained where they were. But they both knew that, when they exploded, they were goners. They had a little over three hours to figure out if they wanted to be martyrs or not.

Padraig and Pete were watching Oleg intently. They saw him move, but they couldn't figure out where the nuke cases were from their vantage point. Maybe Oleg just needed to change his position. In any case they felt they had him covered, along with his two accomplices. Little did the three Russians know that, at every step, their heads were in the gunsights of three sharpshooters just waiting for the command.

At exactly one o'clock, the Miami Dolphins kicked off to the New York Giants. Also at one the sixteen gunships near both military bases where the coup forces had departed flew over the compounds and blasted the hell out of all the gates before any reinforcements could think about leaving. They also took down all the communications towers so the troops on the way to Moscow were isolated from the rest of their comrades. It was executed so quickly and carefully that the troops in the bases just gave up and threw down their arms. Stage one was complete, and Alexei smiled. He knew that, once Drygin lost communication with the compounds, he would figure out that they were on to him. But how long it would be before he tried to communicate with them? Hopefully he would be more focused on the troops marching on Moscow and would only contact the bases if he needed backup. The plan was that, once Alexei knew he had the reinforcements cut off, the signal would go out to trap the two battalions before they knew what hit them.

When Generals Titonov and Alekseev got the command from Alexei, they were ready and waiting. The units consisted of forty tanks, fifteen gunships, and a contingent of five hundred troops apiece. Based on the reconnaissance they received, they wanted to be a little stronger than the coup forces, and as the enemy had no air backup, the gunships were key.

They had stationed General Alekseev's units in the Terletskiy Park off the Gor'kovskoye Shoase, about ten miles from the city center. As soon as the first tank turned the corner, Alekseev's men blasted away with all they had and stopped them in their tracks. The men who didn't die came scrambling out on fire, screaming. The rest of the tanks went in all directions, as they weren't sure where the shots had come from. Within a few seconds, the gunships came barreling down, firing on the troops who also scattered in every direction. It was utter chaos, and Alekseev knew that if he could cut off the men from the tanks, all would be over before it started. He ordered his tank division to split the area among the enemy troops, and they did just that. Within fifteen minutes the enemy tanks were surrounded, and the men were facedown on the street. Military coup battalion number one was deactivated.

Things weren't as easy for General Titonov. When the enemy approached the part of the highway that changes into the Prospekt Mira near the Platforma Seventyanin stop on the metro, a funny thing happened. They actually received good information from the director, who had been on the radio with General Yachenko when his battalion was ambushed. As soon as he was aware that he was going to be attacked, General Levenski went into action, and his troops were ready for the onslaught when it happened. He knew he was on his own because, when he got the initial radio call from Drygin, he called his base for backup and the line was dead.

Titonov had seen action in WWII and commanded a division in Afghanistan. He immediately radioed Alexei and asked him to get to General Alekseev to have any gunships and personnel they could spare to fly northwest and cut off the enemy. The area to the east of the battle was called Losiny Ostrov National Park. It was their only escape route. The main part of the battle was being fought near the street and under the metro stop. But as the government troops gained some ground, the enemy filtered out into the park and dispersed in all directions. When the troops began deserting, General Levenski couldn't believe his eyes. He saw a machine gun in the hands of one of his dead soldiers, picked it up, and fired in all directions. He didn't know who he was shooting at, and he didn't care. He was a dead man either way. When they pulled his body from the carnage, he was riddled with holes.

When the enemy fell apart and scattered, Alekseev's gunships swooped down on them and corralled them like cattle. Some of the enemy made it to the forests, but it was a matter of minutes before they were captured. Alexei's plan had worked, and the first part of the day was a success.

"Yakov, this is Alexei. Both military units have been stopped. Please pass the information on to President Vasilyev. Handle the game, and let me know," Alexei said into the radio.

"Ten four, Alexei, and good going. I'll pass on the information. Please get to Pete and advise," Yakov came back.

"Will do, Yakov. Good luck."

President Vasilyev was still old school, and military coups needed to be squashed immediately unless he wanted further uprisings. On his orders all bases were locked down until further notice, and he would begin to handle the problem immediately after the game. As per Russian protocol, no one at the game would have any idea that a coup had been stopped and there had been a battle in the national park. President Vasilyev might have been opening up his country to the West in hopes of enriching the economy, but there was no way the world needed to know everything that went on.

After finishing the work in the owner's suite, Anton and his partner Timor walked slowly out of the stadium to a trailer hidden behind the far fences out of sight of the security teams. They had set the cases and would now wait until there was ten minutes left in the second quarter to detonate the nukes by remote. As planned, if that didn't work, they would proceed to each of the cases and detonate them by hand. The wait was excruciating, but they couldn't do much to speed it along. American football was slow and boring to them, and they thought it would never catch on in Russia. Plus it was a Western game, and that would never do.

"Almost time to blow up the nukes," Anton said with way too much excitement in his voice.

No one really knew what impact the bomb would have, as only two of them had been detonated so far. The one in Odessa had blown up a few blocks, and the devastation was massive, but the one on the steppes was tiny.

At the allotted time, they took out the remotes and pushed the buttons. The apprehension was unbelievable, but it was short-lived as nothing happened. They pushed the remote buttons again. Nothing.

"What the fuck," Anton swore under his breath.

He knew now that the only way to make them go off was with the hand detonation, and there was no chance of survival. He took a big swig of vodka and ran out of the trailer, yelling for his partner to follow. "Timor, take the owner's suite upstairs, and I'll handle the locker room down here."

They split up. When he was close to the Giants locker room, he could see a lot of action near the alley way that led to the door. While he waited, he saw a bunch of KGB agents running that way and figured it was too late to do anything down here. Hopefully the nuke case in the Dolphins owner's suite hadn't been found. At this point he could only slowly walk out the portal at the far end of the stadium and rush back to the trailer.

*It's the shoes. The fuckin' shoes.*

A few minutes before halftime, Mickey's mind drifted back to the electricians.

*The shoes. That was it.*

They both wore soft brown loafers rather than work boots. He had to get to Yakov, but before he could he heard, "All units report to Giants locker room immediately. A suspicious case is in the backroom."

The head trainer for the Giants spotted a case that he knew wasn't part of the team equipment in one of the backrooms off the main area. Mickey knew his route well, and he would be first down to the locker room.

On the way he radioed Yakov, "Be on the lookout for two guys dressed as electricians in putrid green coveralls but wearing brown loafers. They were up in the owner's suites, and I knew something about them was bothering me."

While running, Mickey was aware that this could possibly be it. Ivan was a few steps behind him, with Petra following as they made it to the lower level. Coming out of the ramp and into the hallway, Yakov, who was out of breath, met them.

"They spotted one of your guys over by the Dolphins locker room, and we're searching for the other one. We have removed the case from the Giants room, and we're transporting it away from the stadium and then will disarm it. We aren't sure if another one is in the stadium, but we need to find that other electrician."

When Yakov finished his remarks, Olga came around the corner and caught the last few words.

"Yakov, there was an electrician up in the Dolphins owner's suite as we left to get down here."

All of them just looked at each other.

"Mickey, you and Mikhail go with Petra and see if you can find your electrician here on the lower level. Ivan and Olga, come with me."

It was a lot longer getting back up to the suite than it was going down. When they headed into the suite, the guy in the electrician's coverall was holding what looked like a remote and pointing it at the console where all the glasses where stored. Before Yakov could make a move, Ivan jumped him and knocked the remote from his hands. The electrician was stunned for a moment but reached into his tool belt and pulled out his gun. When Ivan got up and moved to get his gun, he heard a shot from behind him and realized that Olga had fired.

"No." He gasped as the electrician fired and hit Olga under the left breast.

She died instantly. At the same moment, Yakov fired, and the shot pierced through the left eye of the electrician, killing him immediately. There was stunned silence all around the suite, and the female members of the owner's family were in a state of shock. Olga just laid there with her eyes wide open.

Yakov reported. "One agent down, and the nuke case in the locker room is a decoy. We're checking the one we found in the owner's suite, and it looks to be real. Be on the lookout for one electrician with brown loafers."

When halftime came the teams went into the locker rooms as if nothing happened. It all happened so fast that there had been no time to stop the teams, and it was too late now. They knew they were playing a game of roulette, but they couldn't do much else. Neither country would be held hostage by a threat, especially a threat from within.

When Anton walked out of the stadium, he was surprised that he hadn't heard an explosion. As far as he knew, the cases were the real thing, and something must be wrong. He turned to return into the portal to check on his man up in the Dolphins suite when he saw three agents running up the corridor toward him. He had only one choice, and as they got closer, he bolted back the way he had come and ran as fast as he could to escape the three agents and get out of the stadium.

"There he is!" Mickey yelled.

Mikhail didn't miss a step, and Mickey with Petra were close behind. When they turned the corner and ran on the outside of the stadium, they spotted Anton as he was running toward a bunch of parked cars. All of a sudden a car door opened, and out jumped Dmitri, gun in hand with his sights on Anton. The electrician didn't know what to do as he was trapped. The shot took him off his feet.

Dmitri yelled, "Mikhail, Mickey, let's go. We need to get to Drygin." It was just what Mikhail wanted to hear.

"Petra, stay here and get back up to the owner's suites to help Yakov. We'll report on our way into Moscow," Mikhail ordered.

Petra turned and ran back to the upper level, not knowing that Olga was dead.

"Dmitri, you speak English?" Mickey shook his head.

"Yes, I do, Mickey, and I shoot pretty well, too. I also know my way around Gorky Park." He smiled.

They all jumped in the car and sped off toward Moscow's city center and KGB headquarters.

To Mickey, it was like old times, his buddy Dmitri driving him into Moscow.

On the ride to Moscow, they got confirmation that Olga was dead and the nuke in the owner's suite was real. They knew they had saved the day at the game, but there was always a price to pay. Mickey thought about Petra and made a mental note that, as soon as they finished with Drygin, he would go to her.

Mikhail was just pissed. "That motherfucker. He did Boris in, tried to fuck up my NFL game, and now has killed Olga. There will be hell to pay."

Dmitri explained what was going on and passed on the instructions from Alexei. "Alexei thinks Drygin still has the other nuke cases, but at least one of them is in Berlin. He wants us to get to Drygin and hold him until he can get over there from the Kremlin. We'll enter through a secret passageway that will get us into the office unnoticed. Also, the remotes at the game were sabotaged, and Alexei thinks the scientist Putinov had something to do with this."

Mikhail remembered finding Putinov in the small house near the shore at the mansion in Yalta. "I knew he didn't let us down. Hopefully all the remotes are no good, but we'll not know for sure."

They passed through Red Square and finally got to the Metropole. When they ran through the kitchen, Mikhail was aware that this was the same way he secretly entered Alexei's office. However about halfway in, Dmitri took a left through a hidden door up a few alleys and stopped. They were in the closet, and Drygin was in a conversation with himself.

"That friggin' Asimov! I knew he'd fuck it up. The remotes have been sabotaged, and who knows what ones really work."

He noticed the clock on the wall had struck three. The explosion rocked the foundation of KGB headquarters, and Drygin was ecstatic. He looked out his window to see the smoke and destruction but was surprised that it hadn't done more damage. The impact had leveled the tomb, and a huge section of the Kremlin wall was destroyed. People were running all over the place in mass confusion, and who knew how many had died. He rubbed his hands, and the sweat felt good. When he examined the first explosion in more detail, he heard a voice behind him.

"You are a sick man, Leonid." Alexei had made it to the office just in time to see the explosion as well. Yakov had a gun in his hand, and he was ready to gun down the director. "How much destruction do you think we can allow you to put on our own people?"

"That really isn't for you to decide." Drygin made his way back to his desk.

*Hopefully the last two remotes on my desk will work, and I'll be able to hold off Yakov before he pulls the trigger. We would all be dead, and I don't care if we all died at this point.*

The coup had failed, and he knew the cases at the NFL game were found. He also realized that he had just blown up Lenin's tomb and sent a message to the world. If Oleg could hold up his end of the deal, the U.S. president would be dead, and Berlin would be a mess.

He held one of the remotes and pointed it at Yakov. "Please, Yakov, do me a favor, and pull the trigger. As you do I'll hit this button, and we'll all be killed."

Yakov looked at Drygin and focused his gunsight between his eyes. Yakov wasn't sure what he should do. Alexei was sure that Drygin wasn't bluffing but realized he couldn't let this man get away. Just as he was about to speak, the closet door behind Drygin opened.

The shot blew off the top part of the director's head, and the remote fell helplessly to the ground. Alexei looked past Mikhail to see Mickey and Dmitri coming out of the closet with their guns drawn. Mikhail looked at Drygin, who was facedown on his desk.

"Watch out for Boris wherever you are going," Mikhail remarked. "Payback is a bitch."

"That leaves four cases, and if one of them is in Berlin, the other three need to be somewhere close. We know they didn't leave Moscow so they have to be here," Yakov said.

Alexei looked around as if he had sensed that they were near. "He was a madman, and madmen usually keep their weapons of destruction close to them. The other remotes were in the desk so the nukes should be near."

While in the closet, Mickey had noticed a few big items off in the corner and went back in to inspect the objects. "Two cases right in here. Shit, if he ever hit that button, we were all doomed."

"You were dead either way! Welcome to the game," Dmitri said.

After they secured the area as well as the nuke case that was under Drygin's desk and the two in the closet, Alexei looked at his watch and noticed it was four-thirty. *One more hour and the president would be making his speech at the wall.* He needed to get in touch with Pete and let him know what had happened and to get a feel for what Pete was thinking.

The final troops of the renegade force had been found hiding in the swamps of the park, and all military bases were back under the control of Alexei and President Vasilyev. The president was still at the game and welcomed the call he received from Alexei letting him know that everything in Moscow was under control with the exception of the explosion at the tomb. The president excused himself and returned to the Kremlin. He was grateful that the bomb wasn't nuclear, but he realized that, with the United States, they needed to get control of all nuclear arsenals and slowly start to dismantle them. Madmen like Drygin would always be around, and it was essential to prevent them having access to such dangerous killing tools.

Everything had fallen into place so far, and causalities were at a minimum. The tomb was gone, and the walls of the Kremlin were destroyed, but they could replace them. They would also replace the body of Lenin with the ashes of Drygin. No one would ever know where he had gone.

All the information pointed to having one more remaining nuke case that was live. There was no doubt in Pete's mind that one of the two units they were chasing was real. Whether the remote would work or whether one of Oleg's two agents would blow it up and a few blocks with it was still to be seen. But they couldn't take out the two agents as they needed to have them line up their shots before killing them. That would be a delicate maneuver, but they had to take that chance. Oleg, on the other hand, was a different story. It had always made sense to Pete that they should take him out now, but for some reason he was waiting to make that call.

Padraig was on the scene and had his eyes on Oleg as he sat on the hill. He was about two hundred yards from him sitting in a chair, looking like any citizen enjoying the day and the festivities. While Padraig sat there, he saw Oleg get up and go to the ice cream vendor at the bottom of the hill. After paying the vendor, he went back up and resumed his previous position. Padraig's heart skipped a beat as the beeper was going off, letting him know that Oleg was on the move. But Oleg was still sitting in the same spot. Padraig knew immediately what had happened, and as the ice cream vendor made his way toward the Brandenburg Gates, he knew the coin was in the vendor's pocket. The surveillance coin had done its job but would no longer be useful.

"Pete, the coin was used to buy some ice cream so we need to be sure we keep him within our sights," Padraig advised.

Pete was busy studying the layout of the park and the places where the three Russian agents were located. He also noted where the three snipers were in relation to their targets, and he was fine with their placement. The two Russian agents were separated with one of them on the left side looking into the Gate. One agent was on the roof of the Reichstag, looking into his target at a forty-five-degree angle. His trash canister was a quarter mile from the Gate. The second Russian agent was hidden at a construction site at a left angle to his target, which was much closer than the other agent's target. The snipers, under Pete's control, were located in the buildings on either side of the Gate, looking out into the park and their targets. They had a direct line of sight on both the Russians at a distance of four-hundred yards and had made this shot many times.

"Padraig, keep tabs on Oleg. I want to go to the stage area and take one last look around. Maybe we missed something the last few days that will help us. If he moves let me know."

Pete left to get to the Brandenburg Gate. This was a covert mission so the German authorities were unaware of what was taking place. Pete had, however, compromised a little with one of his German counterparts to get access to the buildings near the gate. The two superpowers decided that, if they let too many countries in on the situation, it would leak and stop the process. They had to locate all the missing cases and do it without the world knowing what had happened. One was left, and it was somewhere in the vicinity of the Berlin Wall at the Brandenburg Gate.

The stage area was around thirty yards in front of the gates. The German secret service had the place wired, and the agents in charge of the president were working in tandem with them to be sure the area was secure. The president would come up through the back of the Gate, which gave him direct access to the stage. He had stayed the night before in the Hotel Aldon Kempinski, which was behind the gate near the Pariser Platz so there was a pathway created for him and all the other dignitaries who were taking part in the program.

Donald was in constant contact with Pete and had clearance to get into the suite at the Kempinski. When Pete arrived at the lobby, Donald met him. Donald took Pete to see the president immediately. It was a few hours before his speech, and he was watching the game in Moscow on ESPN International when Pete interrupted him.

"I guess you know by now that the game has been secured. Alexei called and advised that one bomb was real, but the remote was sabotaged. We aren't sure if that's the case with all of the remotes."

"That's good news, Pete. Have they secured any of the other cases?" the president asked.

"Not yet. But they're on the way to confront Drygin now, and hopefully this will help us find some of them."

"And what about the coup?"

"Stopped in its tracks. All the bases are being secured as we speak. There were some casualties on the enemy's side, but Alexei's boys came out just fine. One of our KGB agents went down."

"Too bad about the agent, but good job so far, guys. It seems that luck is on our side. Let's hope it stays that way. When do you think you'll hear from Alexei again?" President Reed asked.

"I would think any minute as the last time we talked was over an hour ago."

The president looked at Donald. "You need to let me know when everything has been handled. I want to put out a challenge to Vasilyev, but before I do that, I need to know that all is secured. Do you understand?"

Donald looked at Pete, and they both nodded. At that moment Pete's radio crackled, and he excused himself and went into the other room. When he returned he had a slight smile on his face.

"Moscow is under control, and four of the cases have been found. Unfortunately a bomb went off in the Red Square and annihilated Lenin's tomb, but it wasn't nuclear. There were minimal causalities."

"The man is a fucking nutcase," the president said.

"Not anymore," Pete replied. "They blew his head off."

"So all that is left is one more case, and we think it's near the Brandenburg Gate. Is that correct?"

"Yes, Mr. President," Donald answered. "We feel confident we have the matter under control, but are you still all right being so close to a possible nuclear blast?"

"We discussed this at our first meeting, and nothing has changed. We can't allow a madman or terrorists to stop us in our pursuit for freedom. The Russians stood up to their part of the bargain, and we'll do the same."

President Reed thanked them both and dismissed them to carry on with their duties. On the way out, they discussed a few of the minor details, but Donald made sure Pete understood that, as soon as everything was secured, he needed a call.

"Pete, be sure to get to me when it's all done. I'm not sure what he's up to, but he smirks every time he mentions it."

"Not a problem, Donald, and let's hope it goes our way. It's the last quarter. Let's win one for the Gipper."

Oleg was getting antsy. He hadn't heard from Drygin in a few hours and was concerned that something was wrong in Moscow. He wasn't aware of the full plot, but he was sure there was more to this than just what was happening in Berlin. From the start he thought it was something big because the director himself was in charge. Usually Anton would be his point man, but on this mission the director was in full charge. He had heard rumblings of a possible coup, but nothing had surfaced on his radar to confirm that. He knew he was a pawn in the game, but he had his own mission and realized he had to complete his objective and then get back across the Wall to East Germany. He thought back over the last two days, and he only regretted killing Gertrude. He wasn't sure why he did it, but he now had to find another partner on this side of the Wall.

The parade was making its final pass past the viewing area near the stage so the speeches would begin very shortly. The festivities were being held to honor the seven hundred and fiftieth anniversary of Berlin. On the stage sat the dignitaries, but Oleg was only concentrating on the president of the United States. He was seated between the chancellor of Germany and the president of France. The program called for him to be the fourth speaker after the French president. Oleg had changed the plan and decided to blow up the munitions factory in East Germany before President Reed took the podium. He wanted complete pandemonium prior to the U.S. president's speech, as he had an unknown advantage that not even Drygin knew about. He had set up his own operation, to kill the president of the United States.

He figured the other two agents could shoot at the decoys with the bazookas, and that would leave him open to act on his own to get the president.

*Shit, the agents were dead anyway, so they might as well pull the trigger.*

At five minutes after four, he decided to start his leisurely walk to the stage area and to get rid of anyone who might be following him. He wasn't sure if there were anyone, but he wouldn't take any chances. He hadn't seen Padraig.

While he walked Oleg couldn't believe the thoughts that were bombarding through his mind.

*If I can pull this off, I'll be the man. Imagine assassinating the president of the United States and holding onto a half-million dollars. That bomb better go off. Will the credentials work? How close will I be able to get to Reed? Should I shoot just him or go for a few others as well?*

Oleg was in a trance as he sauntered down the path, looking completely happy and worry-free, just a single man on a lonely stroll through the park.

Padraig couldn't believe what he was seeing. He radioed Pete to tell him that Oleg was on the move but couldn't reach him.

He'd need to keep trying, but his main priority at this point was to stay in touch with Oleg and not lose him. That wouldn't be very easy if he mingled in the crowd, and Padraig knew that was just what he was going to do. While they walked down the tree-lined walkways, Padraig could see the mass of people ahead of them. He got as close to Oleg as he could, but he still felt he would lose him in the crowd. There had to be over a half-million people in the area, and it was up to Padraig to stay with one person in order to save his mission. He tried Pete one more time and finally got him.

"Pete, he's on the move and approaching the crowd at two o'clock from the podium. I'm not sure if I can stay on him, and at this point I think we should take him out when we get the chance."

"Ten-four. The other remotes didn't work, and if we're lucky, maybe the ones Oleg has will be useless." Pete cursed himself for not taking Oleg down earlier.

"I don't think he even has it on him, Pete. It looks like he wants to get to the stage in a hurry."

"Shit, the president. Padraig, stay with him and keep me posted."

Oleg disappeared into the crowd and couldn't be found anywhere. Padraig could only make a beeline to the front of the stage and hope he caught a glimpse of him.

"Pete, he doesn't have a rifle so he must have a handgun on him. He'll need to get close to the president if he's going to kill him."

"But how's he going to get the shot?"

"He has to be getting to him from the back of the stage. There's no way he can get close enough from the front with the guards and the barriers. Meet me at the eastern end of the backstage."

Padraig wasn't sure what they were going to do, but it seemed the best option. Pete knew Padraig was right, and as he started to head back to the stage, he realized that Oleg would need some type of credentials to get him through the checkpoints. He also realized that he would need the same thing, and he knew he didn't have them.

*Shit, I'm out of luck.*

It took him ten minutes to fight the crowd, but he made it to the back of the stage and met Padraig. Padraig had concluded the same thing that, without credentials, the security wouldn't let them through.

"Donald Smith!" Pete said aloud. "That's our only chance."

But with all the speeches going on and all the people near the stage, Pete wasn't sure if he could get to Donald.

At exactly four thirty, there was a massive explosion somewhere on the other side of the Wall. The smoke was bellowing into the sky, and the flames could be seen behind the stage.

When the French president was finishing his speech, the two Russian agents lowered their bazookas at the targets. At the same time, the snipers pulled the triggers on their long-range rifles. Russian agent number one was hit right between the eyes and never got his shot off. By the direction of his aim, the agent watching the construction site could see that the target had to be the trash canister located toward the main stage area off to the right. Little did they know that they were both decoys. Russian agent number two was also hit between the eyes before he had the chance to pull the trigger.

Oleg timed his move to coincide with the explosion and the conclusion of the French president's speech. The shot rang out, but with all the applause and confusion, it went unnoticed except for a West German agent standing behind the dignitaries. The agent pulled his gun and got off two shots that hit Oleg in the chest and dropped him where he stood. The look on Oleg's face was one of shock. Before he hit the ground, President Reed turned around and looked at him. The last thing Oleg noticed was a streak of blood on the president's right temple. The damage was only superficial.

The immediate reaction of the massive crowd was bewilderment, but they didn't scatter. It was like a TV show taking place in front of them, and before they realized it, the whole area was secured and under the control of the West Berlin security forces.

Before the president rose to give his speech, Donald leaned over and whispered something in his ear. A grin came over the president's face as he walked up to the podium. He stood there for a few seconds and let it all sink in. He cleared his throat, wiped the last remnants of blood from his face, and began his speech.

"President Vasilyev, open this Gate and tear down this Wall!"

The half-million people at the festival went crazy.

"Pete, this is Yakov. Come in, please."

"Yakov, this is Pete. All is secure, but we haven't found the last nuke."

"That means we need to find that last one before this is all over."

"I realize that, but I think we should let Ivan and Mickey handle that. We're too old for this!"

It was time to call Mickey. Pete's last job was done, and it was time to smile.

# AUTHOR BIOGRAPHY

After his college days at the University of Connecticut, Bob Robustelli worked in the family corporate travel and sports marketing business. His responsibilities included promoting American football in Mexico, Europe, and Russia. Robustelli's father played for the New York Giants and is a member of the NFL Hall of Fame, credentials that helped with his associations with football. Throughout his travels, which took him to all parts of the world, he read thrillers and always thought his job was a good cover for a CIA agent. The idea for *TeamWork* had been formulating with Robustelli for some time, when three years ago he committed to writing it, taking courses at the Westport Writers Workshops and attending numerous seminars. He's enjoyed the process of learning the trade, but realizes there is much more to learn. He's looking forward to the journey.